THE BATTLE

The attack on America has changed everything. And the new war has sparked another—igniting a devastating fire that could consume the world.

In the chaos of the first major conflict of the twenty-first century, an old enemy sees the opportunity to strike. Seeking to exploit America's preoccupation with its foes in the Middle East, the People's Republic of China sets out to "reclaim" by force the territories it considers its own: the Spratly Islands in the South China Sea . . . and Taiwan. China's arsenal is awesome and deadly, including a pair of Akula nuclear-powered subs purchased from a cash-hungry Russia. As Chinese missiles fly across the Straits of Taiwan, the casualties mount at an alarming rate—with American servicemen numbered among the many dead.

World War Three now seems inevitable. And the fate of the Earth suddenly rests with the commander and crew of the U.S.S. *Seawolf*, lead boat of America's newest class of ultra-silent attack submarines. For this battle can only be won beneath the surface of a turbulent sea—where the enemy rules in firepower and numbers . . . and will not relent, even at the cost of the future.

Other *Silent Service* Titles
by H. Jay Riker

LOS ANGELES CLASS
GRAYBACK CLASS

THE
SILENT
SERVICE

SEAWOLF CLASS

H. JAY RIKER

AVON BOOKS
An Imprint of HarperCollinsPublishers

This is a work of fiction. Names, characters, places, and incidents are products of the author's imagination or are used fictitiously and are not to be construed as real. Any resemblance to actual events, locales, organizations, or persons, living or dead, is entirely coincidental.

AVON BOOKS
An Imprint of HarperCollins*Publishers*
10 East 53rd Street
New York, New York 10022-5299

Copyright © 2002 by Bill Fawcett & Associates
ISBN: 0-380-80468-9
www.avonbooks.com

First Avon Books paperback printing: August 2002

Avon Trademark Reg. U.S. Pat. Off. and in Other Countries, Marca Registrada, Hecho en U.S.A.
HarperCollins® is a registered trademark of HarperCollins Publishers Inc.

Printed in the U.S.A.

10 9 8 7 6 5 4 3 2 1

THE
SILENT
SERVICE

SEAWOLF CLASS

PROLOGUE

Tuesday, 1 July 1997

Russian Federation Embassy
Beijing, People's Republic of China
2145 hours, local time

Fireworks lit the night, a stuttering, popping, thunderous display of light and color flashing and strobing across the sky to the southwest. Vasili Andreevitch Mikhailin sat on the veranda of the main embassy building with his guest, sipping strong black tea and pretending to admire the celestial spectacle. The portly man sitting to his left, Admiral Li Guofeng, was all smiles and camaraderie, but Mikhailin didn't trust him further than he could throw him. Given their respective differences in size, he thought wryly, that was not very far at all.

"A new age beginning, Comrade Mikhailin," Li said in badly accented Russian, raising his own cup in a toast. "To our business partnership, and to our glorious future!"

"To our future," Mikhailin replied, but with an enthusiasm he could not feel. He did not point out that Li's continued use of the honorific "Comrade" was not only dated, but in decidedly poor taste. Didn't this fool know, wasn't he *aware*, that the world had changed?

Mikhailin hated Beijing. He'd hated it when he'd been a military attaché here at the embassy fifteen years ago, and he hated it even more now. Beijing was a grand-looking sprawl of a city, to be sure, with its miles of museums, monuments, boulevards, temples, and people's halls, but it remained a lie all the same, a gleaming facade masking the wretched poverty of the people both beyond the capital precincts and within the twisting back streets and alleyways of the city itself. It was rumored that the Beijing government had turned off the hot water for most of the city's inhabitants for the duration of these festivities; the pollution pouring from the local coal-fired power plants was not something that visiting foreign dignitaries should be allowed to see.

Throughout that week, he and others of the Russian Special Trade Delegation had been feted by their opposite numbers in the PRC Defense Ministry. That morning they'd been taken to the Beijing Zoo, a squalid collection of tiny cages and flea-bitten animals crowded between the Olympic Hotel and the Beijing Exhibition Center. Mikhailin loved animals, loved nature and the outdoor wilderness. The sight of those miserable creatures sweltering and pacing in their filthy cages had moved him more than the squalor he remembered of the peasants out in the country beyond the capital sprawl. The two giant pandas just inside the front gate were mangy and half dead.

The conditions—worse, the lack of empathy for the poor beasts—appalled him. Visitors to the zoo could actually buy toy guns that fired plastic pellets for the express purpose of letting their children shoot at the helplessly caged and tormented animals; at one point he'd watched a gang of adolescents hurling rocks at the monkeys while guards stood impassively by . . . and felt a small stab of vengeful amusement when the shrieking monkeys retaliated with fistfuls of their own feces.

The experience had soured Mikhailin completely. You could not trust a people, he reasoned, who treated their own natural inheritance in so callous a manner. Resources, money, neighbors, allies, all were mere assets to be *used* until they were used up. Granted, China was a country with extraordinary problems, not least of which were a population approaching 1.2 billion and a geography that had lost something like a fifth of its agricultural land to desertification and soil erosion in the past fifty years.

Still, to Mikhailin's way of thinking the People's Republic was a giant slowly strangling on its own filth.

"This day is only the beginning, comrade. By returning our territory to our rightful possession, the western imperialists have acknowledged that we are a world power, and one to be reckoned with!"

"Indeed, Comrade Admiral," Mikhailin replied with a blandly polite smile. "There can never be a question of that. The whole world knows and respects the might of the People's Republic of China."

"The surrender of Hong Kong to our sovereign jurisdiction," Li continued, "is only the first step. We shall soon regain control over our renegade twenty-third province in the east, and of our territorial islands in the South China Sea. And you and your people at Krasnaya Sormova, Comrade Mikhailin, will be instrumental in effecting that change."

Another crackle and rumble of explosions sounded from the sky to the southwest, above Tiananmen Square and the Forbidden City. Mikhailin could also hear, beneath the concussions, the heavy beat of music accompanying a troupe of ribbon dancers. Beijing was going all out to celebrate this day and Britain's long-awaited return of Hong Kong to the sovereign rule of the People.

"Our business agreement will be of immense benefit to both of us, Comrade Admiral," Mikhailin replied. "What you do with our . . . product is, of course, entirely up to you."

"With ten of your Varshavyanka and two of your new Barrakuda in our service, plus the might of our own growing fleet, the People's Republic will again become a maritime nation to be respected and feared. We will fear no foreign power, no trespass on our territorial sovereignty."

A particularly dazzling spray of red and green sparks cascaded across the sky. Mikhailin leaned back, watching the avalanche of light, and wondered how long it would be before the Russian Federation regretted its shortsighted marketing policies.

Ever since the final collapse of the Communist state, the new Federation's economy had been struggling along, never quite, as the Americans liked to say, making ends meet. Desperate for hard currency, Moscow had begun aggressively selling arms of all types to anyone with cash and the desire to play catch-up in the world arms race. MiG fighters, T-80 tanks, munitions, automatic rifles . . . the worldwide demand, fortunately for Russia's financial problems, was insatiable.

Perhaps the most lucrative trade item in Moscow's marketplace, however, was the diesel-electric submarine known as the Varshavyanka class. Small, superbly silent, and a real bargain at only $300 million dollars apiece, the efficient little hunter-killer had proven to be one of Russia's most sought-after exports. And as for the nuclear-powered Barrakuda . . .

Mikhailin sighed. How long before these deficit-balancing trade goods were turned against the *rodina*? he wondered. Moscow, he feared, had lost sight of the dangers in the quest for income. The People's Republic of China might be primarily interested in Taiwan and the Spratly Islands for now, but he could not forget that Beijing had longstanding territorial claims in Siberia as well. A fleet of ten Varshavyankas and a couple of the deadly Barrakudas could easily blockade Vladivostok and the approaches to the Sea of Okhotsk, cripple the weakened Soviet Far East Fleet, and perhaps even force the surrender of the Maritime Provinces.

It seemed unlikely, though, that the Americans would allow the People's Republic to take over Taiwan without a fight. Perhaps, in the long run, Moscow would find itself in a kind of strange and highly improbable alliance with Washington against the machinations of the Beijing militarists. He would need to discuss the matter with his contacts in the State Security Service upon his return home.

Home. He missed her. It would be good to be home when this round of negotiations was completed. Good to be with Masha again, and the kids and their families. He was getting too old for these international junkets, no matter how important they were supposed to be to the national economy.

"It is nearly time, Comrade Mikhailin," Li said, glancing at his watch. "We should leave."

Mikhailin nodded. Another banquet, more dancers, more fireworks.

At least he could inform his superiors that the deal,

worth some thirty trillion rubles over the next ten years, had gone through as planned. Russia would get the money she so desperately needed in order to continue pretending that she was no longer a third-world country.

And China would receive a fleet of the deadliest warships known to man, and a free hand at last with her old enemies across the Taiwan Strait.

Thursday, 23 September 1999

Operation Buster
Northern Pacific Ocean
48° 16' N, 178° 02' E
0312 hours Zulu

Lieutenant John Calhoun Morton, "Jack" to his friends, turned the hatch release and pushed, easing the round hatch of the forward escape trunk up and out. With MM2 Theodore Hanson close behind, he pulled himself through the narrow opening and into the ocean. Pale light spilled up through the hatchway from the caged battle lantern in the escape trunk but was almost immediately swallowed by the inky blackness of the water. The target was still distant enough that they could risk showing the light.

By that wan glow, he could just make out the vast, shadowy bulk of the USS *Pittsburgh*, a Los Angeles-class submarine, hull number SSN-720, hovering in the midnight-black water beneath his gently kicking, flippered feet.

The other SEALs of First Platoon were already working in the near-total darkness, unshipping the pair of Combat Rubber Raider Crafts from the temporary deck housing aft of the conning tower and inflating them from the attached CO_2 cylinders. The *Pittsburgh*'s conning tower—her "sail" in submariner's parlance—rose like a black, knife-edged cliff above the SEAL platoon. Then Hanson closed the deck hatch, cutting off the thin mist of light from below.

The team had practiced this maneuver in total darkness many times, however, and in moments, the inflatable CRRCs were unfolding, rising rapidly to the surface as the fourteen men of First Platoon followed them up. Morton broke the surface, spitting his rebreather mouthpiece from between his teeth and pushing his mask back on his head. There was more light here than there'd been below, but not by much. The night was black and the sky overcast, with a strong wind slicing across the surface in a fine, ice-cold spray that cut his exposed skin like a knife. Without their wet suits, the water, at forty-six degrees, would have leeched the heat from their bodies in minutes, and the SEALs would have lost consciousness to hypothermia.

Seven men piled into each inflatable boat . . . a close fit for large men and their gear. TM1 Cyzynski unpacked the small outboard motor from its case, screwed it down on the stern engine mount, and connected the waterproof battery. Morton, meanwhile, pulled out his Motorola headset and slipped it on, holding the needle mike close to his ice-cold lips. "Whalesong, Hammerhead. Radio check. Over."

Pittsburgh's periscope array rose like heavy, upright pipes from the water a few yards away, almost invisible in the darkness with their mottled pattern of light and dark gray camouflage paint. A special radio antenna mounted to the radar mast would provide communications for the team . . . so long as the *Pittsburgh* was able to remain at periscope depth. They needed that radar perched well above the wave crests to home them in on their target.

"Hammerhead, Whalesong" was the reply, barely heard above the keening wind and hissing spray. "Check okay." There was a pause. "Objective now bearing three-five-zero, range eight-three-five."

"Objective bearing three-five-zero, range eight-three-five," Morton repeated. "I copy. Hammerhead out."

"Good luck, Hammerhead. We'll keep a light on in the window for you."

His wrist compass showed them the correct direction, a little west of due north. When his second-in-command, Lieutenant j.g. Brad Conyers, had completed his communications check from the other CRRC, they fired up their engines and began easing away from the towering masts of the submerged *Pittsburgh*.

They moved against a heavy swell, and the wind battled them across the crown of every cresting wave. Lightning flared on the western horizon, briefly lighting the clouds in a stuttering white flash; a squall line was approaching. In part, the oncoming storm had dictated the decision to go with the op now, rather than waiting for a more propitious moment or a better angle of approach. The ocean swell preceding the storm, however, was going to make the approach a bit hairier than usual.

Eight hundred yards . . . eight football fields . . . but the objective was completely invisible in the dark and sleeting spray. If they maintained their heading, however, and a steady speed of five knots, despite the best efforts of the wind to slow them . . .

"Hammerhead, Whalesong."

"Whalesong, Hammerhead. Go ahead."

"Hammerhead, be advised target is changing heading to one-eight-zero at twelve knots. Recommend you come to new heading . . . make it three-one-zero to intercept."

"Coming to new heading three-one-zero. Copy."

Morton could just make out the second ISB to port, with Lieutenant Conyers at the tiller. He switched to the tactical channel. "Hammer Two, this is One. You copy that, Two-IC?"

"One, Two, I copy. Coming over now."

Together, the two inflatable boats nosed to the left, coming onto the new heading that, according to the plot board in *Pittsburgh*'s CIC, would let them still intercept the target. A course change. Damn . . . did they suspect? Morton wondered. Had they picked up a radar pulse . . . or the encrypted, low-wattage comm signal and been warned off?

Minute followed bone-chilling minute with no new change of course from the target. Apparently, they were altering course in an attempt to stay ahead of the weather, which was growing steadily worse.

"Contact!" RM1 Schiff called back from the bow of the rubber duck. He was holding a portable radar gun, a smaller, waterproofed combat version of the device used by state troopers to catch speeders. "He's dead ahead!"

An instant later, as the CRRC crested the next wave, the objective emerged from the darkness . . . a ghost ship, blacker than the surrounding night, with only running lights and a red glow from her bridge to reveal her shape through the mist.

"Whalesong, Hammerhead. We have visual, repeat visual . . . dead ahead, range fifty yards. Request permission to execute Plan Victor."

"Roger that, Hammerhead." There was a lengthy pause, filled with static. "You are go for Victor. Execute, I say again, execute."

As they motored silently closer, the hull of the target ship loomed huge above them. She was an aging freighter, rust-streaked and battered, with a dead-weight tonnage of 4,700 tons, a length at the waterline of ninety-nine meters, and a beam of thirteen. She had the look of a small oiler, with bridge and superstructure well aft and two mast-slung cranes forward. She was the *Kuei Mei* out of Shanghai, and her destination was the port of Los Angeles.

The freighter was plowing steadily south now, at a speed of eight knots. From Morton's low-to-the-water vantage point, it looked as though she'd changed course to better take the heavy following seas on her quarter. It didn't appear that any alarm had been given. No one was visible on deck and there didn't seem to be any excitement or haste. The two rubber raiders shifted their angle of approach slightly to stay ahead of the target vessel; at best, the raiders could manage eighteen knots, but the seas were heavy enough to slow that best considerably, and there was a real danger that the *Kuei Mei* would cruise serenely by, just out of reach.

On this line of approach, the target's port side was visible. The plan of battle called for Morton's boat to take the target from the starboard side, while Conyers's team hit it from port. Morton spent several minutes carefully studying the freighter's movement, trying to judge whether the slower CRRC could cut under the target's stern to reach her starboard side . . . or whether it would be better to have both teams assault from port. Morton tended to be conservative, unwilling to push the all too fragile combat asset of luck, but it looked to him as though there would be plenty of room and time to spare.

If the freighter maintained her heading and speed. She had a top speed of only about twelve knots, and a CRRC could easily outsprint her, but in a long chase the advantage lay with the quarry. In this heavy sea, though, her skipper was keeping her speed to an easily controlled wallow, and the *Pittsburgh* had vectored the team in at just the right angle to maximize their chance of a clean intercept. It looked good.

Judging wind and wave carefully, Morton put the helm over and gunned the battery-powered engine to full throttle. The other six SEALs grabbed hold of the safety lines looped along the rubber boat's gunwales as the flat-bottomed craft slapped and jounced over the cresting waves. Icy spray drenched them all, and visibility was reduced to a wet blur that stung their eyes in salty blasts.

The *Kuei Mei* loomed huge and high to the left as they cut beneath the leviathan's stern and bumped hard through her wake . . .

USS *Pittsburgh*
48° 16' N, 178° 02' E
0402 hours Zulu

"Conn, Sonar!"

Commander Thomas Frederick Garrett picked up the intercom mike beside the periscope housing and held it to his lips. "This is Conn. Whatcha got?"

"Conn, we have a possible contact, bearing two-nine-nine, designated Sierra One-two."

"What do you mean *possible* contact?"

"Sir . . . it's very quiet. More like a hole in the water than anything else. But we picked up some transient mechanicals, and Busy is calling it a sub."

"Stay on it. I'll be right there."

Hanging up the mike, he turned to Lieutenant Commander Keith Stewart and said, "You have the conn, Stew. I'll be in the shack."

"Aye aye, Captain."

The sonar shack was located in a room of its own, aft and on the port side of *Pittsburgh*'s control room. Inside, the overhead lighting had been reduced so the four sonar techs on duty could better watch the vertical cascades of light on their monitors popularly called "the waterfall."

"So show me this hole in the water," Garrett said.

Chief Sonar Tech Wayne Schuster handed him a computer printout. "We've been getting bumps and possibles for maybe five minutes now, Skipper," he said. "And two minutes ago Chesty here was sure he picked up a screw, making slow revs for maybe five knots. But no engine room noise that any of us can hear."

SM1 Chester Andrews nodded. "It was there, sir. I heard it. Then I lost it. And the water out there just sounds . . . well . . . dead. I know that doesn't make sense, Captain."

"It makes fine sense, Chesty," Garrett said, studying the printout. It was an analysis of transient noises made by the sonar room computer, affectionately dubbed "Busy Bee." They showed several spikes of noise picked up by *Pittsburgh*'s sensitive, far-hearing underwater ears. The steady, crawling thrum of the freighter's screw was clearly in evidence, as were the sharper, higher-pitched hums of the electric outboard motors on the inflatable boats. There was the low-frequency hiss and rumble of the surface waves. But behind the obvious noise . . .

The traces were so slight as to be damned near non-existent . . . thumps or bumps that could have been anything from a fish burping . . . to someone dropping a wrench on board another submarine nearby. The characteristics argued against the fish-burp notion. That particular streak on the chart looked mechanical . . . not like a biological at all.

As for the "hole in the water," Garrett knew all too well that sonar operators, the good ones, relied on senses that were as much psychic, as much pure magic, as anything definable and measurable in the real world of science and high-tech computers. Sonar techs bragged that they still did the actual identification of the noises around the sub themselves, with some help from computer sound archives, of course. Manning a sonar station was far more art than science. A feeling that the water was dead in a certain direction might well indicate that something was there, something extremely quiet.

And in submarine warfare, quiet is *always* the ultimate advantage.

The question was, if there was another boat out there in the darkness someplace, whose was it? And why was it here? There were only a few possible answers that occurred to Garrett, and none of them was pleasant.

"Captain? Conn" sounded over the intercom.

"Go ahead, Conn."

"Sir, Hammerhead reports they are in position, ready to climb."

Garrett thought a moment. He had the power—the responsibility, in fact—of calling off the SEAL op if a problem arose, one jeopardizing the success *and* the covert nature of the mission. There was a distinct possibility that the hole in the water was a Chinese sub, one sent to shadow the freighter on the surface.

But so far there wasn't enough to go on. "Pass Hammerhead the word that they're good to go," he said. "And Godspeed."

"Aye aye, sir."

Garrett turned to Schuster. "Can I assist you through maneuver?"

Schuster's brow wrinkled. "Sir, at this point I wouldn't know what to ask for. We don't know the other boat's heading, or even his range, *if* he's there at all."

"Stay on him, then. If you hear anything more, give me a yell."

"Aye, Captain."

"Carry on." Garrett stepped back out of the claustrophobic enclosure of the sonar shack and walked across to one of the two plot tables aft of the side-by-side periscope housings. The freighter had recently come to a new heading, due south, a course that would take her directly across the *Pittsburgh*'s bow in another ten minutes or so. If she was being shadowed by a sub, the other vessel ought to change course as well and might expose herself to *Pittsburgh*'s sensitive sonar arrays.

"Maneuvering," Garrett said. "Come to new course zero-zero-five, ahead dead slow."

"Come to new course zero-zero-five, ahead dead slow, aye aye, sir," Master Chief Alex DePaul repeated from his station between and behind the planesman and helmsman, forward. Aboard American submarines, every order was repeated back verbatim, a carefully, almost religiously choreographed check that orders had been correctly given and correctly received.

This particular set of orders would bring *Pittsburgh* onto a course parallel with but opposite to the target freighter ... and bring into better play her TB-23 towed sonar array streaming aft.

It might give them just a bit of an advantage if the freighter had a silent shadow.

Chinese Freighter *Kuei Mei*
48° 16' N, 178° 02' E
0408 hours Zulu

Morton held the outboard's tiller over as TM2 Ciotti secured the magnetic mooring rings to the hull of the freighter alongside. Ciotti reached well up above the level of the CRRC to give it enough play on the mooring lines so a passing wave wouldn't drag it under ... or leave it dangling high and dry against the ship's side. After crossing under the *Kuei Mei*'s stern, they'd worked their way forward down the starboard side, so that they were now secured beneath the loom of the freighter's bridge and deck housing.

All of the SEALs had removed their diving gear—flippers, masks, rebreather units, weight belts—and stowed them in mesh bags secured to the inside of the rubber raider. Still dressed in their death-black wet suits beneath Nomex hoods and flight suits—plus assault vests, UBA life jackets, and black rubber boots—they carried the standard subsurface assault loadout known as VBSS, the Navy's acronym for Visit, Board, Search, and Seizure. Each man carried his primary weapon, for most an H&K MP5SD3 with attached laser optical sights and integral silencer. MN1 Vandenberg was packing a Remington 300 combat shotgun with folding stock and a cut-down barrel. The men also had secondary weapons—sound-suppressed Smith & Wesson "Hush Puppies"—plus spare ammo, flares, strobes, grenades, bricks of C-4 explosives, detonators, chem lights, flashlights, knives, medical and E&E kits, personal Motorola radio sets, and night vision goggles. Each SEAL Team member looked like an invader from another world, hulking, bulky, and decidedly other than human.

"Whalesong," Morton whispered into his Motorola mike. "Hammerhead One, at the mark. Ready to climb."

"Whalesong," Conyers's voice added a moment later. "Hammerhead Two, at the mark and ready to climb."

"Hammerhead, Whalesong, wait one." Seconds dragged past with agonizing slowness as the CRRC bobbed and slapped alongside the moving freighter. Then, "Hammerhead, Whalesong" came back, slowly and with deliberate emphasis. "You are go for Operation Buster. Repeat, go. Go. Go."

"That's the word," Morton told the others. "Let's do it."

Schiff finished unshipping and assembling the climber's extension pole and grapple—basically a painter's pole equipped with a grappling hook at the business end attached to a rolled-up caving ladder. Letting the ladder unroll, he reached up high, standing in the CRRC with the steadying support of the others, to hook the end of the pole over the freighter's freeboard three meters up, securing it to the gunwale.

In seconds TM2 Ciotti was on his way up the ladder with an ease born of long practice and rigorous training. Schiff went next, vanishing into the darkness overhead, while the remaining five men waited in the bobbing CRRC below. For a long moment there was no sound but the wind and waves, and the heavy chug of the freighter herself as she churned through the swell.

Then a pencil flash signaled once . . . twice . . . then two more times in rapid succession. Morton went up the ladder next, gripping the metal rungs with ridged Nomex gloves and leaning far back to maintain tension for the climb. Vandenberg came up behind him, followed by Young, Cyzynski, and with Hanson bringing up the rear. Like shadows, silent and all but invisible, they swarmed up the ladder, rolled over the railing, and dropped onto the deck, immediately taking up their combat positions, H&Ks covering every direction.

A Chinese sailor lay facedown a few feet away, his blood intensely black in the green-yellow monochromatic glow of Morton's night goggles. He wore civilian clothing, the garb of a merchant mariner, but a Type 56 rifle, the Chinese equivalent of the ubiquitous AK-47, was slung over his back, muzzle down. His throat had been cut.

Young and Hanson heaved the body over the railing, careful to drop it well aft of the moored CRRC below. It vanished with a splash instantly silenced by the wind and the hissing ship's wake.

Morton held up his gloved hand, fingers flickering in well-practiced sign-language gestures. *You . . . you . . . forward. You and you, aft. You two with me . . .*

The huddle of seven black-clad men broke into fire teams, each gliding silently toward memorized and practiced objectives. Having studied the *Kuei Mei*'s deck plans and layout for hours back at Coronado, they knew exactly where they were going. They'd run endlessly through mock-ups of the vessel at the Special Warfare Center, practicing their moves, with the roles of the Chinese crew played by U.S. Marines. Each man knew exactly where he was going and how long he had to get there.

Morton and the two he'd kept with him, Schiff and Vandenberg, made their way forward to a cargo hold access hatch located in the deck just below the loom of the deckhouse and bridge. The hatch cover was secured by steel bars and a padlock, but a moment of Vandenberg's expertise with a pick released the bar and allowed them to quietly slide the cover back. The hold yawning beneath them was dark—reassuring since the lack of light suggested a lack of guards—and one by one they slipped over the hatch combing and made their way down the vertical ladder to the cargo deck below.

VBSS at times resembled a boarding action of the Age of Sail—storm aboard, guns at the ready, taking down the crew and securing the ship before they knew what had hit them. That was SOP so far as raids on suspected drug smugglers went, for instance, or when Intelligence had determined that a suspected terrorist was definitely aboard a certain boat.

There were times, however, when stealth was called for, especially when the intel picture wasn't clear. Intelligence had pinpointed the *Kuei Mei*'s probable cargo as something of interest, but the key word there was *probable*. In the shadow world of military intelligence and espionage, where nothing was quite as it seemed, a strike force sometimes had to develop its own intelligence, at least in so far as confirming Washington's suspicions was concerned.

And that was the first operational goal for Hammerhead, now that they were on board. The hold was too dark even for starlight optics. Pulling flashlights from their combat vests, the three SEALs made their way through the freighter's hold, which was stacked high with cargo pallets and wooden crates. Destination manifests attached to some of the crates identified them, in English and Pinyin, as machine tools and parts destined for the port of Los Angeles.

Using his Mark I diving knife, Morton prized back the lid to the nearest crate. Inside, beneath a layer of packing material, was . . .

Something that looked like a heavy tool die.

Schiff pried open another crate nearby. "Negative here," he whispered over the tactical channel, his voice rough in Morton's earplug speaker. "Machine parts."

"And here," Vandenberg said from another crate, farther aft.

"Keep looking," Morton said. The cargo they were looking for would be only a portion of the freighter's entire load. There would be plenty of legitimate cargo, if only to increase the chances of slipping the illegal stuff past U.S. customs.

They went through several more crates, scattering their choices around the hold to get a fair sampling. Morton finally chose a crate at the aft end of the compartment, one underneath a stack of other crates, so that he had to pry the side off to open it up.

Inside were half a dozen M-22 assault rifles, the export version of the Type 56, wrapped in plastic sheeting and coated with Cosmoline. They were missing their magazines, but Vandenberg found plenty of those a moment later in another crate nearby, while Schiff turned up a third loaded with 7.62mm rounds. The contraband seemed sequestered in the forward port corner of the hold, well away from the deck hatches. As the three men concentrated their search there, they found more crates, all labeled "machine parts" and "machine tools," which contained hundreds of the export assault rifles, plus magazines, ammunition, grenades, explosives, bulletproof vests. One large crate held the Chinese version of the Russian RPG-7 rocket-grenade launcher.

The SEALs continued their sampling, finding still more crates of weaponry. Especially worrying were the RPGs, which could take out a police armored car . . . or an airliner lifting off from a runway.

And all headed for Los Angeles.

"They have enough shit here to start a small war," Vandenberg whispered.

"Maybe that's the idea," Schiff replied.

"The war's already under way," Morton told them. "Beijing just wants to make some money on the side. But they're going to find out that *this* cargo was a damned bad investment."

The Beijing government had tried this before. Early in the Clinton administration the government had sold off the old Navy base at Long Beach, California; the facilities had been purchased by a Chinese firm as a commercial seagoing freight terminal. Despite its ongoing cosmetic overhaul and the occasional free-market protestations, the PRC was still a Communist state, and the trading company at Long Beach was little more than a front. Several Chinese freighters at Long Beach were discovered to be in violation of federal arms import regulations. Their cargoes had included automatic weapons and ammunition apparently brought into Los Angeles for sale to none other than the Crips, the Bloods, and other notorious street gangs.

Beijing's involvement in the bloody gang warfare in America's streets seemed to have less to do with fomenting armed revolution than it did with seeking profit. The People's Republic had been publicly chastised and the incidents largely forgotten.

But the political landscape had been changing rapidly of late. In 1993, Islamic terrorists had detonated a bomb at the base of one of the World Trade Center towers in New York City, in the heart of the downtown financial district. The plan, apparently, had been to topple one of the 110-story towers into the other, causing untold devastation and loss of life.

Those in the know had been briefed on something even more disturbing, something withheld from the general public: Buried in the basement rubble of the blast, a second bomb had been discovered, a chemical device set to release a large amount of cyanide gas well after the first blast. Had that weapon been detonated as planned, hundreds of police, firefighters, and paramedics would have been killed . . . and the poison cloud might well have spread across lower Manhattan, gassing untold thousands of civilians to death.

Few civilians were aware of this as yet. The administration, apparently, wished to avoid panic or a violent anti-Moslem reaction. But terrorism had come to the heart of America with a new and horrifying urgency, awakening the country's defenders to the reality of a new and potent threat. America was under attack by enemies who could slip in and out almost at will, across unguarded borders, by airliner or ocean freighter.

Just because you're paranoid, Morton thought, repeating the old joke to himself, it doesn't mean the bastards aren't out to get you.

"Hammerhead Two, this is Hammerhead One," he called softly, engaging his mike. "Two, this is One. Do you copy?"

No response. Hammerhead Two was investigating the hold forward of the one Morton was in.

"Whalesong, Hammerhead. Do you copy?"

Again no reply. Likely, the massive steel bulkheads

were interfering with the transmission. They'd expected as much. "Okay," he told the other SEALs. "Let's get back on deck and see if we can get a clear signal."

Their op orders required that they buck their discovery up the intel ladder, then wait to see what came back down.

He just hoped they wouldn't have to wait long. Each additional minute on board the freighter increased the chances of their discovery, and this was *not* a good place to be caught.

USS *Pittsburgh*
48° 16' N, 178° 02' E
0412 hours Zulu

"Conn, Sonar!"

"Conn here. Go."

"Sir, we have a definite contact, Sierra One-two, bearing two-eight-four, range approximately six-zero-zero."

"On my way." Commander Garrett hurried across the bridge to the sonar shack, stepping into the narrow room. Chief Schuster was waiting for him with another printout. "Nailed the bastard," he said, grinning. "Course one-eight-zero, slipping along right behind the freighter." He pointed at the printout. "These sounds right here? They're from the freighter . . . and you can see where she cut back on her revs here, slowing down . . . and going to a stop. This over here . . . that's Sierra One-two. He's real, real quiet, but he cut back on his revs a moment ago and started cavitating."

Cavitation occurred when a ship's turning screw slowed too quickly, causing bubbles to collapse against the blades' surfaces—bubbles that popped and crackled with a distinctive signature easily intercepted by a sub's sonar. Turning the *Pittsburgh* parallel to the other vessel's southward course exposed the entire length of her trailing TB-23 streaming sonar array. That made *Pittsburgh*'s underwater ears both more sensitive and more precise, allowing a rough guess at the target's range of about six hundred yards.

"Andrews," Garret said. "Any sign that he's heard us?"

"Can't tell, Skipper," Andrews said. "Target's not acting like it."

"Yeah," Schuster added. "The real question is, does he know yet that the target has visitors . . . and has he guessed that those visitors must have come from another sub in the area?"

"Best guess on class?"

"Definitely a delta-echo, sir," Andrews said, referring to a diesel-electric motor. "Sounds like a Kilo . . . or maybe doesn't sound is a better way to say it. I keep listening and . . . there's just nothing there. Dead, like."

"Something that quiet," Schuster added, "I'd have to go with a Kilo."

"Yeah. That's what I'm thinking," Garrett said, nodding. "Okay. Keep on him. I want to know if he so much as reaches back to scratch his ass."

"You've got it, Captain," the sonar chief replied.

Garrett stepped back out of the sonar shack and returned to his usual position beside the periscope platform. A Kilo, trailing a Chinese freighter. This was not good . . . not good at all.

The SEAL platoon out there might just find itself flat out of luck.

Thursday, 23 September 1999

USS *Pittsburgh*
48° 16' N, 178° 02' E
0414 hours Zulu

Garrett looked across the control room at *Pittsburgh*'s weapons officer, Lieutenant Roger Yantis. "Weps, ready warshots, tubes One and Three. Do not, repeat, not flood the tubes."

"Ready warshots, tubes One and Three," Yantis repeated. "Do not flood the tubes, aye, sir."

"Maneuvering."

"Maneuvering, aye, sir."

"Down scope. Down bubble, ten degrees. Make depth one-two-zero feet."

"Down scope, aye, sir. Make depth one-two-zero feet, aye." The planesman pushed the aircraft-style control yoke forward, and Garrett felt the deck tilting beneath his feet.

They would be quieter completely submerged. When *Pittsburgh*'s periscope and radio masts extended above the surface, the wake caused by the sub's movement and maneuvers could be picked up by a listening enemy. Unfortunately, this would put them out of touch with the SEALs until they could return to periscope depth.

After a moment the deck tipped back to a level plane. "Leveling off at one-two-zero feet, sir," Master Chief DePaul said.

"Helm, come about to port . . . a slow turn to one-eight-four degrees. I want to slip right into that bastard's baffles without him smelling us."

"Come about to port, make course one-eight-four degrees, aye, sir." The order was passed to the helmsman, the acknowledgment passed back up. "Slow turn to port, make course one-eight-four, aye aye, sir."

"Pass the word through the boat—no unnecessary noise. Let's see if we can outquiet a Kilo."

Which wasn't easy. The Russian-built submarine designated by NATO as "Kilo" was one of the quietest in the world. It didn't have the range, tonnage, or staying power of the bigger nuclear boats, but its diesel-electric engine let it travel in almost perfect silence, so long as it stayed below about five or six knots.

The Russians called the Kilo class Varshavyankas, and had made them one of the mainstays of their foreign trade program. Anyone with about $300 million could buy one, and in recent years customers had included Libya, Iran, India, and, most recently, the People's Republic of China.

While that "hole in the water" out there *might* be a neutral foreign sub practicing maneuvers on an unsuspecting freighter, Garrett had to assume that it was an escort, one of the new Chinese Kilos riding shotgun on the freighter and her cargo.

And if that were true, he just might have an explosive situation on his hands. Starting a war with China would not look at all good in his service record.

But the way things were shaping up, it was possible that he wouldn't be given any other options.

Chinese Freighter *Kuei Mei*
48° 16' N, 178° 02' E
0414 hours Zulu

"Whalesong, this is Hammerhead! Whalesong, this is Hammerhead!" Again and again Morton keyed his Motorola, trying to reach the *Pittsburgh* over the scrambled command channel. There was no answer, and since none of the SEALs could raise the sub on any of their radios, there were only two possibilities open. Either the *Pittsburgh*'s communications were out, or the submarine had submerged.

Either way, the timing sucked.

The three SEALs had reemerged from the depths of the freighter's aft cargo hold, and were now crouching in the shelter afforded by some oil drums stacked on the main deck just forward of the bridge house. With flashlights doused, they again wore their starlight masks, which turned the glow from the bridge overhead into a fierce, green-yellow glare and rendered the deck nearly day-bright.

According to the op plan, they needed to get a final go/no-go from Special Operations Command, by way of the *Pittsburgh*'s communications center. Plan Alfa

had them take down the freighter themselves. Bravo
had them return to the sea for recovery aboard the
Pittsburgh, at which point the *Kuei Mei* would either
be sunk by the *Pittsburgh* or boarded by conventional
forces off of an American Coast Guard cutter.

That the matter was still in doubt was a testament to
the incredible power of bureaucracy. The civilians who
needed to make the decision about the *Kuei Mei*'s fate
wanted all of the information before making that decision. Morton understood that. In his line of work,
good, solid intel was worth a hell of a lot more than
gold. But in this case, it deprived the SEAL Team on-site
with the freedom to make their own decisions based on
the tacsit as they saw it. Micromanagement was never a
good option in a combat situation. Jimmy Carter had
tried running the op personally during Operation Eagle's Claw, the attempt to rescue the American hostages
in Iran back in 1980, and in the end General Beckwith,
in command on the ground at Desert One, had elected
to have "communications difficulties."

Morton looked up at the black and unpromising sky.
A light rain, lashed by a stiff wind, was starting to fall.
If they'd brought their own satcom gear, they might
have established a direct link to SOCOM at Fort
Bragg. But the team had already been heavily loaded
for an underwater lockout and approach, so the decision had been made to relay all communications
through the waiting *Pittsburgh*.

Only now the 'Burgh was out of touch. And if they
didn't make contact soon, Morton know he would
have to make his own decision about this cluster fuck
without Washington's help, a notion that at the moment was looking better and better.

USS *Pittsburgh*
48° 16' N, 178° 02' E
0420 hours Zulu

Lieutenant Ralph Henderson, *Pittsburgh*'s navigation officer, looked up from the starboard chart table. "Turn complete," he said. "We're in his baffles, sir."

"*Should* be," Garrett replied. "If he didn't change course while we were swinging around behind him."

Not being able to see, playing the game with sound and maneuver alone, was a real challenge. Things were a lot tougher when you couldn't see the other guy, when even the sound he was making was so faint it was like following whispers down an echo-ridden alley. Worse, passive sonar only gave relative bearing on the target, not range—with only an occasional educated guess on the actual distance if the sonar team was very good. *Pittsburgh*'s sonar people were the best, but Garrett had to keep reminding himself that their determinations were *only* guesses. If the sierra contact up ahead had maintained his speed and course throughout the maneuver, he ought to be about six hundred yards in front of *Pittsburgh*'s bluntly rounded bow. The first law of military tactics, however, was that the other fellow *never* did what he was supposed to do.

"Sonar, this is the Captain. You still have Sierra One-two?"

"Captain, Sonar," Chief Schuster's voice came back. "Intermittent contact, sir. We're picking up some prop wash. Sounds like we're smack in his baffles. Range, I'd make it about five hundred, five hundred fifty yards."

Even the quietest submarine stirred the water astern with its screw. That caused some noise, of course . . . and also left the water turbulent, making sonar reception difficult through the disturbance. The result was that a submarine was largely deaf to the area dead astern; a stalking sub could follow literally in its wake, able to hear the prey without being heard in turn. Tactically, it was the ideal place to be when hunting another submarine.

It was also dangerous. If the Kilo up ahead decided to stop or slow suddenly, *Pittsburgh* could ride right up his wake and smack him in the ass—an embarrassment, to say the least, and a possible international incident best avoided. Back in the wild and woolly days of the Cold War, there'd been a number of collisions between U.S. and Soviet subs hunting one another, boats whose skippers had been unlucky, become careless, or, just as bad, had been too aggressive.

Garrett's first responsibility—after the captain's ever-present responsibility to ship and crew—was to the mission, which meant the safety of the SEAL team aboard that freighter, the successful completion of their operation, and their safe recovery afterward. The Kilo was germane to all of that only in so far as it became a threat—to the *Pittsburgh* first, then to the mission.

Stewart joined Garrett at the chart table. "Skipper, I'm going over it and over it," he said, shaking his head, "and I still can't figure it. What the hell is a Kilo doing way out here?"

"If he is Chinese," Henderson added, "he's a hell of a long way from home. Kilos have a top range of, what? Three thousand miles, before they have to refuel? That would almost take him from the China Sea to the West Coast along the Great Circle . . . and leave him stranded."

"Maybe he's Russian," Stewart said, "operating

out of Petro. That would extend his trans-Pacific range a bit."

"He'd still need to meet with a sub-provisioning ship out here to make it home," Garrett said. "Kilos just aren't meant to be used at long range. Stew, we need some updated intel on ship movements out here, with an emphasis on sub tenders."

"I'll have Sparks get on that, as soon as we can get a transmission out."

"Good."

The problem was, the Kilo *was* a threat, both to the *Pittsburgh* and to the mission. Garrett refused to believe that the other sub was here by accident. It was deliberately trailing the Chinese freighter, which probably meant it was an escort, protecting the freighter and *its* mission. And that meant that the Kilo and the *'Burgh* were already on an intercept course, whatever the plot table might say.

Suddenly, the control room seemed a bit crowded to Garrett . . . as if a whole host of politicians, bureaucrats, and armchair-bound second-guessers were watching over his shoulder. No matter what he did in the next few minutes, there was a better than even chance that someone would very soon be pointing out how he'd made exactly the wrong decision.

"Maneuvering," he said. "Planes, up five degrees. Bring us to periscope depth."

"Planes up five degrees. Set periscope depth, aye, sir."

They couldn't do a thing for the SEALs on board the freighter if they didn't have the sub's radio mast above the water, if they weren't available to pass on communications between the SEALs and SOCOM.

And if that meant risking detection by the Kilo, so be it.

Chinese Freighter *Kuei Mei*
48° 16' N, 178° 02' E
0424 hours Zulu

"We can't wait any longer," Morton told the others, speaking over the tactical channel so every man in the VBSS team could hear him. "Execute Plan Bravo. Repeat, Bravo."

Morton's personal preference would have been to go for Alfa—to take the bastards down and take over the ship—but both training and professionalism dictated a safer course. They would retreat to the sea. To remain on board the freighter much longer was to invite the risk of being discovered and forcing them into a firefight. The freighter was still several days out from U.S. waters; once they reestablished contact with the *'Burgh*, they would let SOCOM and Washington decide what to do with this mess. The trick, of course, was to get in touch with the sub again; there was no way to know what had gone wrong, or why the *Pittsburgh* was currently out of touch. She must have been forced to submerge . . . but why?

They would sort that out later. Right now it was imperative that the SEALs get off the freighter, preferably unnoticed and with their valuable intelligence coup intact. One way or another, the *Kuei Mei* would not be unloading her death-dealing cargo at Long Beach, for distribution to the street and drug gangs of Los Angeles, and that was all that mattered.

"One, Two" sounded in his earphone. "Confirm Plan Bravo. We're moving."

So Conyers and his team, assembled now on the freighter's port side, had the word and were returning to their CRRC. It was time for Morton and his people to do the same. "Let's get the hell out of Dodge," he told Vandenberg, crouched in the shadows at his side. They started moving toward the starboard companionway aft.

The eruption of gunfire was as spectacular as it was sudden, a sharp and thunderous clatter accompanied by stabbing bursts of muzzle flash, dazzling against the night. The first burst, from the port side forward, was matched almost immediately by a second burst from the port wing of the bridge, high above the main deck.

"Hammerhead One, this is Two!" sounded over his earphone. "We are compromised! We are compromised! We are taking fire!"

"Copy, Two! All Hammerheads, we are weapons free, repeat, weapons free! Support Hammerhead Two!"

Powerful searchlights on the bridge wings snapped on, bathing the main deck in an actinic, blue-white glare. Raising himself above part of the base mounting for a deck crane, Morton snapped off the safety on his H&K, shouldered the weapon, and loosed a three-round burst at one of the lights. The searchlight flared, then died in a scattering cascade of sparks and hot, falling shards of glass. A shadowy figure behind the light shrieked something in high-pitched Chinese.

A stabbing blaze of gunfire from the bridge wing nearby sent rounds snapping over Morton's head and clanging wildly off the crane. He returned fire, his H&K chuffing off rounds in near silence, spent brass clinking at his feet as he targeted the shadowy gunman high above the deck. He thought he hit the guy but couldn't tell for sure. More gunfire erupted from the port side as Chinese sailors converged on Conyers and his team.

This was getting very nasty, very fast.

USS *Pittsburgh*
48° 16' N, 178° 02' E
0425 hours Zulu

"Conn, Sonar! I'm picking up what sounds like gun-fire from the freighter! It's pretty noisy up there!"

Shit. The balloon had just gone up.

The deck leveled off beneath Garrett's feet. "Level-ing off at five-eight feet, Captain," the diving officer announced.

"Up periscope. Sonar! Bearing on Sierra One-one and on Sierra One-two!"

"Sierra One-one at one-seven-five degrees, range ap-proximately one thousand. Sierra One-two at one-eight-one degrees, range approximately five hundred."

Sierra 11 was the freighter, 12 the probable Kilo. Right now the Kilo was between the freighter and the *Pittsburgh*, offset by a small amount.

The starboard periscope slid smoothly in its housing, rising in front of Garrett until he could snap down the handles and lean into the viewer. Swinging the scope to five degrees off to the east of due south, he peered into darkness, highlighted by the eerie green-yellow of starlight optics.

There she was, green-lit and stern-on, the Chinese freighter rolling slightly in the heavy swell. He could see the glare from a searchlight forward, mostly masked by the loom of the deckhouse, funnel, and masts.

"Communications!" he rasped. "Get me a channel to Hammerhead."

"We're picking up tactical chatter, sir."

"Put it on speaker."

Now that *Pittsburgh*'s periscope-mounted radio

mast was above the surface again, they could hear the communications chatter from the SEAL Team.

"Watch it! Shooter on the starboard bridge wing! Shooter on the starboard bridge wing!"

"I see him. He's down. Cover me!"

"Cyzynski! On me! Move it!"

The words were sharp and urgent, punctuated by rattling bursts of automatic gunfire and the shriek and chirp of ricochets.

"Conn! Sonar! Cavitation noises from Sierra One-two! He's slowing!"

"Helm! Come right forty-five degrees!"

"Helm right four-five degrees, aye aye, sir!"

"Conn, Sonar! I have ballast noise from Sierra One-two! He's surfacing!"

Garrett swung the periscope slightly to the right, looking for the surfacing sub. Ballast noise meant he was blowing his tanks, replacing water with air to take him to the surface. The fact that he was slowing suddenly meant that the American boat was in immediate danger of ramming him. The *Pittsburgh* was almost 110 meters long and had a submerged displacement of over seven thousand tons. She was currently traveling at eight knots—not fast at all, but you did not stop that much mass on a dime.

"Hammerhead One" rasped from the bulkhead speaker. "This is Two! We need fire support!"

From the sound of things, the SEALs on board the Chinese freighter were fighting for their lives.

And in the next few minutes the *Pittsburgh* might well be doing the same.

Chinese Freighter *Kuei Mei*
48° 16' N, 178° 02' E
0426 hours Zulu

The second spotlight flared and died in a burst of broken glass and sparks. Morton keyed his mike. "All Hammerheads, execute Plan Alfa! Repeat, execute Alfa!" It was always dangerous changing horses in midstream, but if they continued trying to get back to their CRRCs, they risked being pinned down on deck in a deadly gunfight. It was time to go over to the offensive.

In Plan Alfa, Morton, Schiff, and Vandenberg were tasked with securing the *Kuei Mei*'s bridge, which meant moving aft to the starboard companionway, then up a partially enclosed ladder. Schiff opened fire on full auto, spraying the bridge and bridge wings so Vandenberg and Morton could sprint for the partial cover of the deckhouse. A Chinese sailor stepped through an open door in the front of the house, an assault rifle at the ready. Morton triggered a three-round burst as he ran, not even slowing as the other man spun to the side and collapsed. Morton and Vandenberg paused at the ladder, waiting as Schiff pounded across the deck and joined them.

Up the ladder, then, rubber boots almost silent on the metal rungs. The ladder opened onto the first deck above the main deck. Another Chinese sailor with striped shirt and an assault rifle turned as they emerged from the ladder well. Schiff triggered his H&K twice, a double tap on semiauto that punched the sailor back, slammed him against the bulkhead, and put him down with a heavy thump that was louder than the soft chuffing of the sound-suppressed submachine gun.

Around the corner and up another ladder took them to the bridge level, emerging on a partially enclosed passageway leading to the bridge's starboard wing.

An officer—his cap and jacket identified him as such—stood on the wing, staring at them in gapemouthed astonishment. Schiff double-tapped again, but the man was already moving, lunging through the door to the bridge, shrieking warning in a high-pitched singsong.

The door to the bridge slammed, clanking as it was dogged shut. Vandenberg slapped a breaching charge over the hinges, yanked the pull ring on the detonator, and stepped back. There was a sharp crack, then a clang as the heavy door blew partway open.

Morton leaned around the opening and tossed a flash-crash into the bridge compartment as Vandenberg kicked the partially opened watertight door aside. An instant later the darkened bridge lit up like a strobe flash as a deafening crack echoed from steel bulkheads. Morton and Schiff together each loosed a pair of three-round bursts into the compartment as someone inside screamed. Schiff rolled through the opening, followed by Vandenberg; Morton followed close behind, triggering his H&K again, to catch a Chinese sailor in the act of raising his assault rifle to his shoulder. Several more bursts and two men still on their feet went down.

"Hammerhead," Morton said into his mike. "Bridge clear."

The huge, front windscreens enclosing the bridge had been shattered from the earlier exchange of gunfire, and wind and a light, misty rain streamed through the openings. Six bodies lay strewn about on the deck, and the ship's wheel slowly turned on its own. The lights were out, but the scene was painted in sharp luminescence in the SEALs' night vision goggles.

Vandenberg ran aft to the door leading to the freighter's radio room. The door was locked, but the SEAL's shotgun, referred to with wry humor as a "Masterkey," boomed in the smoky, enclosed compartment, shattering the lock. Schiff and Morton rolled through the open door together, catching a Chinese radio officer hunched over the radio. He looked up at them with wide eyes as his hand closed on a pistol holstered at his hip. Schiff took the man down with three rounds to his center of mass.

Vandenberg looked at the radio. "You think he got a call out?"

"Doesn't matter now," Morton said. "Make sure no one else does." Vandenberg's shotgun thundered again, smashing the radio's console.

"Sir!" Schiff called from the starboard side of the bridge. "Look at this!"

Morton joined the other SEAL, looking out the shattered doorway onto the exposed right wing of the bridge. Spray cascaded from the surface of the ocean less than fifty yards off to starboard, where something huge, a night-black whale with a low, squared-off dorsal fin, emerged in an explosion of foam, wind-whipped spindrift, and crashing waves.

His first thought was that the *Pittsburgh* was surfacing . . . in stark and utter betrayal of her orders to avoid possible detection by the enemy.

But he immediately abandoned that idea as he got a clearer view of the sub. The sail was all wrong, too long and not nearly tall enough. Though size was always tough to gauge without known referents, the sub wasn't nearly big enough to be a Los Angeles–class boat by at least a quarter. Other details—the shape of the hull, with a sharply-angled platform rising to a flat deck above the rounded hull, and the lack of diving planes mounted on the sail, the lack of an LA-boat's characteristic gray-mottled camouflage on the periscope masts—all added up to one incontrovertible fact.

That was not the *Pittsburgh* surfacing off the *Kuei Mei*'s starboard beam. It wasn't even American. Morton's knowledge of the submarine classes of other navies was less than expert, but he thought the boat had the look of a Russian sub.

He was pretty sure it was their export diesel boat—a Kilo.

What the hell was a Kilo doing way out here? There was no way to judge the nationality. If it was a Kilo, it might be Russian, or it could belong to China, India, or any of several other nations.

But then, the fact that it was trailing the *Kuei Mei* so closely suggested it was probably one of the new Chinese Kilos, accompanying the freighter as escort. If so, the SEAL op had just encountered one hell of an unexpected twist.

In the spray and rain-lashed darkness, Morton could just make out several shapes appearing in the Kilo's weather cockpit, atop and at the front of the sail, just beneath the periscope array. A loud-hailer squealed, and then he heard a staccato burst of Chinese, calling across the water.

That settled the nationality question, at least.

And it answered the question of what had become of the *Pittsburgh* as well. The American sub must have dropped below periscope depth in order to stalk the Kilo or to avoid being spotted herself.

A searchlight blazed from the Kilo's cockpit, illuminating the *Kuei Mei*'s bridge. More orders were barked in Chinese over a loud-hailer, followed a moment later by a burst of automatic gunfire. A bustle of activity on the sub's forward deck suggested that they were getting a boat ready to send a boarding party across.

There were damned few options open to the SEALs now. They could wait and face capture by the crew of the Chinese submarine. They could fight back, and trigger the international incident they'd been ordered to avoid at all costs. They could try to steer clear of the Chinese boarding party . . . but that could only be carried out for so long.

They could also pray that the *Pittsburgh* returned quickly to radio contact, so the question could be boosted upstairs.

Morton snorted at that idea. The bureaucrats were safely stateside, warm and dry, not here. *He* would decide how to pull his boys out of the fire.

Deciding, he raced across the bridge to the helm station, where the ship's wheel was slowly turning free above the body of the freighter's helmsman. The engine room telegraph was marked off in Chinese characters, but it was easy enough to guess that pulling the red-handled lever all the way back, then shoving it full forward, was the cue to go to full steam ahead. At the same time, he grabbed the ship's wheel and spun it hard to the right. They might be able to avoid a gun battle if he could distract the Chinese submarine for a moment . . . by ramming her.

But the *Kuei Mei* was sluggish and handled slowly, especially wallowing in these heavy seas. Her best speed was twelve knots, about the same as a Kilo on the surface, but the Kilo was far nimbler and more responsive to the helm. Morton's ramming attempt

would work only if he could catch the skipper of the
Chinese sub off guard.

The sub driver was good, though, or at least alert. As
the freighter clumsily swung to starboard, so did the
Chinese submarine, dancing easily out of the *Kuei
Mei*'s reach.

**USS *Pittsburgh*
48° 16' N, 178° 02' E
0430 hours Zulu**

"Conn, Sonar! Change of aspect, on Sierra One-
two! He's turning hard to starboard!"

Which meant the other sub was suddenly cutting
across the *Pittsburgh*'s path.

"Estimated range to Sierra One-two!"

"Estimate . . . two hundred yards, sir!"

"Diving Officer! Emergency dive! Down bubble,
twenty degrees! Helm, come hard right rudder!" The
deck tilted down, sharply, then slanted to starboard as
the *Pittsburgh* dropped into a sharp, plunging turn.
The Kilo's turning radius was tighter than the *Pittsburgh*'s; her shorter hull made for more maneuverability. At six knots, the *Pittsburgh* might slow in time, but
she stood a better chance of turning away from the
other sub and trying to drop beneath her. If he cut
speed, he would lose maneuverability. So many decisions to be made in so short a time . . .

And then there was no time for decision making.
Garrett could hear—they all could hear!—the steady
thrum of the Kilo's screw ahead and above, growing
closer, almost masked by the heavier pounding of the
freighter's propeller. It was going to be close. . . .

Garrett grabbed the microphone and switched it to intercom speaker. "All hands! Brace for collision! Sound collision alert!"

The klaxon sounded its shrill warning squawk, and then they struck with a thunderous impact, dimming the lights and flinging them all hard and to the right. For a horrifying nightmare of a moment it felt like *Pittsburgh* was about to go bellyup. . . .

Thursday, 23 September 1999

USS *Pittsburgh*
48° 16' N, 178° 02' E
0430 hours Zulu

Garrett grabbed hold of the safety railing next to the periscope platform as the *Pittsburgh* heeled over to starboard. The main lights flickered out a second time, replaced by the eerie glow of the emergency lights, before coming back on full. With the deck tilted to a forty-five-degree angle, all he, all any of the men in the control room, could do was hang on, waiting, as a shrill, metallic ripping sound grated through the hull from somewhere overhead.

"Caught her with our conning tower," Stewart said, looking up at the overhead. Then the scraping, ripping sound stopped and the *Pittsburgh* began to right herself, the deck slipping back toward a more reasonable level plane.

They were continuing to descend, however, in obedience to Garrett's last command. "Level off at one hundred feet!" he snapped.

"Make depth one hundred feet," the diving officer replied. There was remarkably little stress evident in his voice, considering what had just happened. "Aye aye!"

Everyone in the control room continued carrying out his assigned tasks, calmly and professionally. There was a terrifying number of things that could go wrong on board a submarine, any of which could kill her and her crew: fire, explosion, exceeding crush depth, collision. Every man aboard knew how close they'd just come to disaster and knew, too, that the threat wasn't past yet.

Collision was a constant danger for a submerged boat, especially for one submerged just beneath the surface. With her awareness of the outside world limited to the less than ideal sense of sound—a sense that could passively give direction but was notoriously vague on distance—she was awkwardly blind in tight quarters.

"Leveling off at one-zero-zero feet, Captain," the diving officer announced.

"Damage control, this is the captain," Garrett called. "What's our status?"

"Still checking, sir," a harried-sounding voice came back. "We have minor flooding in the sail. No other damage that we can track yet."

"Keep on it."

"Captain," the diving officer said. "We're having some problems with the sail planes. I think we took some damage on the port plane."

"How bad?"

"We can work with it . . . but we're going to need to get her back to the World to fix her permanent."

That was inevitable anyway. After a collision of this magnitude, they would need to have the hull damage boys go over her from sail to keel with a toothbrush, looking for dings and dents. And there would be the inquiry as well . . .

Time to think about that, and the future of his Navy career, later. Right now he had a boat and crew to save . . . and if he managed that, there was still the mission to think about.

"Conn, Sonar!"

Now the hell what? "Sonar, Conn. Go ahead."

"Change of aspect on Sierra One-one! He's turning to starboard! I think he's—"

A second grinding, scraping noise of metal on metal sounded through the control room.

Chinese Freighter *Kuei Mei*
48° 16' N, 178° 02' E
0431 hours Zulu

For a moment it looked as though the Kilo was going to easily slip inside of the *Kuei Mei*'s turn to starboard, avoiding the freighter's clumsy sally. Suddenly, though, the surfaced submarine had shuddered, as though she'd run hard aground, and then her blunt prow came swing back to port, straight across the line of the *Kuei Mei*'s charge.

"Hang on!" Morton yelled, and then the freighter's bow slammed against the hull of the Chinese submarine midway between her sail and her rounded prow, shuddering, then rising sharply as the sub's nose was pressed inexorably down into the sea. The *Kuei Mei* heeled over to port by ten degrees, continuing to grind slowly ahead with a shriek of tearing metal. The crane mast jerked forward, halted, then toppled to the deck in a tangle of guy wires and spars. A moment later there was a telltale crack and a thump as the deck dropped a foot or so. It felt as though the freighter may have just broken her back.

"Hey, Skipper?" Schiff called to Morton across the bridge.

"What?"

"Anyone ever tell you you're an awful driver?"

"Hey, it's my first time at the wheel. Cut me some slack."

"He's gonna lose his license for sure," Vandenberg observed.

Morton moved across the sloping deck to the starboard bridge windows and looked down at the Kilo. It didn't look as though the submarine was damaged much at all, but the forward part of the freighter's hull appeared to be buckling. Another long, drawn-out shudder confirmed it. The freighter was old, her hull rusting. The stress of the collision had done her mortal damage.

Which worked. Morton had hoped to pull off a diversion at best, perhaps buy some time. If the *Kuei Mei* was sinking, the question of what to do about her deadly cargo was no longer in the hands of Washington bureaucrats.

But just to make sure . . .

"You two get back down to the aft hold," he told them. "Plant charges on the contraband we found . . . especially the ammo, understand me?"

"Roger that."

"Set it for . . . make it ten minutes. If you can manage to punch a hole in the hull while you're at it, so much the better. It won't look completely like an accident, but it'll confuse the hell out of things. Move it!"

"Aye aye, sir!"

The gun battle seemed to be in abeyance for the moment. Several Chinese sailors were running about on the forward deck, green and yellow shapes against the shadows in the starlight optics. To the freighter's port side, the Chinese submarine was riding at a sharp list, almost beneath the bridge. Morton could look down into the cockpit, only a few feet below the weather bridge, and see several officers and crewmen scrambling out of the sail and down ladder rungs to the sloping deck.

A flare burst into starlike radiance above the entangled vessels, illuminating them both in an uneasily shifting pattern of light and dark. The Chinese submarine would be sending a distress signal by now; he wondered what the closest vessel was . . . Chinese?

Well, the *closest* vessel would be the *Pittsburgh*, somewhere out there, cloaked in night and ocean. Interesting question in international ethics, this: A moment ago, one of his options had been to sink the *Kuei Mei*, an act of deliberate aggression; now she was going down, but accidentally . . . or nearly so. The *Pittsburgh* was out there, supporting the op, yet all vessels were required to respond to a mayday. Commander Garrett was an idiot if he decided to surface and render aid, and yet if he didn't, it was possible he'd be roasted alive by a Board of Inquiry.

Morton was damned glad that he didn't have Garrett's job right now.

And now that he thought about it, the Chinese sub had jolted as if she'd hit something just before swinging back to port to collide with the freighter. Had she hit something unseen beneath the surface?

God above, had she hit the *Pittsburgh*?

He searched the surface, lit in black and silver by the light of the slowly descending flare, but couldn't see anything that was obviously a sign of another sub.

There were men in the water now . . . crewmen from the sinking freighter. Crewmen on the sub were throwing them lines, helping them scramble aboard.

"Hammerhead One-one, this is One-five." That was TM2 Ciotti.

"One-five, One-one. Go ahead."

"Bad news, Skipper. Our CRRC is gone. I think it got torn free in the collision."

"Roger that. Muster on the port side. We'll go out with Hammerhead Two."

"Aye, sir. Moving!"

"Hammerhead One, this is Hammerhead Two."

"Go ahead, Two."

"Can't make it to the engine room, Jack," Conyers said. "Too many hostiles, and it sounds like the engines are dead anyway."

Conyers's team had been tasked by Op Plan Bravo with taking the freighter's engine room and securing it, with the optional possibility of planting explosives to wreck the propeller shaft.

"Change of plan, Brad," Morton said. "She's done for. Fall back to your rubber duck and wait for the rest of us. The other duck is out of action. We'll go out with you."

"Aye aye, sir!"

"Hammerhead One-one, this is One-two!"

"Go ahead, Schiff."

"Can't get to the goodies, Skipper. The aft hold is flooding, and pretty fast. It's suicide to go down there now!"

"Okay. Pull out and fall back to the port side access. We're going out with Hammerhead Two."

"Roger that, Skipper. See you there."

"I'm on my way." There was nothing more to be done here.

But before he left the bridge, Morton took a last look at the Chinese sub, crowded up against the freighter's hull. A lone man stood in the sub's cockpit, less than twenty yards away and a few feet below Morton's position on the bridge. He wore a dark greatcoat and was close enough that, by the light of the dying flare, Morton could see his face, see his expression. The man was staring directly at him, a scowl on his flat features.

Morton was still wearing his starlight goggles, but he wasn't worried about being seen. It was too late to hide the presence of invaders on board the *Kuei Mei*; there would be enough survivors from the freighter to tell of the battle with mysterious boarders.

Casually, almost nonchalantly, Morton raised his hand to his brow, saluting the other officer. The salute was not returned, but Morton could have sworn the man was muttering something, whether to himself or to someone unseen on the sub's sail, it was impossible to tell.

Morton turned away and left by way of the port-side bridge entryway.

They would have to move fast for all of the SEALs to get safely off the stricken ship.

USS *Pittsburgh*
48° 16' N, 178° 02' E
0433 hours Zulu

"The freighter has definitely collided with Sierra One-two, Captain," Chief Schuster said. "We're getting hull-breaking noises and sporadic gunfire. Sounds like our boys are raising hell over there, sir."

Which, of course, was what SEALs were paid to do.

Still, to use the precise military terminology for this sort of affair, this whole operation had devolved into a class-A cluster fuck. The best special ops were those where not a shot was fired. The white hats went in, did their thing silent and unobserved, and slipped out again without anyone knowing they'd been there.

Judging from the sounds they were picking up in the sonar shack, Morton and his people were raising one hell of a ruckus topside, too much of a ruckus for a classically stealthy in-and-out. The question now was how to help them extricate themselves . . . and to preserve both *Pittsburgh*'s safety and anonymity.

"Helm! What's our bearing?"

"Bearing now zero-four-two, Captain."

"Very well. Hard right rudder, and hold her there all the way around to zero-zero-zero."

"Come right to zero-zero-zero, aye aye, sir."

"Sonar, Conn. We're doing an almost-three-sixty. Clear our baffles."

"Conn, Sonar. Clear our baffles, aye."

First and foremost, he wanted to turn the boat clear of the pile-up to port. It wouldn't help anyone if he managed to foul the *Pittsburgh* on the Kilo or the freighter.

Next, the Chinese Kilo had provided one unexpected and unpleasant surprise so far. He wanted to be sure there were no other surprises lurking out there, masked by the sounds of *Pittsburgh*'s own screw.

And finally, by turning around in an almost complete circle, he would bring the *'Burgh* onto a northerly course, but about a couple of thousand yards farther to the west, with the freighter between the American sub and the Kilo.

As for the SEALs, they'd have to take care of their own extraction.

Garrett knew their rep. If any men on the planet could pull it off, it was the Navy SEALs.

Chinese Freighter *Kuei Mei*
48° 16' N, 178° 02' E
0438 hours Zulu

Morton bounded down the port-side companionway ladder and dropped to the main deck. Conyers and his men were already there, holding a perimeter around the spot where the remaining CRRC was tied to the ship's side. The rain was coming down harder now, and the steel deck was slippery. Gunfire crackled from the forward deck, where several Chinese with automatic weapons were trying to get close enough to hit the crouching SEALs. Bullets sang and chirped off metal or snapped through the air overhead.

He did a quick count of goggle-faced SEALs. Twelve . . . two missing.

"All Hammerheads!" he snapped into his mike. "Who's missing muster?"

"One-one, this is One-six." That was Hanson. "I'm pinned down, port side forward! They've got me pretty well zeroed in!"

"One-one, this is One-three!" That was Young. "I'm port side, midships, on the main deck. Pinned down by bad guys forward!"

"Okay, boys, I copy. Watch for your chance and get the hell over here."

"Whattaya gonna do, Skipper?" Conyers asked. He was crouched behind a fifty-five gallon drum, loosing three-round bursts into the fire-streaked darkness.

"I'm leaving you in charge, Two-IC, that's what.

Whatever happens, get everyone you can over the side and out to sea."

"But—"

"Just do it, damn it! I'll be along in a minute!" Slinging his weapon, Morton reached into his combat vest and pulled out both of the blocks of plastic explosive he was carrying. "C'mon," he added, holding the explosives out in his hands. "Let's have 'em!"

The other SEALs contributed their explosives loads, enough to pile into a bundle the size of four loaves of bread.

"Now cover me!"

The SEALs opened up in full-auto mayhem then, spraying the forward deck. Flash-bang grenades detonated, their flashes strobing brilliantly against the night and casting wildly moving shadows across the deck house. Under that fusillade of lead and pyrotechnics, Morton crawled rapidly across the water-slick deck, his progress aided by the fact that the *Kuei Mei* was listing forward and to port now, which meant he was slide-crawling downhill.

He was baffled momentarily by the tangle of the fallen crane, which blocked his way, but was able to wiggle between two fallen yards, pushing his deadly package ahead of him.

The barrage from the SEAL position continued, keeping the oppositions' heads down, but the SEALs had come with only a normal VBSS load of ammo, not enough to carry on a sustained battle. They would have to start conserving their ammunition, and picking their shots, very soon now.

At last Morton reached his destination—the deck hatchway leading down into the after hold. The cover was off and a thin, hard mist of water was spraying up through the opening. He used his flash to check the opening. Vandenberg and Schiff had been right: Water was entering the after hold at a considerable rate. He could see the black and oily surface roiling below, surrounding the stacks of crates and drums. He guessed there was three or four feet of water in the hold already. Either the *Kuei Mei*'s hull was old and brittle, her plates snapped open by the shock of the impact, or the Kilo had caught the freighter a slashing blow with her forward diving planes, ripping open her side like the iceberg gutting the *Titanic*. Either way, the freighter was doomed.

What he was about to do might or might not hasten her end, but what he hoped it would do was convince those of her crew remaining on board to give up the fight and abandon ship. Carefully, he removed two contact detonators from his vest, pushed them into the claylike mass of the plastique, and wired them to a pair of pull-ring igniters, leaving about ten seconds' worth of primacord between them. This done, he yanked both pins, took the explosives package in both hands, and tossed it into the hold.

"Young! Hanson!" he shouted. "Heads down! Fire in the hole! Run for it when you get the opening!"

"Roger that!"

"I copy!"

The explosion hit the deck beneath his belly like the impact of a monster sledgehammer and sent a flash of bright flame geysering up through the open hatch like an erupting volcano. The freighter trembled and pitched at the detonation within her belly; his ears were ringing furiously, though he wasn't even sure he'd heard the actual blast.

He heard the second explosion, though, when it came a moment later. The jolt was less savage, but he could hear the *pop-pop-pop* of ammunition cooking off below the deck. That was a bonus; he'd hoped his little surprise package might set off sympathetic detonations in the cargo of ammo and explosives the *Kuei Mei* was carrying in her hold but hadn't been able to count on it. The ongoing blasts would only emphasize the point he'd made with the first explosion.

And it looked as though the remaining Chinese crewmen had gotten the message. Forward, half glimpsed in the glare from the Kilo's spotlight, three men in striped shirts raced across the deck to the starboard bow and leaped off into the darkness.

"Okay!" he shouted over the tactical channel. "Let's get the hell out of Dodge!"

He saw Hanson rise from cover behind some crates twenty feet away, between the deck house and the hatch cover. Morton rose to follow.

More shapes crowded onto the freighter's forward deck, spilling forward from the starboard side next to the deckhouse. These men were in uniforms and appeared less ragged than the freighter's crew. Morton knew at a glance that they were a boarding party off the Kilo. Several opened up with automatic weapons, and Hanson staggered and dropped.

From his half crouch behind the open hatchway, Morton shouldered his H&K and opened fire, triggering three-round bursts, one after another after another, firing into the dense-packed knot of submariners charging onto the *Kuei Mei*'s forward deck. Two went down . . . then a third. The others returned fire . . . and then Young was kneeling next to Morton, adding his autofire to the barrage, driving the Chinese boarding party back to the shadows beneath the deckhouse.

Morton tossed a flash-crash after them, then raced forward to Hanson. The SEAL was still alive, still conscious, his arms wrapped around a badly bloodied left thigh.

"Gotcha covered, Skipper!" Young shouted. "Go! Go!"

Morton scooped the wounded SEAL up in a rough fireman's carry and sprinted up the sloping deck to the port side. Young, his H&K spitting and hissing, followed, covering the retreat.

They reached the spot where Morton had left Conyers and the others minutes before. Two men, Schiff and Ciotti, were still there, helping to cover the retreat. They waved the three SEALs on. "Time to get wet!" Schiff yelled into the wind.

"Roger that!" Morton called back. He lowered Hanson to the deck. "How about it, Ted?" he asked. "Ready for a swim?"

"Hey," the wounded SEAL said through bloodless lips, "the water is our friend."

The water is our friend. It was a kind of mantra learned by all SEALs since the glory days of Vietnam, when it was discovered that the enemy rarely cared to pursue Navy SEALs into the water. Constant training and conditioning, endurance swims, drown-proofing exercises, all contributed to the mystique of a very special relationship between sea and SEALs. It was *their* element, as much as was the night. They would find relative safety there, at least for the time being.

And if they were lucky, they might even find the *Pittsburgh* out there in all of that rainswept, night-clad ocean.

Maybe . . .

USS *Pittsburgh*
48° 16' N, 178° 02' E
0441 hours Zulu

"What's our heading?"

"Coming around now onto two-seven-five, Captain. Still at hard right rudder."

"Very well. Maintain."

They were crossing astern of the Kilo and the damaged freighter now, three-quarters of the way through their long, clockwise turn. Kilo-class boats mounted six forward torpedo tubes but no stern tubes; they weren't at risk from a Parthian shot, at least, but a wire-guided torp could describe a full circle and hit them no matter which way the other boat was pointed. They would be safer once the freighter was between the *Pittsburgh* and the Kilo.

"Sonar, Conn. Anything new?"

"Nothing since those explosions a few minutes ago, sir. Can't tell for sure, but we think they came from the freighter. There's also been more gunfire."

"Let me know as soon as both sierras come up full abeam."

"Aye aye, sir. You got it."

"And keep a real sharp ear out for anything unusual from the Kilo. Tubes flooding, outer doors opening, anything like that."

The Kilo *must* know the *Pittsburgh* was here . . . but perhaps they had their hands full just now, dealing with damage from the second collision when the freighter had sideswiped them.

"Conn, Damage Control."

"Conn. Go ahead."

"Minor damage to the Type 18, sir. The sail's watertight integrity has been compromised, and there's minor damage to the port sail hydroplane. We've sealed watertight hatches in the sail and jury-rigged repairs on the plane. We're in no immediate difficulty, but we will need to put into port stateside ASAP for repairs."

"Very good. Keep me informed."

"Aye aye, sir."

Good. The damage wasn't nearly as bad as it could have been. Of the three points, the worst was the hit to the *'Burgh*'s Type 18 periscope. The boat had two scopes, riding side by side, the Type 18 to starboard, the Type 2 attack scope to port. The Type 18 was the workhorse periscope for an American submarine, with a low-light operating mode and closed-circuit TV capability, while the Type 2 was a basic periscope with no advanced optics. It might make seeing at night or in heavy weather a problem.

They would deal with that when the time came. "Diving Officer, bring us to periscope depth."

"Make depth periscope depth, aye aye, sir."

They began their ascent.

Chinese Freighter *Kuei Mei*
48° 16' N, 178° 02' E
0441 hours Zulu

Morton finished strapping the barrel of Hanson's H&K to his thigh with plastic ties, a rough-and-ready splint that didn't look pretty but would help them get him into the ocean. "You ready, Ted?"

"As I'll ever be, Skipper," Hanson said through hard-clenched teeth. "Let's do it!"

"Over we go!"

Holding tight to Hanson's body from behind, and

with Young and Ciotti's help, Morton manhandled the wounded SEAL upright next to the railing, got his legs over the side, and jumped.

It was a short fall. The *Kuei Mei*'s freeboard was normally less than three meters, and the freighter had settled a lot in the last few minutes. They hit the icy water with a splash, plunged beneath the surface, then rose again, Morton struggling and kicking to get Hanson's head above the surface. He yanked on the pull ring on the man's swim vest, triggering the CO_2 cartridge, then inflated his own vest and hooked them together with a canvas strap. Above them, Ciotti, Young, and Schiff tossed their now useless weapons overboard, then leaped in after them.

Morton concentrated on swimming, using a one-handed sidestroke to drag himself along, with Hanson in tow. He thought the SEAL was unconscious; the pain of the impact to his leg when they hit the water must have been horrific. He kept pulling, cresting wave after wave, trying to put as much distance as he could between them and the freighter.

Conyers and the rest of the team ought to be out there somewhere, but they would be next to impossible to spot in the dark and rain. Then Schiff, swimming next to him, pulled out a chemical light stick, snapped it, and waved it into a green, phosphorescent glow, holding it above his head.

A moment later, as a wave carried him up to its crest, he spotted a dim, answering glow *that* way. "I see them!" he gasped, spitting out saltwater. "There!"

Moments later several more SEAL swimmers appeared, gathering in the rear guard and escorting them back to the remaining CRRC. The rubber duck was far too small to carry all fourteen SEALs, but they managed to get Hanson up and out of the water and lying in the bottom of the boat, where HM1 Saunders could start administering first aid. Four others stayed in the boat, keeping a lookout for any sign of the *Pittsburgh*, while the other eight clung to the safety lines slung along the rubber duck's side.

"Now we find out if the *'Burgh* stuck around!" Conyers shouted as he dropped a transponder lead over the CRRC's side. Morton could only nod. Exhaustion was weighing him down like a freezing, leaden blanket, and the cold was finally penetrating his wet suit, leaving him weak, his teeth chattering.

Just like BUD/S, he told himself. *Just like training.* SEAL recruits, officers and enlisted men alike, went through some of the most grueling training on Earth to wear the gaudy SEAL Budweiser emblem with its eagle, trident, anchor, and flintlock pistol. Men were pushed to their absolute limits of endurance and beyond. Right now, he felt like he had toward the end of Hell Week, sitting in freezing mud up to his waist, teeth rattling in his skull, too tired to go on.

But he'd lasted it out. He would last *this* out. Just a little longer . . .

The transponder sent out a pulsed sonar signal that the *Pittsburgh* would hear. If she was still in the area . . . if she hadn't been badly damaged by her brush with the Kilo, she would pick up the signal and home on it. If . . . if . . .

And if they found her . . . what then? The *'Burgh* wasn't supposed to surface, but the team had lost half of their diving gear when the other CRRC had been lost. That would hamper recovery. They would have to buddy-pair it going down, sharing rebreathers.

Shit! He wasn't thinking! What about Hanson? The SEAL was unconscious. They would have to request that the sub surface to take him aboard. SEALs did *not* leave their own behind.

"Sir!" Hernandez called from inside the raft, pointing. "Sir! There!"

Morton had to haul himself higher up the side of the CRRC to see, but it was worth the effort. There, just visible through night and rain and spray, a white periscope wake was expanding, boiling wider, giving way to the upthrusting slate-gray cliff of a submarine conning tower. He made himself look hard to make sure it wasn't wishful thinking, that he wasn't seeing the Kilo suddenly surfacing forty yards away, but that submarine—with sail-mounted planes and smoothly rounded hull—was definitely and undeniably a Los Angeles–class boat.

She wasn't supposed to surface . . . and her skipper was taking a hell of a risk doing so. Morton turned to look back and found he could just barely make out the outline of the freighter against the night, backlit by the Kilo's searchlight. Garrett had deliberately maneuvered the *Pittsburgh* around to place the freighter between him and the Chinese sub. The SEALs, seeking only to stay clear of the sub, had hit on the same strategy and found themselves quite close to their ride indeed.

The hatch to the forward escape trunk, located just behind the sail, opened, and work-jacketed sailors started spilling out, putting a light on the swimmers and waving them on. Someone threw a line.

They were going to make it after all.

Just like BUD/S, Morton thought. All except for the part where the op turns into a damned cluster fuck . . .

Wednesday, 6 October 1999

Headquarters Building
SEAL Team Three
Coronado, California
1015 hours

"As stated at the beginning of these proceedings, Lieutenant, this is a Board of Inquiry and not a court-martial. The findings of this board may be applicable in later judicial hearings, and may in fact be used in formal charges and specifications at a later date, but should not, of themselves, be taken as censure or disciplinary action.

"We are interested in learning all pertinent details of the military action of September twenty-third of this year, part of which was carried out under your command. You are not required to answer our questions, although we do, of course, enjoin you to cooperate fully with our investigation.

"You are free to have legal counsel of your choice present or to have one appointed for you by the office of the Judge Advocate General. Do you understand?"

"Yes, sir, I do."

"Do you wish at this time to have legal counsel present?"

"No, sir, I do not." He'd decided there was no point. Either he'd made the correct decisions that night, step by step, or he had not. He'd committed no crimes, at least not under the articles of the Uniform Code of Military Justice, and doubted that a court-martial was in the works—unless, of course, he demanded one later.

His career was on the line, certainly, but a lawyer wouldn't have been much help here. He knew what he'd done that night, and why, and had no interest in concealing or twisting the facts to his favor.

"Very well. You may be seated."

Morton took his seat, a straight-backed chair alone in the center of a large expanse of emptiness in the sparsely furnished room. In front of him, behind a wide desk, three naval officers in dress whites—a commander and two four-stripers, captains—took a final shuffle through the papers before them, as though reluctant to begin. He had the impression that these proceedings were as unpleasant for them as it was for him.

The commander, seated on the far left as Morton faced the board, clasped his hands and leaned forward. His name was Kenneth Randall, and he wore the SEAL Budweiser above row upon row of brightly colored ribbons. "Lieutenant Morton," he said with grave deliberation, "we've so far covered the events of the VBSS up through the time when you and two of your men took control of the *Kuei Mei*'s bridge. We would like to discuss now your decision to take the freighter's helm and ram the Chinese Kilo-class submarine then cruising off your starboard beam."

"Yes, sir."

"Would you tell us, please, in your own words, what happened?"

It was all in the report he'd already submitted, and in his opening statement to the board at the commencement of the inquiry two days before. But the formula had to be followed all the way through to the end.

"The wheel was turning free," he told them. "We were in a rough following sea, and my first thought was that we could broach to. I guess, considering what happened, that might have been a good thing . . . another way of stopping the freighter without actually blowing her up. But I didn't think about that at the time.

"My orders at that point were to contact SOCOM via the *Pittsburgh*'s communications suite, but we were out of communication with the *Pittsburgh*. My interpretation of my orders was that I was to take such action as I deemed necessary to delay or prevent the delivery of contraband military cargo to the continental United States, either by destroying that cargo myself or by arranging for Coast Guard or other U.S. forces to take control of it."

"You've already explained that you were unable to establish contact with higher command authority," Randall said. "Tell us about why you decided to put the *Kuei Mei*'s helm hard over to the right."

"Everything was happening at once. The Kilo surfaced just as we were sorting things out on the bridge, and she presented all sorts of complications to the mission, of course. She was pacing us maybe fifty yards off our starboard beam. We couldn't outrun her. She was probably already radioing for help, if her skipper'd figured out something was wrong aboard the freighter. I assumed she surfaced because she'd picked up sounds of gunfire on her sonar and popped up to investigate. Maybe she tried to radio the freighter and came up when we didn't answer. Anyway, I didn't see too damned many options. Sir."

The man sitting in the middle of the trio facing him looked up from his papers to meet Morton's eye. He was Captain Edward Chaffee, and he'd come all the way out to Coronado from the office of the Joint Chiefs at the Pentagon to sit on this board. He was, Morton sensed, the most critical of the three board members . . . and he was certainly the most senior. "And what, Lieutenant," Chaffee asked, "did you see as your options at the time?"

"Well, sir, I *could* have waited until the sub put a boarding party across. In that eventuality, I could have directed my men to fight them off, though they were already involved in close-quarters combat with the crew of the *Kuei Mei*. Or I could have ordered the VBSS party to E and E immediately."

"And why didn't you take that option?"

"Because it would have left my men sitting ducks on the water. There were still a number of heavily armed men on board the freighter, and the Kilo could have maneuvered to a position to take our CRRC under fire. We might have been able to slip away in the rain and heavy seas, but that didn't seem to be a viable choice at the time. In any case, the Chinese would have been able to secure the freighter and her cargo intact, leaving my mission only partially complete. Sir."

"What about opening fire on the Chinese boarding party?" the third man behind the desk asked. He was Captain Samuel Polowski, and though considerably

Chaffee's junior in seniority, he pulled a fair amount of weight on the board. He was from the Naval Amphibious Base's SPECWAR division office and, though he was no longer in the teams, he wore the SEAL Budweiser.

The fact that two of the three men on the board were SEALs was comforting. They'd *been* there, at the sword's point. They knew what an op was like, what it was like to be under fire, what it was like to have men under you whose lives depended on your clear thinking. Morton knew Randall slightly; he had a rep for pulling through as 2IC on a rough covert op in Lebanon a few years back. Morton didn't know Polowski personally but knew his rep. He'd been CO of Team Three until his promotion several years ago, and before that he'd racked up an impressive list of decorations and commendations. Chaffee was the only real unknown.

He would also be the most *political* of the officers on the board, and the one Morton would have to convince.

But right now Morton wasn't sure what Polowski was getting at. "Sir?"

"You could have had your men open fire on the Chinese submarine from the decks of the freighter. They would not have been able to board under those circumstances."

"Well, sir, at the time that seemed like just the sort of provocation we'd been ordered to avoid. We were there to ascertain whether the *Kuei Mei* was carrying contraband cargo and to take appropriate action as directed by a higher command authority once our inspection was complete. Our orders did not encompass the possibility of getting into a firefight with a foreign national submarine. The idea was to avoid military confrontation. In any case, our ammo loadout was pretty light. We wouldn't have been able to sustain a firefight against any kind of odds for very long."

Polowski made a note on the paper in front of him. "I see. Go on."

"But it did look at the time as though the sub was going to put a boarding party across. If I didn't want to E and E, if I didn't want to fight, then all I could do was make it hard for the crew of the sub to get aboard. That's when I took the wheel."

"Were you considering outrunning the Kilo, Lieutenant?" Chaffee asked.

"Well, it crossed my mind, but I knew I wouldn't be able to play that game for very long."

"Why not?"

"Sir, the *Kuei Mei* was a Zhandou 59-class cargo ship, with a length overall of 328 feet, a beam of forty-three feet, and a deadweight tonnage of something like forty-seven hundred tons. Top speed of maybe twelve, twelve and a half knots.

"A Kilo-class submarine—the standard Russian export model—has a length of 241 feet, a beam of about thirty-two feet, and a dwt of twenty-three hundred tons on the surface. She also has a top speed of twelve knots on the surface . . . about twenty submerged. With two diesel engines to the cargo ship's one, half the tonnage, and three-quarters of the length, she has a *lot* more power-to-mass. With a narrower beam and a shorter loa, the Kilo is a lot more maneuverable. Only reasonable, of course. The Kilo is a combat vessel, while the cargo ship is, well . . . a *truck*."

"So you weren't actually trying to ram the Kilo?" Polowski said. "Just what was it you were you trying to do?"

"I'm not actually sure, sir," Morton replied. "I couldn't outmaneuver the sub, I knew that. Couldn't outrun her. I could make it hard for her to put a boat with a boarding party across . . . at least until the sub skipper got tired of playing games with me. I guess that's what occurred to me first."

"When you put the helm over," Chaffee asked, "were you *trying* to ram the Kilo then?"

Morton let his attention stray to the wall behind the board. Early morning sunlight spilled through two tall windows, framing an array of framed photographs — President Clinton, the Secretary of the Navy, the CNO—as well as a large print of a famous battle in the Age of Sail, the USS *Constellation* against the French *Insurgente* off the island of Nevis in 1799. There was a sense there of longstanding tradition, of military duty, and of the hierarchy of command responsibility.

His reply to the question, he knew well, could end his naval career. Whatever the details of the operation, of the freighter's cargo, of the overall political situation, the United States was not at war with the People's Republic of China. But the outcome of the incident—the *Kuei Mei* had sunk in heavy seas four hours after the collision—had provoked serious international repercussions between Washington and Beijing, and this after tensions between the two were already extremely serious.

"Sir," he said carefully, "I don't think I expected I *could* have deliberately rammed the Kilo. The best I could do was hope to buy some time, to keep them from boarding the freighter. There was a chance they would give up, I suppose. There was also a chance that other Chinese naval units could have been nearby, or that the Kilo would actually take the *Kuei Mei* under fire.

"I put the helm hard over to make the Chinese sub skipper veer off. I suppose I *was* trying to ram him, but given the respective capabilities of our vessels, I had no expectation of the attempt actually succeeding."

"I see," Chaffee said. "What happened next?"

"The Kilo was veering off, as expected, turning to starboard well inside our starboard turn. She then appeared to shudder, as though she'd run aground or hit something. We didn't learn until later, of course, that she'd accidentally hit the submerged *Pittsburgh*.

"Anyway, she swung back to port. The *Pittsburgh*'s conning tower struck the Kilo's after control surfaces and apparently jammed her rudder in a hard-left configuration. At that point we couldn't have avoided her if we'd tried. The *Kuei Mei*'s bow struck the Kilo about halfway between her bow and her sail. We rode up over her forward deck partway, then slid back off. As we did so, the Kilo's forward port diving plane tore into the *Kuei Mei*'s starboard hull forward, opening a gash into both the forward and after cargo holds, and she began sinking by the bow.

"At some point in there, we lost power in the engine room, which, of course, was still under Chinese control. I think they figured out something was wrong down there when we hit the sub, and cut the engine. By that time, I'd decided our mission was effectively concluded, and it was time to evade and escape."

"What led you to believe your mission objectives had been reached?"

"Sir? At that point, I wasn't entirely certain what our mission objectives *were*. Destroy the cargo? Sink the ship? Wait for the Coast Guard? We couldn't call for specific orders, but it felt as though the *Kuei Mei* was sinking. If she was, that would take care of the cargo."

Randall paged through a stack of typewritten sheets. "In your debriefing, you said that you ordered two of your men to return to the aft cargo hold to plant explosives. Correct?"

"Yes, sir."

"Why?"

"To make certain that the cargo was destroyed, even if I was mistaken about the extent of the damage to the ship."

"And why did you change your mind?"

"My men reported that the after hold was flooding. Entering the hold to place explosives would have presented an unacceptable—and unnecessary—risk to them and would not have materially affected the success of the operation. The fact that the hold was filling with water confirmed my earlier feeling that the ship was sinking. I told them to pull out and fall back to the port-side rendezvous point for E and E."

"And yet, a few minutes later," Chaffee went on, "you changed your mind again and returned to the hatch leading to the aft hold in order to drop explosives inside."

"Yes, sir."

"You seemed to be changing your mind a lot that morning. Why?"

"Two of my men reported that they were pinned down on the forward deck by enemy fire. I reasoned that the Chinese forces still aboard the ship knew they were under attack by a naval commando force and were attempting to organize an effective defense, possibly to hold us in place until reinforcements could arrive from the submarine alongside. There wasn't a lot we could do tactically to drive them off or to discourage their attack on the two missing men.

"I did believe it possible, however, that the Chinese crewmen still aboard the freighter knew that their cargo included explosives and munitions—ammunition for the assault rifles and rocket-propelled grenades at the very least. If they thought the cargo was exploding—better yet, if I could make the cargo explode—they might become . . . discouraged and abandon ship."

"And that is, in fact, what happened, isn't it, Lieutenant?" Randall asked.

"I believe so, sir. When the explosives went off, I saw several of the crewmen jumping overboard in some haste. At the same time, though, we came under fire from a boarding party off the Chinese sub."

"And that's when Machinist's Mate Hanson was wounded?" Polowski asked.

"Yes, sir."

The three officers at the table began a low-voiced conversation among themselves then, which lasted several minutes. Morton let his gaze travel past the photographs on the wall to one of the windows. Outside, the gray buildings of the U.S. Navy Amphibious Base at Coronado squatted under a bright, California morning sun. A formation of dungaree-clad Basic Underwater Demolition/SEAL trainees—BUD/S recruits—jogged past on their way to another round of calisthenics and indoctrination under the sharp-barked commands of their instructors. Four years ago Morton had been one of their number, jogging in the hot, California sunshine, bench-pressing creosote-soaked telephone poles with other BUD/S recruits, battling the cold Pacific, the mud, the bone-numbing exhaustion. . . .

Had it been worth it?

"Very well, Lieutenant," Chaffee said at last. "We have no further questions at this time. Your report covers the remaining aspects of the operation—your withdrawal from the *Kuei Mei*, and your subsequent extraction by the USS *Pittsburgh*—in adequate detail. You may withdraw while the board considers its verdict."

There was something about that word, *verdict*, that chilled the blood. This wasn't a court-martial, true, and yet . . .

He stood. Since this was indoors and he was not covered, he did not salute, but he came to attention. "Aye aye, sir." Turning crisply, he strode toward the large, wooden double doors which were flanked by a silent pair of Marine guards and left the room.

The doors opened onto a broad passageway with high ceilings and an institutional green and white linoleum floor. Opposite was an office suite, busy with computer keyboards and sailors in whites, fronted by a reception desk and an arrangement of sofas, chairs, and low, bark-the-shins tables. A soda machine stood sentry on one wall.

Lieutenant Mark Halstead was leaning on the reception desk, chatting with the attractive civilian woman behind it in his most wolfishly charming manner. He looked up as Morton emerged from the inquiry room.

"Well, Jack? How'd it go?"

"Good as can be expected. I guess it all comes down now to whether they're looking for a sacrificial lamb."

"Try not to bleat too loudly, then." He grinned. "You know, I prefer the role of wolf. Silent and deadly."

"I hear you, swim buddy."

Mark Halstead was Morton's best friend. The son of a Vietnam-era SEAL—one of that war's three SEAL Medal of Honor recipients—Halstead had followed in his dad's swim-fin prints, joining the Navy and graduating BUD/S just in time to take part—a highly classified part—in Operation Desert Storm. He'd come home furious about the lack of decent intelligence support in that conflict, gone mustang, and become an officer. As a SEAL platoon commander, he'd been involved in several highly classified ops since then.

His current assignment at the China Lake Naval Weapons Testing Facility had scotched his chances for skippering Operation Buster, the *Kuei Mei* op, but he'd thrown his weight behind Morton, suggesting to a number of brass hats at NAVSPECWAR that Jack Morton was the man for the job.

And the deal had come through. Unfortunately, Morton wasn't entirely sure now that it had been a good thing.

But that certainly wasn't Mark's fault. Luck of the draw, in a universe sometimes frustratingly perverse.

Halstead walked over to the machine, fed it money, and came back with a couple of cans. Morton popped the pull tab of his with a hiss and took a swig.

"So what do you think it'll be?" Halstead asked after a moment. "Make nice to China? Or tough it out?"

"Damfino. I never claimed to understand politics. *Or* politicians."

"Hear hear. The PRC has been spoiling for a fight lately. We might as well get it on. Why stop with their embassy?"

"The idea is *not* to have a war with them," Morton said. "What is it that's worth fighting about. Taiwan?"

"Sinking one of their merchant ships could be considered an act of war," Halstead observed. He had a twinkle in his eye, though, and a bantering lilt to his voice.

"Don't I know it!" Morton jerked his head, indicating the council going on behind closed doors now. "That's what I figure they're talking about now. Am I a hero for standing up to the Chinese dragon? Or another scapegoat, somebody else to apologize for to the Chinese ambassador?"

"Things have been getting pretty damned tight with the PRC," Halstead said, all levity gone. "You know, if we *don't* stand up to them pretty soon, if we *don't* draw a line and say 'no further . . . ' "

He let the thought trail off, unfinished, but it was a topic both men—most SEALs—had discussed frequently of late.

China had been decidedly more aggressive these past few years, especially in confrontations with the government of Taiwan. A major crisis had been brewing a few months back, when Beijing fired several test missiles into Taiwanese waters, rather pointedly demonstrating that they could take their rebellious province, as they thought of Nationalist China, under fire any time they desired.

But the real crisis with Washington had begun in May of that year. The escalating NATO air campaign against Serbia in the Balkans had proven less than effective, and after considerable dithering, air strikes had been directed against targets deeper and deeper within major cities, instead of out in the hinterlands. One promising target had been the Bureau of Supply and Procurement in downtown Belgrade; with laser-guided bombs dropped from stealth F-117s, Washington hoped to bring the war home to Milosevich and his thugs without causing civilian casualties.

A mission had been duly dispatched. At least three bombs had struck the target in the middle of the night.

Unfortunately, the target turned out to be not the nerve center of Milosevich military logistics network but the Chinese Embassy. Working from maps two years out of date, a CIA analyst had managed to bomb the embassy of a country Washington was at that moment negotiating with, hoping to build a solid international front against the Serbs. Thirty people had been in the embassy compound during the attack; three had been killed. Most Chinese assumed the attack was deliberate, pointing to the fact that their flag had been clearly visible above the building; none seemed to understand—or be willing to understand—that such details as a flag flying at night were invisible to the electronic surveillance systems employed by an F-117, which might release the bomb some miles away from the target.

The bombing had to be one of the most disastrous intelligence gaffes in the history of warfare.

As a result, anti-American feeling in the People's Republic had been running at a fever pitch, and each day seemed to bring about new breakdowns in relations between the two countries. Demonstrations, rock-throwing, and flag-burnings at the U.S. Embassy in China. Angry rhetoric at the UN. The incident in the northern Pacific appeared to have brought the two nations to the brink of war, and Beijing's saber-rattling had recently gone so far as to suggest publicly that the U.S. West Coast would not long be beyond the reach of Chinese nuke-tipped missiles.

The world appeared to be on the verge of another round of nuclear superpower confrontations, and inevitably the Teams would be in the thick of things.

The better part of an hour ticked slowly past on the big, round clock on the wall behind the secretary's desk. Morton and Halstead talked some, but much of the time passed in worried silence. Morton caught himself wondering about the verdict . . . and what the delay meant. What was it supposed to be . . . that the longer the jury was out, the better the chances for the accused? He wasn't certain that applied in this case. Either he'd done good, so far as the Navy and the SPECWAR community were concerned, or he hadn't. If they were taking this damned long to make up their minds, there had to be a problem.

Shit. . . .

One of the doors opened and a Marine sentry looked out. "Lieutenant Morton? They're waiting for you, sir."

"Thank you."

"Break a leg, amigo," Halstead told him.

"Just keep the getaway car warmed and ready, in case I have to make a break for Mexico."

"Roger that."

Morton reentered the room and came to attention in front of the desk. The three senior officers did not appear to have moved from their places. They were continuing to confer among themselves and didn't take any immediate notice of him.

Jack Morton was a student of history in general, of Navy history in particular. He couldn't help thinking about an old, old naval tradition that went back to the time of Nelson and the Age of Sail.

In those days, in the Royal Navy, an officer who went before a court-martial board surrendered his sword at the beginning of the proceedings. At the end of the board's deliberations, the officer was called back in to hear their judgment. If, when he walked in, his sword was lying on the desk with its hilt pointed at him, he knew that the inquiry had been decided in his favor. If the sword lay on the table with its point toward the accused, he knew the case had gone against him and he was facing censure, disgrace, professional ruin . . . or worse.

It was a shame, he thought, that the tradition was no

longer in effect. It would have saved him some unpleasant moments there, standing rigidly at attention while waiting for them to finish.

The huddle broke at last, and Chaffee cleared his throat. "Ahem. Lieutenant Morton. It is the judgment of this formal Board of Inquiry that, in regard to the events of the early morning of twenty-three September of this year, while you were engaged in the tactical evolution of Operation Buster as commander of First Platoon, SEAL Team One, you did endeavor to carry out your orders to the best of your abilities, acting in the finest traditions of the naval service." He paused, looking uncomfortable. "Speaking now off the record, Lieutenant, I will say that, while, ah, some on this board questioned the, um, *zeal* with which you carried out your orders—a zeal which resulted in the unfortunate sinking of a commercial vessel of a foreign power with whom we are not currently at war, as well as extensive damage to one of their warships—your orders at the time offered little leeway in the honorable, prompt, and expeditious carrying out of those orders. This board does not hold you responsible for that sinking, which must be classified as an act of God.

"Speaking on the record, again . . . it is, further, this board's conclusion that you, Lieutenant Morton, acted with distinction, decision, and bravery under fire in effecting the recovery of two of your men, one of whom was wounded in the action. We intend to pass to higher command authority this board's recommendation that you receive an official commendation for your action."

"He means we're putting you in for the Silver Star, Jack," Randall said, grinning.

Chaffee glared at the junior member of the board but continued without allowing himself to be sidetracked.

"Congratulations, Lieutenant, on a job well done. This Board of Inquiry is closed."

"Thank you, sir."

"You are dismissed."

"Aye aye, sir!"

Turning, he strode from the room, heels clicking on the hardwood deck.

"You dodged the bullet," Halstead said when he saw Morton emerge from the room. "Son of a bitch, you dodged it!"

"I guess they were full up on lambs this week." He rubbed his stomach. "I don't know about you, friend, but I need a drink!"

"I'm there!" Halstead blew a kiss to the receptionist. "Catch ya later, blue eyes!"

Together, they marched down the passageway and out into the bright California sunshine.

Morton found himself trembling as hard as he'd been trembling with cold and exhaustion in the North Pacific. He'd *survived*.

Damn, it was good to be alive. . . .

Friday, 22 October 1999

Headquarters Building
SUBRON 11
San Diego, California
1512 hours

Commander Tom Garrett, like many naval officers, was a student of history, especially naval history. He was thinking now about a certain old naval tradition—one involving a court-martialed officer's sword.

"Commander Garrett? They're ready for you now, sir."

"Thank you." Rising, his hat with its scrambled-eggs-laden bill in hand, Garrett smoothed the creases from his dress whites as best he could and followed the Marine back to the high, double wooden doors leading to the hearing chamber. Inside, the chair he'd sat in for the past few days had been taken away. He came to attention in front of the long, broad desk. The five senior officers who'd made up the Board of Inquiry—four captains and a rear admiral—sat behind the table, watching him impassively.

Is the sword hilt toward me, he wondered, or the point? He couldn't tell from the carefully shuttered expressions . . . but the shuttering itself gave him an ominous premonition. And they'd taken so long—over three hours—to reach a decision . . .

"Commander Thomas Frederick Garrett," the man at the center of the panel said, glancing down at a sheaf of papers in his hands. He was Rear Admiral Kenneth Bainbridge, commanding officer of Submarine Squadron 11, and Garrett's ultimate boss in the chain of command in San Diego. He wore the golden dolphins of a submarine officer, as did all of the men at the table.

Whatever they'd decided, it would be as fair as possible, as fair, at least, as the current political situation could manage. While they wouldn't play favorites here, at least he knew that all five of these officers had been there at one time or another, commanding a hundred or so men within the claustrophobic confines of a steel coffin deep beneath the ocean's surface.

Bainbridge hesitated a moment, then went on without further preamble. "Regarding the events of the early morning hours of September twenty-third, 1999, during Operation Buster, this Board of Inquiry does not find sufficient evidence concerning your part in that incident to warrant convening a court-martial.

"However, we do find you negligent in your official duties as commanding officer of the nuclear attack submarine *Pittsburgh*.

"First. Upon detecting the presence of a potentially hostile foreign-national submarine within your area of operations, you did fail to notify both the requisite higher command authority and the SEAL element then embarked aboard the operation objective, the PRC merchant vessel *Kuei Mei*. Such a warning would have enabled the SEAL element to disengage from the mission, possibly without engaging in the subsequent firefight. By submerging below periscope depth, as you did, you prevented the SEAL element from contacting higher authority for clarification of their operational orders, thereby endangering the mission.

"Second. Your decision to follow the submarine contact at close range resulted in the grazing collision of the USS *Pittsburgh* with said foreign-national submarine, resulting in minor damage to the vessel under your command. This board acknowledges that the collision was instigated by the foreign submarine's sudden and unexpected maneuver to starboard but notes that you should have been more cognizant of the possibility of collision should the target vessel change course or speed.

"Third. Your decision to surface was in direct violation of your operational orders, which required you to remain unseen for the duration of a covert mission, operating under conditions of high security. This board acknowledges that by so surfacing, you probably saved the lives of at least some of the SEALs then embarked on the operation, one of whom was injured and unable to use closed-circuit scuba gear to reach the submarine escape trunk at depth. However, you could not have been aware of the injury before surfacing, and your decision to surface potentially jeopardized both the mission and your command.

"Fourth. By surfacing and revealing your vessel's presence to foreign national forces present, said forces then operating under emergency conditions, you did fail to render aid to those foreign forces—specifically to the Chinese merchant vessel *Kuei Mei*, which was at the time heavily damaged and sinking. As a result, our government has received an official protest from the government of the People's Republic of China decrying our nation's, I quote, piratical activities, unquote, and condemning our failure to render timely aid to a vessel in distress in international waters. This has resulted in considerable embarrassment to this nation, to the current administration, and to the naval service."

Garrett was having trouble believing he was hearing what he was hearing. *My God, they're out to scuttle me!*

"It is the recommendation of this board," Admiral Bainbridge continued, "that a formal letter of reprimand be issued by the convening authority for inclusion in your personnel records in lieu of further disciplinary action. Commander Garrett, you may, of course, appeal this decision by requesting a formal court-martial. You are strongly advised, however, that such an appeal will only serve to further jeopardize your career in the naval service. . . ."

There was more to the litany, but Garrett scarcely heard the words. They *were* out to scuttle him . . . to sink his career, at least. Technically, and in a rather backhanded way, they'd been lenient, letting him off with a slap on the wrist rather than condemning him to the more formal—and serious—arena of a general court-martial. But by letting stand charges that he'd mishandled his command and his part of Operation Buster—worse, by including those charges in a letter of reprimand that would follow him throughout the rest of his naval career—they were guaranteeing that he would never hold a command again . . . indeed, that the promotion boards would pass him by and he would never make captain.

He would never be allowed to command a submarine again, and that simple fact twisted in his gut like a knife.

Bainbridge had stopped talking, and the five men were watching him with something like academic interest. He was expected to say something.

"I understand, sir."

"Do you feel at this time that you will want to appeal this decision, Commander?" Captain Frank Gordon asked.

"I . . ." He stopped. Did he? At the moment, it felt as though he were supporting some titanic weight on his shoulders and could hardly stand. Could he fight the decision?

Could he *win*?

A court-martial was the only way for him to clear his name now, and he would have to win if he didn't want to see his career slamming into a brick-walled dead end. The "convening authority"—and that meant Bainbridge and SUBRON 11—would fight with every trick at its command. Hell, he might find himself fighting this thing all the way up to the Pentagon, and that wouldn't do his career any good either. The Navy Department would not want to see this affair dragged out into the light of publicity and the evening news.

And promotion boards only favored those officers they considered "team players," those who didn't rock the figurative boat.

"Sir, I will need to consider my options."

Politics. Damn it all, he *hated* military politics! You could devote your entire life to the service of your country, but once you reached the rank of commander, every promotion, every position of authority, depended on who you knew in the old boys' network, and who you'd managed to piss off on your way up.

"You are dismissed." The words were like a final pronouncement of doom.

"Aye aye, sir."

Retaining as much composure and dignity as possible, he about-faced and walked out of the room. Down a passageway, left past the front desk, out the big glass doors into the California sunlight, and down the concrete steps beyond . . .

A ship's horn mourned in the bay, out beyond a row of palms. A Ticonderoga-class CG was rounding North Island on her way to Navy Pier.

Garrett's thoughts blurred and shifted. It was tough to concentrate. Seventeen years of service. He was thirty-nine years old, Annapolis-trained. All his life he'd wanted nothing more than the submarine service. Seventeen years of military life, of training, of duty . . . and now he might as well retire.

Could he fight it?

"Tom! Hey, Tom!"

He turned, aware that someone had been calling his name for several seconds. It was Captain Gordon, trotting down the steps in front of the headquarters building after him.

He came to attention and saluted. Gordon returned it but made a face. "Damn it, Tom, hold up a sec! We need to talk."

"What is there to talk about?" He tried not to let the words carry his bitterness but knew he'd failed.

"I know you feel like you're being railroaded. . . ."

"Oh, is *that* what I'm feeling now?" He started walking again, not sure where. "Thank you, sir. I wasn't sure."

"Can the attitude, Commander. You need to work on your target identification. *I'm* not the enemy."

Garrett stopped, sagged a bit, and turned to face his friend. He'd known Frank Gordon for twelve years.

"I'm sorry, Captain. I guess . . . I'm a little keyed up still."

"Let's head for the O-Club. You look like you could use a drink."

Garrett let the older man steer him toward the Officers Club, where the two took a booth in the rear and gave their orders—bourbon on the rocks for Garrett, a rum and Coke for Gordon—to the civilian waitress. It was almost empty this early in the afternoon, and they had the back of the place to themselves.

Garrett's mind was still racing. What was Gordon's stake in this?

When Garrett had first met Gordon, back in 1987, he'd been a fresh-faced lieutenant j.g. on his first sea tour, and Frank Gordon had been the commanding officer of the USS *Pittsburgh*, his CO. His tour of duty aboard the *'Burgh* had only lasted a year, until his promotion to lieutenant, but Gordon had taken a special interest in the career paths and studies of all of the junior officers under his command. Even after he'd switched career paths to Naval Intelligence and been assigned to shore duty, Gordon had remained one of his chief mentors as he'd worked his way up the promotion ladder, recommending him for Submarine Officer Advanced Course with a glowing letter, and helping him land a billet as SSN XO aboard the *Portsmouth* in '94. He wasn't sure, but he'd always suspected that Frank Gordon had a hand in getting him selected for command of the *Pittsburgh* once he'd made commander. The coincidence, if that was what it was, was too bizarre otherwise.

It had come as a shock as cold and bitter as the north Pacific Ocean to find Gordon on the Board of Inquiry convened to investigate his actions during Operation Buster.

"What the hell is going on, Captain?" he asked. "Did you hear them in there? Did you?"

"I heard."

"All of those charges and specifications. It's bullshit! I couldn't report that Kilo right away without revealing my position. Besides, there was nothing in the orders about checking every detail with Washington! I was well within my command discretion!"

"Agreed."

"I surfaced because I knew the SEALs had been in a firefight, a long one. Damn it, we could *hear* the shooting, underwater! I didn't know they had casualties, sure, but it was a good guess. And a damned lucky one!"

"Also agreed. Keep your voice down."

"I deliberately surfaced on the far side of that freighter from the Kilo and far enough out that they couldn't get a good look at us."

"Intelligence reports that they didn't see you. At least, that Kilo didn't make a report to that effect. They're sure they hit a sub out there—hell, the SEALs had to come from *somewhere*—but they think they sank you when they collided with you." He gave a grim smile. "The way *they* tell it, they won."

"I did run into them," Garrett said. "But it couldn't be avoided! I was doing my job, damn it. I was right where I was supposed to be. You know how fuzzy passive sonar range is. And if I'd gone active, they would have heard the pinging and known I was there. Damn it, Captain, what else was I supposed to *do*?"

"Take it easy, son." Their drinks arrived and Gordon lifted his glass. "It ain't over till it's over. Right?"

Garrett sipped his drink and scowled at the bite. "Bainbridge was out to nail my hide to a tree."

"Bainbridge had an agenda."

"What agenda?"

"To make sure that nothing endangers the current diplomatic negotiations with Beijing. The administration has a lot riding on favored nation trade status for the People's Republic. That means being nice to the Chinese, apologizing for an unfortunate 'incident,' and making sure that nothing, no *one*, rocks the boat."

"That sucks."

"Agreed. The question is, what are you going to do about it?"

"I haven't decided yet."

"It's your right to demand a court."

"I know. And their right to squash me like a bug. Damn it, Captain, no matter *what* I do I'll never have my own command again. I might as well take early retirement!"

"That would be a waste, Tom, and you know it. You have too much invested in your career right now."

"My career." The word was bitter in his mouth. "Claire wouldn't mind seeing me get out. She's been on about it for a couple of years. And it sure as hell doesn't look like I'm going anywhere now."

"That may be your perception now, Tom. It's not necessarily accurate. A lot of it has to do with what you decide. You're not adrift, you know. You can make active choices. Take charge of your own life."

"Look, Frank," Garrett said. It was a sign of his agitation that he'd called Gordon by his given name. They'd been on a comfortable, first-name basis since Garrett had made commander, but never when they were both in uniform. "I'm flattered. I really am. But just what is your interest in this . . . in me?"

"What do you mean?"

"You've been my fairy godmother ever since I came aboard the *'Burgh*, when you were her skipper. And I've appreciated it. But why me?"

Gordon shrugged. "You're a good officer. Talented.

Good potential. I saw that, as you say, when you came aboard in 'eighty-seven. I believe in encouraging talent wherever it's found."

"Yeah? Then . . . don't get me wrong, but why did you sign on with Bainbridge's little crusade this week?"

"I didn't 'sign on,' as you put it. I was volunteered."

"By who?"

"My bosses at ONI." He made a face. "Let's leave it at that."

Gordon rarely talked about his work with the Office of Naval Intelligence. Garrett had the impression that he was a senior analyst with the California branch of the department. "You spooks can never give a straight answer," he said.

"Don't start, Tom. As it happens, us spooks need good, steady people where we can tap them for reliable information. Sources. And sometimes we need sources in our own camp as much as we need them behind enemy lines."

"Are you saying I'm one of your sources?" Garrett was startled. But then, it did make a kind of sense. He remembered now that it was Gordon who'd asked a favor of him several months ago, in finding a radio shack billet for another of his protégés—a radioman first class named DiGiorgio.

"You're a *friend*," Gordon insisted.

"And a part of your personal spy network?"

"More like an old boys' network. I do you a favor, you do me a favor. . . ."

"In other words, manipulation. I don't like it, Captain."

Gordon scowled. "That manipulation, as you call it, just might save your ass. Unless you fold your cards now and get out of the military. You're . . . what? Sixteen, seventeen years in? Three more and you could be out with twenty."

"Is that what you suggest?"

"Negative. I suggest you ride this out. Don't try to fight that letter of reprimand with a court-martial. You'll just dig the hole deeper, and you might not be able to climb out."

"Then what—"

"Trust me, Tom. There's a way to get around Bainbridge and his reprimand, believe me."

"How? By becoming a spook?"

"Would that be so bad?"

Garrett sighed. "I don't know. I don't like desk work, I know that much. I've wanted to be a submariner ever since . . . hell, I don't know since when. Since I was a kid, I guess. Watching *The Enemy Below* and *Das Boote*. I always rooted for the Germans in those."

"*Hunt for Red October*? That was my favorite."

"That, too, though I was already in the Navy when that came out. Sean Connery made a hell of a Russian submarine captain."

"Better than Kurt Jurgens."

"Hell, yeah!"

Gordon nodded. "It's important. How we're portrayed on the big screen."

"Maybe. I always thought we tried to stay out of the limelight, y'know?"

"Sure. That's the way it has to be. But it helps if the public thinks of us as heroic figures. More to the point, it helps if *Congress* thinks of us as heroic figures."

"Amen to that, Captain."

How had Gordon done that? Garrett wondered. Somehow, he'd deflected his anger and gotten him talking about submarine movies and Hollywood stars. The guy was slick, that was sure.

"Look, Captain," he said, "I can't promise anything. I don't know if I have it in me to fight this thing."

"I don't want you to fight it, son. I want you to roll with the punch. Just keep your head down and your nose clean. You'll lose the *Pittsburgh*, of course . . . but there might be another command in your future. *If* you play it cool."

"What, a diesel boat? An SS?" Garrett snorted. "That's a lieutenant commander's billet." He shook his head. "I guess I could skipper a sub tender."

"A minute ago you were telling me you would never have another command and you might as well quit. Now you're telling me what you will or will not accept?"

"No. No, sir, I'm not."

"Good. This is a big navy, and there are lots of opportunities. Just don't go burning your bridges before you've crossed 'em!"

"Aye aye, sir."

"Oh, by the way . . ."

"Yes?"

"Thought you might like to hear. That request you radioed back for information on Chinese sub tenders in the area . . . it paid off."

Despite his mood, Garrett was interested. "Yeah? What did they have?"

"The *J503*. Dalang class. She was loitering about maybe three hundred miles southeast of where you ran into the Kilo." He stopped when he saw Garrett wince, then recognized the unintended pun. "Ouch. Sorry about that. You know what I mean."

"Stands to reason," Garrett said. "A Kilo couldn't make it clear across the Pacific without refueling."

"Exactly. The question, of course, is why they sent a

Kilo. They have nukes. Their Han-class attack boats are pretty good, even by our standards."

"They only have five of those, at last count," Garrett replied. "And Kilos . . . This must be something new."

"Word is the PRC is taking delivery each year on more and more Kilos being built by the Russians up in Komsomolsk-na-Amur. Special order, just for Beijing."

"How many?"

"We're not sure."

"Why? Why the big buildup on diesel boats?"

"Believe me, there are people at ONI spending some *very* sleepless nights over just that question."

"Why are you telling me?"

Gordon shrugged. "I thought you'd be interested. As a friend."

Garrett wasn't sure he was ready to accept anything Gordon told him at face value. The man always seemed to have wheels going within the wheels.

"Yeah, well, I may not have a need to know anymore, Captain. Not if I'm going to lose the *'Burgh*." The thought brought with it a cold tug of depression. He was trying to fight it, but . . .

The waitress appeared beside the table. "You boys be having anything else?"

"Actually, no," Gordon said. "I have to get back to the office."

"Same here," Garrett said. "For a little while, anyway."

For Garrett, "the office" was the *Pittsburgh*, high and dry now in a submarine dry dock. They'd pulled her out of the water almost as soon as she'd limped back to San Diego after Operation Buster. The damage was relatively light—she was getting a new set of periscopes in her refurbished sail, and there'd been some work on the sail-mounted diving planes—but the powers-that-were had decided to take advantage of the opportunity to give the boat a thorough going-over, installing new pumps and a quieter shaft, replacing the screw, which was starting to show signs of wear, as well as the TB-23 towed sonar array that had been jettisoned during the encounter with the Chinese Kilo. All told, the *Pittsburgh* would be in dry dock for a total of four weeks, which meant she would be kissing the water again in another six to eight days.

Garrett wasn't sure how long he would stay in command of the boat. He was half expecting new orders when he arrived aboard . . . then wondered if they would be giving him time to decide to resign first and save them the trouble of finding him a new billet.

The hell with that noise, he thought. His talk with Gordon had stiffened his resolve. He *would* see the thing through, and he wouldn't allow them to railroad him out of the service.

That night he had his last fight with Claire.

At the end of the work day, Garrett drove home in his aging Skylark. He and Claire rented a modest ranch out in La Mesa, a few miles inland from San Diego. He stayed there with her when the *'Burgh* was in port, and she lived there alone when he was at sea, or sometimes stayed instead with her mother up in Bakersfield.

He joined Claire in the kitchen as she finished making dinner, and told her about both the conclusion of the inquiry and his interesting talk with Gordon.

"So . . . what are you saying?" she asked, wooden spoon in hand. "That you're going to *stay*?"

"I know you'd rather I quit," he told her. "But I can't do that. We've discussed this. . . ."

"No. You've *told* me. We haven't *discussed* it. I tell you why I don't like the Navy, and you just ignore me."

She returned the spoon to the spaghetti, stirring hard. "I don't think you even hear me!"

"I do hear you, hon."

"Don't 'hon' me! Look at us! We're barely getting by on your paycheck, even with sea pay and hazardous duty! Now you tell me you probably won't even make captain! When I married you, you were a poor j.g., but you told me you were going to be an admiral someday, and I believed you! O-5 pay just doesn't cut it!"

"I'm thirty-nine years old, Claire. It's a little early to retire, and a little late to start over!"

"Bullshit! Al Jaffey got out in 'ninety-seven, and he's making ninety thousand a year now. And Fred Lee—"

"Fred Lee is—*was*—an aviator, Claire. A Hornet driver. United probably had headhunters jump him the day he set foot off-base as a civilian. And Al is a programmer. Of course he landed something in Silicon Valley. What am I good for on the outside? Driving the submarine ride at Disneyland?"

"You have all that training in nuclear reactors."

"In case you hadn't noticed, Claire, nuclear energy's pretty much a dead issue in this country. Nobody's building 'em anymore."

"Well, you're an officer, for chrissakes!" she shouted. "A manager! You could get a job at any company as an office manager, a department head, a director of—"

"I don't want any job, Claire. I'm a submariner. You knew that when you married me!"

"And maybe I didn't know what a bum ride I was signing on for," she told him, bitter. "You're gone more than you're here. Sea duty three, four months at a stretch. And you just keep smiling and taking all the shit they give you, with a 'please, sir,' and a 'thank you, sir,' and an 'aye aye, sir.' I'm *sick* of it!"

"Claire, it's not like that, and you know it! Frank said today that—"

"*Frank* says! *Frank* says! I'm sick to death of what Frank says! Was he or was he not on that kangaroo-court board of inquiry?"

"He was, but—"

"Some friend! He's using you, using your friendship, and he couldn't even pull one of those strings of his you're always boasting about to get you out of trouble with SUBRON! He's a goddamn spy! You know it, and I know it! I never did trust him!"

"What does his being in Navy Intelligence have to do with it?" Garrett asked, on the defensive. Sometimes, when Claire got into one of her moods . . .

"It means that he's working with the CIA or who-ever, and as soon as something goes wrong with one of their little plots with some dictator somewhere, he'll find someone to blame, like you! It means he uses you, takes advantage of you, and he'll discard you like *that* if it's convenient! The Cold War's over! He should come in from the cold already!"

"You're not making any sense!"

"Neither are you! Damn it, Tom, I'm sick of this life, sick of not having enough money, sick of not having kids, sick of having you gone all the time, sick of wor-rying about you. . . ." She turned, looking up at him. "I've had it, Tom. I really have. I wasn't cut out to be a Navy wife. I want better. I deserve better! Either you leave the Navy . . . or I leave!"

"That's not fair! You can't ask me to just ditch my career on a whim—"

"This isn't a whim! I've been thinking this over for a

long time. Mom agrees with me. Make something better of yourself, for once in your life! Or find yourself someone else who can put up with this nonsense! Like a dog who doesn't mind going to the kennel when you have sea duty!"

He tried to smooth things over, as he'd done in times past, but dinner was eaten in sullen silence, and that night he found the bedroom door locked, with blanket and pillow piled on the sofa. He left the next morning without saying good-bye . . . and she was gone when he returned.

For Garrett, who'd loved Claire deeply—once, at least—it was like a small but intensely bitter ending of the world. . . .

Thursday, 15 May 2003

Fleet Activities Yokosuka
Yokosuka, Japan
0915 hours

"Would you please step out of the vehicle, sir?"

He stepped out of the cab under the watchful eyes of two Marine sentries—both men in full combat dress, with M-16 rifles at port arms, *with* magazines in place. A third Marine, a very young-looking lieutenant, very carefully examined his military ID, comparing the photo to his face.

Gordon waited patiently as the Marine checked him out. He was still feeling a bit sick and jet-lagged after his all-night crossing of the Pacific aboard a Marine C-130 Hercules—"available transportation" in Navyspeak. They'd hit the fringes of a storm south of Kamchatka, and the last three hours of the flight had been a jouncing, thumping, air-pocket-ridden hell that had made all thought of catching up on lost sleep impossible.

The Herky Bird had touched down at last on the runway at the Naval Air Facility at Atsugi, and he'd elected to hire a local cab rather than wait for the next scheduled military bus bound for Yokosuka. He desperately needed a shave, a shower, and about ten hours in the rack—not necessarily in that order—but his scheduled meeting at Fleet Activities HQ was at 1300 hours, and he somehow doubted that he was going to catch up on his sleep first.

The lieutenant finished his inspection of Gordon's ID at last. "Very well, sir," the Marine said. "We'll get your luggage. Corporal!"

"Aye aye, sir!" Yet a fourth Marine trotted forward, careful not to come between the two armed men and the taxi that had brought Gordon out from Atsugi. He pulled Gordon's single small suitcase out of the backseat and carried it off toward the front gate security shack.

"May I check your briefcase, sir?" the lieutenant asked, eyeing the attaché case Gordon was carrying.

"No, Lieutenant," he replied, reaching into his inside jacket pocket. "Here's my clearance."

The Marine studied the paper, which listed the security classification for the contents of the briefcase and exempted it from search. "Thank you, Captain," the lieutenant said, handing the document back to Gordon. "You may go through, sir."

It was, Gordon thought, further evidence of a world changed beyond all sane recognition.

The destruction of the World Trade Center in New York in 2001 had awakened America to the realpolitik of a world fast sinking into a new Dark Age of barbarism, warlords, and terror, and *all* threats to the nation's boundaries were being met with a vigor that was at times almost paranoid.

And reasonably so, Gordon thought. The War on Terrorism was in its second year now and still showed no sign of abating. One of the most obvious signs of that war's far-reaching effects worldwide was the increase in security at airport terminals, at international border crossings, at embassies . . . and at military bases. At installations like the Fleet Activities base here at Yokosuka, even official vehicles could no longer simply drive through the main gate without close inspection, and foreign vehicles were turned aside by armed guards and rows of concrete dragons' teeth blocking the road. No one was permitted on base without careful scrutiny.

Especially high-profile bases like this one. The Commander Fleet Activities for the Western Pacific, COM-FLEACTWESTPAC, was responsible for the logistical support of all Navy forces on this side of the Pacific. Yokosuka—pronounced "yoh-koo-ska" rather than the way the name looked—was the largest naval shore facility in the Far East, covering something like five hundred acres. Thirteen hundred families lived on base, with another four hundred quartered at the Negishi Housing Area at Yokohama, seventeen miles to the north, and perhaps twelve or thirteen hundred families more living off base in private rentals. If Al Qaida terrorists were looking for a target that combined American military prestige with sheer numbers of potential casualties, as well as one with strategic value, Yokosuka was a prime candidate. Military security, for that reason, was extremely tight and had been ever since the bloody infamy of September 2001.

A Marine driver ushered Gordon into a gray-painted sedan and whisked him into the depths of the huge

base, past the on-base McDonald's, a cluster of bowl-
ing alleys, swimming pools, and other recreational cen-
ters, and the A-33, a popular fleet exchange carrying a
bewildering array of electronic equipment, cameras,
computers, and the like.

The base was crackling with activity, with sailors
and Marines everywhere. East, toward the waterfront
on the Uraga Channel, a forest of radar masts and antennae rose above the skyline of nearer buildings,
marking the moorings for the fair-sized fleet of American warships in port. Overhead, a pair of F/A-18 Hornets thundered high just beneath the overcast, lazily
circling on patrol. All ships, bases, and facilities were
on the highest level of alert with the worsening of this
latest international crisis.

The driver deposited him in front of the BOQ—the
Bachelor Officers' Quarters—where he reported in and
was assigned a room. Three hours later, he emerged,
clean and clean-shaven, and wearing a fresh uniform,
but with only a fraction of the catch-up sleep he
needed. Informed of his arrival, Admiral Hartwell had
dispatched a car and driver and suggested that he
might like to grab a bite to eat at the facility O-Club.
Gordon didn't feel like eating yet—his stomach was
still operating on California time—so he elected to
forgo lunch and hike to the HQ.

As he approached the building's front steps, he spotted a familiar figure on the sidewalk up ahead. "Good
afternoon, Commander," he called when the other officer didn't see him right away.

Commander Garrett started, visibly surprised.
"Frank!" He came to attention and saluted. "Captain
Gordon! What are *you* doing here!"

"The same thing you are, most likely," Gordon said,
returning the salute. "Thirteen hundred briefing?"

"Y-yes, sir! How did? . . ."

Gordon hefted his briefcase. "I'm giving the briefing. It's good to see you again, Tom. It's been a while."

"Three years, has it been?" Garrett said. "Yeah, it's been too damned long."

At least Garrett didn't seem to be holding a grudge still for what had happened at the inquest back in '99, Gordon thought. A good thing. Garrett didn't know it yet, but his career was about to do yet another wild one-eighty.

"How's it going?" Gordon asked.

Garrett's eyes appeared shuttered. Cautious. "Well enough."

"I . . . heard about you and Claire. I'm sorry."

Garrett shrugged. "Things had been heading in that direction for a long time. It was bound to come to a head sooner or later." He glanced at his watch. "Maybe we should be getting inside?"

"Affirmative. I . . . think you'll like the little surprise I've arranged today."

"Oh?" Garrett's expression became, if anything, even more opaque. "Anything I should know about, Captain?"

"Don't sweat it. It's good. I need you to volunteer for a pet project of mine."

"I don't know if that's a good thing or not, sir. The first lesson I learned in the Navy was 'never volunteer.'"

"That's okay. You were volunteered while you were out of the room. Let's get on inside, shall we?"

"Aye aye, sir."

"Believe me, Tom, it's *not* a death sentence."

Together, they walked up the steps and into the building.

The briefing room was occupied by a long, broad

table and plenty of chairs, most of which were already occupied by the time Gordon finished his preliminary talk with Admiral Hartwell and strode into the room. A senior chief entered a moment later, saying, "Gentlemen, attention on deck! COMFLEACTWESTPAC arriving."

The assembled officers, most of them Navy, but with a few Marines adding khaki to the ranks of blue, rose to their feet. Admiral Charles B. Hartwell entered with a brisk "As you were" and took his place at the head of the table. An aide, a Navy captain with a name tag reading OSTER, followed at his heels, taking his place at a podium at the far end of the room, in front of a large, rear-projection screen.

"Gentlemen," Captain Oster began without other preamble. "The Taiwan Crisis, as the press back home are calling it, is heating up. At zero-six-hundred hours this morning the PLA launched a CSS-1 intermediate-range ballistic missile with a high-explosive warhead from a launch facility outside Fuzhou. The warhead detonated on a runway at the Chiang Kai-shek International Airport, causing extensive damage and a number of casualties . . . probably at last two hundred casualties, as of our latest update, and including several American citizens.

"During the past week the People's Republic has launched no fewer than eight missiles in what they've described as a 'military exercise.' All of these missiles detonated harmlessly in the Strait of Formosa and were intended to generate fear and dissension within the Taipei government and the Taiwanese population in general.

"The attack this morning, the first directed against a specific target on land, was accompanied by what can only be regarded as an ultimatum. Taipei is to send a delegation with full powers of negotiation to Beijing by the end of this month in order to draft and sign formal documents of reunification with the People's Republic. Such documents would, of course, mean the end of the Republic of China, and the end of an independent Taiwan.

"The United States government, of course, though it has distanced itself in recent history from open support of Taiwan in order to avoid jeopardizing relations with Mainland China, remains committed to the independence of Taiwan. The President has, therefore, directed all military forces to maintain the highest alert status and readiness levels, and to deploy several key military units to the Taiwan Area of Operations." The briefing officer paused, then looked at Gordon. "Captain Gordon, of the ONI, has flown out this morning from CONUS to give us the latest brief on PRC forces and their projected intentions. Captain Gordon?"

Gordon rose and walked to the podium. He hadn't had much time to prepare his presentation—his sleepless night aboard the Herky Bird had been the best he could manage—but there was little to prepare for. "Lights, please," he said, and as the room lights dimmed, he added, "First slide."

The projection operator in the next room brought up the first image on the screen at Gordon's back. It was a full color picture of high detail and remarkable clarity, looking down obliquely on a submarine at sea . . . a Kilo-class boat with the characteristic long, low sail of Russian designs. It appeared to be lashed alongside a larger ship, an old and sharp-prowed surface vessel with "J503" painted on the bow in very large characters. The two were making their way through heavy swells, with a heavy fuel line strung between them. Evidently, the Kilo was taking on fuel at sea.

"Some of you," Gordon said, "will remember the incident south of the Aleutian Islands in 'ninety-nine, when one of our Los Angeles boats tangled with a Chinese freighter escorted by a Kilo-class diesel submarine. The details of Operation Buster remain highly classified, both for the mission itself and for the particulars of the ensuing collision and the sinking of the Chinese merchant vessel *Kuei Mei*."

Several heads at the conference table turned, as various participants looked at Commander Garrett. Those who didn't, Gordon thought, were likely those who didn't know that the *Pittsburgh*'s former skipper was in the room.

"This is the Kilo involved in the Operation Buster incident," he went on. "We caught her about thirty hours after the collision with one of our reconnaissance aircraft. The surface ship, incidentally, is a Dalang-class submarine support vessel that just *happened* to be in the area."

Several chuckles arose from around the table at that.

"What is interesting about this is the way the Chinese were employing this boat. The Kilo-class submarine has a submerged displacement of 2,900 tons and a top submerged speed of twenty, maybe twenty-five knots, no more. She has two diesel engines that can only be run on the surface, or while snorkeling, and a rechargeable electric drive for use when submerged. A crew of sixty.

"The Kilo is classified as a medium-range sub, with a top range, on the surface or while snorkeling, of about six thousand miles. That, of course, means that if this Kilo was trying to escort the *Kuei Mei* all the way across the Pacific, she was going to need refueling in order to make it back.

"The question is why the Chinese were using a diesel submarine as a transoceanic escort. Their Han nuclear boats would be much better choices, in terms of range, since they can go around the world without refueling. At ONI, we could only arrive at two possibilities.

"One, the Kilo was on a mission requiring extreme stealth. Kilos are quiet, *very* quiet, at least so long as they're submerged and running on their electric motors. Nuclear subs, because of the various cooling plants and pumps associated with their power plants, are noisy . . . and the Hans are especially so."

"Wait a minute, Captain," Admiral Hartwell said, interrupting. "You can't be saying that that Kilo was crossing the Pacific on her batteries, can you?"

"No, sir. A Kilo can only travel a few hundred miles on her electric drive before she has to recharge, either by surfacing or by running submerged on her snorkel. And both of those options are damned noisy. No, the idea was that our Los Angeles just happened to intercept the Kilo while it was running on batteries, but that it periodically either surfaced or used its snorkel to recharge. If that submarine was intended for some stealthy mission, it would have been somewhere close to our coast, probably within our coastal waters. ONI thinks it possible they were traveling with the freighter, in order to mask the noise they made when snorkeling."

"That," Hartwell said with a frown, "is disquieting."

Gordon was tempted to say something about the admiral's pun but thought better of it. It was probably unintentional.

"I should say that the CIA is partial to this idea. There is another possibility, however, one that some of us at ONI think is more likely. The Kilo was escorting the freighter, as we originally surmised. A Kilo drew the mission rather than a Han because they were training the crew."

"Training the crew?" Hartwell said. "For what?"

"Blue-water operations. Missions far from the Chinese coast. And *that*, Admiral, gentlemen, is what is truly disquieting." He paused, watching the implications sink into the various members of his audience. Some still looked puzzled, or lost. Most were beginning to get the idea.

"You see," he continued, "short- and medium-range submarines are generally intended for a defensive role. They're kept in close to the home country's coastline, where they can be employed against foreign maritime intruders that may be entering coastal waters, or to escort local shipping.

"But as every sailor knows, things get a lot different when you push off outside of coastal waters. Some of us believe that the Kilo was on a training exercise intended to give her captain and crew a taste of operations in deep water, far from home. She would have escorted the freighter most of the way across the Pacific, but left the *Kuei Mei* in order to rendezvous with the sub tender and refuel. Then she would return, either alone or with the *Kuei Mei*, on her return voyage."

"Navies do not undertake such training missions unless there is a serious need," Hartwell pointed out. "The risk of a serious training accident is so grave . . ."

"Exactly," Gordon said. "This is an especially alarming development coming from the People's Republic. China continues to think of herself as the 'Middle Kingdom,' a central land of civilization surrounded by not-very-interesting barbarians. For a long time now they've been hampered by that worldview, with the result that they've never bothered developing a navy with a truly global outreach. The PLA Navy—and that should tell us something right there, that their navy is still a part of the People's Liberation *Army*—

was designed strictly for coastal defense, repelling invasions, protecting their territorial waters, that sort of thing.

"Lately, though, there's been a distinct shift in Chinese military philosophy. Their first Xia-class ballistic missile submarine was launched in 1986. Their Han nuclear attack sub dates back to the seventies, but with a few exceptions, they've rarely ventured with them very far from their home waters. Recently, however, the Chinese have been flexing their naval muscles. They appear to have taken delivery on a number of Kilo-class submarines from the Russians, of which this boat was one. Our estimates on the total number of submarines delivered by the Russians at this time range from eight to ten boats, all produced at the Komsomolsk Shipyards.

"And over the past few months, the Chinese have become particularly active in the South China Sea, around the Paracel and Spratly Islands, both of which they consider to be their territory. Blue-water training missions would give their diesel boat crews valuable experience in transiting to key overseas operational areas. A fleet of Kilo-class boats operating out of a Chinese base in the Spratly Islands, for instance, could play havoc with shipping lanes through that region. But the Spratlys are a thousand miles south of mainland China. That's a long haul for sub crews who haven't been trained to operate in deep water."

Admiral Harold Kohl, the commander of the *John C. Stennis* carrier battle group, turned to Hartwell, seated on his left. "Still seems strange sending a Kilo on escort duty across six thousand miles of the North Pacific, doesn't it, Chuck?"

"Not if you're trying to jump-start your submarine force into something with a global reach," Hartwell replied, his voice grim. "Having the PRC operating a strike force of very quiet submarines in the Spratlys or the Paracels would *not* be a good thing."

"In fact," Gordon continued, "the Chinese submarine fleet may not be deploying that far afield . . . at least, not yet. Next slide, please."

The Kilo and the sub tender on the screen were replaced by another high-resolution photo, this one in black and white, shot from a considerable altitude above a seaport or naval facility. Large traveling cranes were clearly visible, as were smokestacks, warehouses, piers, and even individual workers. Of greatest interest was a pair of cigar-shaped vessels moored side by side at one of the piers. A number of white-clad sailors were visible on their decks and on the pier itself. A crane embraced the vessel closest to the pier, which appeared to be swallowing a long, blunt-tipped pencil through a hatch on its forward deck.

"This was taken by one of our intelligence satellites four days ago," Gordon said. "We are looking down on the Huludao Shipyard, two hundred kilometers northeast of Beijing, in Liao Ning Province. We keep a close eye on this port, of course, since it's the same facility where both the Chinese Xia-class ballistic missile submarine and the Han-class nuclear attack submarine were first built and launched.

"These vessels, however, are not of Chinese manufacture. They are Kilo-class diesel boats, purchased within the past few years from Russia. As you can see, they're outfitting at least one of these boats for patrol. That is a twenty-one-inch 'long' antiship torpedo they're wrestling into the weapons loading hatch. Next slide, please."

The next shot was similar to the first. A pair of submarines was moored at a pier in front of a busy military port. Torpedoes were being unloaded from trucks on the pier. Several shorter, stubbier torpedoes were visible as well, apparently being loaded *onto* the trucks.

"The Jiangnan Shipyard at Shanghai," Gordon explained. "Also four days ago. What's interesting here is that they appear to be unloading twenty-one-inch antisubmarine torps from the Kilos and replacing them with the longer antiship torpedoes."

He took them through more slides, each of shipyards, each showing bustling activity around moored submarines. "We're seeing the same thing at ports all along the Chinese coast," he said. "Luda Shipyard, up at Dalian. Hongyi. Donglang Guangzhou and Zhonghua. We have counted a total of eight Kilo-class submarines in various ports up and down the Chinese coast, all being outfitted for patrol at the same time. We have also counted all five of their Han-class nuclear attack boats in port, plus all three of the older Ming-class diesel boats, and even a significant number—eight—of their old Romeo- and Whiskey-class boats . . . clunkers, obsolete boats purchased from the Soviets in the sixties, or built on license for export since then.

"Next slide, please."

This photograph, taken from a different angle, showed the Huludao Shipyard again . . . and the same pier. Both Kilos, however, were gone.

"This one, as you see from the time stamp, was taken yesterday morning, at about zero-seven-hundred hours, local time. And next . . ."

Another repeat, this time Jiangnan. Again the two Kilos were gone.

"As of yesterday morning, gentlemen, the Chinese submarine fleet appears to have set sail. *All* of it. It's the same story at every port on the Chinese coast. Their attack submarines, both nuclear and diesel, and including all of their new Russian Kilos, are now at sea.

"And we don't know where they are headed."

"My God," someone in the audience said, the words startling in the shocked silence.

"Captain Oster has already told us about the missile fired at Chiang Kai-shek International this morning," Gordon continued. "Beijing has been steadily escalating the crisis over Taiwan for the past six months, and it is possible that this is the payoff. One of the scenarios they're looking at back in Washington right now is the possibility that the PRC is about to invade Taiwan. Ten Kilo-class submarines would be sufficient to shut down *all* commercial and military sea traffic in the Strait of Formosa. If they can block the Seventh Fleet from Taiwan waters, they could well have a free hand for an invasion.

"Another possibility we're looking at is the idea that the Kilos have all been dispatched to either the Paracel Islands or, more likely, the Spratly Islands, in order to secure the PRC claim to those regions.

"In either case, the Chinese are gambling on the American reluctance to engage them in a full, stand-up war. The War on Terrorism is tying down a large percentage of our military assets now, worldwide. Beijing may have decided that we're overextended and that this is the best opportunity they've had in a good many years to rush in and grab Taiwan out from under our noses. Once the PLA is entrenched on Taiwan, of course, we're not going to be able to evict them without a protracted and extremely bitter engagement on the land, something Washington wants to avoid at all costs. If we're going to stop the bastards, it *has* to be at sea, before they land.

"And that, we think, is why they have acquired those

Kilos. One carrier battle group could block a Chinese invasion force across the strait without too much trouble. But even a single Kilo, operating in stealthy mode, would be almost impossible to detect and could play havoc with our CBG. Ten kilos could destroy the Seventh Fleet."

"The hell they could," Admiral Kohl rumbled, but Gordon could still feel the wheels turning behind those angry eyes. Attack submarines were the greatest threat faced by a modern carrier battle group. A CBG had plenty of aircraft, missiles, and CIWS Phoenix Gatling mounts to take out incoming missiles, but the only counters to hostile submarines were the group's ASW assets—LAMP helos, Viking S-3 aircraft, and, most important, the pair of Los Angeles-class hunter-killer submarines attached to each group.

But the Kilos were so damned *silent*. Finding them all before they had the range on an American carrier might be almost impossible, even with the vast array of American military technology at the battle group's disposal.

"We have one more piece of bad news," Gordon told the group. He waited a moment for the murmur of conversation to die down before adding, "Slide, please."

Again the screen showed a satellite view of a busy naval facility, with cranes, docks, and pier-side buildings. A submarine was moored to one of the piers.

This one was different from the Kilos, longer, thicker, heavier, and with a long, low, and streamlined-looking sail. Aft, a teardrop-shaped nacelle rode atop a vertical fin.

"Gentlemen," Gordon said, "this is a Walker-class boat."

A few chuckles from around the briefing table greeted the weak joke. The nuclear attack sub on the screen had been first deployed by the old Soviet Union in 1984, just before the discovery of the treason by the infamous Walker Spy Ring.

John Walker had been a Navy chief warrant officer who, from 1968 to 1985, had quietly funneled to his Soviet KGB handlers over one million top secret naval communications and the decryption keys to read them. During those seventeen years, he'd recruited his brother, a lieutenant commander in the submarine service; his son, a communications specialist; and Jerry Whitworth, a Navy radioman. The Walker Spy Ring, as the family business became known, had produced a hemorrhage of the Navy's most vital secrets. The Soviet defector Vitaly Yurchenko had claimed to the CIA that had the Soviet Union and the United States gotten into a war in the 1970s or 1980s, Russia would have won simply because of the importance of the material the Walker Ring was channeling to Moscow. Walker's treason had been at least as important and as far-reaching for the Soviets in their understanding of U.S. secret communications as Ultra had been for the Allies in World War II.

A vital corollary of that understanding was that the Soviets had learned in detail from the Walker information just how vulnerable their submarines were to detection, how easily U.S. sonar and SOSUS nets could track them . . . and how far behind the Americans they were in submarine technology.

The Office of Naval Intelligence had been working for a long time to assess the damage done to the United States by the Walker ring. The full depth and breadth of that damage might well never be known, but one outcome of Walker's treason was on the projection screen now.

"The Russians call her the 'Barrakuda,'" Gordon went on. "NATO dubbed her 'Akula,' the Russian word for shark, after we ran out of phonetic alphabet code names like Sierra, Tango, and Foxtrot. Ten thousand tons' displacement submerged. One hundred thirteen meters long. Top speed submerged estimated at thirty-five to forty knots, but it may be considerably higher.

"And gentlemen, she is as quiet as Death himself. There are many in ONI and the CIA who firmly believe that the Russians built this submarine using technology made possible by the Walker Spy Ring—hence the name 'Walker class.' There are also some in the submarine community who believe the Akula is superior in all respects to our own Los Angeles boats, that it may even be better than the *Seawolf*."

Gordon didn't add what many in the room knew but was still highly classified—that he himself had faced a Soviet Akula back in 1987, during a sneak-and-peek mission with the *Pittsburgh* into the Soviet bastion of the Sea of Okhotsk. A Russian Akula skipper had been just a bit too eager and pursued him into Japanese territorial waters; the Russian boat had been destroyed, but it had been a near thing.

What still counted most in sub versus sub engagements, rather than the technology, was the skill and daring of the men on board, officers and enlisted alike.

"This photo was taken two days ago by a spy satellite over Guangzhou . . . that's Canton, up the Pearl River from Hong Kong. That is the Guangzhou Shipyard.

"What we do not yet know is whether this Akula submarine in Canton is a Russian boat on a show-the-flag visit or one the Russians have sold to the PRC. There have been rumors floating about lately that the Russians were putting together an arms deal with China, one worth *trillions* of rubles, and that the deal included a number of Kilo-class diesel boats and something else, something better and bigger and far more deadly.

"Something like an Akula . . ."

"Wait!" Hartwell said. "Captain . . . you're saying that the Chinese might have bought themselves an Akula?"

"It is a possibility. The ONI would be very interested in confirming that sale, if it really happened. As I said, this could be a simple visit by a Russian submarine to a Chinese port of call. However, we have not been able to identify this particular Akula. That means she's new . . . but the Russians have not been adding to their own fleet lately. Upkeep has been too expensive, and too many of their first-line warships are already rusting to death in ports from the Baltic to the Pacific. If this is a new build, she may have been launched solely for sale to an export market.

"I don't need to add that even one Akula in the PLA naval forces would drastically tip things in their favor in any naval confrontation over Taiwan or the South China Sea. Ten Kilos are bad enough. An Akula is a nuke boat with unlimited range, almost as quiet as a Kilo . . . quieter than one of our Los Angeles boats, in fact. Besides torpedoes, she can launch SS-N-15, -16, and -17 missiles . . . the equivalent of our Tomahawks. One Akula could decimate a carrier battle group. One Akula supported by a wolfpack of Kilos could threaten the entire U.S. Seventh Fleet."

He paused, gauging the temper of the men in the room. They were all listening with grim intensity; Hartwell's fingers were drumming lightly and quickly on the polished mahogany surface of the table.

"Gentlemen, we need hard intel. We need to know exactly what the Chinese have in their inventory . . . and we especially need to know whether they have an Akula in their fleet. Washington had worked out a plan to garner that intelligence, but the missile attack on

Taiwan this morning may have stolen a march from us.

"Nevertheless, Washington's orders are to proceed with the operation, which has been dubbed 'Red Dragon,' with modifications along the way as necessary. We are immediately deploying the attack submarine *Seawolf* to the Strait of Formosa, where she will listen for PLA submarines and attempt to gather acoustical data on their presence and operations there. She will make a special effort to find and identify the Akula in the Hong Kong area and make an attempt to determine her nationality.

"In the meantime, the *Stennis* battle group will deploy to the Strait of Formosa to present Beijing with a show of our determination to stand by Taiwan. Should war break out between China and the United States, the *Seawolf* will already be in position to strike PLA assets along the coast between Hong Kong and Fuzhou. Commander Lawless? Is your boat ready to sail?"

One of the naval officers at the table nodded. He was Commander George Lawless, the current skipper of SSN-21, the USS *Seawolf*. "Yes, sir," Lawless said. "We're ready to sail on twenty-four hours' notice. My wardroom is still down by an XO, however. Commander Joslin was airlifted out to San Diego three days ago."

"I know." Lieutenant Peter Joslin, *Seawolf*'s exec, had developed sudden and severe heart problems, problems severe enough that *Seawolf* had put into Yokesuka, the nearest major Navy port at the time, to transfer Joslin to the naval hospital there. He'd been transferred back to the States when it became clear that he needed better hospital facilities to treat his condition.

For Frank Gordon, Joslin's illness had provided an unexpected but most welcome opportunity. He'd been arguing for the past month that he needed one of his people on board the *Seawolf* if that boat was to be sent

hunting for Kilos in the Formosa Strait. But even Sea-
wolfs were crowded, and no skipper wanted people on
board who weren't pulling their own weight. There'd
been resistance to the idea.

"Some of you may know Commander Tom Gar-
rett," he went on, "by reputation if not in person. He is
a former skipper of a Los Angeles boat—*my* old boat,
in fact—the USS *Pittsburgh*. In addition, he has particular expertise tracking Kilo-class submarines. I would
like to suggest him as a temporary executive officer for
the *Seawolf*. You may find his skills damned useful on
this one, Commander."

"As long as he's not driving," Lawless said. He made
it sound like a joke, and several at the table chuckled,
but Gordon knew that Lawless still didn't like the idea.
He'd broached it to him by phone yesterday and received a lot of static . . . mostly having to do with the
fact that Garrett was still under a cloud after his collision with a Chinese sub and the subsequent hearing.

Gordon also knew that Lawless would go along with
the idea. Admiral Dulany, back in San Diego, had been
most emphatic. Gordon wanted a particular man on
the *Seawolf* for Operation Red Dragon, and he would
have that man, no questions asked.

And Gordon wanted Garrett on the *Seawolf*.

He wondered how Garrett felt about that.

Thursday, 15 May 2003

Fleet Activities Yokosuka
Yokosuka, Japan
1210 hours

Garrett drove his battered, secondhand Toyota down Nimitz Avenue, then turned at the bustle of the Alliance Club—a sprawling structure billed as the largest enlisted men's club in the world, three floors of discos, bars, and restaurants. It was lunchtime, and he knew he ought to be hungry, but the briefing he'd just attended had jolted him hard, leaving him weak, a bit shaken, and not at all interested in food. He wanted to make it down to the dockside area.

He wanted, no, he *needed* to see the *Seawolf*.

He was going to be assigned to a submarine again . . . and *such* a submarine! *Seawolf* . . .

It was the stuff dreams were made of. The problem was, nightmares were dreams, too. Could he do this?

His career track had definitely taken a negative turn since '99. He hadn't fallen off the straight and narrow yet, but things were definitely closing in on him. According to the charts, his expected professional development path would have seen him commanding a submarine like the *Pittsburgh* until he had eighteen years or a bit more in-service, then had him rotate ashore for a postcommand stretch at a SUBRON HQ or other sub-related shore facility. He might also find himself selected for a senior service college or a major command, once he hit his twenty-year mark . . . and all of it would be aimed at grooming him for selection as captain and a posting to a major command.

He'd now been in the Navy for twenty years. At twenty-one he would have been able to make captain, but that was such a distant dream now it wasn't even worth considering. Once you hit O-5 in this man's Navy—the rank of commander—you'd pretty much risen as far as it was possible to go without some pretty serious politicking and good friends within the infamous Old Boys' Network.

And where was he? His first command had been aborted halfway in. After leaving the *Pittsburgh*, he'd ended up shuffling papers at the Naval Supply Center Command in Pearl Harbor. Hawaii was a true paradise, but it had been exile nonetheless. They might as well have posted him to Adak, Alaska. Submarine skippers had their share of paper shuffling and bureaucracy, sure, but Supply had been an absolute horror of boredom with its endless paperwork, forms, and requisitions.

And after a year at Pearl he'd been transferred again, this time across the Pacific to Atsugi. That was after the divorce with Claire became final, and at least he didn't have to worry about finding housing for her in Japan, where long waiting lists made good housing on- or off-base hard to come by.

Fortune had smiled in another way, too. He'd been assigned to the Foreign Technologies Department at Atsugi, where the DIA and ONI kept a close watch on such developments as quieter Russian submarines out of the Komsomolsk shipyards, or the acquisition of Kilo sub exports by Beijing. Since he'd actually encountered one of those Kilos, Garrett had arrived at Atsugi as a minor celebrity and was assigned to an office processing all incoming data on Chinese Kilos.

He'd become the Navy's Far East expert on Kilos; in fact, he'd been summoned to the meeting this morning in order to brief the assembled admirals and captains on the Kilo and its current capabilities. He'd done so after Frank Gordon had finished his presentation, and managed to get through the material despite the spinning clutter of thoughts in his skull.

He found himself wondering if Gordon had had a hand in putting him at Atsugi in the first place. Damn the man, it wouldn't be beyond his powers. Garrett didn't know whether to be happy about that or furious at the meddling in his career. His career might be going nowhere right now, thanks to the Operation Buster incident, but damn it all, it was his career, and he wanted to make it or go belly up on *his* merits, talents, and sweat, not his friendship with a senior submariner.

He reached the dockside and found a parking place for his car. He had to stroll a few hundred yards to reach a good vantage point. The air was cool and quite wet; a storm was moving in from the Pacific, and clouds were gathering above the base, promising rain. Shafts of bright sunlight, however, were slashing down out of the cloud-mountains, sparkling on the dark water and illuminating the ranks of submarines moored to the piers.

There she is . . .

A security perimeter had been established to keep the curious well away from her moorings, but it was possible to get a good view from where he stood. She was long, low, and dark gray, a beautiful, elegant lady. White, magnetic numerals reading *21* clung to the side of her sail. They would be removed when the vessel put out to sea, but for now they identified her as SSN 21, the first attack submarine of the twenty-first century, arguably the most modern attack boat in the world. Forget what the experts thought about the Akula; *Seawolf* was the Queen of Deep Water.

She looked huge. Her sail appeared small compared to the bulk of her hull, and the wedge at the forward foot of the sail, which gave it a sweeping, smoothly curved look instead of the usual right angle between deck and conning tower, made the boat look a bit alien to Garrett's eye. At just over 106 meters in length overall, she was actually three meters shorter than the lean and slender *Pittsburgh*, but her lines were heavier, bulkier, and her submerged displacement was almost a third again greater than a Los Angeles boat. Despite that, she could manage thirty-five-plus knots underwater and had been built to travel at twenty knots in almost complete silence. Everything about her had been designed with quiet in mind. She was to the dark and quiet world of submarines what the F-117 Stealth Fighter was to the skies. In fact, it was said of the *Seawolf* that she was quieter moving at tactical speed than a Los Angeles-class boat was tied up to the pier.

Unlike *Pittsburgh* and the earlier L.A. boats—but like all of the newer L.A. boats numbered 751 and later—she had her planes mounted on her bow rather than on her sail. The public explanation was that this allowed her to surface through the ice with fewer problems during operations beneath the Pole. In fact, sail-mounted planes had been discovered to be a serious source of unwanted sound at higher submerged speeds, and moving them to the bow was yet another effort to achieve perfect undersea silence.

Her complement would be something like 115 men and twelve officers, about the same as on board an L.A.-class. But there were only two Seawolf-class submarines afloat now, with one more, the *Jimmy Carter*, due to launch in another year. Quite a noisy battle had been fought in the corridors of the Pentagon and on Capitol Hill as to whether there would ever be any more, and eventually the Seawolf program had been killed in favor of the smaller, cheaper Virginia-class New Attack Submarines. Competition for a berth on board *Seawolf*, or on her sister boat *Connecticut*, was fierce and unrelenting, especially among officers who saw the prestigious assignment as a big leap up the career ladder.

And now he was going to be the *Seawolf*'s executive officer.

"She's a real beauty, isn't she?"

Garrett didn't need to turn around to see the speaker. He knew the voice well. "Yes, sir," he said. "And I'm standing here wondering just how much you had to do with getting me this billet." He turned then and saluted Captain Gordon, stiff and rigidly precise. He needed to keep a tight-fisted control on his emotions just now.

Dream come true? Or nightmare?

Gordon returned the salute with a perfunctory snap of his arm. "You can't think I'm responsible for Commander Joslin's heart condition."

"Hm. I guess not. But every time my career goes any-where, up or down, you seem to be somewhere in the wings."

"At this point, Tom, I'm more worried about my ca-reer than yours. This Chinese Kilo thing caught us all napping . . . and that Akula up at Canton makes it much, much worse. Intelligence is going to take it in the neck if Taiwan falls to the PLA."

"That's the usual way of it, isn't it?" Garrett said with a rare grin. "Shoot the messengers."

"Especially if the messengers didn't bring the mes-sage in time. Or if the message was . . . unpalatable. Right now there's a lynch mob forming up at the Pen-tagon. ONI isn't in real good odor at the moment."

Garrett chuckled. As usual, Gordon had a way of disarming him with easy wit and a comfortable change of topic.

"So . . . can *Seawolf* bail out the ONI?"

"If it's possible, she can," Gordon replied. "We need intel, and we need it badly. *Seawolf* is the best platform in the world for this kind of work."

"That's what they say. Last I heard, the *Seawolf* was still a boat in search of a mission."

Work on *Seawolf* had begun in 1989, with a design intended to counter the newer, quieter Soviet boats like Akula and the Sierra, but when the Soviet empire had died, *Seawolf* lost her major projected opponents.

So *Seawolf* had gone to sea in the mid-1990s with a broad range of capabilities, with mission and growth potential that far exceeded the L.A.-class boats. She was designed to carry out a variety of crucial opera-tions anywhere from under the Arctic ice to littoral regions anywhere in the world, with missions includ-ing surveillance, intelligence collection, special warfare, covert cruise-missile strike ops, mine warfare, and both conventional antisubmarine and antisurface ship operations. The question was whether this extremely expensive submarine was even necessary anymore in a world where the Soviet Union no longer existed.

The Navy had pushed hard to keep the Seawolf program in place despite the cost-cutting efforts of the post–Cold War Congress. They'd managed to save a fragment of the original program, but unfortunately, cost overruns had kicked the price tag for *Seawolf* up to over a billion dollars per boat—ten billion for the first five, and thirty billion more for the next twenty-five—and the original planned complement of thirty Seawolf-class submarines had long ago been scaled back to three.

"She *has* a mission, Tom," Gordon said after a long moment. "Operation Red Dragon. Surveillance, intelligence-gathering . . . and ASW support for the *Stennis* CBG."

"You realize, of course, that she's going to be pretty badly outnumbered . . . hunting for ten Kilos, plus that Akula if she's part of the PLA Navy."

"Well, that's what keeps the Navy life interesting. Think of it as a challenge."

"Will we have backup?"

"There will be other subs deploying to the Chinese littoral, sure," Gordon admitted. "But they'll have their own patrol areas and their own missions. And there are two L.A.-class boats with the *Stennis* CBG—the *Salt Lake City* and the *Jefferson City*. If things really heat up, the *Kitty Hawk* CBG will be operating north of Taiwan."

"If things heat up. Is it going to be war, do you think?"

"Up till yesterday I didn't think so. The Chinese have been rattling sabers at Taiwan since 1949. But after this morning and the attack on Chiang Kai-shek International . . . I just don't know. It doesn't look good. A lot is going to be riding on the *Seawolf*, on what she can learn, and on what she can do to persuade Beijing that a war right now is just not in their best interests."

A gray sedan with official government markings pulled up in the pier-side parking lot a few yards away, and a tall, slightly stooped man in khakis climbed out of the back seat. Garrett recognized him—Commander George Lawless, the *Seawolf*'s CO.

"Captain," Lawless said, saluting Gordon. "Commander Garrett." He sounded preoccupied.

"Good afternoon, Skipper," Garrett replied. The protocol of the moment was fuzzy. Both men carried the rank of commander, O-5, but Lawless was captain of the *Seawolf* and Garrett's commanding officer . . . or he *would* be when Garrett reported aboard with his orders, which wouldn't be ready until tomorrow morning. Garrett wanted to establish a friendly footing with the man he would soon be working for, and calling him "Commander Lawless" seemed a bit too formal for the occasion. The informal "Skipper" seemed to fit the moment.

"I am not your commanding officer *yet*, Commander," Lawless said with a voice like ice. "When I am, I expect you to address me with proper respect."

"Aye aye, Commander Lawless," Garrett said stiffly, his voice held carefully neutral.

"I'm not exactly pleased at this *intrusion* on board my command," Lawless added. "A Seawolf rates an O-4 for the XO billet."

"Commander Garrett has specialized knowledge,

Commander," Gordon said, "as I told you on the phone the other day."

"So you said. So you said. I still don't have to like it. Sir." He paused, as if considering something. "I'll tell you this, gentlemen. Jos Joslin is one of the best officers in this fleet. My men respect him. My crew is a well-oiled, smoothly operating, highly efficient machine. I will *not* tolerate any disruption to that machinery. Am I clear?"

"Quite clear, Commander," Garrett replied.

"I don't care what sort of sneaky-Pete shenanigans you're engaged in. On my boat you will serve as my XO, and you will maintain the high efficiency and standards of my crew. What boat were you exec aboard?"

"*Cheyenne*, SSN-773, from 'ninety-eight to 'ninety-nine."

That got a grudging nod from Lawless. "A good boat. Do as well on the *Seawolf* and we'll get on okay. Just one thing."

"Yes, Commander?"

"When you stand the OOD watch, you will *not* run my submarine into any other submarine or surface vessel. Am I understood?"

"Yes, Commander."

"Good." The man stalked off, passing through *Seawolf*'s security checkpoint with a wave at the sentries standing guard there.

"Was that supposed to be a joke?" Garrett asked.

"If it wasn't, pretend that it was, Tom. Don't let them get to you."

"Shit. I'm never going to live the *Kuei Mei* down, am I?"

"Maybe not. Or maybe you'll do something positive, something so positive that it erases that memory."

"I suppose. I'm beginning to wonder if my career is worth this."

"It is," Gordon said. "Trust me. C'mon. I'm starved. Let's find someplace to eat."

"I'm not very hungry."

"Cut the crap, Commander. This base has everything. KFC. The Mammy Shack. Shakey's Pizza. McDonald's. Or we can go off-base for McSushi at the local Japanese McD."

"You do know how to cheer a man up." Garrett held his stomach. "Gah!"

"I take it you've already enjoyed the experience."

"Occasionally. Up at Atsugi. It's actually not that bad, but I think I'll stick with American food for now."

"Gringo."

"No, here it's *gaijin*," Garrett said. "And proud of it. Let's go hit the O-Club. It's pretty good here."

"Affirmative."

Before they left, though, Garrett stopped and took a last, long look at the USS *Seawolf*. Lawless was striding up the gangplank now, as a boatswain piped him aboard and a voice over the 1MC called out, "*Seawolf*, arriving."

In the submarine service, a man had to earn the dolphins he wore on his uniform. Enlisted personnel served on board for up to a year, rotating through each department, before they were eligible to pin on that coveted badge. Garrett had put in his months as an apprentice back on board the *Pittsburgh*, under then-Commander Frank Gordon. The entire wardroom had lined up to pound the dolphin pin into his chest, one after another in time-honored, bruising tradition. Grinning malevolently, Gordon had been first in line.

Garrett wondered how long it would take to earn his dolphins all over again.

Kaohsiung Airport
Kaohsiung, Taiwan
2020 hours

The C-17 transport dropped smoothly out of the fast-gathering darkness, touching down on the main runway with a howl of reversing jet engines. Taxiing past the main terminal, the cargo plane, bearing USAF markings, wound its way toward the Taiwanese military base at the far end of the facility, parking at last in front of a ready line of needle-nosed, Chinese Nationalist F-5E Tiger II interceptors.

The rear ramp came down and twenty-four dungaree-clad men trotted down and out onto the tarmac, falling into double ranks, each shouldering his own seabag. They wore blue ballcaps, rather than white hats, but otherwise looked like any other group of U.S. Navy sailors.

Six officers in khakis accompanied them. Lieutenant Commander John Calhoun Morton was the senior officer. As Lieutenant Reese took the roll call, he turned and saluted the small contingent of men in camouflage utilities who approached them.

"Commander Morton?" the senior Chinese officer said. "I am your counterpart, Commander Tse Chung On. Welcome to China."

Morton suppressed a smile. Alone in all the world, the Taiwanese continued to insist that *their* China was the *real* China, holdout legacy of their retreat in 1949 to this island stronghold. It was, he thought, evidence of Taiwan's ongoing siege mentality.

"Thank you, Commander," he replied. "It's good to be here again."

The last time Morton had been in Kaohsiung, it was in 1997, and he'd been 2IC of a SEAL platoon deployed to Taiwan to assist the Nationalist Chinese in a training program. Nationalist China maintained a special warfare group called the Parafrogman Assault Unit, a team similar to the Navy SEALs in training, equipment, and operational technique. Nationalist parafrogmen often operated deep inside Mainland China as the active arm of both the Military Intelligence Bureau and Taiwan's Special Operations Command. Together with the Long-Range Amphibious Reconnaissance Commandos, Taiwan's other premier covert ops force, the parafrogs had long been the West's primary source of intelligence on military capabilities and deployments within the PRC.

The SEALs and parafrogs frequently trained together, both in Taiwan and back in the States, at Coronado and elsewhere, but this time around the visit was not about training. "My orders," Morton said, handing Tse a packet of documents.

Tse gave a slight bow and gave them only a cursory examination. "We have been waiting for your arrival. You have heard the news?"

"About the missile attack at the Taipei airport? Yes."

"Beijing has issued an ultimatum. We are to send them a delegation to begin negotiations for formal reunification."

"What's the 'or else'?"

Tse's brow crinkled. "Pardon?"

"What happens if you don't comply?"

"Ah! That is not stated. However, it hardly needs to be, yes? Taipei has, of course, refused."

"Let's get my men to their quarters, Commander. Then we can talk."

"Of course. This way, if you please?"

Lieutenant Reese called the company to attention. They then reshouldered seabags and began walking single file toward a trio of trucks waiting in the twilight.

First Company, SEAL Team Three, was on its way to war.

Kamiseya, Japan
2130 hours

Garrett walked up to the apartment foyer and pressed the three-button number on the telephone keypad. A moment later a woman's voice answered the phone. *"Moshe-moshe!"*

"Kazuko? It's me!"

"Tom? Let me buzz you in!"

The inner door lock buzzed as he hung up the phone. He pushed through and made his way to the elevator.

It was a western-style apartment, but there were still two pairs of shoes by the mat outside the door. One of Kazuko's roommates must be home. He knocked.

The door opened and Kazuko's smile greeted him, warm radiance and sunshine. "Tom!"

"Konichi-wa, Kazuko-san! Nani yatteta-no?"

"Betsu-ni," she replied, then giggled. "Your accent is still atrocious, you know."

He sighed. "You'll just have to keep working on me, I guess. Are you going to invite me in?"

"Of course. Come in!"

Stooping, he untied his shoes and left them and his socks outside.

"You know we don't have the apartment to ourselves tonight," she told him as she shut the door at his back. "Yukio is in town."

Kazuko shared the apartment with three other women. All were flight attendants with JAL, and it was always a crapshoot as to how many of them would be home on a given evening or weekend.

"I know." He looked around the living room—tidy and minimally furnished. "Where is she?"

"In the bedroom, to give us a bit of privacy. Your phone call sounded urgent. What's the matter?"

"First, I need a hug."

She slipped into his arms, smelling of lavender and warmth. Kazuko Mitsui was the best thing that had happened to Garrett since his being stationed at Atsugi. Born on Okinawa, she'd moved with her parents to California when she was three, growing up in San Francisco and attending college at USC before moving back to Japan. She was a natural linguist, speaking perfect and colloquial English, as well as Cantonese, French, and a bit of Russian.

He'd met her one afternoon a year ago, while visiting the shrine at Kamakura with its huge, ancient, carved Buddha. A walk together had turned into coffee . . . then dinner. She'd done a lot since then to heal the wounds Claire had left in his soul, though finding privacy with so many roommates was sometimes a bit difficult. More than once he and Kazuko had settled for a hotel room, avoiding the so-called Japanese "love motels" that charged by the hour, for something a bit classier and more romantic . . . like the Kamiseya Holiday Inn.

"I . . . I got new orders today. Sea duty."

Her eyes widened and she drew back. "No! I thought you were going to be at Atsugi for at least another year!"

"I thought so, too. And I should be back at Atsugi afterward. They're sending me out just for the one mission, as a kind of expert, I guess."

"How long?"

"I don't know. At least a few weeks. There's no way to know."

"No, I mean how long before you go?"

"Tomorrow night."

She hugged him close again. "Well, we knew it would happen."

"It's not like this is the end for us. You know?"

"Of course not. But . . . well, it's been good having you so close." She held him for a long moment more. "Tom?"

"Yes?"

"Is this . . . does it have to do with what's happening in Taiwan?"

"You know I can't talk about it, one way or the other."

"I know. But if there's going to be shooting, I just . . . well, I want to know."

The need for tight security was an integral part of the way Garrett thought and acted, as much as the need for air or human companionship. Submariners never talked about their jobs with others, and his stint with the ONI had only reinforced that bedrock instinct. He'd been officially questioned several times about Kazuko; there were those within the intelligence community who got nervous about fraternization with non-Americans, especially since the War on Terrorism had begun. He trusted Kazuko absolutely, in a way he hadn't even with Claire . . . but he still kept the operational details to himself.

Always.

"You know there's always a chance of shooting," he told her gently. "Especially these days. That's part of the territory with the service, to go in harm's way, right?"

"I guess so. I don't have to like it."

"I don't either, but it goes with the job."

"You'll be careful?"

"Hey. Submariners are nothing *but* careful. The idea is to stay so quiet no one even knows we're there."

She managed a sad smile. "I know. I'll be thinking about you."

He thought it best to change the subject. "Have you eaten?"

She nodded. "Before your call. But I wouldn't mind going someplace quiet where we can be together. When do you have to be back at the base?"

"Oh seven hundred tomorrow."

"Would you like . . . to get a room?"

"I already called the Holiday Inn."

"Let me get my overnight bag."

"You do that."

Much later he lay with her in bed, feeling her gentle breathing in the darkness, feeling her warmth, smelling the sweet musk of their lovemaking. He'd been unwilling to sacrifice his career for Claire. Kazuko, though . . . his need for her seemed deeper, sweeter, more powerful every time he was with her. Was it time to move on to another career, he wondered, something more settled that would allow him to enjoy what he had, what he *could* have with this woman?

He didn't know.

But he knew he'd never known such peace as when he was in her arms.

Friday, 16 May 2003

Captain's Office, USS *Seawolf*
Pier 4, Fleet Activities Facility
Yokosuka, Japan
1345 hours

"Commander Thomas Garrett, reporting aboard, sir."

He stood in the narrow doorway leading into the captain's office, a cramped space at best, even aboard a modern Seawolf-class boat, tucked away next to the captain's quarters off the main forward passageway. Captain Lawless was squeezed in behind his small desk, on which a laptop computer was perched. Opposite, a master chief in khakis, a burly man in his fifties with a crisp mustache and eyes that missed nothing, leaned back in a chair, cradling a mug of steaming coffee. The mug bore the legend "COB."

Lawless held out his hand, and Garrett passed him the bulky manila government envelope containing his orders and personnel records. The captain unwound the string tie, pulled out the cover sheet, and scanned it briefly. "Okay, Garrett. Welcome aboard." He nodded at the chief. "Master Chief Kevin Dougherty. Chief of the Boat."

"Master Chief."

"Good t'meet you, sir," Dougherty said, reaching across and shaking his hand. "Welcome aboard."

"Commander Garrett will be replacing Mr. Joslin as XO," Lawless explained. "*Temporarily.*" He came down hard on the final word.

Dougherty gave him a scrutinizing scan, top to bottom and back again. "Weren't you skipper of—"

"Yes, COB," Garrett replied.

"I think I'll have our XO take us out this afternoon, COB. Any problem with that?"

"No, sir. None at all." Dougherty grinned as though he shared a secret with the captain. "We'll just have the fender crews standing by!"

"No need, COB," Garrett said. He grinned. If he was going to be accepted by the *Seawolf*'s crew, if he was going to have a prayer of fitting in, he would need to join in the fun. "I'll be fine . . . unless, of course, there are any *Russian* subs tied up at Yokosuka."

Dougherty laughed. "Heh! I'll be sure to have the lookouts keep a sharp watch!"

Lawless was going through Garrett's service records. He'd pulled out the thick folder that included his health records and began thumbing through the pages. Uh-oh, Garrett thought. Here it comes.

"Interesting" was Lawless's only comment, at least for several long moments as he stopped to read a page. "I find this somewhat disturbing, Commander," Lawless said at last. "You are under prescription for moderate to severe clinical depression."

"Yes, sir." He glanced briefly at Dougherty, who was carefully studying his coffee. The contents of a man's health records were confidential. While his commanding officer would have access to them, by rights no one else on board save the medical staff would normally be privy to their contents. A submarine's Chief of the Boat, however, was a special case, a minor deity who served as the direct link between the enlisted personnel and the officers—especially the boat's executive officer, who was responsible for the crew's performance. He needed to build trust with Dougherty, needed to build it both ways, and to build it quickly. Chances were, Lawless would share the information with the COB in any case. "Zoloft, one hundred milligrams."

"Is this something stemming from what happened with your former command?"

"That was a contributing factor, sir. As were my divorce and the apparent sidetracking of my career. You'll note, sir, that I have a clean bill of mental health."

"So long as you take your pills." Lawless frowned. "I am sorry to hear about your *personal* troubles, Commander. But this medical condition worries me. Depression is a killer. It is also a primary occupational hazard on board a submarine. Most submariners suffer from depression, to one extent or another, at some point in their careers. But if you are to be my exec, I need to know that you will function efficiently, without question, without hesitation. And I need to know that you will work well with my crew, that you will always be available to them, that you will not degrade their performance with your problems."

"You don't need to worry about that, Captain."

"I *do* need to worry about it, Commander. The Navy pays me to worry. I need to know I'll be able to count on you when the pressure's on. I expect you to do things by the *book,* Mr. Garrett, by the book."

"All I can say, sir, is that you'll have to give me a chance to prove myself."

"That is exactly what I intend to do. You'll have your chance. One. That's all I ever give anyone. Am I clear?"

"Yes, sir."

Lawless continued to page through Garrett's personnel record as if searching for something more, something to use. Garrett wondered if he'd been dismissed.

Lawless looked up. "Ah, Commander? One more thing."

"Yes, sir?"

He tapped the open folder he was going through. "Do you know what this is?"

Garrett couldn't see it from where he stood. "No, sir."

"Your security file." Lawless studied it a moment more. "Says here you've been dating a Japanese girl."

Garrett felt a cold fist closing in his gut. "That's right."

"That's a bit unusual, isn't it? Someone working for ONI, having a relationship with a foreign national?"

He had reported his relationship with Kazuko, as was required. Especially *these* days, the authorities were nervous about the possibility of terrorists getting hold of intelligence dealing with U.S. military deployments, base plans, or security.

"No, sir. Some of the guys at ONI are married to locals. Sir."

"I wouldn't want one of my officers to have trouble with enemy identification."

Anger flooded Garrett, coloring his face, but he kept his response rigidly under control. "That is *not* a problem with Ms. Mitsui, Captain."

"It had better not be. She only needs to *gook* us once—"

The racist epithet, used as a verb, burned. "*That* is uncalled for! Sir!"

"Is it?"

Garrett forced himself to unclench his fists. To relax. To press back the white fury. "Yes, sir. It is. Is there anything else? Sir."

He sighed. "No, no. Not now. Dismissed, Commander. COB? Why don't you show our new exec to his quarters, get him settled in."

"Aye aye, sir."

Garrett found himself trembling as he stepped out into the passageway. *That damn racist bastard!* Was it possible people still thought that way, felt that way in this day and age?

He took a deep breath. Yes, of course it was, unfortunately. Since September 11 and the start of the War on Terrorism, anyone not obviously American-born was suspect, along with anyone, American or not, who was a Moslem.

"This way, sir," Dougherty said, squeezing past him. A short way down the passageway to a cabin marked EXECUTIVE OFFICER.

"Thank you, Master Chief."

"No problem, sir. Uh . . . listen . . ."

"Yes?"

"Don't let the Old Man get under your skin, Commander. He has a knack for pushing hard to find weakness, y'know?"

"Is that what you call it?"

"Don't get me wrong, sir. The captain's great. The men love him. But he can be damned tough on you until he gets your measure, until he knows what you're made of, you understand? He'll really put the pressure on in order to check out your crush depth, if y'take my meaning. Don't let him get your goat."

Garrett relaxed a bit. "Thank you, COB. I'll try to remember that."

"This is a good boat. The captain worked hard to get this assignment. He beat out I don't know how many other qualified submarine skippers to land it. The men are good, too, the very best of the very best. Only the best would get duty aboard the 'Wolf."

"I would have expected nothing less."

"Good. So, if you'd like to come on aft to the wardroom, I'll start introducing you around."

"Thanks, COB. I'd like that."

Four of the Seawolf's officers were in the wardroom, seated around the table that nearly filled a compartment that was relatively large by submariner standards.

"Lieutenant David Ward, our weapons officer," Dougherty said. "Lieutenant Ronald Simms, navigation. If we get lost, it's his fault."

"Fuck you, COB."

"Any time, sir, anyplace. The tall, gangly guy in the corner there is Lieutenant Tollini, our dive officer. And over by the door, where he can make a quick getaway, is Lieutenant j.g. Neimeyer, fresh out of sub school and ready to conn the Seawolf all by his lonesome. Gentlemen, this is Commander Garrett, our new exec."

The four nodded and murmured greetings. "Fresh meat!" Ward added. "You seen the skipper yet, sir?"

"Just did."

"Then you know what to expect. Seawolf is a tight boat."

"The brasswork shines," Simms added. "And if it doesn't, the Old Man'll damn well know why. By the book, people, by the book!"

"Good to meet all of you," Garrett said. They

looked like a good group . . . but wary. All submariners, in Garrett's experience, were a bit reserved
with newcomers and outsiders. It had to do with the
job, where silence was more than golden, where secrecy was the rule, and where you depended on the
other members of the crew to work together to make
sure you returned to the sunlight alive after each time
the boat dived.

It had been a while since Garrett had been aboard a
submarine, or even associated closely with submariners. Was it their natural Silent Service reticence
he sensed? Or something more?

He would have to get to know them better to decide.

Crew's Mess, USS *Seawolf*
Pier 4, Fleet Activities Facility
Yokosuka, Japan
1410 hours

"So, anyone get a load of the new XO when he came
aboard?" Torpedoman's Mate First Class Jordan
Larimer asked the others. Midday dinner was over and
the mess tables wiped down. Larimer and four other
Seawolf sailors had gathered there for a break and some
scuttlebutt with cups of coffee or juice before getting
back to the routine of preparing the sub for departure.

"I saw him," Engineman Second Class Bennett said.
He shrugged. "Didn't look like much. Another ring-
knocker."

"Annapolis, huh?" Sonar Tech Chief Eric Toynbee
said. "Takes more'n that to turn out a good submariner. Right, Queenie?"

He slapped the youngster on the bench next to him

hard enough so the kid almost spilled his bug juice. Ken Queensly was *Seawolf's* newest sonar tech, a skinny, gangly looking kid with Coke-bottle glasses and the awkward air of a computer geek.

"Right, Chief," Queensly said. "I heard he was a full commander, though. What are we going to do with two commanders on board?"

"Stay out of trouble," Larimer said, and the others laughed.

"On a ship," Toynbee explained, "and in the boats, the guy running the show is *always* 'Captain,' no matter what his rank. And if he's captain of a boat, he's God Almighty Hisself. There is *no* question who is in charge."

"But, I mean, do we call him 'Commander' or 'Mister Whatsisname'?" Queensly asked.

It was a fair question. In Navy rank protocol, a lieutenant commander was generally called "Mister" and addressed by name, while full commanders and up were addressed by their rank and name . . . unless, of course, they were captain of a ship, in which case they were always called "Captain."

"Well," Toynbee said, stroking his chin, "*sir* will do until he makes his wishes known."

"How the hell'd we manage to get an O-5 as XO?" Bennett wanted to know.

"The way I heard it," Radioman First Class Wayne Shaeffer said, "this guy *had* a boat of his own, the *Greeneville*. He collided with a Jap fishing boat off Hawaii and—"

"You're full of shit," Toynbee said, laughing. "*That* guy was booted clear out of the Navy. Excuse me . . . he took early retirement as an option. This ain't the same guy."

"Naw, I'm telling you it is," Shaeffer said. He leaned forward and let his voice drop to a conspiratorial murmur. "I got a buddy at Pearl, stationed at the comm center. He said there was orders for this guy to take Mr. Joslin's place, only he'd been a sub driver before and got busted for colliding with a Jap ship a few years ago."

"Then your buddy's full of shit," Toynbee insisted.

"You gentlemen are talking about the *Ehime Maru*," a new voice said. They turned in their seats as a man in officer's khakis with the three gold bars on his shoulder boards of a full commander stepped through the watertight door and onto the mess deck. The COB was close behind him.

"Attention on deck!" Toynbee barked, but before any of them could rise, the newcomer waved them back.

"As you were," he said. "Don't mind me. I just happened to catch your conversation coming down the passageway. The boat you're talking about was the USS *Greeneville*, a Los Angeles-class submarine, SSN 772. She surfaced under a Japanese fishing boat nine miles south of Diamond Head, Oahu, in February of 2001. The *Ehime Maru* was a Japanese research-fishing vessel carrying a number of students on board. She was torn open when the *Greeneville* performed an emergency surface exercise under her, and she sank in two thousand feet of water. Nine Japanese nationals were killed, creating a serious international incident and ruining several promising Navy careers.

"*Greeneville*'s skipper was Commander Scott Waddle. I didn't know him personally, but by all accounts he was a good man and an excellent sub driver. According to the testimony at his Board of Inquiry, he did not receive key sonar information on the Japanese vessel's location in time before surfacing . . . and his routine periscope sweep before the exercise indicated the area was clear. The chief, here, is right, though. Commander Waddle retired from the service shortly after the incident. A damned shame. It was a sad end to a promising naval career."

An awkward silence followed. Chief Toynbee finally said, "Uh, thank you, sir,"

"Don't mention it. Always glad to be of help."

"As I was saying, sir," Dougherty said, "this here's the enlisted mess. And since it's the largest common area on the boat, it doubles as our rec center, movie theater, and all-round hangout joint. These goldbricking gentlemen are Chief Toynbee, our head sonar tech ... TM1 Larimer ... RM1 Shaeffer ... EM2 Bennett ... and ST3 Queensly." He looked at the men around the mess table. "*This,* people, is Commander Garrett, our new XO."

"Gentlemen," Garrett said, smiling pleasantly. "Good to meet all of you."

"Welcome aboard, sir," Toynbee said.

"Thanks, Chief. I like what I see so far."

"If you'll come this way, sir . . ." the COB said, ushering Garrett toward the aft passageway.

They waited in silence for several moments, until the new officer was out of earshot. "Whew!" Bennett said. "What do you make of *that*?"

"Seemed like an okay guy," Toynbee said. "Not stuck-up, like some ring-knockers I've known."

"I dunno," Larimer said. "He was laying it on pretty thick with that lecture. Like he was tryin' to make a point or something."

" 'Course he was," Toynbee said. "He was telling us that he'd heard us talking about him!"

"Man!" Queensly said, adjusting his glasses on his nose and staring at the door through which the two had exited the mess deck. "His ears must be as good as mine!"

Ken Queensly had been assigned to the *Seawolf* straight out of sonar tech school, with one of the highest grade averages ever recorded. Though he would be spending the next several months rotating through all of the *Seawolf*'s departments before winning the coveted submariner's dolphins, it was clear that his true talent lay with the gang in the sonar shack. He was one of those rare and gifted individuals who could pull the slenderest threads of information out of garbled noise, working at a level beyond the capabilities even of most computer-assisted electronics, a level that seemed to be nothing less than psychic to others. His hearing was incredibly acute, and his assessment of Garrett's hearing high praise indeed.

"Bullshit, Queenie," Toynbee said. "He heard us, all right . . . but *you* didn't hear *him* coming!"

The others laughed, and after a moment Queensly joined in. "This is going to be an interesting deployment," he said. "We're going to have to watch every word we say!"

**Sail, USS *Seawolf*
Pier 4, Fleet Activities Facility
Yokosuka, Japan
2005 hours**

Garrett stood on the *Seawolf*'s weather bridge, looking past the lines of Navy ships moored to the Yokosuka piers at the dark waters of Tokyo Bay beyond. The sun had just set in red-orange glory behind a stretch of clear sky to the west; the rest of the sky was overcast, with the promise, borne of a fresh, wet, northeasterly breeze, of more rain to come.

The city lights were on all the way north up the coast, from Yokosuka itself to Kawasaki to the vast, illuminated sprawl of Tokyo over the horizon. The gleam and glow of brightly colored lights caught the moving waters of the bay in dancing shimmers of reflected illumination, a magnificent sight.

"Bridge, Conn," a voice called over the 1MC. "Pilot tug reports they are ready to guide us out."

Garrett could see the tug, standing off astern and to starboard, one of the ugly, chunky powerhouse workhorses of any naval facility. She was accompanied by a harbor patrol boat that would escort them clear of Tokyo Bay.

"Conn, Sail. Acknowledged." Captain Lawless turned and looked at Garrett. "Well, *Mister* Garrett," he said, emphasizing the title. "You have the conn. Take us out, if you please."

"Aye aye, sir," he acknowledged. "I have the conn."

It was possible that the captain's use of "Mr. Garrett" was a calculated insult, a way of forcibly reminding him that he was *Seawolf's* executive officer and operating only under the captain's orders and at his sufferance, but Garrett didn't care, *couldn't* care one way or the other. He was in command of a submarine once again . . . and what a submarine! The *Seawolf,* SSN-21. He could almost feel the quiet, steady hum of power running through the soles of his shoes and the tips of his fingers, ready and responsive to his direction.

He touched a switch on the comm console in front of him. "Deck party!" he called. "Make all preparations for getting under way. Secure the brow! Line handling parties, fore and aft, stand by the lines."

"Secure the brow, aye, sir" came back from Chief

Boatswain's Mate Sterling, in charge of the deck crew below. In moments the ramp connecting *Seawolf's* aft deck with the pier to port had been swung away and secured on the pier. Line-handling parties fore and aft, each man wearing a bright orange life jacket over his dungarees, began queuing up, ready to release the *Seawolf* from the dock.

Back in the old days, all of a submarine's surface maneuvers were conned from the weather bridge atop the sail. Now it was possible to conn a sub in or out of port from her control room, but there remained an air of tradition, of rightness in skippering the boat away from the dock and out onto the high sea from the bridge. Garrett had only rudimentary instrumentation to rely on—a compass and bearing indicator, a speed indicator, the intercom link with the control room and through the headphones of the men bossing the deck details.

"The brow is cleared away, sir," Sterling said over the 1MC.

"Very well. Single up lines fore and aft. Prepare to cast off."

"Single up lines fore and aft, aye aye, sir."

"Lookouts, check astern."

"Clear astern, sir!"

The crew, Garrett was pleased to note, was moving with crisp efficiency. They were well-trained and they were good. They worked together to clear away all of the lines holding *Seawolf* to the pier, save for a single line off the bow, another off the stern. A diver in full rig stood ready on the deck in case anyone fell in. This was a dangerous evolution, given the submarine's smooth, wet deck, and with the safety rails taken down and stowed. A misstep could mean disaster at worst, embarrassment and delay at best.

He took a last look around. The water was clear

astern and to starboard. Behind him, *Seawolf's* two
lookouts continued scanning the area, checking for
anything, from drifting trash that might foul the screw
to the sudden appearance of an aircraft carrier that
might threaten the boat's maneuver.

"Maneuvering, Bridge. Rudder to starboard. Come
aft, dead slow."

"Bridge, Maneuver. Rudder to starboard, come aft,
dead slow, aye aye."

Gently, gently, *Seawolf's* stern edged away from the
dock. The line handlers aft let the line out, bracing
themselves against the movement.

"Cast off aft."

"Cast off aft, aye!" A moment later Chief Sterling's
bull voice bellowed out, "Aft line handlers! Cast off!"
The line astern flipped over to the pier, where it was
caught by shore-side handlers.

Garrett watched the angle between *Seawolf* and the
straight slash of the pier growing larger. When her
blunt prow almost touched the pier, he called out,
"Cast off forward!"

"Cast off forward, aye aye!"

"Conn, Bridge. Give me three blasts on the horn."

"Bridge, Conn. Three blasts on the horn, aye." *Seawolf's* horn shrilled, three sharp honks echoing across
the bay, signaling that she was backing down.

"Maneuvering, Bridge. Bring rudder amidships.
Maintain aft revs for dead slow."

"Bridge, Maneuvering. Rudder amidships, maintain
aft revs, dead slow."

Slowly, the 331-foot bulk of the *Seawolf* slid backward through still, black water, edging away from the
pier. The tug gave a mournful blast from her whistle,
answered by the patrol boat. Garrett leaned over the
combing of the weather bridge, watching carefully to

make sure that the bow planes safely cleared the pier, that no stray lines—"Irish pennants"—were trailing in the water, that no one in either the deck or shore parties had fallen into the water and was in danger of being run down. The remaining tatters of light in the sky were failing fast, and though the dance and sparkle of harbor lights reflected on the water grew more intense by contrast, visibility overall was quickly fading.

Seawolf's nose was well clear of the end of the pier now. The sailors in the shore working party stood in small groups, watching the submarine slowly back into the bay.

"Maneuvering, Bridge," he said. "Make revs for ahead, slow. Helm, bring us to port, four-five degrees."

"Bridge, Maneuvering. Make revs for ahead, slow. Helm to port, four-five degrees, aye aye, sir."

Seawolf gave a slight bump in the water as her screw stopped, then changed direction, nudging her gently forward. Her helm came over and she began swinging sharply to port, putting the pier and the watching sailors ashore to starboard.

"Maneuvering, increase speed. Make revs for eight knots."

"Make revs for eight knots, aye, sir."

The breeze freshened in Garrett's face. *God*, it was good to be here again. He'd missed the sea, and he'd missed driving a sub. He turned to Lawless, who was leaning against the side of the weather bridge, staring out across Tokyo Bay.

"I've seen better," Lawless said with a gruff lack of enthusiasm. "You could've made the break past the end of the pier sharper, more crisp."

"Yes, sir." Garrett had already made up his mind that he was not going to let Lawless's attitude ruin this moment.

"All in all, though," Lawless admitted, "not too shabby."

"Thank you, sir."

A blast from the horn of the harbor pilot boat, cruising up ahead, interrupted any further exchange.

"Civilian small craft," the port lookout called out, "five points off the starboard bow!"

Garrett raised his binoculars to his eyes, peering into the gathering gloom in the indicated direction. There . . . hard to see in the twilight . . . but he could make out a civilian boat—a cabin cruiser, it looked like—just beyond the harbor boat. A number of people were crowded into the aft well deck or hanging off the boat's flying bridge, and some were waving bottles. Several held a large cardboard sign over the side, crudely lettered NO TO NUKES!

"What are they, Greenpeace?" Lawless asked.

"I don't think so, sir. Looks like a local protest."

"Slant shitheads," Lawless muttered.

Garrett didn't reply. Greenpeace was an international organization that frequently tried to rally local protests against American nuclear presence throughout the world, but they tended to be well-organized and equipped . . . usually with high-speed Zodiacs, chase boats, and plenty of news coverage. *That* looked like a drunken boat party. They didn't even have running lights on.

Shitheads those people might be—that was a given if they were mixing alcohol with a cruise on Tokyo Bay at twilight—but the racist epithet bothered Garrett, as had the earlier comment in the captain's office.

Japan had a long history of protest against nuclear power, though the Tokyo government continued to flirt with some highly suspect technologies, like breeder reactors. The carrier currently homeported here at Yokosuka was the *Kitty Hawk,* one of America's non-nuclear carriers, precisely because the Japanese wouldn't tolerate a nuclear warship based in their territory. They were less stringent with visiting nuclear warships, like the *Seawolf,* and the U.S. Navy maintained its custom of never admitting whether any of its vessels had nuclear weapons on board. Still, protests occurred from time to time, assembled by citizens with sincere beliefs . . . and an occasional appalling lack of understanding.

"What do you intend to do, Mr. Garrett?" Lawless asked.

He thought about it. There was no threat from the intruder, and the harbor patrol craft astern was already coming up abeam to intercept the trespassers.

Still . . .

"Control Room, Bridge. Alert the harbor pilot that I intend to pass him to port."

"Aye aye, sir."

"I think I'd like to put some distance between us and them, Captain," Garrett explained. "Sometimes they stage little surprise ambushes . . . Ah! Like that!"

They were passing a headland at the edge of the naval base, just beyond the spot where the cabin cruiser was trying to get under way. A number of other civilian boats were there, sheltered behind the headland.

"If they can get in our way, they will," Garrett added.

"Show them our heels, Mr. Garrett."

"Aye aye, sir. That was my intention." He opened the intercom channel again. "Maneuvering, come left ten degrees. Make revolutions for fifteen knots."

"Bridge, Maneuvering, come left ten degrees, aye, sir. Make revs for fifteen knots, aye."

Seawolf's prow slid farther from the land to starboard and farther from the tangle of civilian boats. She accelerated smoothly through the dark water, gliding up on the tug. At Garrett's command they gave one toot on the horn—passing to port—and continued on past. It was a kind of football play, Garrett thought, with the *Seawolf* making the end run while the tug and patrol boat blocked the opposition.

It was a hell of a way start a deployment, though, having to dodge the forces of people theoretically on your own side.

He wondered if it was an omen of rough waters ahead.

Saturday, 17 May 2003

Republic of China Naval Amphibious Base
Kaohsiung, Taiwan
0930 hours

"You mean the entire ROC has only four sub-marines?" Jack Morton was only now receiving a per-sonal briefing on the readiness state of Taiwan's parafrogman program from Commander Tse. "I would have thought that would be your strongest force!"

Tse shrugged and manage to look apologetic. "It is a political thing," he explained. "In China—I mean, in Nationalist China—all things are political to one de-gree or another."

Morton looked at the two aging submarines moored to the Kaohsiung Naval Facility docks. "But those two are relics!"

"Indeed. U.S. Guppy II class submarines. The one on the left is the *Hai Shih* . . . formerly the USS *Cutlass*,

SS-478. She was launched in 1944 and in service by March 1945. The other is her sister, the *Hai Pao*, originally the USS *Tusk*, SS-794. She has been in service since 1946. Both vessels were transferred to the Republic of China in 1973 for antisubmarine warfare training . . . with their torpedo tubes welded shut, I might add.

"We have only two other submersibles in our navy. Both are modified Dutch Zwaardvis-class vessels." Tse stumbled over the alien name and made a face. "They are *Hai Lung* and *Hai Hu*—the *Sea Dragon* and the *Sea Tiger*. They were ordered by Taiwan in 1980, over Mainland China's strong protests. *Sea Dragon* was not delivered to us until 1986 and then only as deck cargo on a heavy-lift freighter.

"There were orders for two additional submarines of the class," Tse continued, "plus options for a fifth and a sixth. All were cancelled by the Dutch after heavy political pressure was brought to bear on them by Beijing. Does this tell you anything?"

"Beijing doesn't want you to have submarines," Morton said, nodding.

"We are at war, Commander," Tse said with matter-of-fact bluntness. "We have been at war with the Communists since the beginning of our civil war in 1927. Taiwan has stood alone against the Communist monsters since we were forced to withdraw here in 1949."

Morton raised an eyebrow at that but said nothing. Taiwan had not exactly been alone throughout the long years of the Cold War, and the U.S. Navy still served as buffer and guarantee for the holdout island's freedom. And . . . he'd done some reading up on the history of the Chinese Civil War, which, as far as the rest of the world was concerned, had ended in 1949. It had begun in 1927 with the Shanghai Massacre—when Chiang Kai-shek turned on his erstwhile Communist allies in a surprise attack, capturing and executing five or six thousand of them on the spot. The blood feud between Nationalist and Communist in this war-sick country was old, bitter, and exceedingly deep, and neither side held the moral high ground any longer—indeed, if either had ever held it.

A pox on both your houses was what he wanted to say, but his orders were to cooperate with his Taiwanese hosts and assist them in the upcoming op. The question was how that op was going to be deployed. The best idea for such a mission would have involved insertion by a submarine outfitted for commando-type operations close inshore.

But that wasn't going to be possible with *this* submarine fleet.

Operation Dragon Slayer had been assigned to SEAL Team Three during the flurry of excitement over Beijing's sudden, restless churnings in the western Pacific. The missiles fired at Taiwan had so far been of two calibers—Long March ballistic missiles fired from a test center west of Beijing, and a new, uprated version of the venerable Silkworm surface-to-surface missile, fired from a group of mobile launchers clustered near the coast opposite Taiwan at a village called Tong'an.

The Long March sites were deep within China's borders and well out of reach of anything but a U.S. air strike or an extremely large and complex covert operation. The mobile launchers, however, offered mission planners in Washington an almost irresistible temptation—a high-profile target within easy striking distance by a small team of Special Forces operators. Hitting those launchers would send a clear political message to Beijing: stop the bombardment of Taiwan or face a much larger, much more devastating response.

Satellite reconnaissance had pinpointed the mobile

launcher site. Of course, the fact that those launchers were *mobile* made them an ephemeral target; Operation Dragon Slayer had to be what was known as a hasty strike, an attack put together from scratch with almost no preparation time at all. That was why the decision had been made to join elements of SEAL Team Three with their parafrogman counterparts in Taiwan.

The SEALs trained endlessly for just this sort of operation. The Taiwanese commandos had actual operational experience on the mainland. It should be possible for the two to work together to slip into the PRC, sabotage the launchers, and get out again before the PLA even knew they were there.

The getting in, however, was the tough part. Right now, the Strait of Formosa was heavily patrolled and swept by search and weapons radar. Infiltrating a large commando strike force into Mainland China was not going to be easy.

And as for getting them out again afterward . . .

"Okay," Morton said, "I give up. How do you put operators ashore on the mainland, then, if you can't use submersibles?"

"Small boats, most often," Tse replied. "Sometimes we use HAHO or HALO parachute drops from aircraft. And sometimes we go in aboard larger ships which call at major ports, like Hong Kong or Shanghai. Our men slip over the side as the freighter moves into Communist waters."

"I see." None of those methods was going to work well for this op. HAHO assaults—High-Altitude/High-Opening parachute drops that allowed the infiltrators to maneuver steerable chutes for twenty miles or more—and HALO assaults—High-Altitude/Low Opening drops that required the infiltrators to free-fall to within a thousand feet or less of the ground before opening their chutes—required exceptional levels of training to keep the operations team together. Making that kind of insertion without practicing with the Nationalist forces first was guaranteed to scatter them all across the mainland in hopeless and ineffectual confusion.

Besides, the PRC was going to be real touchy about aircraft entering their airspace right now, and it might be difficult to get within twenty miles of the objective.

By boat? Possible . . . but, again, the Mainland Chinese were going to be nervous about everything from freighters to traditional fishing junks to high-speed cigarette boats. The waters of the Formosa Strait had to be one of the most heavily radar-blanketed regions in the world right now. A sparrow wouldn't make it through that hundred-mile stretch of water without a challenge.

They would need to try another approach.

"So how else can we get over there?" he asked Tse. "It sounds to me like every avenue is blocked."

"Not quite all," Tse replied.

"You're not thinking of packaging us up and mailing us to the mainland, are you?"

Tse looked puzzled, then brightened as he realized Morton was making a joke. "Ah! No. We will use helocast."

Morton's eyes widened. Helocast—having frogmen jump out of helicopters as they skimmed the wave tops—would work within a mile or so of an enemy coast, but they would have to get within swimming range. SEALs were good, as were their Nationalist counterparts, but even they couldn't carry out an op ashore after a twenty-mile submerged swim to get through Chinese territorial waters.

"If we can't get an aircraft or a boat close enough to the mainland to do any good," he said, "what makes you think the Communists will let us come right up to their coastline in helicopters?"

"Simple, Commander Morton," Tse said with a smile. "We will be operating out of *our* territory, at Kinmen."

Sonar Room, USS *Seawolf*
East China Sea
1430 hours

Garrett stood just inside the doorway leading to the *Seawolf's* control room. Chief Toynbee stood next to him, watching three other sonar techs sitting at the boards, ears encased in headsets. On the screens before them cascades of light—"waterfalls," in sonar parlance—made the sounds filling the surrounding water visible.

"We've been picking up good solid contacts all day," Toynbee said. "It's finding the needles in the proverbial haystacks that's problematical. This is one of the busiest international shipping channels on the planet, after all."

"Conn, Sonar. New contact, designated Sierra Five-four," ST3 Queensly reported. "Bearing zero-seven-one, estimated range ten thousand."

"See?" Toynbee said. "That's fifty-three separate individual sonar contacts since this cruise began."

"I'd have thought most of that international shipping would have cleared out to the Formosa Strait by now," Garrett said. "With Chinese missiles flying overhead, this can't be the healthiest piece of aquatic real estate in the world."

"Sierra Five-four tentatively identified as another

trawler," ST2 Juarez said. "I've got drag sounds from the nets. He's making revs for twelve knots."

"Most of them have cleared out, as of two days ago," Toynbee told Morton. "What's left are local junks, fishing trawlers, coastal traffic, most of 'em under a thousand tons. Their livelihood is the sea—this sea. They're sure as hell not going to pack up and leave just because Beijing and Taipei are shooting at each other again."

"The real trick is finding the Kilos in all that clutter," ST1 Roger Grossman said, leaning back in his seat and looking up at the two khaki-clad men in the doorway. "Junks and trawlers are noisy. Against that kind of background, Kilos are damned near invisible."

"Wait a sec!" Queensly said, leaning forward and pressing his headset tightly against his ears. "I've got something, guys."

For a moment all three techs strained against their equipment, trying to drag order out of chaos. "I just hear the trawler, Sierra Five-four," Grossman said with a frustrated shake of his head.

"No," Queensly insisted. "*Behind* the trawler. Listen hard . . ."

"Let me hear," Garrett said.

Toynbee jacked in an extra set of headphones and handed them to Garrett. He set them over his ears and listened.

He could hear the gentle, background whoosh of moving water . . . the noisy hammering of an ancient diesel engine. That would be the trawler. He could also make out a kind of muffled clattering, hissing noise, the sound of a heavy seine net moving through the water.

And just beneath and behind those covering sounds . . .

"He's right," Garrett said. "He's snorkeling."

"I'm calling it," Queensly said excitedly. "Conn,

Sonar! New contact, designated Sierra Five-five. Bearing zero-seven-three, estimated range twelve thousand, speed twelve knots. Probable diesel submarine running submerged on snorkel."

"Sonar, Conn!" Lawless's voice snapped back over the intercom. "Verify that last!"

As Queensly repeated his call, Garrett focused on the soft, almost smothered sounds all but lost in the sea ahead. Diesel engines needed air—and lots of it—to run. Running them while submerged swiftly poisoned a submarine's air supply with carbon monoxide. The alternative was to run the sub on its batteries when it was submerged, surfacing periodically when the batteries ran low in order to recharge them off the diesels.

Surfacing, however, was the next best thing to a death sentence for any submarine in this modern era of ASW—antisubmarine warfare. German submariners had solved the problem, at least partially: hook the diesels to a rigid hose—the "snorkel"—and run it to the surface just abaft of the periscope array. The sub could then cruise along at periscope depth with only its snorkel above water, recharging its batteries while remaining hidden.

Snorkels did not render a submarine invisible, however, nor did they keep it silent. Diesel motors were noisy all by themselves, and snorkels used rather noisy pumps to draw in fresh air from the surface and to expel exhaust fumes. They also made noise dragging through the interface between air and water, and the snorkel could be spotted by day by sharp-eyed surface observers, and any time by radar.

From the sound of things, this sub was trying to mask the sounds made by its own engine and the wake of its snorkel by snuggling in close to an even noisier fishing trawler. It was a good strategy, but not a foolproof one. Garrett could just barely hear the *thud-thud-thud* of a diesel engine, and the duller thump of air pumps, all but masked by the louder pounding of the surface ship.

The *Seawolf* was running south through the Strait of Formosa, midway, roughly, between Taiwan and the coast of Mainland China. She had arrived on-station that morning after an all-night passage south from Yokosuka. She was submerged, moving at a depth of three hundred feet, while her various sonar arrays strained useful data from the welter of noise around her. Contact Sierra Five-five was about six to seven miles to the east-north-east, in the direction of the Taiwan coast.

Garrett handed the headset back. "Good listening, Queenie," he told the third-class sonar tech. "That's a tough one to differentiate."

"Th-Thank you, sir!" He blinked owlishly behind his glasses. "Thanks a lot!"

"Stay on the bastard," Toynbee added. "I don't want him to so much as stealth-fart without our hearing the bubbles."

In the control room, Lawless was giving orders to come to periscope depth. The command was relayed back from Lieutenant Tollini, "Make my depth, periscope depth, aye aye, sir." He then spoke quietly to the sailor on duty at the dive planes station; the sailor pulled back gently on the aircraft-style control yoke, and the deck tilted slightly beneath their feet. *Seawolf* was moving up out of the darkness, gradually approaching the light of day far above.

Lawless looked across the control room as Garrett walked toward the chart tables behind the periscope housings. "I'll want to radio this one in to Mother Hen," he said. "They can decide whether that trawler is a PLA decoy or an innocent fisherman being used by that Kilo."

"I'd put my money on the former, sir," Garrett said. "That trawler has his nets down, but he's going at a hell of a clip for fishing. He must be doing twelve knots, maybe a little better."

"Agreed," Lawless said. "But it's not our job to sort 'em out. That's a job for the Taiwan Navy."

Garrett could see that Lawless was playing this very strictly by the book. Submarine officers were by nature conservative, unwilling to take risks with the lives of their men and the safety of their boats on the line. But they also tended to temper that conservative nature with a daring commensurate with their skill, the daring that in World War II had let Gunter Prien slip the U-47 into the heavily guarded British base at Scapa Flow to torpedo the British battleship *Royal Oak* . . . or a host of American sub skippers to penetrate Tokyo Bay itself. In the Cold War, U.S. submarine skippers had repeatedly taken their commands deep inside Soviet territorial waters to spy on their arch rival . . . and to glean bits of intelligence firsthand that might have proven invaluable if war had ever broken out between East and West.

Garrett had no doubts about Lawless's skill as a submarine skipper, but so far he hadn't shown the initiative, the sheer guts, that Garrett associated with good attack boat drivers. He was acting more like a boomer skipper—the captain of a ballistic missile submarine, which was supposed to stay hidden, out of sight and off the enemy's sonar displays, with survival as the watchword.

His assessment, of course, wasn't entirely fair. Garrett knew that *Seawolf's* mission required stealth, patience, and a hunter's cunning . . . which included the ability to observe without being observed, to watch without being seen.

He couldn't help watching Lawless command the *Seawolf* without wondering what he would do in the same situation. In this case, he thought his best option would have been to approach the new contacts—especially the surface contact, Sierra Five-four—and take them under direct observation through *Seawolf's* Mark 18 scope. Were the crewmen aboard that trawler fishermen, or would he see uniforms? Weapons? A high-tech radio mast that had no business being mounted on board a civilian fishing junk? The visual inspection by a good, old-fashioned Mark I Mod 0 human eyeball could provide invaluable additional data that went a long way toward expanding the wealth of purely electronic data gathered by the *Seawolf's* sensor suites.

And yet, Lawless was right. By simply identifying the trawler as a possible PLA screening vessel, he'd given the local navy something to go on. It was Taipei's responsibility now to stop and board that ship, or let it continue on its way.

He felt the deck leveling beneath his feet. "Leveling off now at five-eight feet," the diving officer announced. "Periscope depth."

"Very well," Lawless said, stepping to the periscope platform. "Up scope."

The periscope slid up in its housing, and Lawless rode the handles as they opened, walking the scope in a complete circle as he scanned the surface overhead. "We're clear," he said. "Radio Shack! Let's raise Mother Hen."

"Radio Shack, aye!"

Mother Hen was the code name for the submarine command facility on Taiwan, which was linked electronically and via satellite both with elements of the U.S. Seventh Fleet and with Pearl Harbor. They would relay *Seawolf's* sneak-and-peek discoveries to the appropriate channels.

"Conn, E-2 sensor suite. We're being painted. Can't tell if they've fingered us yet, but we're getting a lot of military-grade radar out there."

"Roger that. Keep monitoring."

"Conn, Radio Shack. We're patched through to Mother Hen."

"Very well." Lawless began rattling off the specs of the two latest sonar contacts, giving ranges, bearings, and probable identification, and recommending an overflight by local ASW assets.

"Are we going to track that Kilo, sir?" Garrett asked.

"If your intelligence is accurate, Mr. Garrett, there are nine other Kilos out here and possibly an Akula as well. We can't waste time following one lone PLA boat. We'll wait for the ASW people to pick them up and continue with our assigned patrol. By the *book*, Mr. Garrett, by the book."

By the book. Garrett had about decided that if he heard the captain's pet phrase one more time, he was going to Section 8 right out of the service—that mythological medical classification that said you were too nuts to be in the military. He shook his head ruefully at the thought. He'd had his chance to get out with some remaining measure of dignity three years ago and turned it down cold. It was way too late to think about that now.

"Captain, Radio Shack" came over the 1MC.

"This is the captain. Go ahead."

"Sir, we have incoming SATCOM radio traffic. It's headed 'Titan Spear,' 'Top Secret,' and 'Urgent.'"

"On my way."

Lawless left the control room. Leaving the OOD in charge, Garrett returned to the Sonar Shack to listen to the subtle thud and rumble of the presumed Chinese diesel sub. A Titan Spear message meant something from Washington and from pretty high up on the chain of command. Garrett wondered, though, why the message had been sent by UHF transmission, especially if it was Top Secret.

Staying in touch with the Navy's fleet of submarines, especially when they were submerged, had long been a tough technical problem. There were a variety of communications modes: VLF, LF, HF, UHF, ELF, and even blue-green OSCAR laser pulses fired from geostationary communications satellites.

Extremely Low Frequency transmissions could penetrate the upper levels of the ocean and be received by a submarine at depths of a hundred meters or more. Because the wavelength of an ELF signal was so long—about four thousand kilometers—the transmission rate was painfully slow. It could take hours to send just a few characters, and the method was usually reserved for "bell-ringer" messages, an alert to come to shallow depths and receive a longer message by VLF or other means.

Other modes of communication required the sub to trail a long antenna in its wake or to use a buoy that drew the antenna up to within a few meters of the surface. Very Low Frequency transmissions were routinely received this way, and most communications with submerged submarines on a deployment were handled through this mode. Low-frequency, high-frequency, and ultrahigh frequency transmissions could only be picked up by the sub when its radio mast was extended above the surface, from periscope depth. Optical Submarine Communications by Aerospace Relay—OSCAR—was still experimental, expensive, and limited in scope, but the *Seawolf* was equipped to receive blue-green laser messages and could do so without trailing long receiving antennae or buoys.

Standard communications procedures had messages for deployed submarines—attack boats on ASW duty in particular—stored for burst transmissions from orbiting communications satellites at specified times of the day. The sub skipper needed only to bring his boat to receiving depth and trail the antenna at a specified time to pick up his mail. Garrett looked at his watch. *Seawolf's* next scheduled CVLF receiving time was set for 1720, another three hours. Having the Titan Spear message transmitted by satellite rather than waiting for the VLF window seemed a hit-or-miss way of doing things. Either the message was of very low priority or someone back in the World didn't know what the hell they were doing.

And that hardly bode well for the cruise.

However, until the skipper decided to share the contents of the message with the other officers of the boat, it wasn't his worry. Garrett continued listening to the snorkeling noises of the Kilo, pulling them from the heavier pounding of the surface traffic, burning them into his brain until he was sure he could recognize their distinctive feel at another time.

"Mr. Simms, Mr. Garrett. This is the captain. Report to my office, on the double."

Toynbee looked at Garrett, then rolled his eyes. "No rest for the wicked, sir?"

"True enough, Chief."

"*Now* what did he do?" Grossman asked just before Garrett was out of earshot.

Garrett couldn't help a lightly malicious chuckle at that. Apparently the crew had noticed how hard Lawless was riding him. It suggested that they both liked and respected him, which was important. A boat's XO needed a close rapport with the crew.

The fact that the captain had called for both him

and *Seawolf's* Nav officer suggested that they were about to learn the contents of that UHF message. Garrett had expected Lawless to sit on it for as long as he could, if only to show that he had the power to do so. Much of Lawless's behavior, Garrett thought, seemed centered on his need to prove to all concerned that *he* was in command.

Then another thought occurred to him: What if that UHF message had been transmitted as it had just in case *Seawolf* was on or near the surface? That might mean considerable urgency in the matter.

And the only thing Garrett could think of that might be that urgent was the possibility that the United States was now at war with the People's Republic of China. Washington would want to warn its most valuable submarine asset in this part of the world as soon as possible, without waiting for the 1720 VLF transmission window.

A war with China . . . and the *Seawolf* was already in the middle of it.

Captain's Office, USS *Seawolf*
East China Sea
1448 hours

Captain George Lawless looked again at the printout flimsy in his hands, fresh from the radio shack and decoding. "I still don't know what to make of this, COB," he said.

Master Chief Dougherty had been in the control room when Lawless had emerged from the radio shack, and he was summoned to the office with a curt wave of the hand. They were just waiting for—

Three sharp raps on the door announced their arrival. "Enter."

Garrett and Simms came in. "You wanted to see us, Skipper?" Simms said.

"Sit," Lawless said, nodding at a pair of empty chairs squeezed into the claustrophobic space. "Read."

He handed Garrett the message flimsy and watched with mild amusement the play of emotions over the man's face: worry . . . puzzlement . . . surprise . . . consternation . . .

Garrett handed the message to Simms and said, "I don't understand this, Captain. It's insane!"

"Neither the hell do I," Lawless replied. "Neither the hell do I!"

"It doesn't strike me as an especially sound decision tactically," Simms said.

"I was expecting a message to the effect that we were at war," Garrett added. He almost sounded disappointed. "What does it mean?"

"Damfino," Lawless replied, taking the flimsy back from Simms. "But we *will* follow orders. By the *book*, gentlemen, by the book!"

He looked at the flimsy again, reading the decoded message.

CLASSIFIED: TOP SECRET
FROM: OFFICE OF MILITARY AFFAIRS LIAISON,
        STATE DEPARTMENT, WASHINGTON, D.C.
TO: NAVY DEPARTMENT, PENTAGON, ARLINGTON, VA
CC: COMSUBPAC, COMFLEACTWESTPAC, COCBG 24, COSSN-21
DATE: 17 MAY 2003
TIME: 1210 HRS, LOCAL

OPENING OF NEW NEGOTIATIONS WITH BEIJING AIMED AT DEFUSING CURRENT CRISES OVER TAIWAN MAKES IT NECESSARY TO ASSUME OPEN, PEACEFUL POSTURE IN EAST CHINA SEA/SOUTH CHINA SEA AO. PURSUANT TO PRESIDENTIAL DIRECTIVE THIS DATE, SUBMARINE SEAWOLF, SSN-21, IS HEREBY DIRECTED TO PUT IN TO PORT AT HONG KONG AT EARLIEST OPPORTUNITY BOTH TO SHOW AMERICAN PRESENCE IN AO AND TO ASSURE PRC OF AMERICAN FRIENDLY INTENTIONS.

FOR DURATION OF VISIT, OFFICERS AND CREW OF U.S. VESSELS MAY GO ASHORE AS PER SOP. HOWEVER, ALL PERSONNEL MUST BE ENJOINED TO OBSERVE PROPER PROTOCOL AND THE MAINTENANCE OF FRIENDLY RE-LATIONS WITH THE HOST NATION . . .

There was more, a lot more, but most of it was little more than bureaucratic garble about the need to impress China with America's essentially peaceful posture in the West Pacific. It was signed by none less than Paul Duggin, Undersecretary of State.

But Garrett was right. The whole thing was categorically insane.

But the USS *Seawolf* was going to follow orders.

By the *book*.

Saturday, 17 May 2003

ROC Army Listening Post
Kuningtou, Kinmen Island
Fujian Province, China
2010 hours

The locals called it Kinmen. The island had another name, however . . . and westerners who knew something of China's bloody recent history knew the place by that name: Quemoy.

Jack Morton stood on the outside parapet of a concrete tower, binoculars in his hands, staring north toward the lush, green folds of the foothills of the Shiniu Shan Mountains. That was Mainland China over there, fading into the evening mist across a scant three miles of open water. He raised the binoculars to his eyes and studied the far shore. He could see the beach, the play of low surf on rock. A water buffalo chewed endlessly on whatever it was that buffalo chewed. Tangles of barbed wire lined the beach above the high-tide line.

Westward, to the left, a military base or fortification of some sort sprouted in ungainly, weedlike fashion from sand and tropical greenery. The flag flying over the walls was the bloodred banner of the People's Republic. Morton could see a sentry on a parapet behind the gray wall, staring south across the water toward Kinmen. He couldn't make out the soldier's expression but had to assume it was a bored one. The silence was heightened by the gentle hiss and splash of the surf. The place seemed unnaturally peaceful.

"That, my friend, is our objective," Commander Tse told him. "Do not let the fortifications daunt you. We infiltrate people through that beach all the time."

"And they do the same on this beach, I would imagine."

Tse scowled. "Not so often as you might imagine. Not successfully at any rate."

Morton said nothing. The Taiwanese defenders would only know of the failed infiltrations, the ones that had been detected. No matter. Both sides continued to play their deadly games. It was curious, though, that as the war of words was heating up between Taipei and Beijing, as missiles flew across the strait as exclamation marks to Beijing's harangues, this bit of coastline was preternaturally peaceful and quiet.

Tse turned away, and Morton sensed that he'd ruffled the man's feelings. *Remember your orders*, he thought. *Keep your hosts happy.*

"This is the place where the Communists invaded Kinmen, isn't it?" he asked. "I was reading about Taiwan and saw an article about the battle."

"Yes!" Tse said, turning back with a smile on his broad face. "You can read about the whole action at the Kuningtou Battlefield Museum." He gestured toward the northwest and a low promontory of land extending north into the channel. "It is there, at that point."

"Military history is a weakness of mine," Morton explained. "I'll have to see it while I'm here."

"Ah! It was a glorious battle! October twenty-fifth, 1949. The Generalissimo's forces had suffered many sad defeats on the mainland, and his forces were falling back to Taiwan. Communist forces stormed ashore on this very beach at two in the morning. They walked headlong into a column of PRC tanks behind the beach. Kuomintang forces swiftly closed in with air attacks and ships. The Communists were forced back on that point of land . . . there . . . with their backs to the sea. After twenty-five hours, more Communists landed, but by that time reinforcements had been rushed in from Taiwan. After a fifty-six-hour battle, the last surviving Communists surrendered, at ten A.M., October twenty-seventh. It was a desperately needed victory for Generalissimo Chiang. As a result, Kinmen Island remained free, along with Matsu, further up the coast."

Morton nodded. He had read about the affair, and Tse had not exaggerated the battle's importance. Fifteen thousand Chinese had died in that single, bloody bit of fratricide.

Though the West had largely forgotten about them now, the two small islands of Kinmen and Liehyu, and the archipelago of eighteen tiny islets that comprised Matsu about 170 miles northeast up the China coast, had been very much in the news in 1958, when the People's Republic under Mao had demanded their surrender. The Soviet premier, Krushchev, had been trying to rein in Mao's impetuous adventurism; for his part, Mao rankled that Krushchev didn't consider China a full equal of both the U.S. and the USSR in the world political arena. The two leaders had met secretly for three days in July 1958. Mao's response to Krushchev's patronizing efforts at diplomacy had been to open a forty-four-day bombardment of Quemoy and Matsu. Almost half a million artillery shells rained down on tiny Kinmen alone during that six-week onslaught between August twenty-third and October sixth. The entire world had held its breath, expecting that this was the beginning of World War III.

Morton and raised his binoculars again. A small PLA patrol boat was motoring slowly east along the coast. Her awkward silhouette with a central, squared-off pilot house identified her as a Beihai-class craft, eighty tons and less than thirty meters long, with quad-mounted 25mm antiaircraft guns forward and a second mount aft. She wasn't flying a flag or ensign and probably belonged to a local Communist militia. She chugged slowly along the coast, just outside of the surf line next to the mainland, making perhaps twelve knots.

"Right on time," Tse said, noticing that Morton was tracking the patrol boat with his binoculars. "We will time our approach to avoid their maritime patrols, of course. These days, they are not as zealous in their rounds as they once were."

"Do they have anything larger in the area?"

"A few Huangfeng-class missile patrol boats . . . that is a PLA-built version of the old Soviet Osa I. And there is at least one Hainan-class patrol boat in the area, but its appearances are infrequent. Our biggest tactical problem, though, will be the large number of armed trawlers. The PLA and local militias employ hundreds of them up and down the coast. They are ordinary fishing trawlers of one or two hundred tons, but armed, usually with one or two machine guns. They perform double duty . . . as legitimate fishing boats and as fisheries patrol craft, and therefore they have no set patrol schedule."

"No sophisticated sensors or sonar equipment, though?"

"No. Absolutely not." Tse grinned. "Not even fish-finders! Keep in mind that in many ways we are still dealing with a third world nation. The PLA believes in numbers, not in technology."

Tse's confidence on that point was worrisome. In general, yes, Mainland China employed military technologies twenty to thirty or more years behind those of the United States . . . but they still fielded a well-equipped, well-trained, and fanatically dedicated military force, one intent on catching up to the West in all respects.

The sound of footsteps on wet concrete coming up the stairs behind him interrupted his thoughts. Lieutenant Commander Chris Logan joined them, saluting as he approached.

"Excuse me . . . Commander Morton? Commander Tse?"

"Good evening, Commander Logan," Tse said. He bowed slightly to Morton. "I shall allow you two to talk."

"Thank you, sir." As Tse drew off, Garrett addressed his 2IC. "Hey, Jammer. Whatcha got?"

"The men are all squared away at the new barracks, Skipper. No problem there. Flying roaches the size of your hand. Some of the guys are threatening to start hunting them, secure a little extra protein with the meal rations."

"Sounds good."

"We may have a problem with the local ammo, though. The stuff's ancient."

"Five five-six?"

"Yessir. The parafrogs mostly carry Taiwan copies of the M-16A1. Fires 5.56 by 45mm rounds. But they have old stuff, too. Even thirty-cal M-1 rifles, World War Two vintage."

"They've had to make do a long time. I've seen some of the soldiers here on Kinmen carrying Taiwan copies of Thompson submachine guns."

"Cool. Good weapons."

"What kind of weapons do they have in the specfor armory? Chicom gear?"

"Lots of Chinese Communist stuff, yeah. Plenty of Type 68s and Type 73s." Those were various Chinese copies of the Soviet AK-47.

"And lots of seven six-two to go with them?"

"Yes, sir. And it looks to be in pretty good shape."

"I think I'm going to suggest that we go in carrying Chicom weapons," Morton said. "We're allowed to use our initiative on this one, but our orders are damned specific about not alerting the PLA to an American force trespassing on their territory."

"Some of the guys were talking about using suppressed H and Ks. Of course," Logan added with a grin, "if we actually get into a firefight, we've screwed up."

"Always," Morton replied. "Okay, I guess I wouldn't mind having a couple of H and Ks along for quiet wet work."

"What about Tse's people?"

"That's up to them." He shook his head. "I don't have a good feeling about this one, Jammer."

"I know what you mean, Skipper. No time to train, no time to get to know our opposite numbers."

"And we're going to be completely in their hands. They've routinely infiltrated over there. We haven't. I don't know why SOCOM doesn't just have them take out those launchers. Definitely high-risk, with low pay-off. I have the feeling we're here just for show, for *politics*, and that's never good."

"Well, if we get into trouble over there, we can always call for help. We know we can get artillery support, and if we're *real* lucky, maybe they'll send us sexy underwear."

Both SEALs laughed. Taiwan's use of women's underwear had provided endless amusement for the platoon since they'd first heard the story.

After the initial bombardment of Kinmen and Matsu in 1958, Mao, when confronted by the very real possibility of U.S. naval intervention, made a remarkable offer. If the U.S. Navy stayed out of the Strait of Formosa, he would bombard Kinmen and Matsu only every other day. The offer had been rejected, but Mao, after a unilateral one-week cease-fire was extended to three weeks, had begun the on-again, off-again bombardment on his own.

The Taiwanese had replied in kind. For the next twenty years the PLA had launched symbolic artillery bombardments on Kinmen every Tuesday, Thursday, and Saturday, while Taiwan had fired at the mainland every Monday, Wednesday, and Friday. Sunday, by unspoken agreement, was a holiday for both sides, a day of rest. By the time the ritual duels ended in 1978, 570 ROC soldiers had died . . . along with an unknown number of PLA troops on the mainland.

As a sideline to the artillery duels, though, Taiwan had engaged in extensive propaganda attacks on the mainland. At one point the largest neon sign in the world had stood above this very beach, with characters large enough to be read from the port city of Xiamen on the mainland. It had read, "Three Principles of the People: Reunify China," which, interestingly enough, was a popular slogan on both sides of the Strait of Formosa. The sign, evidently, had become a major tourist attraction on the mainland; when Taiwan finally took it down, the city council of Xiamen had formally complained.

Loudspeakers, also claimed to be the largest in the world, had been set up on both sides of the channel, blaring propaganda broadcasts back and forth. Morton couldn't quite imagine what that cacophony must have been like. And, since artillery shells loaded with leaflets didn't travel all that far, Taiwan had begun a program of launching balloons from Kinmen bearing canisters loaded with top-secret propaganda material for dispersal across the mainland.

The world finally learned the true nature of this propaganda, however, when one balloon actually traveled halfway around the planet and was intercepted in Israel. The canister was opened, and it contained . . .

Transparent women's underwear.

Evidently, Taipei thought the frilly airborne gifts would undermine PLA morale, inducing large numbers of them to defect.

The balloon drops had their serious side. During 1989, balloons had carried Taiwanese newspapers across the channel, to keep the mainlanders informed of what was going on at Tiananmen Square, and it was said that some people in Fujian Province relied on the air drops for news in the same way that folks in Nazi-occupied Europe had tuned in to the BBC on illegal radio sets.

But for the SEALs, the idea of bombarding the enemy with sexy lingerie was priceless, "worth every penny of admission," as MN1 Fuentes had put it.

"Maybe we should pack a few hundred rounds of *Playboy*," Logan added. "You know, bring out the really big guns."

"That might go against the Geneva Convention, Jammer. Cruel and unusual."

"Okay, okay. We'll save the skin magazines for the terrorist suicide bombers . . . you know, the ones who grow up as Islamic fundamentalists, not even allowed to look at a woman until after they get married."

"You have a nasty and fiendishly twisted mind, Jammer. I like that."

"Why, *thank* you, sir!"

Morton's mood sobered, however, after his 2IC completed his report and returned to the barracks. Taiwan and Mainland China had been playing a very strange, very deadly game for over fifty years, and as the U.S. government had estranged itself more and more from Taipei, they'd understood that game, understood its nature, understood its sheer deadliness less and less.

And First Company was smack in the middle of play.

Over the years, tensions between Taiwan and the mainland had gone up and down. In general, and from the West's perspective, things had gotten better. As diplomatic overtures were made to the People's Republic, as Washington and the rest of the world distanced itself from the Nationalists, Beijing's rhetoric had toned down and the threat of an invasion across the Strait of Formosa had grown more remote. This was due in large part to the growth of Taiwan's economic presence on the mainland; nowadays, Taiwan did more business with Mainland China than they did with the United States. Kinmen, once a base for 70,000 ROC troops on an island with a total population of only 52,000, now maintained a garrison of only about 10,000 men. Frogmen still used the island to stage intelligence-gathering incursions across the channel, but not with the regularity—or the sheer viciousness—of years past. Today the island was a tourist attraction, and the main port of embarkation from which illegal Chinese immigrants to Taiwan were shipped back to the mainland.

But the situation had changed sharply just in recent years . . . and ironically, the change had been brought about by Taiwan's democratization. Kinmen and Matsu had been under direct martial rule until 1993; the islands had even maintained their own currency, to keep all the money, and the people, from fleeing to Taipei. The Nationalists had ruled Taiwan with an iron hand, first under Generalissimo Chiang Kai-shek, then under his son, Chiang Chingkuo. An opposition political party—the Democratic Progressive Party—had been permitted only grudgingly, and after 1986.

The Nationalist party, the Kuomintang, or KMT, had maintained all along that it was the rightful ruling government of *all* of China; in fact, over 460 KMT legislators pretending to represent mainland constituencies had retained their seats in the government—since they were unable to stand for reelection in their districts—until they were at last forced to retire in 1991. The nation's first truly free elections had been held shortly after that.

And Beijing continued to insist that Taiwan was a rebellious province of the People's Republic, that Taiwan *would* be invaded if the island ever made a formal declaration of independence, or if it dragged its feet in negotiations to reunify with the PRC. Beijing had not made any moves in that direction beyond diplomatic pressure against attempts to sell weapons to Taiwan, which they considered to be interference in China's internal affairs, and a great deal of rhetoric. With Taiwan investing in more and more mainland businesses, Beijing was not anxious to shut down the flow of hard cash.

But with the arrival of the DPP on the political scene, things had been changing, changing fast, and not necessarily changing for the better. The Democratic Progressives were calling for the creation of an independent Taiwan, a Republic of Taiwan that would have no claims to the mainland but would also be free of Beijing's rule. They'd been making other moves as well—requesting a seat in the UN for the ROC in 1994, for example, though they'd been expelled from that organization in favor of the PRC in 1971. When Taiwan's president, Lee Tengui, made a high-profile visit to the United States in 1995, Beijing had responded by holding "missile tests," dropping test warheads into the sea twelve miles from Taiwan's coast . . . and letting it be known that Los Angeles was within range of China's nuclear arsenal.

The missiles had flown again in 1996, in a transparent attempt to scare Taiwanese voters away from Lee. This ham-fisted version of diplomacy backfired when the U.S. Navy sent two carrier battle groups to Taiwanese waters and Lee won a landslide. Beijing had resorted to missile diplomacy yet again in 2000 to prevent the election of a DPP presidential candidate—Chen Shuibian—and again their attempt to control Taiwanese elections had failed.

But now the DPP was pushing harder than ever for an independent Taiwan, and that was flatly and completely counter to Beijing's will. Though the ROC continued to pretend that things were getting better, the mainland was casting a longer and darker shadow across the strait than ever. Pundits wrote that Taiwan held a very angry dragon by the tail and that now they were clinging to it for dear life. The latest use of missiles against Taiwan merely underscored Beijing's determination. Their "renegade province" would not be granted independence, whatever the rulers in Taipei might imagine.

No one believed that the ROC's military—outnumbered by the PLA by at least ten to one, and without the best and most modern military equipment—could repulse an invasion alone. Everything depended on whether the United States would be willing to come to little Taiwan's defense.

That was the big question, of course, and one very much on the minds of Beijing's rulers. The United States had been steadily distancing itself from Taiwan ever since Washington had withdrawn diplomatic recognition from the ROC in favor of the PRC in 1979. And ever since September 2001 the U.S. military had been increasingly committed to the War on Terrorism, in places ranging from Afghanistan and Iraq to Mexico and the continental United States. Beijing might feel certain that the U.S. would not involve itself in yet another war, especially a war in such an unpopular cause as Taiwan's independence.

Which left First Company, SEAL Team Three, in an awkward and unpleasantly exposed position. With orders to take out mobile launchers on the mainland near Xiamen as a symbolic gesture of defiance, they could find their presence suddenly denied by the government that had sent them. To Morton's eye, this one had the smell of a suicide mission.

And he didn't like that one bit.

Crew's Mess
USS *Seawolf*
2045 hours

"The trouble with America's China policy is that Washington never knows what the hell it's doing when it comes to either Mainland China *or* Taiwan!" Chief Toynbee said, with all the royally self-assured air of one of *Seawolf*'s bona fide China experts. "In short, our China policy *sucks!*"

Garrett laughed, along with most of the men, officers and enlisted both, gathered in the mess hall for an informal bull session. News of *Seawolf*'s impending visit to Hong Kong had spread through the submarine at something greater than the speed of light, with most of the hands in the know even before Lawless had made the formal announcement at 1500 hours that afternoon.

The upcoming visit to Mainland China, then, was on everyone's mind and in every conversation. Mess tables had been cleared off and wiped down after evening chow, and off-duty members of the crew were beginning to gather in expectation of that night's scheduled movie.

By one of those eerie twists of serendipity that serve to make truth stranger than fiction, the movie that evening was *The Sand Pebbles*, with Steve McQueen. The epic story of an American gunboat in the 1930s-era China of warlords and revolution seemed uncannily appropriate. Originally, the extra-long movie was scheduled to be shown in two parts spread over two nights, but the CO had decreed that since the *Seawolf* would be in Hong Kong the following night, the entire three-hour film would be aired in one sitting.

"Look how long we backed Chiang!" Toynbee continued. "And him claiming all along that he and the KMT were the *real* government of all of China! And until Nixon came along, that's the way we believed it, too. Talk about your tail wagging your big-ass dog!"

"Nixon just saw a chance for the big corporations

to make some money in the PRC," someone in the back said.

"Sure," Master Chief Dougherty said. "And what's wrong with that? The idea was to keep the peace, not to go to war with the most populous nation in the world over a bit of real estate the size of Maryland. Backing Chiang all those years was nuts."

"My point exactly," Toynbee said. "It *was* nuts. But then we started trying to appease Beijing, and we all know that appeasement never works worth shit. We booted Taiwan out of the United Nations and started dealing with them kind of under the table, hoping Beijing wouldn't notice. We kept selling them weapons . . . but not *too* many weapons or weapons that were too advanced, because that would make Beijing mad. We wanted to preserve the possibility of doing business with China, but we didn't want to lose the economic miracle that was Taiwan. We tried to keep it *both* ways."

"Come off it, Chief," Larimer said. " 'Economic miracle'? The Kuomintang ran one of the dirtiest, most corrupt governments in the world."

"Yeah," someone in the crowd called out. "They were corrupt, despotic bastards, but at least they were *our* corrupt, despotic bastards!"

"The KMT was booted out of office in 'ninety-six, Chief," Garrett pointed out. He'd been reading up on the political situation in Taiwan over the past couple of days. "Their candidate came in a very poor third."

"And who were we supporting in those elections?" Toynbee asked. "Who were we hoping would win? The KMT! And even though the new government has done more real political reform in Taiwan in a few years than the KMT did in fifty-five years of one-government rule, we're still treating Taiwan like some sort of invisible, poor relation. No embassy. No formal relations. All trade handled through the American Institute, a private corporation in Virginia."

"So what's your point, Chief?" Garrett asked. "It was useless to try keeping Communist China isolated, and pure idiocy to just ignore them, to pretend they didn't exist. It's better to talk and trade with them than to fight, right?"

"Yes, sir, it is. But there's such a thing as looking out for your friends, y'know?"

"The KMT was friends with American money," a second-class yeoman named Michaels said. "In fact, they were friends with *everybody's* money, including every drug lord in the West Pacific! Chiang was the biggest crook and maybe the biggest dictator going out here. Like Diem. Or Noriega."

"Chiang was a puppet," someone else said.

Toynbee shook his head. "Shit, people! I'm not talking about the Kuomintang. Yeah, Chiang was a dictator, and I suppose he was a political tool for us, like Diem was in South Vietnam. Someone we could prop up as a local rallying cry against the Communists. And maybe we should've helped him more, and maybe not. What I'm talking about is the *people* of Taiwan. The ordinary folks who just want to be free to live their own lives and not have the government—I don't care if it's the KMT in Taipei or the Communists in Beijing—breathing down their necks."

"We've been protecting Taiwan right along," Dougherty pointed out. "The Communists were all set to invade Taiwan fifty-some years ago. And we sent a couple of carrier task forces to the Strait of Formosa and made 'em back down. The way I heard it, there were aircraft on those carriers armed with nukes. We were on the verge of a nuclear shooting war with Red China, and maybe the Soviet Union, too, and all to keep Taiwan from being taken over."

"That was then," Toynbee said, stubborn. "That was before Nixon went to China and we decided to cozy up with Beijing. That was before we decided that Communist China was a legitimate nation, and Taiwan wasn't."

"Come off it, Chief," Lieutenant Tollini said, laughing. "Do you seriously think we should have kept recognizing Taiwan as the only real China?"

"No. I'm just sayin' that our China policy has never made sense. We backed Chiang long after common sense said we should have written him off . . . but we dumped him when it became convenient. We still guarantee Taiwan's right to exist . . . but as a kind of nonnation. An aberration on the map. An aberration that's still home to twenty-two million people.

"And now, just when we're up against it and about to go to the wall for Taiwan again, some bureaucrat in D.C. gets the collywobbles and pulls the plug on us. Sends us to fucking Hong Kong on a show-the-flag public relations cruise! Man, it just don't make sense!"

"Hey, Chief Toynbee," one sailor called out from the back of the mess hall. "You're married to a Formosan girl, ain't you?"

"Yeah, Burke, I am." Suddenly, Toynbee's voice was cold, with a hard, wary edge to it. "What of it?"

"Just that kind of explains why you like the chinks so much, huh?"

"What's to explain?" The question was a growl. Toynbee lurched to his feet, his fists clenched, his expression dangerous. "We're talkin' about *people* here. Not chinks. Not slants. Not—"

"Yeah, yeah, okay, Chief. No offense, right?"

"I'm not so sure about that. Sometimes I find you *damned* offensive, Burke."

"Easy there, people," Garrett said. "Both of you stand down!"

"Maybe I will after I swab the deck with that damned snipe," Toynbee said.

"*Cool* it, Chief!" Dougherty snapped. "You heard the XO!"

Another chief, EMC Yolander, was already on his feet at the other end of the compartment, talking quietly with Burke. After a moment Burke got up and left with Yolander, who was the *Seawolf*'s Master at Arms—essentially the boat's senior policeman. But if Burke was a "snipe," as Toynbee had called him, he was also part of *Seawolf*'s engine room gang and therefore in Yolander's division. A quiet word with the man in the passageway outside ought to be enough to settle things, at least for now. Garrett made a mental note to talk with the MAA at the first opportunity and see if there was an ongoing problem here.

The near confrontation left Garrett thoughtful as the movie began a few minutes later. The U.S. Navy was an interesting cross-sectional mix of American culture, beliefs, and attitudes, with some cultural peculiarities all its own thrown in for good measure. People did not shed their prejudices and small-town bigotry with their civvies when they signed up. In boot camp, new recruits from Smalltown, Ohio, found themselves living with former gang members from Chicago, Black Muslim street kids from Philadelphia, Latinos from Miami, Moslems from Los Angeles. The Navy was a melting pot of cultures, religions, and ethnic backgrounds.

And sometimes—especially aboard ships or within the claustrophobic confines of a submarine—the pot became something more like a pressure cooker.

That had always been the case. During Vietnam, the Navy had struggled with racism and racial hatreds, mostly between blacks, whites, and Latinos. In World War II, African Americans in the Navy had been largely restricted to duty as mess attendants and stewards' mates, conveniently ignored, while officialdom struggled with widespread prejudice against Italians, Eastern Europeans, and Jews. Always, it seemed, there was *someone* to hate, someone over whom you could feel superior.

But in the years since the September 11 terrorist attack, especially, traditional American isolationism had been more manifest as a mistrust, a fear, as an outright hatred of *anyone* different—anyone who spoke a different language, worshiped a different God, expressed a different culture. Lately, in fact, Navy personnel had been required to attend sensitivity training classes, view movies, engage in cross-cultural role playing, and receive special counseling, all in the name of keeping the lid on the bubbling stew of religious and ethnic bigotry.

At the same time, Navy personnel were far better traveled than most American kids, both those from small-town America and the street kids from the cities. "Join the Navy and see the world" was more than a recruiting slogan. It was a big part of what life in the Navy was all about, and those people willing to have their eyes opened quickly found that *different* could be interesting, fun, even beautiful. Every duty station where Garrett had been had its share of sailors who loved the place because it was new and foreign and exotic, balanced by its share of men who hated it because it was different.

Quite a few old hands who'd been in the service long enough to be stationed overseas for several years had married local girls. A higher-than-usual percentage of

Navy chiefs and first-class petty officers were married to women they'd met while stationed in Japan or the Philippines, or while on liberty in Taiwan, Hong Kong, or Thailand.

Hell, Garrett thought, he'd been thinking seriously about asking Kazuko to marry him, a year after meeting her at Atsugi. He wasn't sure yet that he wanted to take that step so soon after the divorce from Claire, but he loved her deeply. The idea of crossing cultural—or racial—boundaries didn't bother him in the least.

But there were lots of men who *were* bothered, men who assumed that different was bad or, at the least, inferior.

And those kinds of assumptions could be big trouble when bottled up on board a submarine.

Garrett found himself becoming absorbed in the movie. He'd forgotten that Steve McQueen's character had a Chinese girlfriend and that the movie dealt heavily with the racial and cultural tensions between the fictional *San Pablo*'s American crew and the Chinese. Had things changed so little since the historically realistic days of the movie's setting? That was pretty damned depressing.

He did wonder how the sudden change in the *Seawolf*'s mission would affect things on board. Tensions had been on the rise since he'd joined her in Japan. Everyone knew that the PLA had a brand new fleet of hunter-killer submarines out and that they were tossing warheads at Taiwan. If every man on board didn't expect a war to break out soon with China, at least every man was braced for that possibility. That realization put a lot of stress on the crew.

Then a radio message from Washington arrived, directing them to cruise into Hong Kong with flag flying, ambassadors of American goodwill. That kind of thing could cause an acute case of emotional whiplash. Pent-up stress could be released in unexpected ways. How well captain and crew handled that release, Garrett thought, would tell a lot about their training, their experience, and their dedication to the boat.

He just wished he could be sure the Chinese were as interested in *Seawolf*'s goodwill visit as the State Department seemed to be. *Seawolf* was an extremely valuable, extremely expensive American asset, and moored to a dock in Hong Kong, she would be in-the-crosshairs vulnerable.

This, he decided, was going to be a damned interesting cruise.

Sunday, 18 May 2003

Control Room
USS *Seawolf*
1512 hours

"All clear topside," Garrett said, walking the scope around in a full circle. "Take us up, Mr. Tollini."

"Now surface, surface, surface," Tollini called over the boat's intercom. "Up bubble, ten degrees. Helm, steady as you go."

"Up bubble, ten degrees, aye aye," the planesman announced.

"Helm steady as she goes, aye," the helmsman added.

"Blow main ballast," Garrett said.

"Blow main ballast, aye." Tollini brought his palm down on the main ballast release, sending high-pressure air into the sub's ballast tanks.

The deck tilted, and *Seawolf* rose from the darkness of the ocean depths.

This was, Garrett thought, an unnatural act, akin to a reluctant paratrooper's lament about jumping out of a perfectly good airplane. Modern submarines did *not* belong on the surface . . . and he hadn't needed the Board of Inquiry after Operation Buster three years ago to tell him that. Submerged, an attack submarine was one of the deadliest and most formidable of all modern weapons platforms, hard to find, hard to kill; on the surface, she was remarkably vulnerable and weak, visible to all, with a hull so thin even a lightly armed patrol boat or aircraft could take her out.

And surfacing *here*, just twenty miles off the mainland Chinese coast . . .

"Feeling a case of the jitters, XO?" Captain Lawless asked from the passageway forward.

Did it show that much? "No, sir." He grinned. "Not much, anyway."

Garrett had the watch as OOD, but Lawless had dropped in moments before to watch the surface maneuver. He hadn't taken command but silently looked on as Garrett checked the area for surface vessels, then gave the orders to surface.

He felt the slight shudder in the hull as the sail broke the surface, creating a sudden drag as the rising sub churned up a wake. The hull broke the surface a moment later, leveling off as the bow planes stopped biting water.

"We are on the surface, sir," Tollini announced. "Running smooth and normal."

"Very good," Lawless said. "I've got the deck now. Lookouts topside. XO? Care to accompany me?"

"Gladly, sir."

They climbed the ladder through the narrow confines of the sail, cracking the overhead hatch and letting a splash of cold seawater rain down on them. The lookouts went up first, climbing into their respective sail stations. Garrett was first onto the weather bridge, followed a moment later by Lawless.

Garrett blinked in the bright, afternoon sunlight glaring from a steel-blue sea. Ahead, to the north and northwest, lay Mainland China, low, rolling hills aglow in golden light, beneath cumulous clouds towering into the heavens. To left and right, huge numbers of surface craft crowded the water, though the *Seawolf* was being given a generously wide berth. Most of the boats were junks and fishing yawls; one ominous watcher, though, was running parallel to *Seawolf*, a kilometer off her starboard beam: a Luda-class destroyer, superficially like the old Soviet Kotlin class, but larger, with a flat transom aft and a bulkier superstructure. Flying astern of the destroyer was a Kaman SH-2F LAMPS I helicopter, an American design sold to the People's Republic of China in the past few years specifically for antisubmarine work.

It would be one hell of a note, Garrett thought, if the 'Wolf was to come under attack by a former American ASW helo.

Destroyer and helicopter appeared to be shadowing the *Seawolf*, not coming too close but staying where their presence would serve as a warning. *We see you, Yankee, and we are ready for you. . . .*

They maintained their northwesterly heading through flat seas, accompanied by clouds of civilian craft, fishing boats, junks, cabin cruisers, sailboats. The hills ahead slowly resolved into sharper focus . . . impossibly green and strangely humped, rising from the blue mirror of the ocean. Garrett had been here before, once, when the USS *Portsmouth* made a show-the-flag call back in '95. Hong Kong had still been a British colony then. So far, it didn't look as though much had changed in the intervening years or with the hand-over of the territory to the PRC.

"What are you thinking, XO?" Lawless asked.

It seemed an uncharacteristic question, and it caught Garrett off guard. Still, to his surprise during the past few days, Garrett had found himself understanding Lawless better. Dougherty had been right. The captain was tough, hard, and supremely demanding. He was also fair and devoted to the 'Wolf's crew. The only fault Garrett could find with the man—aside from his occasional bigotry against people of Asian descent—was his habit of not pushing that extra hundred yards to close with a potential enemy or gather the extra bit of hard intel. And that could be explained easily enough by his desire not to put his men or his boat needlessly in harm's way.

"I'm thinking, sir," he replied, "that the conversation on the mess deck last night before the movie didn't do justice to this by half."

"What conversation was that?" Lawless had not attended the movie.

"Some of the guys were saying that our foreign policy so far as the People's Republic goes doesn't make sense. First we spent a couple of decades propping up Chiang's claim that he represented all of China. Then we tried to make up to Beijing and dumped Chiang, but gently . . . trying to keep him on as a trading partner without admitting that Taiwan was a country or making Beijing mad. Then we're helping Taiwan again, when Beijing starts tossing missiles and trying to intimidate us and Taipei. And *now . . .*"

"And now they pull another switch and make kissy-face to Beijing," Lawless said, completing the thought. "Suffering from whiplash yet?"

"Not quite, but it's getting there. What do you make of it, sir?"

Lawless shrugged. "That it's pretty much business as usual. Washington doesn't want a war with China. We want to do business with both the mainland *and* with Taiwan, which makes sense, since trading partners are more fun to play with than military enemies or radioactive deserts. But Beijing and Taipei don't want to play nice with each other, which leaves us in a hell of a position. Either we support Taiwan and get ourselves into one hell of a war . . . or we prove to the rest of the world that our word can't be trusted, that we don't stand by our friends."

"The rest of the world probably got that message when we stopped recognizing the Taipei regime as legitimate."

"Maybe. Of course, nobody else in the world recognizes Taiwan as a real government anymore, except twenty-odd nations that are either too small to be noticed by Beijing or are outcast states anyway. South Africa. Israel. Singapore." He chuckled. "Did you know that Lithuania tried to recognize Taiwan when they got their independence from the Soviet Union? Beijing landed on them hard, threatening all kinds of diplomatic bluster and thunder. Lithuania had to back down finally. They couldn't afford that kind of pressure."

"I hadn't known that."

"S'truth. China, the PRC, has been playing this game for a long time, and they've been playing hardball. They're patient. They haven't wanted a war, either. But they're also determined to get their way, to get their rebellious province back in line."

"So why are they pushing so hard now?" Garrett asked.

"Combination of factors. First, they know that if the PDP stays in power, there's a good chance they'll finally win recognition as an independent state, the Republic of Taiwan. Once that happens, Beijing can't claim that other countries are interfering in their internal affairs by recognizing Taipei, by selling them up-to-date arms and munitions, or by forming trade or defense alliances with them.

"And second . . . there's the Terrorist War. This must be a God-given chance for Beijing, with our military stretched to the limit right now in Iraq, Afghanistan, and half a dozen other places scattered all over the globe. They know we can't commit to a big war here, or a long one, or an expensive one. They're gambling that when they push hard enough, we're going to back down, that Taiwan is a small price to pay for peace."

"They know us pretty well."

"We don't exactly make it hard for them," Lawless said. "China has a culture going back a couple of millennia. They're used to taking the long view. To being patient. Like a cat at a mouse hole."

"And right now I feel like the mouse." Garrett smiled. "So why are we sailing blithely into Hong Kong harbor, with the cat waiting to pounce?"

"Damfino. At a guess, I'd say some lead-asses in the State Department see their careers tied to good relations with Beijing and are willing to do or say just about anything to keep things friendly."

"Sometimes, Captain, I think the world is drowning in stupidity."

"The two most common elements in the universe, Mr. Garrett, are hydrogen and stupidity. I forget who said that."

"Hm. You know, sir, sailing a three-billion-dollar Seawolf-class submarine into the middle of a potential enemy harbor is not exactly a friendly gesture."

"Sure it is. You think the PLA is going to start anything with us in the middle of one of their busiest harbors? Cruise missiles make wonderful equalizers. They'll be *very* friendly."

"Yes, sir, and you know as well as I do that those cruise missiles would be better employed from a weapons platform that was safely tucked away out of sight a couple of hundred miles offshore, and under about three hundred feet of water. If Beijing decides to cut off talks while we're parked in there, we're going to have a hell of a time getting clear." He cast an uneasy glance toward the swarm of small craft to starboard, just beyond the ominous gray shark-shape of the PLA destroyer. "You know, I keep looking at all of those small boats and remembering that these waters used to be pirate hangouts."

"You think they may try to board and storm us?"

Garrett shook his head. "They wouldn't get through the deck hatches. But I do think about the *Cole*."

The USS *Cole* was the Arleigh Burke-class guided-missile destroyer savaged in Aden Harbor by bin Laden's Al Qaida terrorists eleven months before the attacks on New York and the Pentagon in 2001. The *Cole* had been in the process of preparing to take on fuel when a small boat came alongside and exploded, ripping a gaping hole in her side, killing seventeen sailors and wounding thirty-nine others. Most Navy personnel today thought of that attack as bin Laden's true declaration of war, a declaration that had been ignored at the time.

"So we keep the *Cole* in mind and don't let security slip for an instant," Lawless said. "What do you recommend?"

"Armed guards on deck. No local boat allowed to approach within fifty meters."

"That might be tough to enforce in that harbor."

"Yes, sir. Other than that . . ." He stopped. "Are you authorizing liberty, Captain?"

"Yes. This is supposed to be a diplomatic call, remember. Business as usual . . . and, no, you guys *haven't* been shooting live missiles at our friends across the Formosa Strait." He shrugged. "My call, of course, but our orders specified that liberty was to be permitted."

"Then I suggest a word to the hands about security before they go ashore. Small groups ashore one at a time only, rather than port and starboard liberty. We'll want a full watch on board at all times. And let 'em know they could be called back on board at any time, if the situation changes. We treat this as a high-threat situation, and we let *no one* come close aboard without a real good look-see."

Lawless nodded. "Pretty much what I was going to recommend. Very good, Mr. Garrett. We'll make a sub skipper out of you yet."

The words rankled, but Garrett pushed the jibe aside. Half the time, he still couldn't tell whether Lawless was being humorous but clumsy, or deliberately abusive.

"I do wish I knew what State hoped to accomplish by having us go in there," Garrett said.

"Eh? That's simple. Two birds with one stone, and all that. They demonstrate to Beijing that we're friendly but prepared . . . and they keep us out of trouble."

"Us? Out of trouble? How do you figure, sir?"

"Easy. Washington knows there are ten-plus Kilo boats operating out here, and us deployed to track them. Right now, the bureaucrats and armchair admirals are wetting their collective pants over the thought that we might go and trigger World War Three . . . by, just for instance, bumping into one of those Kilos by accident?"

Garrett frowned. "That's not very funny, sir."

"It wasn't intended to be. You know how often our boats brushed with the Russians during the bad old days of the Cold War. The situation is a lot more tense out there now. State is hoping to defuse things a bit . . . keep us in the area and very visible, but also off somewhere where we won't accidentally trigger a shooting war."

True enough. American attack boat skippers had long had the rep of being particularly aggressive when shadowing Soviet boats. More than once they'd run into the subs they were following, often with damage to both vessels.

And Garrett had had his own run-in with a Chinese Kilo under exactly those circumstances.

"So, to keep us from starting World War Three," Garrett said, "Washington wants us to let those Kilos run free in the strait while we hole up inside a harbor that, twenty-four hours ago, would have been considered an enemy harbor . . . and which could turn into enemy territory again at any moment." He shook his head in disgust. "Whose side are they on, anyway?"

"All in the cause of world peace, Mr. Garrett. All in the cause of world peace. Have faith in your government. They *care* for you."

Garrett chuckled, but the sound carried little in the way of humor. "Of *course* you can trust the government. Just ask any Indian!"

"Have some respect, Mr. Garrett. That's 'Native American,' if you please."

"Aye aye, sir."

The easy banter was interrupted as a harbor tug approached, an ugly little workhorse flying the PRC flag.

Local pilots were emphatically not permitted on board a Navy vessel, but the *Seawolf* was required to follow the tug into port. The craft signaled its intent with impatient hoots from its whistle, then came about and began leading the *Seawolf* into the harbor approaches.

And a good thing, too. As the *Seawolf* slowly rounded the island of Tung Lung Chau and entered Tathong Channel, the tangle of shipping and small craft crowding the waterways around the myriad islands grew denser and even more chaotic. It would be easy to lose oneself in these approaches without a firm knowledge of the waters and the local conditions.

Hong Kong Island proper was a roughly football-shaped land mass perhaps twelve miles across. A semicircular bite snatched out of the northern coast formed the basis for Victoria Harbor and the setting for the busy downtown of Hong Kong itself, the district known as Central. North, across the bay, Kowloon thrust southward like a dagger; beyond, to the north, lay the New Territories and the unimaginably vast sprawl of Mainland China. Ships approached Victoria Bay from east or from west, through winding channels and labyrinths comprised of hundreds of islands, ranging from mere bare rocks and reefs to huge Lantau in the west, an island twice the size of the island of Hong Kong. The crowding, the clutter, the chaos, the noise—all were indescribable.

Past Quarry Bay and around North Point, the harbor pilot tug led the *Seawolf* slowly into Hong Kong's Victoria Harbor, a seething, teeming traffic jam of boats, ships, and watercraft of every size, tonnage, and description. Hong Kong may have belonged to the PRC for the past six years, but so far Beijing had kept its promise here to enforce "one China, two systems" . . . allowing Hong Kong's flamboyantly capitalist economic system to continue more or less unchecked, demanding only that Beijing be responsible for its military defense and foreign affairs policy.

The gleaming gold and silver skyscrapers lining the harbor shone as brightly in the afternoon sun as ever, potent symbols of the former British colony's rampant glorification of consumerism and business interspersed with towering advertising boards and signs. The landmarks stood just as they had during the capitalist era: the garish gold, silver, and ceramic facade of the Central Plaza Building; the oddly geometric glass tower of the Bank of China; the stolid polished granite and glass stacks of Exchange Square; and the bizarre steel anvil shape of the Peak Tower atop Victoria Peak, among dozens of other buildings of every shape and description. The futuristic cityscape provided a dramatic, sun-gilded backdrop to fleets of junks that might well have just emerged from the thirteenth century and a starkly alien contrast to the more squalid tenements, condominiums, office buildings, and shacks crowded into the district of Kowloon on the north side of the bay.

Garrett wondered how long Beijing would leave Hong Kong to pursue its gods of commerce and dollars in peace. It was widely assumed throughout the Naval Intelligence community that the PRC was on its best behavior with Hong Kong in hopes of convincing its "renegade province," Taiwan, of the benefits of peaceful assimilation.

Besides, Hong Kong and Taiwan both were the commercial jewels of the west Pacific Rim. Strangling their economies for the sake of ideology would quite literally be killing the goose that laid the golden eggs.

Garrett decided that was the most comforting thought. The PRC wasn't about to start a war when they could win what they wanted through negotiations, persistence, and patience. *Seawolf* would be safe enough inside Victoria Harbor; after all, an attack on her would bring down upon the PRC the full weight of America's military, a confrontation that Beijing simply could not afford to face.

He did wish, though, that he could shake some of the scenes from last night's movie . . . especially those about an American warship isolated far up a Chinese river, surrounded by hostile forces.

The tug led them to the left, into the harbor in front of the district known as the Admiralty, beneath the former Government House and the looming towers of the Bank of China and the Bank of America. Other warships, Garrett noted, were already at their moorings— the British carrier *Hermes*, a Russian Krivak II-class frigate, and the *Jean de Vienne,* a French guided-missile destroyer.

He noticed another foreign vessel in port . . . not a warship, exactly, but an interesting visitor nonetheless. She was a Russian Onega-class GKS vessel. GKS stood for Gidroakusticheskoye Kontrol'noye Sudno, meaning "Hydroacoustic Monitoring Ship," a seagoing sensor platform designed specifically to detect, record, and measure the acoustical signatures of other ships. A number of her crewmen were on deck as the *Seawolf* cruised slowly past, watching the American submarine. He wondered if they'd learned the *Seawolf* was paying a visit and arranged to be here just so they could listen to the submarine's near-silence. *Maybe* they were here by chance.

Seawolf's deck party swarmed smartly up out of the hatches and stood by to handle lines. With Captain Lawless giving commands over the intercom hookup from the sail bridge to the control room, the submarine gentled herself up to a pier, port-side to, where a Chinese shore party waited with monkey fists ready. As the *Seawolf* edged in close enough, the monkey fists—large balls of heavy, knotted cable attached to slender tethers called "small stuff"—were tossed across the water and the sub's deck, where the line handlers could grab them and haul in the heavier mooring lines waiting coiled on the pier. Within a few moments *Seawolf* was spring-tied to bollards fore and aft, and Lawless had given the order, "All stop, now secure engine."

A small cluster of Chinese government officials, customs police, and military officers stood at the head of the pier, quietly waiting. "I'd better get the formalities out of the way, XO," Lawless said. "If you would address the matter of security?"

"Aye aye, sir."

He clambered back down the sail hatch, descending the ladder to the control deck.

"Mr. Garrett?" One of the kids from the radio room was waiting for him as he stepped off the ladder and into the control room.

"Yes, Zollner. What is it?"

"We went ahead and started taking in radio traffic as soon as we surfaced. Got this for you. It's a family gram."

"Oh?" He accepted the message printout from Zollner.

Family grams had evolved as a means of letting submarine crew members stay in touch with family and loved ones ashore. Normally they were reserved for enlisted personnel and their families, especially for crews aboard the big boomers that might be at sea for months at a time without surfacing to permit normal ship-to-shore communications. On a typical cruise, each man was allowed to get about eight fifty-word family grams. Sometimes they arrived in code that only the captain could decrypt . . . so that he could decide whether to give the crewman news from home about a death or a dear John.

This one was dated May 17—yesterday—which was pretty quick. Sometimes, censors ashore would hold up family gram transmissions, again to check them for news that might adversely affect a member of the sub's crew.

> DEAREST TOM. JUST LEARNED ON WCN YOU'RE GOING
> TO HONG KONG. I HAVE LAYOVER THERE MONDAY
> NIGHT THROUGH WEDNESDAY, CAN WE MEET FOR DIN-
> NER AND A LION? NO ROOMMATES THIS TIME. I'LL BE
> AT AIRPORT REGAL, LANTAU, AFTER 2000 MONDAY.
> CALL WHEN YOU CAN. ILY. KAZUKO.

Garrett took a deep breath. Forty-six words, just under the limit, filled with promise. "ILY" was standard family gram code, turning the three words of "I love you" into a single word. The reference to the lion, however, was purely their own, personal code . . . a reference to the time when Garrett had stalked on all fours across the bed, roaring like a lion, before pouncing on the squealing Kazuko.

And the no-roommates bit was delightfully self-explanatory.

Kazuko was going to be in Hong Kong? It would be good to see her, assuming he could get an evening free. They'd done this before several times when he'd been traveling on ONI business to the Philippines, Bangkok, and Singapore, and she by coincidence was working flights to those same cities.

The one thing that was disquieting about the message was her reference to WCN. He didn't like the idea that the World Cable Network news had learned and announced *Seawolf*'s visit to Hong Kong almost at the same time that the '*Wolf* herself had received the orders. What the hell was going on?

It was something he would have to take up with the skipper. For now, though, he needed to make sure that *Seawolf*'s security detachments were clear on their orders. No one was going to get close to the *Seawolf* while she was in port.

Not without a hell of a fight.

Crew's Mess
USS *Seawolf*
1505 hours

"Aw, man, it was one *hell* of a fight!" Chief Toynbee leaned back against one of the mess tables as he regaled the sailors gathered around on the recollected joys of liberty in Hong Kong. "The British Royal Marines, they're pretty good, see. As good as our Marines, or at least that's what they'll tell you. Our jarheads claim descent from the Royal Marines.

"Anyway, there we were, toe-to-toe with the queen's finest, and neither of us about to back down. One of 'em made a crack about 'colonials living in sewer pipes,' and that was it. We waded in and decked 'em!"

"How many Brits did you say there were, Chief?" Quartermaster Chief Thompson asked.

"Five of them, against the four of us. And we gave as good as we got, let me tell ya!"

"Now, the way I heard it," Thompson said with a laugh, "was that it was you and three other guys against two British Marines. And they mopped the deck with you!"

"That's a damned lie! Who said such a thing?"

"Doberly, for one. He was there!"

"Shit! Dobie can't count to two without using the fingers of both hands. And he transferred out when we were at Yokosuka. You gonna believe me, or a lying sonuvabitch who ain't even here?"

"Dobie said he got fifteen stitches in his scalp when one of the Brit jarheads clobbered him with a bottle. And he said you ended up in the sick bay aboard the *Inchon* for a week with a concussion!"

"It was only three days, damn it. I *told* ya he was a lyin' sonuvabitch!"

"So after *you* mopped the deck with *them*," HM1 Ritthouser said with a grin, "what happened?"

"The SPs showed up and cleared the joint out."

"How would you know, Chief?" RM2 Meyers asked. "You had a concussion, remember?"

"Actually, I don't remember much of anything. But man, that was one hell of a *great* Hong Kong liberty!"

"Are you going back there, Chief?" Ritthouser asked.

"Sure am, Doc. Ya wanna come? Best little whorehouse in Hong Kong, I tell ya!"

Seawolf's corpsman shook his head. "I don't know about that, Chief. I'm supposed to be warning you poor, benighted souls about the dangers of places like that, remember?"

"Aw, c'mon, Doc!" TM1 O'Malley laughed. "How ya gonna know what to warn us about if you ain't been there yourself?"

"I'm also married!"

"So? What's that got to do with it, Doc?" YM1

Haskell asked. "We won't tell on you!" The others laughed and hooted.

"It's gonna be an interestin' visit, though," Chief Toynbee said. "That was . . . lessee, I was a first class then. It was, yeah, 'ninety-five. This is my first visit back to this port since the Commies took the place over. Now, they say nothin's changed, but I wonder if the old fleet watering holes are the same."

"Of course they are, Chief," Thompson said. "Half the port must live off the various navies that visit here. That's not going to change just because of a little switch of government. People are still people, and sailors still have more cash than sense when they get liberty."

"Well, it's not like the old days, when we always had ships calling at Hong Kong."

"No, but they still do," Thompson said. "I think the Navy likes to run L.A. boats and the occasional carrier through here just to remind the Chinese we're here, y'know?"

"Well, I know one thing," Toynbee said. "And let this be a warnin' to each and every one of you guys. Stay out of trouble! Back in the old days, the local Hong Kong police boys were efficient, but they were also friendly and they could be real reasonable if you had American dollars. I don't know that I'd want to try to bribe a Chicom cop, know what I mean?"

"Cops are cops everywhere," Ritthouser said. "Maybe you just need to make their acquaintance!"

"And maybe a certain smart-aleck corpsman is going to see Hong Kong by way of the number one torpedo tube!"

"Attention on deck!"

The men started to come to their feet, but Garrett waved them all back down. "As you were. What's up?"

"I, ah, was just filling the guys in on personal hygiene, sir," Ritthouser said. "Especially on how *not* to come back aboard with STDs."

"Yeah," Meyers said. "He was telling us how guys' dicks fall off when they visit HK cat houses."

"Sounds like a cool lecture, Doc. Wish I'd heard it."

"Yes, sir."

"Chief Toynbee? I understand you've been in Hong Kong before."

"Uh . . . yes, sir. A long time ago . . ."

"I need to talk to you."

The XO led Toynbee off to the side of the compartment, where they began speaking in low voices. Meyers looked at the others. "I say the new XO is okay!"

"He'll do," Ritthouser said. "Meanwhile . . . tell me about this whorehouse. . . ."

"Well," Haskell said, "it's called the Fuk Wai, and you'll *know* why when you see the girls. . . ."

Monday, 19 May 2003

Fujian Province
People's Republic of China
0035 hours

Thundering through the night, the line of Huey UH-1 helicopters clattered scant feet above the waves, unseen in the darkness below. Jack Morton sat on the edge of the cargo deck of the lead helo, his feet braced on the landing skid as the warm, wet wind slapped and tugged madly at his assault gear.

Four helicopters, thirty-two men, eight to a bird. Sixteen men from Third Platoon, First Company SEAL Team Three, and sixteen more from the Taiwan parafrogmen commando unit. It was a larger insertion than Morton liked. While he'd trained in large-scale assaults, the SEALs were at their best in small-unit deployments, usually in eight-man squads or, at most, a sixteen-man platoon. More men than that and the operation could become badly confused real fast, especially if you weren't sure where all of your men were at any given moment.

This was a lot worse, too, because half of the assault force was made up of strangers, the Taiwanese parafrogs. Oh, there was no question whatsoever that they were *good*. Their training was closely modeled on the insanely rigorous BUD/S training the American SEALs went through. But the Third Platoon had the advantage of having worked and trained together for a long time, to the point that every man knew every other better than a brother, knew him so well you could damned near tell where he was and what he was doing by some arcane sixth sense.

But the SEALs were also trained to take part in hasty insertions, and this op was about as hasty as they came. Fortunately, it was relatively straightforward. Get in, find the PLA mobile launchers a few miles inland, wham-and-scram, and exfiltrate.

They were riding heavily on trust on this one—trusting Tse and his people to be as good as they were supposed to be, trusting the Taiwanese helo pilots to be as good as *they* were supposed to be, and trusting a Taiwanese patrol boat to meet them at a certain point with a certain signal to get them the hell out of Dodge when the time came. That level of trust came damned hard for SEALs. They knew they could count on one another . . . but who the hell were *these* guys?

Morton had been a kid running around with his shirttails out at Swissvale Elementary School during most of the Vietnam War, but he'd heard plenty of stories, especially from TEAM old-timers, now retired, about the love-hate relationship the Teams had developed with intelligence bureaus in general and with the CIA in particular. Intel on enemy movements, deployments, and strength had been so piss-poor dreadful that the SEALs had swiftly formed their own intelligence networks, relying on their own people to deliver when the cowboy hat and shades–sporting boys from the Company had nothing to offer but guesses and hot air.

The situation here was similar—depending on sources of intel about enemy strength and presence that were reputedly good, but untried by Third Platoon. Only the parafrogs' reputation among the SEALs, thanks to other Team members who'd worked with them, made this operation even conceivable.

The copilot of Morton's helo turned in his seat, reached back, and slapped Morton on the shoulder, before holding up three gloved fingers. Morton nodded his understanding and gave a thumbs-up in reply.

Three minutes.

He nudged Chief Bohanski at his left and passed on the three-minute warning. Each of the eight SEALs aboard the Huey began giving one another a final going-over, checking for hanging straps, unhooked buckles, or loose gear.

The SEALs were in full war paint, their faces heavily coated with black and green swaths of an oil-based paint that would not come off in seawater. They wore diving gear—Draeger rebreathers and masks—over combat vests tightly packed with explosives and demo gear, spare magazines, sheathed knives, plastic-wrapped main weapons, and personal radio equipment.

They'd made a final check with USSOCOM by communications satellite relay that afternoon, and received the command "Red Dragon takes flight." The op was a go, their last set of intel downloads on the objective still good.

For a time over the past forty-eight hours, Morton had wondered if the mission might be called off before they deployed. Taiwan television had been full of news reports for the past couple of days of a "friendly visit" by an American nuclear submarine to Hong Kong. That sort of flag-showing happened from time to time, but only rarely in times of crisis as tight as this. The news also carried stories of the possibility of new talks with Beijing, aimed at defusing the Taiwan crisis. Taiwan, however, had not been invited to join those talks, at least not yet, and until that happened it was still business as usual for the ROC parafrogs.

He felt the Huey swerve slightly and slow. The pilot, in the right-hand seat, was wearing a heavy, masklike headset that covered his eyes, with night-vision goggles that let him pick out details of surface and surroundings in near-total darkness. According to Tse, these helo crews were expert at finding their way to particular unmarked patches of ocean in the middle of a moonless night with uncanny precision. He just hoped their sense of altitude was good in those things; they were flying at something like twenty feet above the waves, way too low for the altimeter to be at all useful, low enough that the slightest miscalculation could slam them into the water and end their mission right then and there. The other three helicopters should be strung out behind the leader, staggered in echelon formation so that jumpers from one helo wouldn't come down on top of other jumpers already in the water.

If these guys knew what they were doing.

Their speed should be dropping to about twenty or thirty knots, no more. Any faster and the SEALs would slam into the water hard enough that it would feel like a stone wall. Men had been killed in training accidents when pilots had signaled the helocasters to jump and were flying too high or too fast. Morton leaned forward, looking down into blackness. The moon had set several hours before, and the night was overcast and dark. He could just make out a glimmer of light reflecting from a black, oily surface, but it was almost impossible to gauge altitude by eye alone.

Time for a final equipment check, to pull masks down over painted faces . . . and turn on the gas flow from rebreathers.

The copilot reached back again, gave a clenched-fist signal, then pointed. It was time . . . *now!*

Two by two, from the open cargo deck doors on either side of the Huey, the SEALs planted their feet on the helicopter's runners and pushed themselves off backward into black emptiness. Morton shoved hard with his feet, holding his breath and squeezing his mask down hard against his face. An instant later a cold, explosive collision engulfed him when he hit the churning black water.

Helocasting was only a slightly updated form of the original UDT deployments off patrol boats or landing craft during World War II and Korea. Frogmen trained to jump off the side of a speeding boat into a raft secured to the boat's side, and then on command to roll over the edge of the raft and into the water. The maneuver permitted them to deploy with considerable precision, carefully spacing the combat swimmers out in a line.

This was much the same, but from a low, slow-flying helicopter instead of a boat. Aircraft gave them considerably better maneuverability than boats would have allowed. Their flight path had been carefully contrived to take them north from Kinmen toward the mainland, then swinging west parallel to the invisible border between ROC and PRC territory. Kinmen was only about four miles off the Chinese coast; the line of UH-1s would have been apparent on every PLA radar screen from Xiamen to Shenhu. The watchers along the coast might even suspect that a frogman insertion was under way, but they would have no way of telling exactly where the commandos had dropped off.

Kicking gently, Morton approached the surface. When his head broke through to open air once more, he could hear the dwindling flutter of the helicopters continuing to fly west, parallel to the border. Eventually they would swing south, out over the strait, and make their way back to Taiwan.

But thirty-two black-clad combat swimmers remained, moving through the inky darkness with slow, silent kicks. The luminous LED compass on Morton's wrist gave him his bearing of 325 degrees; the mainland coast ought to be just over two miles ahead, *that* way . . . an easy swim.

And a lonely one. He knew there were thirty-one other men out there, but he could see nothing, could hear nothing but the hiss of his own breathing, the thud of his own heartbeat in his sea-muffled ears. Slipping back beneath the water, he concentrated on holding his stroke to a measured beat per second, counting each kick in order to estimate his progress.

At a yard per kick, seventeen hundred and some yards per mile . . . call it an hour to cover two miles. Kick . . . kick . . . kick . . .

His progress was helped by the inflowing tide, and a two-knot current along the coast, running east to west, had been accounted for in the op planning. Now was the time, though, to wonder what they'd missed, what factor, forgotten, was going to turn around and bite them. Kick . . . kick . . . kick . . .

SEALs were trained to be patient, to hold on, to endure. Thrusting steadily along, he stayed just beneath the surface. Once, thirty minutes into the deployment, he heard the growling rasp of a boat's engine growing louder, and he jackknifed at the waist, going deeper. He had to be careful of his depth. Draeger units had the unfortunate habit of causing oxygen poisoning at depths much below thirty-two feet. The growl grew louder, louder . . . then faded away behind him. Presumably, the PLA had boats out on patrol, guarding against just such a visitation as this one. They would also have listening devices of various sorts planted . . . and possibly mines as well. They would not have motion detectors, since those could be triggered by any large, passing fish. And there might be nets, but they couldn't encase the entire coast in antiswimmer netting.

He heard a sudden, dull thump and felt a quick pressure in his ears. He stopped, hovering in the darkness, listening. Another thump, farther off this time. Those were explosions . . . probably hand grenades tossed into the water. He felt a stab of concern, then pushed the emotion down. Almost certainly, a PLA surface patrol was tossing grenades into the water at random, hoping either to catch enemy swimmers by chance or to bluff them into showing themselves. If they'd actually spotted some of the Red Dragon swimmers . . . well, there wasn't a lot that could be done, save to press on. After another three distant explosions the thumps ended.

Morton kept swimming.

Almost an hour after the helocast, his flippers brushed against stony bottom. He swam on a few more yards, then carefully maneuvered himself upright and again broke the surface.

He was adrift in a gentle offshore swell. He could see the coast clearly a few hundred yards ahead, the city of Xiamen was close, a mile or so to the southwest, and the sky glow reflected off overcast and water made the surroundings visible, especially to eyes dark-adapted by an hour of swimming in pitch-darkness.

For a long, long time Morton floated there, watching the coast. He could see the beach as a gray streak edged by the slash and churn of rolling surf. Above the beach was forest, black and impenetrable. There were lights on a hill in the distance—a house, perhaps, or a small building. There were no nearer signs of habitation.

Ten minutes passed. He could feel himself being dragged east by the current and kicked slowly to hold himself in place. This was one of the crucial points of the insertion. Somehow, thirty-two swimmers who'd jumped into the ocean an hour ago and two miles away from that beach had to rendezvous with absolute stealth and silence. The only way to do that was to have two men—Petty Officer Second Class Li Ho and PO First Class Chiang Soon—go in first and alone as pathfinders. Once they found the right spot of beach and made sure it was clear, they would—

Yes! There! A light winked briefly above the beach to the right—two shorts and a long, the agreed-upon signal. Morton began kicking again, striking out toward the indicated section of beach.

He felt the bottom rising beneath him, felt the surf grow stronger, more turbulent, roiling the surface and propelling him forward. He let an incoming wave lift him and send him gliding forward; he hit wet sand and clung there as the wave burst over his back and head and shoulders, hissing, then trickled away, leaving him on wet and gleaming sand. He crawled forward, staying flat, as another wave broke across his legs and splashed around his face.

Reaching behind him, he unsnapped the Chinese Type 73 assault rifle and pulled the plugs sealing barrel and receiver. Dragging back the charging lever, he chambered a round, carefully studying the dark forest ahead as the surf continued to splash and hiss around him.

To his left a barely seen shadow, black against the black of the water, moved forward in a crouch. A second shape joined the first. Another signal light winked from the forest, and the SEALs, death-silent, moved forward.

The body of a PLA sentry lay at the edge of the beach, the back of his neck pierced and his spine severed by a swift stab from a diving knife. Li was in the process of dragging the body back into the woods where it could be hidden.

The Team members were already fanning out through the night, silently taking up positions on a large perimeter, facing all directions. As more and more of the SEAL and Taiwanese commandos arrived, rising out of the surf like black, shapeless sea monsters, they began forming up into squads of eight men each, the better to move quietly and efficiently through the woods.

Before they set out, however, Chief Merriam assembled the compact SATCOM dish, connected the power supply, and punched out a coded signal to USSOCOM, a brief message meaning, simply, *We're here.*

The answer came moments later. *Go.*

Still in utter silence, the SEALs and Taiwan commandos slipped deeper into the forest, leaving the splash and wash of the surf behind. They had a long way to go.

Bottoms Up Bar
Hankow Road, Tsim Sha Tsui
Kowloon, People's Republic of China
1910 hours

There were no two ways about it, Chief Toynbee thought. Ken Queensly hadn't been to many bars in his life, but Toynbee and another sonar tech, ST1 Kellerman, had insisted that if he was going to see Hong Kong, he *had* to see the watering holes of Kowloon. Hell, forget the usual tourist sights—the tram up Victoria Peak, Government House, Hong Kong Park, or the Space Museum. You hadn't seen Hong Kong until you'd seen the Bottoms Up.

Kowloon, with its business district of Tsim Sha Tsui, lay directly north across the bay from Hong Kong proper, occupying a blunt peninsula thrusting south into Victoria Harbor. Until the new airport had been opened on Lantau Island in 1998, all of Hong Kong's air traffic had been handled by the old Kai Tak Airport on Kowloon's southeast corner—a single runway extending out into the harbor, which had offered stomach-dropping views of the city during the precipitously daring landings and takeoffs.

Kai Tak was closed now, but Kowloon murmured and jostled and festered as enthusiastically as ever, a seething anthill of people, shops, tenements, high-rise condos, market places, and mercantile mayhem. The skyline wasn't as modern, as thrilling, or as high as Hong Kong's; incoming aircraft had to skim Kowloon's rooftops during their approaches, resulting in stringent height restrictions to the buildings, though most of the development money had migrated anyway to the financial district across the harbor. Still, the sheer busyness of the place had Queensly wide-eyed and a bit dazed. Toynbee had to take his elbow to guide him through the looming doorway of the Bottoms Up.

Queensly's experience with bars had been limited to the joints along the main drag outside of the Great Lakes Naval Training Center during his boot leave, and to an identical stretch of bars, tattoo parlors, uniform tailoring shops, strip clubs, tobacconists, and massage parlors outside the sub school complex at Groton. Some of those places had been pretty sleazy— shockingly so for a wet-behind-the-ears kid from Zanesville, Ohio—but none of them had been as sleazy as this place.

Tobacco smoke mingled with other, curiously exotic and alien scents filling the air, making both breathing and navigation difficult. Grease, spilled drinks, and dirt covered the floor and most other surfaces in sight; garish red lighting and pulsing disco strobes made it hard to see the larger-than-life James Bond posters on the walls.

There were seven Seawolves in the shore party— Toynbee, Queensly, Larimer, Bennett, Shaeffer, Haskell, and Ritthouser. They were wearing civilian clothing, as was expected on liberty nowadays in a world where military personnel were told to keep a low profile, but it was easy enough to pick them out as Navy, with their short haircuts, loud banter, and good-natured camaraderie. More, it was possible to pick them out as submariners. Their skins were uniformly pasty under the garish bar lighting.

"This place is real big on Bond . . . *James* Bond," Toynbee said with a snicker. "One of the Bond movies had some scenes shot in here, and they never let you forget it!"

"They've done some redecorating since the last time I was in here," Haskell said. "But it still looks pretty much the same."

"The Communists promised hands off for fifty years," Larimer pointed out. "They can't shut decadent places like this down until 2047."

"So we got that long, at least, to enjoy!" Ritthouser said. "Decadent is *good*!"

"I thought we were going to that other place you were talking about," Queensly said as a hostess led them to a table almost lost within the caliginous, smoke-wreathed recesses of the place.

"The Fuk Wai?" Haskell said, scraping his chair back and taking a seat. "Don't worry, Queenie! We'll get there!"

"Queenie's a little anxious, huh?" Bennett said.

"Wouldn't you be?" Shaeffer said, laughing. "His first *real* liberty?"

"Patience, Queenie, patience!" Toynbee said. "There's a proper order to these things. First, a few drinks here. Then we mosey up the street to the Fuk Wai and find *out* why. . . ."

Shaeffer laughed. "I remember my first time ashore. Wow! It was in the Patpong in Bangkok—"

"Ha! Did *you* dip your dong in the ol' Patpong?" Toynbee asked.

"What's the Patpong?" Queensly asked.

"Red light district," Shaeffer explained. "Where all the bars and whorehouses are. Oh, man! There was this sweet, sweet little Thai girl, couldn't've been more than fifteen—"

"I don't want to even hear that shit, man," Ritthouser warned.

"Aw, it's the way things are there, Doc! You know! Cultural differences!"

"Don't make that kind of thing *right,*" Bennett said.

"So?" Shaeffer said, eyebrows raised. "You tell that to a fifteen-year-old kid who comes in from the sticks, ends up alone in the city and has to find a way to eat!"

"We've got that back in the States," Ritthouser said. He nodded toward a cage where a teenage Chinese girl in a G-string gyrated to the thump of western hard rock. "And maybe here, too!"

Their waitress arrived and took their drink orders . . . scotch or bourbon for all but Toynbee, who ordered beer, and Queensly, who asked for *kekou kele*—a Coke—to the guffaws and good-natured jibes of the others.

"Maybe *that's* a cultural difference!" Haskell said, laughing.

"Speaking of cultural differences," Toynbee said, "get a load of *them*!"

Another party of westerners was being ushered into the back of the bar, eight men in white naval uniforms that showed horizontally striped T-shirts under the jumpers' V-necks. Their haircuts were distinctive as well, their scalps as closely shorn as those of any punk-rocker skinhead. The black patches giving their ship's name on their sleeves were picked out in Cyrillic letters.

"What are they, Russians?" Bennett asked, squinting through the smoke.

"Off that GKS in the harbor, I'll wager," Larimer said, nodding.

"I don't think so," Toynbee said, his expression turning serious.

"How do you know?"

"GKS vessels don't have names, they have numbers—GKS-83, GKS-95, like that. Those name patches read . . . can't quite make them out from here. Looks like *Admiral . . .* something."

"*Admiral G. L. Nevolin,*" Larimer said, squinting hard. "Maybe the GKS ships have names now?"

"Or that's the name of that Krivak Two we saw in port," Shaeffer suggested.

"Nah," Toynbee said. "Krivaks all have names like

'Lively' or 'Wrathful.' One-word names, and they wouldn't be Admiral Somebody-or-other."

"They're submariners," Ritthouser said.

"How can you tell, Doc?"

"Look at their skin, Bennett! Those guys haven't seen the light of day for months!"

"Makes sense, I guess," Larimer said. "Wasn't Nevolin a Soviet sub guy?"

"We'll need to check that with the skipper when we get back aboard," Toynbee said. He watched the Russians for a moment more. They were loudly ordering drinks in a mix of Russian and badly broken English.

"So what Russian sub is in Hong Kong?" Shaeffer wanted to know.

"The *G. L. Nevolin*?" Haskell asked.

"Asshole. No, I mean there wasn't any Russian sub in Victoria Harbor when we came in."

"Maybe they just got here today," Bennett pointed out.

"Negative," Larimer said. "We'd have seen her posted on the port arrivals board on the *'Wolf*."

"Or they could be visiting up the Pearl River, at Shanghai," Toynbee suggested. "There are military bases up there, and a big fleet facility."

"That could be. But I wonder why a bunch of Russki submariners are in port now, just when we get here."

"Chief, you're paranoid," Larimer said.

"And you're ugly. What's your point?"

"Uh-oh," Haskell said. "They've noticed us."

Several of the Russian sailors were openly staring at the Americans now. One laughed and said something in Russian, unintelligible, but loud enough to be heard . . . and to sound insulting. Two others stood up, grinning, then sauntered toward the Seawolves.

"You were staring too hard, Lar," Ritthouser said.

"Stay cool, people," Toynbee ordered. "This is a friendly night out on the town, we have a right to be here . . . and so do they."

"I saw a Star Trek episode like this once," Bennett said. "Klingons and Federation on a space station. Ended in a bar fight."

"There will be *no* fighting," Toynbee said. "Best behavior, remember?"

"Even if they draw their phasers first," Ritthouser said. "Where's a damned tribble when you need one?"

If the Russians heard or recognized the Star Trek reference, they didn't react. "You are Americanski navy, *da*?" one of the Russians said through a shallow, crooked-toothed grin. He slurred the words a bit. He'd been drinking hard for some time and was already approaching the proverbial four sheets to the wind. Drunken Russian sailors. This was *not* good.

"We are Americanski navy, *da*!" Larimer said. He raised his glass of scotch. "*Dasvidanya*, comrade!"

The Russian's eyes narrowed and the grin vanished. "It is not 'comrade.' There *are* no comrades any more!"

"But there are *tovarischii, da*?" Larimer asked. "Friends?"

Toynbee raised his glass. "To the end of the Cold War! And to new friends!"

The two Russians studied the Americans at the table for a moment, and then, magically, the grins returned, deep and sincere this time, and the moment's tension evaporated. "*Da! Da!* No more war! No more enemy! You join us at table, *da*?"

"Whatcha say, guys?" Toynbee asked.

"Suits me!" Shaeffer said.

"Let's do it," Larimer said. "I'm curious, anyway."

They ended up pushing the two tables together and

spreading out around them both. This is about a quarter past bizarre, Toynbee thought ruefully as he carried his beer over and sat down. Times do change. Sitting in a bar in Communist Hong Kong sharing drinks and jokes with Russian sailors . . .

"So, what ship?" Larimer asked one of the Russians as the women left. He touched the man's shoulder patch. "*Shtoh sudno?*"

"*Eta podv*—"

"Is frigate," one of the Russian sailor's companions said, interrupting hastily, with a sharp look at the man. "*Admiral Nevolin*. Out of Vladivostok. We hunt American submarines for fun!"

The other Russians at the table laughed, but Toynbee thought he detected a trace of nervousness. What had that first Russian been about to say? Toynbee didn't speak Russian—not as well as Larimer, anyway—but he knew a few technical words that had a bearing on his career. The word *podvodnaya*, for instance. *Submarine*.

Had that guy been about to admit that the *Nevolin* was a sub?

And why was it so important that the American submariners not know this?

He joined in the laughter and offered to buy the next round of drinks. It might be interesting, he thought, to listen closely to what else they had to say.

After all, the chances were excellent it was exactly what the Russians were doing with them.

Monday, 19 May 2003

Chep Lap Kok International Airport
Lantau Island, Hong Kong
1945 hours

Garrett walked onto the main concourse of Hong Kong's airport, feeling a bit dazed. The place was *titanic*, everything built on a scale of giants, as if to make ordinary mortals feel even smaller and more helpless than they were.

It was a place of superlatives. He'd heard that the Chep Lap Kok terminal was the largest single airport building in the world, and the world's largest enclosed public space—an area of 500,000 square meters, or ten times the size of Wembley Stadium in the United Kingdom. Someone had told him that the baggage claim area alone was the size of Yankee Stadium in New York City. The place was supposed to be handling eighty million passengers a year in another decade or

two, making it the busiest airport in the world, as well
as the world's largest.

As he passed into the East Hall, he entered what was
touted as the largest retail space in any airport, dozens
upon dozens of shops, restaurants, cafés and snack
shops . . . even public rest rooms, which were in shockingly short supply throughout Hong Kong itself.

The place seemed curiously empty at the moment,
however. With the Taiwan Crisis in full vigor, many
flights into Hong Kong had been cancelled, and many
more were coming in almost empty. Those passengers
visible in the concourse were huddled in tiny knots
about various shops and counters. The majority appeared to be business people trying to book flights out
of the country as quickly as possible.

War, Garrett thought wryly, can be very bad for
business.

At the security checkpoint, they weren't allowing
nonticketed passengers through to the gate area. Even
the PRC was clamping down at its airports, guarding
against what had so far been primarily a scourge in the
West—the use of hijacked airliners as guided missiles in
the War on Terrorism. PLA soldiers and militia, in red-
trimmed olive uniforms and with AK assault rifles
slung over their shoulders, stood at key access points
around the concourse and at the security gates, scrutinizing everyone who passed—especially the non-Asiat-
ics. Garrett was stopped twice by soldiers and asked to
produce his papers; his Navy ID let him pass each time,
but the hassle was annoying.

He thought it intriguing that, though the Taiwan
Crisis was turning into a face-off between China and
the United States, he wasn't being stopped because he
was American, and in the military, albeit in civilian

clothing. They were looking for terrorists, and stopping him because he was foreign, even though he didn't fit the profiling guidelines.

And no matter what his race, nationality, or occupation, they would not let him through the security checkpoint without a ticket.

So he found a comfortable place to wait, taking a bench where he could watch the trickle of people flowing in from the Y-shaped gate corridors beyond. It was fortunate the crowds were so light. The arching entranceway was broad enough that it would have been tough to pick out an individual in the usual mobs that filled the place in more relaxed times. A bank of flight information monitors reassured him that the JAL flight from Tokyo was on time.

And, just thirty-five minutes after her flight was due in, there she was, walking out of the gateway in her trim, dark, flight-attendant's uniform, trundling her small suitcase on its casters behind her. He rose from the bench and went to meet her.

"Tom!"

He grinned as he took her in his arms. "*Konichiwa*, beautiful."

"*K-Konichiwa* yourself. I wasn't expecting you to *meet* me!"

"Thought I'd surprise you. Things were squared away on the boat and they didn't need me as OOD, so . . ." They kissed.

The kiss started as a quick smooch, but swiftly degenerated into a long, comfortable hello, with rich promise for later. Garrett pulled back when he realized a number of people in the concourse were staring at them.

"Uh, we might need to find a place more private," he said.

She laughed. "There you go, Tom, frightening the locals again!"

"Well, watching's free."

"Uh-huh. And maybe we should take this show inside."

He looked around. "We *are* inside."

His eyes met those of a Chinese man standing near the security checkpoint, perhaps twenty yards across the concourse. It was hard to read the bland expression, but Garrett thought he saw disapproval there, and possibly anger.

Different people, different customs. The Chinese tended to be conservative and traditional. Expressions of public affection between men and women were frowned upon, though allowances were made for foreigners, who were automatically thought of as a bit crazy to begin with. It was the same in Japan, actually. Kazuko was so thoroughly western in her attitudes, beliefs, dress, and speech that it was easy to forget and give her a hug or a kiss or simply walk with her hand in hand, and garner disapproving stares from the local people. "Frightening the locals" was their private, joking term for it.

Kazuko noticed the watching man. Others in the concourse were looking at the two of them as well, openly staring, but only the first man seemed to be doing so with open hostility. "I think that guy doesn't like *gwailos*."

"Let's get out of here. Have you eaten?"

"Actually, yes. At the airport in Tokyo, before the flight." She gave him a sidelong look. "You?"

"I'm fine. What I want to eat *doesn't* involve food."

"Oooh, I was hoping you'd say that. Come on, Lion. Let's check into my room, and we'll see about dessert."

Arm in arm, they walked across the East Hall toward the airport hotel.

Hankow Road, Tsim Sha Tsui
Kowloon, People's Republic of China
2215 hours

The entire group, American and Russian, was steadily sinking deeper into a buzzing, light-headed whirl of inebriation. The Russians clearly had the head start in that direction, but the Seawolves were coming on strong. Ken Queensly alone maintained a reasonably clear head . . . clear, at least, of alcoholic fumes. The strangeness of the evening, the surroundings, and the company, plus the promise of things to come, however, had him feeling a bit drunk himself, and he'd had nothing stronger than a succession of overpriced soft drinks.

"We should get over to the Fuk Wai," Larimer said at last, slamming an empty glass onto the tabletop with an air of finality. "Have to teach Queenie what . . . what life is all about!"

"Suits me," Toynbee said. "Much more of this panther piss and I'm sozzled."

"Sozzled?" Ritthouser said. "Chief, you were sozzle—sozz—sozzelated an hour ago."

"That's what I said, isn't it? You ready, Queenie?"

"I'm . . . not so sure about this, Chief."

"*Sure* y'are! We got a fund goin', the guys an' me. Guarantees ya an A-number-one time."

"What is this Fuk you are talking?" one of the Russians asked. He was a burly *michman*, the equivalent of a warrant officer in the Russian Navy, and his name was Dimitri. Queensly hadn't heard a last name.

For some reason, that made the other Americans at the table crumble into gales of laughter. "It's this place up the road," Queensly explained to the bemused Russians as the others fought for breath. "A, um, brothel."

"No, not a brothel!" Toynbee managed to say, gasping past the laughter. "Not quite! This is a high-class joint. A hostess club. But, um, if you have the money, you can make special arrangements with the girls. . . ."

The Russians found this most fascinating, and for several moments they spoke among themselves in rapid-fire Russian, punctuated by bursts of, *"Da, da, da!"*

"Why don't you guys come along, Dimitri?" Larimer asked. "Make this a truly international party?"

"In spirit of comrades and—and good friendship, *da*!"

They paid their tabs and made their way out onto the street. Somehow, they ended up walking arm in arm up the middle of Hankow Road, past the shops and kiosks and garishly lit bars, with the Russians singing the "Internationale" and the Americans, who knew the tune but not the words, humming along in ragged chorus.

The Fuk Wai was on Hankow close to the intersection with Peking Road, with an almost invisible door tucked in between a tattoo parlor and an electronics store. Narrow and rickety steps led up to a larger, gold-painted door with an ornate, dragon-headed knocker. The sailors were admitted by a tough-looking fireplug of a man in a pinstripe suit and dark glasses who looked like the perfect parody of a Hong Kong gangster film.

Inside was an odd mix of bar and lounge, with comfortable sofas, garish lighting, and tons of crimson gossamer curtains. A stage and runway at one end provided the venue for a pair of naked women bumping and grinding away to the thump of rock music. Other customers were scattered about on the sofas or at tables, most in the company of attractive young women wearing high heels, jewelry, brightly colored panties, and nothing else.

A quartet of topless women met the sailors as they gathered in the entranceway. "Ooh, I want *this* one," one of them said, running her hands over Toynbee's beefy arm. "He so strong!"

"Thanks, baby, but why don't you spend some time with my buddy Queenie, here?" He winked. "There'll be a good tip in it if you treat him *extra* nice!"

"You got it, sailor. You come with *me*, Queenie. . . ."

"Uh . . . it's 'Queensly.' "

She made a face. "That what I say. You like Hong Kong?"

The next half hour was one of the stranger periods of time in Queensly's life. The woman, who said her name was either "DeeDee" or "TiTi"—even Queensly's sharp ears couldn't quite cut through the thick layers of her accent—led him to a table where she ordered drinks. He tried for another Coke, but she wanted him to order a mao-tai. "You try! You try!" she insisted, then leaned over and nibbled on his earlobe for emphasis. "You like lots, you see!" she whispered, and the sensation that sizzled up his spine was like a lightning bolt, guaranteed to make him agree to just-damn-about anything.

TiTi seemed like a nice girl to him. They talked about this and that . . . the sights in Hong Kong, the pleasant weather, the *mao-tai*—which, when it arrived, was colorless, odorless, and slightly greasy—but his tentative first sip went down with a sudden spurt of raw flame that left Queensly gasping for air and brought tears to his eyes.

"No, no, you drink all, drink quick," TiTi told him. *"Gon bui! Gon bui!"*

He drank the rest quickly, marveling as he did so that the second swallow wasn't quite as vicious as the first. TiTi ordered another round for them both; she was drinking something dark and sweet, which smelled like tea. He wondered why she wasn't drinking mao-tais.

After his second drink, that didn't seem to matter, much.

They continued talking, with TiTi leaning close on folded arms that framed and nicely accentuated her naked breasts. He learned that she was from a village in the interior of Guangdong Province called Lianping, and she claimed to be just seventeen years old . . . though the crow's-feet showing through the makeup at the corners of her eyes made him suspect she was exaggerating on the low side for the tourist trade. She was fascinated by his stories of growing up in small-town Ohio and seemed dismayed that Ohio had neither rice fields nor sugarcane.

The idea, he assumed, was to have sex with this woman eventually, but she didn't seem to be in a hurry. He was embarrassed about not knowing the rules of the game and even more embarrassed about not knowing how to talk to this woman about it. He *had* had sex . . . once . . . two days before he'd reported to Great Lakes for boot camp. That had been with Tricia Brown in the backseat of his dad's Chevy, in the driveway of Trish's suburban home. Trish had never taken off anything but her underpants, though, for fear that passing drivers would see the two of them grappling in the car, and the exercise had been awkward, clumsy, and conducted almost entirely by touch. TiTi was wearing nothing but bright green thong panties, little more, really, than a tiny delta of silk and some string, and the sight of her small, perfect breasts transfixed him to the point where he was having trouble looking up at her face.

Damn. The closest he'd ever been to a woman's bared nipples before had been in the pages of *Playboy*. These nipples were large, erect, and appeared to be rouged, and there were tiny silver sprinkles adhering to the skin of her breasts. He wanted to reach out with his fingertips and see if the glitter came off . . . but still wasn't sure about the rules for such things.

For her part, TiTi chattered on in her accented singsong English, talking about this and that, but without any real erotic content to the conversation at all, which confused him. A third mao-tai appeared at the table . . . or was this the fourth? He couldn't remember. And by then TiTi was pressed up against him in a most arousing manner, her right hand kneading his thigh while her left rested on his shoulder or playfully stroked the back of his neck and ears.

"I . . . think I've had enough," he said. He felt strange, woozy and light-headed, unwilling to even try to stand up. He had doubts about whether he would be able to stay standing if he did.

"No, you finish drink, yes?" she said. *"Gon bui!"*

"What does *'gon bui'* mean?"

"Is like . . . empty your glass. Drink up! Be happy!"

"I'm happy. But if I drink another of these things, I'm not going to be happy."

"You feel . . . sick?"

"No. I'm not feeling much of anything right now. Sort of like I'm dead."

"Okay, then, sailor. You rest now." She got up,

picked up her drink, and walked away, buttocks twitching enticingly around her thong panties. He struggled to sit upright. Had he said something wrong? TiTi was joining three of the Russians and another topless hostess at another table, laughing vivaciously.

After a long time, he decided the need to use the rest room was overcoming his need to stay safely and immobilely seated. He managed to find the toilets, but a beefy guard demanded twenty Hong Kong dollars for the privilege of using them. By the time he made it back to the main room, an argument was in progress.

"*Nyet! Nyet!* Is not fair!" Dimitri was towering over one of the women, shouting at her. She was standing toe-to-toe with the Russian, staring at him defiantly and shouting right back in bursts of staccato Chinese.

Queensly joined Toynbee, Larimer, Ritthouser, and Bennett at one of the tables. "What's going on?"

"I think our Russian friends are a little bent about the bar tab."

"Hell," Bennett added. "I don't blame them! Do you know we're paying just for the privilege of *talking* to these girls?"

"Huh? What do you mean?"

"Here's yours," Toynbee said. "They brought it out while you were in the head."

He studied the slip of paper for a moment, with dawning horror. If he was understanding these figures right, he was paying for five mai-tais, five "specials," whatever those were, and an hour of "companionship," plus a cover charge for the stage show, and tip . . . the total came to nearly HK$2,500.

The current exchange rate was about eight Hong

Kong dollars per U.S. dollar, but still, over three hundred dollars for a few drinks and a discussion about why you couldn't grow sugarcane in Ohio seemed a little steep.

"I don't think I had this many drinks," Queensly said, frowning.

Ritthouser looked at his tab and shook his head mournfully. "I had a different notion about what it meant to come here and get screwed."

"So did the Russkis," Toynbee observed. "Heads up, people. We've got trouble."

A pair of the tough-looking, gangster-stylish thugs had appeared, incongruous in their Hollywood-image dark glasses. One was the fireplug who'd met them at the door. The other was overweight and belligerent, but young, possibly still in his teens. They were confronting several of the Russians, shouting at them in broken English and rapid-fire Chinese. "You pay!" was the most intelligible refrain. "You pay and get out!"

"You know," Toynbee said, "I think the management of this place has changed. They didn't used to be this unfriendly."

The rest of the Russians were gathering around their shipmates, followed by several of the hostesses. Queensly saw with surprise that Haskell and Shaeffer were with them, enthusiastically joining in with the argument.

"We'd better get those two out of here," Larimer observed.

"Who's going to get *us* out?" Bennett said. He nodded toward another couple of teenage bouncers who'd just appeared behind them, blocking the way out. Both kids had their hands theatrically inside their jackets, as though drawing hardware.

"You make trouble, too?" one demanded. "You pay now!"

"You guys have a lot to learn about good public relations," Toynbee said. He reached for his wallet. . . .

Queensly wasn't sure who threw the first punch. The fight appeared to break out among the Russians, but in an instant Ritthouser and Larimer had tackled one of the nearer thugs, and Toynbee and Bennett were wrestling with the other. Behind him, one of the Russians was flying head first across the bar as hostesses shrieked and scattered. Glass exploded. The naked dancers on the stage screamed and ducked behind the curtains.

A semiautomatic handgun skittered across the parquet floor. Almost without thinking, Queensly scooped the weapon up, fumbled with the safety, then pointed the muzzle toward the ceiling. "*Attention on deck!*" he screamed, his voice a little too shrill. He squeezed the trigger. But nothing happened. Two more bouncer types had entered the room, guns drawn. They didn't seem to notice that Queensly was armed, though; he dragged the slide back and chambered a round, then fired at the ceiling again.

The pistol banged, the noise impossibly loud in the curtain-draped room. "I said attention on deck! You guys, drop 'em!"

The bouncers, eyes masked by their sunglasses but jaws agape, dropped their pistols and raised their hands. The fistfight ended as suddenly as it began, and Russians and Americans were disentangling themselves from the Chinese.

What the hell am I doing? Queensly thought wildly. *This is getting way out of hand!* "Let's get out of here!" he shouted. One of the bouncers took a step forward, and Queensly fired a second shot into the ceiling, sending glass spraying from a crystal-dripping chandelier. That stopped the advance, but two of the Chinese had the Russian who'd gone over the bar in their grip. The Russian sailor appeared to be dazed or unconscious. Two of his buddies started toward him, shouting at the bouncers.

That started another fight, and a wild struggle over the dazed man's body. Larimer and Ritthouser joined the fray then, knocking the Chinese away while one of the Russians slung their buddy over his shoulder and started for the stairs.

"Time to get the hell out of Dodge!" Toynbee shouted. "Come on, you guys!"

And that, Queensly thought, was an excellent idea.

But one that came too late. The Americans and Russians were moving together toward the front door when the shrill squeal of whistles sounded from outside and in the stairwell. A moment later a mix of Hong Kong police and PLA militia were spilling into the lounge, all of them with drawn weapons, their response time a little too quick to be believed.

Bennett collided with a PLA militia man, and the two struggled at the front door. The bouncers charged again, one of them straight into a chair swung roundhouse-style by Dimitri.

Someone shrieked something in Chinese, and Toynbee added, "Queensly! Drop the gun! Move slow!"

Queensly was suddenly aware that a half-dozen men were standing around him in a ragged semicircle, guns drawn, every weapon pointed straight at him. Moving very slowly, he put the pistol on the floor, then straightened up, hands in the air. The police closed in.

And something hard connected with the back of Queensly's skull in an explosion of light and pain and swiftly expanding darkness.

Regal Hotel
Chep Lap Kok International Airport
Lantau Island, Hong Kong
2348 hours

Garrett lay in bed next to Kazuko, savoring the warm, moist fragrance of her body, the warmth of her skin, the perfume of her hair spilling across the pillow. Their lovemaking had been enthusiastic and repeated, and they both floated in the pleasant, warm afterglow of close, loving sex.

"Again?" she asked him, her hand restlessly caressing.

"Jeez, give a guy a break, will you? I need some recovery time here."

"And here I thought you American sailors were *always* ready!"

"That's the Boy Scouts."

"No, they're always prepared. We're going to have to fortify you, give you vitamins."

"I'll give you vitamins." He nipped her playfully on the neck.

"Ah! I know. There's a drink you have to try," she told him. "An Okinawan variety of sake."

"Oh?"

"Very good for impotency."

"Hey! Who said I was impotent? I just came three times!"

"Who's counting?"

"You are, evidently. What's this Okinawan sake? I'm not much of a drinker, you know."

"Oh, you would like this. You take sake . . . place within it the body of a small, dead, poisonous snake—"

"Whoa, babe! You just lost me, right there! No snakes, dead or otherwise!"

"—and let it ripen for one month. The snake is completely dissolved except for the skeleton."

"And I thought doing the worm with a bottle of tequila was disgusting!"

"Doing the worm?"

"Never mind. This stuff cures impotency? I'd think it would kill you!"

"I suppose you could call it kill or cure. . . ."

Someone pounded on the hotel room door, a heavy *thump-thump-thump* demanding entrance. A sharp voice barked something in Chinese outside.

"What the hell?" Garrett said. He sat up in the bed, reaching for the light.

The door opened and a small mob poured into the room. All were in civilian clothing, but their close-cropped hair and hard eyes gave them the look of military personnel. One was waving a Makarov pistol that looked government-issue, and the others had Chinese-model AKs. A maid was with them, wide-eyed and crying and holding a set of room keys; one of the men shouted at her and she fled.

Garrett rose to confront them, furious, "What the hell are—"

"Quiet! You stand! Up hands! Back of head! Now!"

Two men dragged Kazuko from the bed kicking and struggling; Garrett lunged forward, grappling with the man with the pistol. *"Let her go!"*

A rifle butt slammed into Garrett's back with a dizzying explosion of pain, knocking him to his knees. The one with the pistol kicked him viciously in the side. "You stand! You stand!"

One of them hit Kazuko in the face, then slammed her up against the wall, pinning her there. Rough hands dragged Garrett to his feet and shoved him into line next to her. The one with the pistol—the leader,

Garrett thought—jammed the muzzle of his weapon hard up under the angle of his jaw.

They were forced to stand there, stark naked, side by side, their hands clasped behind their heads as two of the intruders proceeded to empty Kazuko's suitcase on the floor, paw through her travel case in the bathroom, and pull every drawer out of the dresser. One then produced a knife and began slicing the lining of her suitcase, ripping open seams and tearing out the pockets.

They were looking for something, obviously. Drugs? Hong Kong was the center of a flourishing trade in heroin, opium, cocaine, and most other drugs. Sometimes the Beijing authorities cracked down on the trade, but since they received a hefty share of the profits in taxes and payoffs, they more often looked the other way. Besides, Hong Kong's economic activities were supposed to be off limits to Beijing for the next forty-four years. What was their interest in a Japanese flight attendant?

And that raised another question. Who were these guys? Hong Kong police? PRC militia? PLA? Or even Intelligence? The civilian clothing argued against their being local police, and that wasn't good.

They might also be unconnected with the government at all . . . triad gang members engaged in a quick hit-and-run raid on some vulnerable-looking foreigners. But foreigners, Garrett knew, rarely encountered the triads unless they deliberately ventured into Hong Kong's criminal territory, getting involved in prostitution or gambling or one of the local rackets.

"What is it you want?" he said, trying to keep his voice level against the cold pressure of the pistol barrel. "Money?"

"You quiet!" the leader snapped.

"If you'll just tell us what—"

One of the other men whirled and slammed his rifle

butt into Garrett's stomach. Garrett doubled over, retching. Kazuko dropped her hands from her neck and grabbed his shoulders, shouting something at the invaders in Cantonese.

Someone grabbed Garrett and hauled him upright, shoving him back hard against the wall, then ramming the muzzle of an AK against the side of his head. Another man shoved Kazuko back, holding her arms. The leader was screaming into Kazuko's face now, a barrage of Cantonese unintelligible to Garrett except for the primal message of raw fury. These guys weren't there to rob them, he realized through a haze of hurt and nausea. And this wasn't some sort of haze-the-foreigner hassle. These guys were damn well *pissed*. . . .

Kazuko tried answering in Cantonese, but the leader shouted her down. Reaching out, he roughly grabbed her left breast, squeezing hard until she yelped and swore.

Despite the gun on him, Garrett stepped forward. "Leave her alone, damn you!"

The rifle butt caught him on the back of the head this time, driving him facedown into the carpet. He heard Kazuko scream, but far off, through a black haze of red-shot numbness that threatened to engulf him.

He fought the darkness, the pain, the dizziness, trying to roll over, but he was aware now that two of the intruders were hammering at him with their rifles. He tasted the sharp, salty tang of his own blood.

Suddenly, the blows stopped. Squinting through the pain, he could make out one of the men showing something to the leader . . . his military ID, it looked like, and Kazuko's passport and JAL identification card, pulled from her pocketbook. The leader scowled as he thumbed through cards and papers, then barked an order.

The one holding Kazuko didn't like the order. He snapped back, and slid his hand between Kazuko's thighs. The leader slashed out with his pistol, catching the man on the side of the face and spinning him away.

Kazuko crumpled to the floor next to Garrett, holding him. The leader stared down at them a moment more, as if trying to make up his mind . . . then whirled and strode for the door. The other three followed.

Garrett tried to say something comforting, but his brain was no longer working.

Helpless, he sank into oblivion. . . .

Tuesday, 20 May 2003

Near Tong'an
Fujian Province
People's Republic of China
0825 hours

The composite SEAL–Taiwan commando team had hidden in the forest throughout the first day, taking turns standing perimeter watch while the rest slept, exhausted, concealed by the heavy underbrush filling the clearing opened by the fall of a monster tree. Four of Tse's men pushed on ahead, with orders to reconnoiter the objective.

With nightfall, they'd begun moving once more, covering ground swiftly as they moved deeper inland. Four hours before dawn they reached their planned hide, a hilltop at the edge of the woods overlooking the village of Tong'an from the east. There, they used entrenching tools to dig fighting positions, roofing them over with logs, earth, and tree fronds until they were effectively invisible.

And then they settled down to wait.

SEALs were very good at waiting. During their forging as the most elite of America's fighting units, in Vietnam, they were notorious—and dreaded by the enemy—for their ability to force-march a hundred miles, then *wait*, more patiently than any cat by a mouse hole. SEALs were trained to deliberately place themselves in uncomfortable positions in order to stay awake, to outwait the enemy, to always—above all else—do the unexpected. SEALs who were questioned about why Navy personnel were carrying out operations so far from blue water learned to reply that the water in their canteens was all they needed.

Tong'an was a relatively small town tucked in beneath the loom of the mountains to the north and a swift-flowing river to the west. South lay farmland and open fields; east, the wooded mountain foothills. A large encampment, obviously military, had been erected on the southern outskirts of the town, complete with supply dump and a small airfield, and surrounded by entrenchments, barbed wire, and guard towers. They could not see their objective—a collection of vehicle-mounted IRBM launchers—but were confident that a search of the area would turn them up. Tse's men had been out searching the surrounding hills and forests for them for two days now.

Once the launchers were spotted, they would break out the laser target designator and call in the air strike. It would be ROC aircraft making the hit, but they would be launching laser-guided munitions that would home in on the LTD's reflected light to destroy the targets, no matter how well hidden or protected they might be.

At least, that was the idea. The first thing they needed

to do was find out where the enemy launchers were actually hidden. Satellite reconnaissance had identified the camp next to Tong'an as the base nearest the probable launch site, but so far no one had produced an actual mobile launcher . . . or even a tire track.

One of the first bits of housekeeping Morton took care of at their new location was setting up the satcom link. A small, dish antenna was aimed at a particular spot in the southern sky, the location of a military communications satellite in geosynchronous orbit 22,300 miles above the Earth's equator. RM1 Haggarty and RM2 Knowles, the team's radio men, set up the LST-5 radio, plugged it into the antenna, and powered up the unit.

The LST-5 operated on two channels simultaneously, one for transmission, one for reception. The Team was to maintain radio silence unless specifically ordered to communicate with headquarters. They switched on every other hour on the half hour, listening for a steady relay tone from the satellite. That tone was their lifeline to headquarters. If it were to stop . . .

Morton lay at the slit opening to the hidey-hole designated Team HQ, peering through a set of binoculars at the encampment below. He heard a slither of loose earth and turned as Commander Tse scrambled down. "The recon has returned," he said.

"Anything?"

Tse nodded. Moving to the slit, he pointed past the encampment, past the town, and up into the forest-clad slopes of the mountains beyond. "In those hills," he said. "Just there. Four mobile launchers at an old logging camp clearing. They're heavily camouflaged."

"They would be, of course." The PLA would be most concerned with U.S. Navy or Taiwanese air strikes taking out their launchers, and with American spy satellites finding them in the first place, and would have hidden them accordingly. The general location had been identified using spy sats equipped with infrared tracking gear that had picked up the heat flash of launch and followed the trail of each missile as it hurtled across the Strait of Formosa.

"The recon team has located a good site for an OP. We could move there tonight."

"Good. I'd like—" Morton stopped as MN2 Grollemeir crawled into the bunker. "What is it?"

"Message from Knowles, sir. We've lost the signal."

Shit. "I'll be right there." Morton looked at Tse. "It seems someone wants us to phone home."

Tse's eyes widened behind his grease paint. "We've gone to a war footing, perhaps?"

"That I doubt." Morton nodded toward the slit opening and the military camp beyond. "There's been damned little activity down there. If war had broken out, I'd expect the place to be buzzing like a kicked-over bees' hive."

"It won't be a recall, not now. . . ."

"Let's go find out, shall we?"

Tse nodded and wormed his way out of the hide. Morton followed.

The communications bunker was another covered-over hole in the ground a few dozen yards away, on the reverse slope of the hill away from the town. The LST-5 satcom antenna was perched on top of the branch and earth covering, carefully aligned with the satellite, invisible in the southern sky.

RM2 Chuck Knowles was crouched inside the hide, crouched over the radio. He looked up as Tse and Morton slithered into the bunker. "Hey, Skipper. Commander Tse. Incoming traffic." He handed Morton the headset.

Morton pressed the receiver against his ear, listening to the decrypted transmission. Once the steady tone had stopped, Knowles sent a coded, burst transmission, relayed by the comsat to SEAL Team Three headquarters at Coronado. Moments later a burst transmission had come back down on the receiver frequency.

"Red Dragon, Red Dragon," the voice on the headset was saying, "Cincinnati, Cincinnati . . . Red Dragon, Red Dragon, Cincinnati . . ."

"Acknowledge."

"Yes, sir," Knowles replied.

Morton looked at Tse. "It's an abort."

"No . . ." The word was soft, a hiss of indrawn breath.

"The negotiations might have borne fruit," he said with a shrug. "At any rate, they don't want us screwing up the—"

"We *have* our orders," Tse said quietly.

"Yes. We're to abort the op."

"No. I mean my people. The parafrogmen. We have orders of our own. We are *not* operating under the umbrella of USSOCOM or SEAL Team Three."

Morton felt a cold chill. "Commander Tse—"

"We will, of course, give you and your people time to withdraw from the AO."

"Commander Tse," Morton repeated, "listen to me! You and your team can't go charging off like a loose cannon! If Washington and Beijing have reached some sort of deal—"

"It is a deal to which the Republic of China is not a party, Commander Morton. Washington has operated in its own interests for decades now. We have learned that we must rely on our own resources to . . . how do you Americans say it? To stand on our own two feet to maintain our freedom."

"We have the laser designator," Morton said. "It's going back with us."

Tse shrugged, unconcerned. "You Americans are far too caught up with the magic of technology. We will carry on as we always have."

Which meant Tse and his men had all of the explosives and detonators they needed to take down the objective themselves without calling in an air strike, a classic commando op.

"Damn it, Tse, do you think the Republic of China can fight the PRC alone?" Morton demanded.

"As I said, we have been alone for a long time, since the rest of the world turned their backs on us. You, of all people, should know how vital it is to stand up to an aggressor!"

And Morton knew exactly what Tse meant. Bin Laden's Al Qaida, and the War on Terrorism . . .

"I understand, Tse. But there's a hell of a lot more at stake here than—"

"You do not understand, Commander. No non-Chinese could." And he turned and left the communications bunker.

St. Elizabeth's Hospital
Kowloon, People's Republic of China
0914 hours

"What do you mean, there's nothing you can do?" Garrett swung his legs off the hospital bed and sat up . . . and was immediately sorry he had. He hid the stab of pain, however, and the dizziness, keeping his eyes hard and cold on the pair of Hong Kong police officers standing before him.

The nurse who was with them let out a burst of singsong Chinese, then shifted to broken English. "You no get up! You no get up! You hurt!"

"I want my clothes," he told her. "Please. I need to get back to my . . . ship."

Submariners always referred to their vessel as their *boat*, not ship, but the word would have sounded faintly silly here, and Garrett desperately needed to be taken seriously. He looked across the room at Kazuko. She was sitting in a chair near the door, looking pale and worn. He'd only learned this morning that after he lost consciousness the night before, Kazuko had called for an ambulance to bring him to the emergency room at St. Elizabeth's in Kowloon. Evidently, she'd also spent some time arguing security issues with the manager at the airport hotel and called both the American and the Japanese embassies.

Garrett had awakened in the emergency room, feeling woozy, but not that much the worse for wear save for the bruises and a throbbing head. The E.R. doctor, fearing concussion or internal injury, had insisted on admitting him, and he'd been transferred to a semiprivate room.

The two Hong Kong police officers showed up at 0900 hours, one speaking perfect English, the other no English at all. Neither one was very helpful.

Garrett managed to stand up, but a wave of dizziness swept over him. He touched the side of his head and felt blood on the white gauze bandage wrapping it. The nurse pushed past the police officers and firmly pressed him back down onto the bed. "You no move!"

"I no move," he agreed. "But *please*, I want my clothes." It was impossible to maintain a sense of proper dignity for an interview with the local police while wearing a hospital gown.

He looked up at the policemen and said again, "What do you mean there's nothing you can do? One of the guys who attacked us has a nasty cut, right here." He stroked the left side of his face, showing where one of the intruders had been pistol-whipped. "And his blood's on the carpet in that hotel room."

He didn't add the obvious, that his own blood was there, too. Christ, what a beating they'd given him. . . .

"Sir, I'm afraid you overestimate our resources." The man had a pleasant, richly English accent. He'd given his name as Kuo Jung Wang. "*And* our abilities. Your attackers are long gone by now. Out of our jurisdiction."

"Attacking an American naval officer has got to be one hell of a serious crime. Don't you think Beijing is going to want to hear about this? They're going to hear about it from the American and Japanese embassies, that's for damned sure!"

"Commander Garrett," the officer said slowly, "it won't make any difference. These unfortunate things . . . happen."

"What makes you think they are gone?" Kazuko asked. She added something in Cantonese, which made the policemen look uncomfortable.

"As . . . your friend suggested, miss, attacking foreigners is a serious crime. They will have fled for the interior, where the Hong Kong authorities cannot track them."

"I'd still like to know exactly what the crime *was*," Garrett put in. "Aside from breaking and entering, assault, attempted rape, terrorist threats—"

"You did say that nothing was taken?" the officer said.

"Yeah, so it wasn't a robbery. They took off when they found my ID and Kazuko's passport."

"They were idiots," Kazuko added. "Their leader

just kept going on about me being with a *gwailo*. They seemed to think that I was Chinese."

Gwailo, Garrett knew, was a Chinese word meaning "ghost." For the past two centuries the Chinese had used it as a term for foreigners, a term translated into English as "foreign devils."

"Is that what this is all about?" Garrett asked. "Racism? They thought she was Chinese and were scolding her for having a date with an American?"

"There are . . . traditional elements in our society, Mr. Garrett," the policeman said, "elements that are unhappy at the thought of Chinese girls mingling with . . . foreigners. They may have wished to point out to the lady of the impropriety of her—"

"Impropriety my ass!" Kazuko snapped. "That bastard pinned me against the wall and screamed obscenities into my face. Half of the words he used I didn't even know, which is saying something, believe me!"

"Well, miss, perhaps you just didn't—"

"My Cantonese is excellent, thank you." She added something in Chinese, and Kuo looked startled.

"And what did he tell you that you understood?"

"He kept telling me that I shouldn't mingle the pure blood of the Middle Kingdom with . . . with *gwailo* slime. When I told him I was Japanese, he didn't believe me, told me I was shaming my parents, being like that with a foreigner. They wouldn't believe me until they found my passport."

"Officer Kuo," Garrett said, "these weren't just racist street thugs. Three of them were carrying AK assault rifles. The leader had a military-issue pistol. They were organized, and they were looking for us, specifically. I think they got the maid to show them where we were staying and to let them in."

"Yes, sir." He looked thoughtful. "These are . . . difficult times, sir. Between your government and mine. I suggest you return to your ship and do your best to forget about this."

"That's bullshit! This wasn't political!"

"Can you be certain of that, sir? In my country, nearly everything is political to one extent or another, even if politics are rarely discussed openly. Especially politics of a . . . military nature."

Garrett was about to reply, then stopped. Those four intruders last night had been military men, of that he was sure. The close-cropped hair, the hard faces, the military weapons . . . There'd been a discipline about them, too, except for that one moment at the end, when one had accosted Kazuko and been hit by the leader. And even that suggested a military hierarchy of some sort, confirming that the man with the pistol had held rank.

For some reason, he thought about Frank Gordon. The attackers hadn't been nearly as pleasant or as laid-back mellow as his old friend, but there was something about them, about their manner—their attitude, perhaps—that suggested military intelligence.

And that sent a cold shock down Garrett's spine. An American submarine officer would be a damned juicy target for a military-intelligence sting operation.

So . . . which had it been? Four well-armed thugs terrorizing someone they thought to be Chinese, sleeping with a foreigner? Or four operators out of PLA Intelligence, finding what they thought was an American submarine officer with a Chinese woman and using the situation to . . . what? Intimidate him? Compromise him? Blackmail?

There were too damned many unknowns. If they had been milint people, why had they fled when they did? Maybe they'd had orders not to involve foreign nationals other than their target. Maybe they didn't want an incident with Japan. Maybe . . .

There was no way to know, but he was sure of one thing now. The Hong Kong cops had a reputation for being very good, very thorough . . . but these two men were afraid.

And that clarified a lot. Hong Kong might be operating under the "one country, two systems" rule, but the local police were still under the thumb of Beijing's governors. They wouldn't want to find themselves in the middle, between the U.S. government and the rulers of the PRC. No doubt they would do or say anything just to make the problem go away.

"You're not going to help us, are you?" he said bluntly.

Kuo looked embarrassed. "Sir, as I told you, there is little we can do in this instance. Our jurisdiction is quite . . . limited."

"I understand. It's not your fault."

Kuo pulled a business card from his jacket and placed it on the bedside table. It had the address of a Kowloon police station, on Public Square Street. "If you wish to talk to us again, sir . . ."

"Thank you." He waited until they'd left the room before turning again to Kazuko. "I need to get back to the boat."

"You no go!" the nurse said. "You hurt!"

"Kazuko, explain to the young lady, please, that we were attacked last night by members of the Chinese military intelligence directorate, possibly in an attempt to get me to answer some questions. If she persists in keeping me here, there is every possibility that those men will come back. To this hospital. To this floor. To find me. Ask her if she wants to get caught in the middle of *that*."

He didn't like using strong-arm tactics, but there seemed no faster way to cut through the bureaucracy. Within fifteen minutes the nurse had both produced his clothing and found a doctor to sign the discharge papers. In the meantime, he'd used his room phone to reach Master Chief Dougherty, by calling the American consulate in Hong Kong and having them patch a radio call through to the *Seawolf* via the consulate's military liaison office.

"Commander Garrett!" Dougherty said. "It's damn good to hear your voice. Your friend called earlier and told us you were at St. Elizabeth's."

"That's affirmative, COB. I'm getting processed out of here now. But listen up. I think what happened to us last night might have been an intelligence sting. I think they were trying to set me up so I'd be willing to talk to them."

There was a long pause on the line. "I'm very sorry to hear about that, sir. We seem to have another ... situation."

"Talk to me, COB."

"Seven of our people have been arrested in Kowloon. They're being held at the local police lockup on Public Square Street. The word we have here is that there was a gunfight."

"Shit! Where?"

"A Kowloon hostess club. And—get this, sir—there are Russians involved."

"Interesting." He thought for a moment. "Can you put the captain on the line?"

"Uh ... nossir. He's ashore with Mr. Tollini ... at the U.S. Consulate, trying to straighten things out."

"I see." He took a deep breath. "Okay, we'll do this one ourselves. See if you can check that police station on a map. It can't be too far from where I am now."

"Right, sir."

"And round up the boat's MAA and . . . make it seven men. *With* arms. Post them on the dock, and don't let *any* local near the boat. I don't like the way this is shaping up."

"No, sir. I'm with you."

"I'll try to get the captain at the consulate. But if I can't reach him, I may need an armed shore party to come get me. COB, we might just be the sharp pointy end of a whole new war. . . ."

Near Tong'an
Fujian Province
People's Republic of China
1045 hours

"Got Commander Randall on the horn, Skipper."

About fucking time!

Morton took the handset to the LST-5. "Commander? This is Morton."

"Hello, Jack," the voice at the other end of the line said. There was the faintest of a pause between transmission and reception, partly due to the speed-of-light time lag between Earth and the communications satellite, and partly to the processor time needed to encrypt and decrypt the signal at each end. Commander Kenneth Randall, who'd been on the *Kuei Mei* Board of Inquiry three years before, was now executive officer of SEAL Team Three back in Coronado and the senior SEAL officer on the operational planning staff for this mission.

He sounded tired. "What time is it there, sir? Did I get you up?" Morton asked.

"Nah. It's about eighteen forty-five. They caught me when I got home from the base. What's up?"

"A cluster fuck in the making, sir. What the hell is going on back there?"

"Your mission's been put on hold," Randall said. "What's this I hear about you already being deployed?"

"It's true, Commander. We're on the mainland now. And my counterpart has his own orders. He's not aborting."

The pause at the other end of the line was much longer than any geosynch time lag. "You'd best start at the beginning, Jack. Give it to me slow."

Morton began filling him in on the situation.

The hell of it was, he found himself in sympathy with Tse. The Taiwanese commando was right. It *was* impossible for a non-Chinese to fully understand the long struggle—both physical and emotional—between Mainland China and Taiwan. But Morton understood perfectly the need to negotiate from strength, to not show weakness when dealing with an implacable enemy, and especially the need to hit back, and hit back *hard*, to convince the bully that further aggression was useless.

When Osama bin Laden's terrorist cells had struck at American targets—embassies in Africa, the USS *Cole* at Aden, a car bomb explosion beneath one of the World Trade Center towers in New York City—American response had been tepid at best. After the *Cole* incident, President Clinton had launched cruise missiles at terrorist camps in Afghanistan that were most likely empty by the time they were targeted. President Bush had later categorized the strike as using a ten-million-dollar cruise missile to blow up a ten-dollar tent . . . and hit a camel in the ass. The lack of a forceful response, apparently, had only emboldened the bin

Laden network . . . with tragic, unforgettably night-mare consequences in the late summer of 2001.

And as a direct result, the United States was now engaged in a full-fledged and bloody war spreading across most of the eastern hemisphere; a low-level, mostly guerrilla-style war, to be sure, but a war nonetheless. A war that had given Beijing the opportunity to make a grab for Taiwan, in hopes that the United States was too preoccupied elsewhere to respond.

If the United States had acted decisively and firmly with the first American deaths, Morton thought, if bin Laden had not been dismissed as a disaffected Saudi nutcase bankrolling his network of revolutionary fanatics, perhaps the tragic events of September 11 would never have happened in the first place.

If Neville Chamberlain hadn't given part of Czecho-slovakia to Hitler in a bid for peace in our time . . .

Hell, there was no way to second-guess history like that, he told himself. The causes of World War II lay in more than Chamberlain's political myopia, and the peace would have ended sooner or later. But certain principles were clear. Bullies rarely respected offers of negotiation, save as another form of warfare, a means of improving their position before the real fighting began. Tse's government hoped that a strong response—a *military* response—to Beijing's missile-rattling would make Beijing think twice and perhaps step back from the idea of invasion.

Wishful thinking, perhaps. Taiwan could not long resist an all-out invasion by the PRC. But if they promised that the effort would be costly enough, perhaps Taiwan could win time and even the security of world opinion.

Morton understood all of this and more. His immediate responsibility was not to the regime in Taipei, however, but to SEAL Team Three, to Washington's concept of this operation . . . and to the fifteen American SEALs stuck with him out here in the Chinese hinterlands, and not at all necessarily in that order. Getting his team out of China would have been tricky at best; without the active help and participation of Tse and his men, extraction was going to be a real bitch.

"Roger that, Commander," Randall said when Morton finished relating the situation. "Let me get back to you. Make it . . . eighteen hundred hours, your time?"

"Roger that. I copy. Eighteen hundred."

"In the meantime, keep your head down. Don't go sinking any Chinese freighters and calling attention to yourself."

"That's the submariners' job, sir. We're just along for the ride. Besides, we're a good fifty klicks inland. There's not a freighter in sight."

"I hear you. Randall out."

Another eight hours? Well, they wouldn't be able to move before dark anyway. Even Tse's men, while they'd pulled off by themselves into the woods nearby, would not be moving out before sunset. Who knew? Maybe orders would come through for the SEAL platoon to stick with the Taiwanese and help them take down those launchers.

At least the decision was out of his hands, Morton reflected. He settled down to wait.

SEALs were *very* good at waiting. . . .

Tuesday, 20 May 2003

Kowloon Police Station
Public Square Street, Kowloon
1200 hours

The sound of the old cannon banged out across Victoria Harbor on the dot of noon, just as it had every day for much of the last century. The old three-pounder, a relic from 1901, was one of the better-known landmarks in Causeway Bay, thanks to Noel Coward's 1924 song about mad dogs, Englishmen, and the noonday sun. Even though it was a reminder of British rule, it continued to sound each day in Communist-controlled Hong Kong, if only because it was now a popular tourist attraction.

Garrett was about three miles away, trotting up the steps to the Kowloon police station where the Seawolves were being held. The sound carried well across the water, however, and the distant *bang,* loud enough

254

to be heard above the traffic and street noise and echoing off distant buildings, startled him. It was a reminder that he was very much alone in hostile terrain . . . alone and unarmed.

Kazuko was on her way back to the airport. Funny. She'd seemed less shaken by the attack than Garrett. "I was talking to the people at the Japanese Consulate on the phone," she'd told him an hour ago, before they left the hospital. "It seems there've been several incidents like this happen to tourists in Mainland China. Someone breaks into a hotel room, threatens the occupants . . . racism pure and simple. They told me there was even at least one incident where an American was found with an Asian girl. They thought she was Chinese, but she was actually Japanese and the guy's wife at that." She'd shrugged. "Mistakes happen."

"That was no damned mistake," he'd told her. "Even if it was, that kind of racist crap is unacceptable no matter what the circumstances. They don't like you and me being together? They can damn well get over it.

"But everything about those creeps points to them being MMI—Ministry of Military Intelligence. They're not going to care two *yuan* who I'm dating . . . not unless it helps them somehow. And just maybe we can use that to our advantage. . . ."

He strode into the police station, a dingy, noisy place with rubbish on the floor and the mingled scents of alcohol and urine. The place must have been doing a heavy business in drunks the night before. On one wall, a large portrait of the Chinese president was flanked by a pair of bright red PRC flags.

The desk lieutenant barked something in Chinese as Garrett walked up to the desk, then looked up, saw that he was a westerner, and shifted to accented English. "Yes? You want?" A name plate on the desk had a row of Chinese characters, and the man's rank and name in English: LIEUTENANT XIAN GAO.

Garrett flashed his ID. "Commander Garrett, U.S. Navy. I need to talk to whoever's in charge here."

"I in charge," Xian said stiffly.

"You don't have a captain here?"

"This satellite station. Captain Yuen at main station, downtown. You want?"

"I want my men," he said. He was aware of how alarming he must look—an American in civilian clothes, with a bloodied gauze bandage tied around his head. "Seven men, sailors off the USS *Seawolf*. They were brought in here last night after a fight."

The man's eyes narrowed. "Your captain already call. These men held for trial. Bad, very bad. They shoot up place." He held up his hand, thumb and forefinger extended to imitate a pistol, and added, *"Chow! Chow!"*

Garrett kept his face bland. "Was anyone hurt?"

"No hurt, no bad. But much damage to place."

"My men were not armed when they went there, Lieutenant," he said quietly. "Where did the guns come from?"

"I not know. When police arrive at Fuk Wai, one of your men is holding gun, shooting at ceiling. He very lucky he not shot by police."

"Your men are well-trained, sir. If he had a gun, he must have taken it off of someone else. Who? Not your police, surely."

Lieutenant Xian looked uncomfortable. "Employees at Fuk Wai hostess club have guns."

"Ah. Did they shoot at my men first? Who started it?"

"They say they try get your men pay bill. A fight start. One of your men grab gun, shoot."

Garrett nodded. He was dancing pretty close to the

edge, not knowing exactly what had happened. He did know that U.S. sailors wouldn't have had guns while they were on liberty. Someone had been trying to impress them with a show of hardware, it sounded like, and overstepped some bounds.

"This place, the . . . what did you call, it?"

"Fuk Wai. Hostess bar. Very clean, very honest place. *Good* place."

"I'm sure it is. And the bouncers obviously had guns. What are they . . . Triad?"

He was guessing now, but at least it was an educated guess, one based on some research he'd done before leaving the boat. Many of the bars, brothels, and hostess clubs in Hong Kong either paid protection money to or were owned outright by one or another of the city's notorious triads, criminal gangs that were the Chinese equivalent of the Mafia. The triads supposedly traced their ancestry back to revolutionary groups fighting the Manchus and had helped bring that brutal regime down in 1911. Flaunting snappy names like 14K and the Bamboo Union, they were active throughout southern China in everything from youth gangs to the sellers of Swiss watch copies in the streets, and from bodyguards for wealthy visitors to the vastly powerful masterminds of sprawling and competing criminal empires.

The triads rarely had anything to do with *gwailos*; their targets of choice tended to be local businesses, the Hong Kong movie industry, Macau's gambling concessions, wealthy Chinese visitors both in China and abroad, and the traditional rackets of extortion, prostitution, loan sharking, smuggling, and corrupt politics. But western visitors might run afoul of them in the streets or in some of the sleazier hostess clubs and bars. Kazuko had told him once that some of the more colorful triad characters affected the criminal "look" made popular by Hong Kong martial arts movies— flashy suits and dark glasses.

The Communists had smashed the triad hold on the opium business in and around Shanghai back in 1949 and helped make them a truly international empire; nowadays, the triads worked hand in black hand with the PLA and with corrupt government officials. Hong Kong had always valiantly, if mostly unsuccessfully, tried to resist the gangs. The ICAC—the Independent Commission Against Corruption—had so far done a good job at exposing triad infiltration into local police and government.

But it was a losing battle, especially now that Beijing had arrived on the scene with its own ideas of how government and the Hong Kong police should be run, its own choices of personnel, its own agenda.

Xian appeared uncomfortable at the mention of the triads. "There . . . is no triad," he said. "That old story. *False* story."

Denial. A longtime favorite of politicians and city administrators everywhere when faced with a problem that would not go away. "Uh-huh. So . . . if we have local bouncers packing guns, and there's no such thing as triads, that suggests they work for someone else. Maybe . . . the PLA? The MMI?"

"What you say?"

The man's English might be broken, but Garrett knew better than to assume that poor English meant poor thinking. His eyes were hard and sharp. He knew exactly what Garrett had just suggested.

Garrett pulled the business card Officer Kuo had given him from his wallet and passed it across the desk. "This gentleman came to St. Elizabeth's and talked to me just this morning. It seems the MMI was trying to roust *me* as well, out at the airport hotel." Reaching up, he touched the bandage on his head, felt the sticky wetness on his fingertips. "They did *this* to me and assaulted my girlfriend, a foreign national. Do you detect a common thread here?"

"What are you talking about?"

Interesting. The lieutenant's English had just become a lot sharper, and more polished as well.

"I and my men are from an American nuclear submarine in Victoria Harbor. The crisis between China and the United States almost came to a head the other day. My guess is that the Ministry of Military Intelligence thought it could grab some people off that sub, make it look like an ordinary assault or a bar fight . . . and maybe pick up some information on one of America's latest submarines. What do you think?"

"Your men were arrested and brought here, sir," the lieutenant said slowly. He was looking at the business card, as though reading it carefully. "But that had nothing to do with . . . outside agencies. They were involved in a fight with the club's management, and with some Russian guests."

"Ah, yes. A group of Russian sailors. How do they figure into this?"

The man shook his head. "They not want to pay bill."

His English was slipping again. "Were they fighting with my men?"

"No. Your men . . . help Russians, when people at club try to get Russians to pay."

Garrett nodded sagely. "The old story, huh? A rip-off? A con? Put hidden charges on the patrons' bills, then threaten them with arrest or worse when they don't pay?"

The lieutenant nodded. "That . . . appears to be what happened."

"That sounds like a triad tactic. But if there's no triad, it must be an MMI trap. Which do you think?"

The police lieutenant blinked, then leaned far back in his chair. He'd just been put in a nasty double bind. He could admit to being either part of a triad con or part of an MMI sting operation against foreign nationals.

"What is it you want?"

Garrett spread his hands expressively. "I want to do what's right. The *Seawolf* has a sailors' fund, money we can use to pay for the damages and, ah, for any inconvenience. But my boat is leaving, and those seven sailors are going to be on her. Today."

He had to be careful here. He wasn't sure whether Lieutenant Xian was amenable to a bribe or not. If he wasn't, Garrett knew his offer of money had to be made in such a way that Xian could overlook it as a bribe and accept it as payment for damages.

"There are really just two ways to handle this, Lieutenant Xian," he continued. "I can walk out of here with my men and leave you the money to pay that hostess club for any damages . . . or you can keep them here and start an international incident. Our countries are close enough to war as it is, don't you think? If I were you, I'd hate to think I was the one who'd called down a cruise missile attack on Hong Kong."

"If I kept your sailors here," Xian said, all pretense of broken English gone now, "it would be because *they* had started the international incident. Not me." But he was clearly thinking about this hard. "Damages at the Fuk Wai total at least a thousand dollars, American."

Garrett doubted that was true, but in any case he didn't have that much money on him. At least it sounded as though Xian was willing to cooperate. "May I use your phone?"

The lieutenant gestured to his desk phone.

Routing the call through the American consulate again, Garrett talked with Dougherty on board the *Seawolf*. Lawless, he learned, would be back on board in a few minutes.

"Okay, COB," Garrett said. "I'll try to see the men here. Round up a shore party, as many as you can spare. Armed. Fill the captain in on the situation, and see if the paymaster can put together a thousand dollars in cash."

"What are we doing, paying ransom?"

"No. Damages. If we can settle this peacefully, we will." He glanced at the lieutenant, who was openly eavesdropping. "If *they* won't settle peacefully, though, we're going to finish this."

"Yes, *sir!*"

He hung up the phone. "Lieutenant, I'd like to see my men."

There was a moment's hesitation. "I do not yet know that I can release them into your custody."

"Lieutenant Xian, I am the executive officer of the USS *Seawolf*. That makes me responsible for the men in my command, for their behavior, for their discipline. And I assure you that they *will* be disciplined."

"And the damage at the Fuk Wai?"

"You heard me ask for the money to be brought here."

"Yes." Xian thought for a moment, calculations flicking behind dark, nearly expressionless eyes. "Very well. I'll have them brought up here."

A few minutes later the seven Seawolves were led into the station's receiving area. They had scuffs, bruises, and disarrayed clothing, but nothing worse. They walked with slow, shuffling steps, their shoelaces were gone.

Garrett caught Toynbee's eye and winked.

"All right, you miserable *excuses for human beings!"* he shouted in his best parade ground bellow. He'd been Cadet Petty Officer in Charge at Annapolis and could do a fair imitation of a drill instructor. "Fall in! Fall in on this line!"

Startled, the men toed an imaginary line in front of the police lieutenant's desk, standing at rigid attention. Pacing up the line, Garrett launched into a sulfurous tirade. "God damn it to hell! *What* were you people thinking? *Were* you even thinking at all? I am going to have your miserable, sorry hides flayed, dried, tanned, and *nailed* to the *Seawolf*'s mess deck as a warning to the rest of them!"

He reached Chief Toynbee at the end of the line, took his elbow and led him aside. "What's the word, Chief?" he said, sotto voce.

"Hey, sir." Toynbee's tired face brightened. "Good t'see you. Good t'see a goddamn friendly face."

"I hear you. You and the men okay?"

"Yeah, pretty much. Some of us were roughed up a bit when they took us in."

"Tell me what happened."

In a low-voiced murmur, Toynbee began going through the previous evening's events, ending with the gun battle in the hostess club. "Actually, I figure they was trying to hustle the Russkies. Somehow we got mixed up in it. If it wasn't for Queenie, there . . . I mean, he made those damned gorillas back down. If the cops hadn't shown up when they did—"

"Okay, okay. You have your personal stuff? Wallets, ID?"

"Nossir. They took all that shit when they brought us in here. Even took our belts and shoelaces."

"Back in line." Garrett turned on Xian. "Lieutenant, my people are going to be here in just a few minutes, and when they arrive, they are going to want to take custody of these men. I want these men's personal effects here. Now. Wallets. Papers. Everything signed, sealed, and delivered."

"Sir, I'm afraid that would be . . . difficult to arrange. You see—"

"Lieutenant Xian. Have you heard the expression 'the ugly American'? You have? Good. Because you have no idea just how ugly I can get when I am provoked. You are going to have a whole roomful of very ugly Americans in just another few minutes.

"Now . . . you are going to decide how we play this. We can assume that, um, criminal elements tried to hustle my men last night. They fought back, completely in self-defense. We are sorry for any breakages and will pay for the damages. My men go back to the *Seawolf* with me now. I assure you, on my word as a U.S. naval officer, that they will be punished for their part in the fracas last night.

"*Or* we can assume that what happened last night was a rather heavy-handed Military Intelligence operation, one that went very bad. As such, it becomes an act of war, and I and my people will respond appropriately. I will take these people out of here. Afterward, I will order that this station be targeted by a cruise missile. You've heard of them? Very accurate." He slammed his palm down on the lieutenant's desk, making him jump. "One could land precisely on *this* spot if I gave the order. Do we understand one another, sir?"

The lieutenant nodded slowly, the color draining from his face.

"Good. Frankly, if I were you, I would be looking for a way to defuse this situation before you find yourself in a hole you can't get out of. Your superiors are not going to be happy about being caught up in any

MMI plots, are they? Or in being forced publicly to acknowledge the triad presence in Kowloon. You have
more important things to do, I'm sure, than babysit
drunken American sailors *or* be the tool of PLA Military Intelligence."

Xian and Garrett locked eyes for a long moment,
neither man blinking, neither looking away. This was
the payoff, Garrett thought. He'd given Xian a way to
back down without losing face. Whether there were
gangsters behind this mess or PLA spooks, he couldn't
possibly want to have anything to do with the situation. If Xian would just let him show the way out . . .

Suddenly, Xian barked an order. Moments later several policemen arrived with boxes, the men's personal
effects. "Queensly, Kenneth," one of the officers said,
reading from a card.

"Get your things when they call you," Garrett ordered, "then get back in line. No talking."

"Uh . . . permission to speak, sir?" Toynbee said.

"What is it, Chief?"

"Well, sir . . . they got those Russians locked up
back there still. Doesn't seem right, us getting off and
them being in jail, y'know?"

Garrett sighed and looked away. "That's stretching
it, Chief," he said quietly. "I don't know if I can get you
guys out, much less the Russian Navy!"

"They're good people, sir."

"Drinking buddies? You just met them last night!"

"Well, yessir. What's your point? Like I say, they're
good people, and we shouldn't leave 'em behind. Those
cells back there are god-awful, sir."

Garrett took a deep breath, again catching the stink
of the front room. The cell areas in the back must reek
he thought. If the cleanliness of the front reception area

was any indication as to how well the police force was supported by the new government . . .

"Back in line, Chief. I'll see what I can do."

He walked over to Xian's desk. The lieutenant looked up. "I am calling my captain," he said. "This is all very irregular."

"You go ahead and call. But when my people get here, we're going out through that door."

"You Americans are very sure of yourselves."

"No. Not at all. We just don't like being pushed around by people who think they can take advantage of us." He nodded toward the doorway leading to the cell blocks. "What about the Russians you brought in with my men?"

"What about them?"

"We have established that my men may have been guilty of damaging some private property. There were several Russian naval personnel involved as well. Why should my men walk free and the Russians stay in jail?"

"Your men may not walk free, sir! And the charges are very serious! Discharging firearms within city limits . . . drunk and disorderly conduct . . ."

"The firearms were used to threaten my people first, Lieutenant. You know it and I know it. They acted in self-defense—and with considerable restraint, I might add, if they didn't outright shoot anyone. Drunk and disorderly, well, that's Navy men on liberty. Isn't the first time it's happened, now, is it? I told you, I'll pay for the damages, and if you want to put the whole city of Hong Kong and Kowloon off limits to Americans and to American money in the future, well, that's your business.

"But right now you have to decide whether you're going to be the trip wire for an international incident . . . or have the common sense and decency to let these people go. *All* of them!"

They fenced back and forth for several minutes more, but Garrett could see Xian's resolve weakening. The lieutenant did not make the threatened phone call, and after a while he gave the order to have the Russian prisoners and their effects brought to the front as well.

Garrett continued to parade back and forth in front of the Seawolves, tearing into them for everything from their disrespect of authority to their slovenly personal habits. They would, he assured them, be chipping paint for the rest of the cruise, if they didn't all wind up in Portsmouth Naval Prison for insulting their hosts in a foreign port.

It was an act, of course, and the men knew it. They played along, however, wearing expressions that ran from bland self-control to something just short of terror.

It was nearly 1300 hours when the front door to the police station opened and Master Chief Dougherty himself entered. He was wearing a Sam Browne belt with a holstered 9mm Beretta and was carrying a thick manila envelope tied shut with string.

"The skipper's outside, sir," Dougherty told him, handing him the package. "He didn't want to come in and screw up anything you had going in here. Do you need him to take over? Or the shore party?"

"Have them stand by, COB. We should be out of here in a few minutes. Transport?"

"Covered, sir."

"Great. Tell 'em we'll be out in a few minutes."

"Aye aye, sir."

He handed the envelope to Xian, who took it, unwrapped the string, and began paging through the sheaf of bills inside.

"Will that cover the damages, sir?" Garrett asked.

"Yes. Yes, this should do nicely." He looked at Garrett. "You know, I should wait until my captain gets here. I do not have the authority to release these men."

Garrett tensed. Was the whole deal going to fall through after all?

"However, Hong Kong is still in charge of her own internal affairs," Xian went on. "She takes orders from Beijing, relies on Beijing to handle all matters of self-defense and treaties. But in most ways we continue as we always have."

"I understand that, Lieutenant."

"Many of us involved in the civic administration of Hong Kong do not appreciate the . . . the interference of other groups in our affairs. Or the fact that such groups would *use* us to their own ends. There are some people flying here from Beijing now to interview your men. I recommend that you and your ship be gone by the time they get here." He tied the manila envelope closed again. "You did *not* hear this from me, however." He cracked a sudden, unexpected grin. "My English . . . not so good, no?"

Garrett extended his arm and shook Xian's hand. "Thank you, sir. Good luck to you."

"And to you, Commander."

Garrett marched the fourteen former prisoners out of the police station and into the dazzle of Kowloon's midday sun. Three large, Chinese flatbed trucks were parked outside, with a dozen of *Seawolf*'s men posted on and around them. Garrett assumed the trucks had come from the city docks—requisitioned or hijacked, he didn't know.

Captain Lawless was there in uniform, arms crossed and a fierce look on his thin face. Incongruously, there was a beefy-looking man in a Russian naval officer's uniform standing next to him, and several Russian sailors in their striped T-shirts mingled with the American sailors.

Garrett didn't salute Lawless—he was not in uniform himself—but he walked over to the captain and came to attention. "Our people are secure, sir," he said. "But I recommend we get back to the boat as quickly as we can and make all preparations for getting under way. We may be sitting on a hornet's nest here."

"So I gathered." Lawless nodded toward the Russian officer. "This is Captain First Rank Yuri Shtyrov, formerly of the Russian attack submarine *Nevolin*."

"Pleased to meet you, sir," Garrett said, bowing slightly.

"And you, Commander," the Russian said. "You have freed my men as well?"

"Yes, sir. The seven who came in with our people, at least."

"Thank you, Commander. Sometimes, after a long cruise, the men get . . . restive. They are eager to enjoy the accommodations of a foreign port and sometimes celebrate too hard."

"From the sound of it, a hostess club was trying to rip them off. That led to the fight."

" 'Rip . . . them off'?"

"Take advantage of them. Take their money."

"Ah."

"You said formerly of the *Nevolin*, sir?"

"*Da.*" He hesitated, as though measuring the two American officers. "I should perhaps warn you both. We—my crew and I—brought *Nevolin* here to turn him over to the Chinese. He is a new submarine, very fast, very powerful."

"What we call the Sierra class," Lawless said. "We knew she was in Canton. We didn't know her, uh . . .

his status." Russians always referred to their vessels as masculine.

"As of several days ago he was officially part of the PLA Navy," Shtyrov said. "We bring him to Guangzhou, turn him over to Chinese Navy. We will return on board our electronic listening vessel in Victoria Harbor. I . . . should not tell you more."

"We appreciate the word, Captain Shtyrov," Lawless said. "I suggest that right now we get the hell out of here."

"*Da*. There is a lot of hell here to get out of."

"Have your men get aboard the trucks, Captain. We'll take you to your ship."

"Thank you, Captain."

Garrett clambered into the back of one of the flatbeds, along with the men he'd retrieved from the station and several of the shore party. Dougherty handed him a Sam Browne belt with a holstered Beretta and three loaded magazines. "Just in case, sir," he said.

But the drive back to Victoria Harbor was uneventful. The little convoy picked up Hong Chong Road and followed it through the Cross-Harbor Tunnel, emerging on Hong Kong Island at Causeway Bay next to the former Royal Yacht Club. They followed Gloucester Road west then, in light traffic, reaching the naval piers at just before 1330 hours.

As the Russians climbed off the truck, Garrett and Lawless joined Shtyrov for a final good-bye. "Take care of yourselves, gentlemen," the Russian said. "I recommend that you get clear of the harbor before the *Nevolin* comes down the Pearl River. He is a good boat, with excellent ears . . . and . . . let us say he has been working closely of late with our GKS."

"Thank you, Yuri," Lawless said. "We won't forget this."

"It is we who thank you, Captain. This . . . incident would have had unfortunate repercussions, both in Moscow and in Washington."

"Until next time, then."

"Da. Dasvidanya."

"Let's get back to the *Seawolf,* Mr. Garrett," Lawless said. "It's time, as they say, to get out of Dodge."

"Aye aye, sir."

"And . . ."

"Sir?"

"Good work getting our people out of there. I was getting nowhere through the consulate."

"Seemed best to cut through the red tape, sir."

"Red in more ways than one. I was told Beijing had an interest in our people."

"It may have been an MMI sting, sir. I can't be sure . . . but I was able to use the possibility to scare the local cops. They don't like Military Intelligence screwing around in their affairs any more than we do."

"Most folks just want to be left alone, Commander. Most folks just want to be left alone."

"That, sir, is a universal given."

The trio of requisitioned trucks hurried them back to the *Seawolf.*

Tuesday, 20 May 2003

Sonar Room
USS *Seawolf*
Victoria Harbor, Hong Kong
1515 hours

"Jesus H. Fucking Christ!" Toynbee exploded as he, Queensly, Grossman, and Juarez filed into the sonar room and took their seats. "You guys should have seen Commander Garrett in action! The guy was fucking incredible!"

"Queenie here was already telling us," Juarez said. "He was hot to trot, huh?"

"He put those local cops through the hoops, let me tell ya! I ain't seen the like since I was a third class on the old *Grayback*!"

"I thought he was going to eat us for breakfast," Queensly put in. "Having us stand at attention like that? Chewing us out like a Marine D.I.?"

"That, my boy, was pure theater," Toynbee said, "and brilliantly done, too, I might add! He was doing it to let that Hong Kong police lieutenant know we would get our just desserts back on the boat and also to give the guy a way to save face."

"Are you guys gonna get any fallout?" Grossman wanted to know.

"Ah, we might get some shit details. Mr. Garrett hasn't confided in me. But I'll tell you what. Right now, I would follow Commander Garrett any damned place on Earth or off of it, just on his say-so. That man is okay in my book!"

"You guys said you were going to show me an interesting time," Queensly said, flicking on the switches on his sonar board and adjusting his headphones. "You weren't kidding, though I had kind of a different idea of what to expect."

The waterfall came to life on his screen, a glowing cascade of yellows and greens. The harbor was noisy with small craft engines, the throb of diesels, the clatter of submarine metal, chains, lines, creaking hulls, and all the rest, making it the acoustical equivalent of opaque.

"Yeah. The ol' Fuk Wai has changed management or something," Toynbee said. "Didn't use to be a rip-off joint. That's really pretty disappointing. Now, when we get back to San Diego, we'll have to take you to this place we know on the main drag in from the waterfront. Man, I tell you, the girls there are so—"

"Chief Toynbee?" Captain Lawless was standing in the doorway to the sonar shack. "When you're through with your dissertation, I would appreciate some *work* from you for a change. We're supposed to be listening to noise here, not making it."

"Sir. Yes, sir."

"You other gentlemen squared away all right?"

"Yes, sir," Grossman said. "Can't hear shit out there, though. Harbor crap."

"Understood. But keep a close watch anyway. Once we get under way, we might have some interest from the harbor patrol, if nothing else. And I want you to be especially sharp on the lookout for other subs. This is the perfect place for us to pick up a tail."

"Could a sub follow us submerged in here, Captain?" Queensly wanted to know.

"I don't know, Queensly. I wouldn't want to try it if I didn't know the channel well and have some damned good charts. But we can expect that the Chinese have just that, and I don't want to be surprised."

"We're going to have the devil's own hell of a time picking up a tail in that clutter, sir," Toynbee pointed out. "And the channel's so narrow, we won't be able to clear our baffles."

"I know. Do your best. I don't expect miracles out of you people. Just magic."

"Aye aye, sir."

When the skipper had left, Toynbee let out a whoosh of pent-up breath. "Man. He does not sound happy."

"Would you be, Chief?" Grossman pointed out. "You're in command of *the* most expensive submarine in the U.S. fleet, and your bosses tell you to take it into a potentially enemy harbor just as sweet as if you-please. Then some of your people screw up and get the locals mad, and you have to get out before things turn ugly. How would you feel?"

"Yeah. I see what you mean."

"Kind of like steering a brand new Rolls-Royce into a demolition derby, huh?" Juarez said with a grin. "Or the local megamall at Christmas rush!"

"Submariners need blue water," Toynbee said philo-sophically. "And lots of it. Let's see what we can hear out there for the skipper, guys."

Radio Shack
USS *Seawolf*
Victoria Harbor, Hong Kong
1520 hours

"Man, it is *so* good to hear your voice," Garrett said, pressing the telephone handset against his ear. "Thanks for making the call."

At the other end of the line, Kazuko laughed. "I'm just sorry our good-byes were so . . . abrupt!"

The line crackled with static. Kazuko had put the call through from a phone on board the JAL jetliner that was at this moment passing out of Chinese air-space and over the South China Sea. The call was being routed to the U.S. Consulate and then to the *Seawolf* by a ship-to-shore line, and the numerous connections made for bad hearing.

Still, it was so good to hear her voice.

"I'm just glad to know you're off the ground and on the way home, hon."

"Yes. My office put me on the first plane back to Tokyo. I'm flying as a passenger, no less! I feel like a queen!"

"You are one, love."

"Flatterer. Anyway, there's talk of them giving me some time off, with pay, because of what happened."

"I'm jealous."

"So . . . when are *you* getting out of Hong Kong?"

"I . . . don't know." It was a lie, of course, the typical submariner's secrecy reflex. There was no telling who might be listening in on this line, even if it was supposed to be secure. "Pretty soon, I imagine." In another two hours or so, in fact.

"I was hoping we could pick up on unfinished good-byes back in Tokyo."

"You know I'll call as soon as I get in, hon. As soon as I can. But I don't know when that will be."

"I know." He heard the sadness in her voice. "I know. I've been listening to the news. Have you?"

"They have CNN going on a box in the wardroom."

"The negotiations are going pretty well, they say. Maybe there won't be a war after all."

"That," he said with heartfelt warmth, "would be wonderful." He'd read, once, that no one loved peace more than the warriors who had to do the fighting. He could not have agreed with that sentiment more.

"I'm looking out the window now," she told him. "We're above the ocean. I'll be home in a few hours. I'll . . . be waiting for you, Tom."

"And I'll be with you just as quick as the situation permits, love."

"What did you say?" Her voice was very far away, thick with static.

"I said I love you!"

"I'm having trouble hearing you, Tom . . . and this call is really expensive. I'd better go. I love you."

"Love you!" he practically shouted.

And then she was gone.

He hung up the handset and turned to find Captain Lawless standing in the passageway outside.

"Your girl okay, Commander?"

"Yes, sir."

"I, ah, didn't mean to eavesdrop on a private conversation."

"It was hardly that, sir. Not when I have to shout to be heard."

"I just wanted to be sure she was squared away and safe."

"Thank you, sir. Her airline is flying her out. She's in the air now, in fact."

"I'm glad. That sounded like a hell of a bad experience you two had last night."

"It wasn't fun, sir," he said, lightly touching the gauze wrapped around his head. His body ached all over. "I feel like I've been through a meat grinder."

"And you look worse."

"Thank you, sir, so very much. That's the nicest thing anyone's said to me all day."

"Well, let me say something else nice . . . and that will be my quota for the month. You did good, getting our people out of that Kowloon jail. Well done, Tom."

"Thank you, sir. Just doing my job as XO."

"A boat's executive officer has the responsibility of looking after the men of his command, of seeing to the discipline, morale, training, and smooth functioning of all personnel on board," he agreed, as though reciting from a naval officer's textbook. "Absolutely correct. But a lot of XOs would have let the COB take care of bailing the men out of jail. They wouldn't have bothered to get their hands dirty."

"I was close to the police station, sir. And I'd already talked with one of the cops. It just seemed like the right thing to do."

"Well, I appreciate it. If we'd waited and tried to go through channels, God knows how long we would have been tied up here in port."

"Yes, sir."

"Do you have recommendations for disciplinary action?"

"Sir, from the sound of it, our people were being hustled. If you want a captain's mast—"

"I want to know what you think should be done."

"Captain," he said formally, "it is my opinion that ignoring the whole incident will not have an adverse effect on the discipline of this vessel."

"I'm not sure we can ignore the incident. They were drunken and disorderly, and we had to damn near hijack three port authority trucks to get them out of there. I'm still trying to figure out how I'm going to explain sending an armed shore party into Kowloon on my report."

"Yes, sir. But the days of Americans letting themselves get shoved around by the rest of the world just because we're Americans, because we're supposed to be the good guys, are over. And a damned good thing, too, if you ask me. Sir."

Lawless nodded, and sighed. "Agreed. Well, I'll take that under advisement. I do want a complete report from you on what happened to you and your friend at the hotel last night, and another report on what happened at the police station. I will also expect you to debrief the men involved, get their official versions of the story down on hard copy."

"Yes, sir."

"God knows what CINCSUBPAC is going to make of this mess."

Garrett grinned. "With luck, sir, there'll be a war, and no one will care."

"In which case, God help us all."

Near Tong'an
Fujian Province
People's Republic of China
1625 hours

Tse's men left the commando hide in the afternoon, long before sunset. Twice, PLA helicopters—big, lumbering Mi-8 transports—passed overhead, circling above the hills as if carrying out a search. Tse thought that those transports might be looking for the commando team and ordered his men to move off through the woods. "We cannot wait any longer, Commander," he told Morton. "If we stay here, the enemy will sniff us out. I strongly recommend that you get your people back to the beach as quickly as possible. Wait for dark, then swim across to Kinmen. You have the passwords and security information. . . ."

"I don't like this, Commander Tse," Morton told him. "We're trained not to leave our own behind."

Tse smiled. "Thank you for including us with your company, sir. We are honored. However, this is something my people must do . . . for ourselves, whether we have your country's help or not."

"I understand."

Morton watched the Taiwanese commandos slip off into the woods, almost invisible in their bracken-camouflaged jackets and gear, as silent and as tightly disciplined as any SEAL platoon. He was still waiting to hear from the World but had little hope that Washington or SOCOM would be able to clarify this muddle. From the sound of it, the SEALs had been deployed across the Formosa Strait, then forgotten.

Or were they part of some larger picture, something SOCOM hadn't bothered to share with the men on the ground?

The worst of it was, the SEALs were not equipped to fight a major battle. The whole idea of covert ops was to stay covert, to stay hidden, to carry out your mission and, ideally, never even let the enemy know you'd been there, until it was too late.

And nothing could screw a good covert op faster than a cluster fuck somewhere back in the rear echelons. That was what every SEAL, every SEAL commander, dreaded above all else: being sent into a hot operations area with bad intelligence, with no clear idea of what was going on, with a poorly conceived or fuzzy set of mission parameters, without adequate backup and support.

Morton and the SEALs were now running completely blind, deep in hostile territory with no idea what their status might be. Their contact with the folks back home was intermittent and frustratingly piecemeal, and from the sound of it, *they* didn't know what was going on either. *Not* good. Not good at all.

They waited. Tse's advice—to pack up and move out—was good, but Morton didn't want to dismantle the satellite dish until he'd heard from Randall. It was a lot safer to move at night in any case. The SEALs didn't know the ground here the way the Taiwanese did.

Damn it all, what was going on back in the States?

A loud clatter sounded overhead, coming from above the woods to the east. A moment later another Mi-8 transport thundered low above the SEAL OP, flying toward the town of Tong'an. What the hell was going on down there?

He didn't think they would have to wait much longer to find out.

USS *Seawolf*
Victoria Harbor, Hong Kong
1648 hours

"Cast off all lines, fore and aft," Lawless said over his radio headset. He and Garrett stood in *Seawolf*'s narrow weather bridge, high atop the sail, looking down on the deck party in their bright orange life jackets as they took in the mooring lines.

"Cast off all lines, fore and aft, aye, sir," the response came back over the radio speaker on the small sail console.

It was late afternoon, and the sun was hovering low above the mountains to the west—Victoria Peak and Mount Davis. The harbor, as always, was crowded with small craft, junks, yachts, sailboats, fishing craft, and shipping of every size and description.

"Maneuvering, Bridge. Slow astern."

"Bridge, Maneuvering, aye. Slow astern, aye aye."

Three blasts from *Seawolf*'s whistle warned craft astern that she was backing down. Gently, the *Seawolf* began moving away from the pier. The trucks they'd used to escape from Kowloon had been left on the dockside. A cursory radio message had just been sent to the Hong Kong Port Authority informing them that *Seawolf* was under way. A longer and far more detailed message had been sent to COMSUBPAC, informing them of the incident in Kowloon and of the need to get *Seawolf* clear of the harbor and into the safety of deep water. No submariner felt truly secure on the surface, and *Seawolf* would not be able to submerge until she reached open blue water, around the curve of Hong Kong Island and well past Cape Collinson.

There was no reason to think that the authorities would try to stop the *Seawolf* now. And yet . . .

"It'll be good to be in blue water again," Lawless said. "What did you think of Shtyrov?"

"He seemed to be a decent enough sort. He was trying to warn us that the Russian GKS had given the Chinese our signature. I'd guess that they sold them the data, along with that boat. Part of a package deal."

"Yes."

Seawolf might be the most silent of all submarines in the sea, but all vessels made some noise, simply by having their screws turn through the water. GKS acoustic listening vessels like the one in Victoria Harbor now were designed to make recordings of the sounds other ships made, specifically for the libraries in Russian sonar shacks. Evidently, the Russians had sold the Sierra to the Chinese Navy and included sound tapes of various American vessels the sub might one day soon be facing in combat. They would, of course, have recorded the *Seawolf*'s acoustical signature as she entered the harbor on Sunday, and that would have been part of the package.

If the Chinese had *Seawolf*'s signature, it would be easier for them to track her, to pick out the little sound she did make from the background noises of the sea. It would also help them with weapons targeting, by giving acoustical homing torpedoes a specific sound to track.

Seawolf was well out into the harbor now. "Maneuvering, Bridge," Lawless said. "Left full rudder. Come to zero-nine-zero. Make revolutions for five knots."

Seawolf began churning slowly forward through the crowded harbor.

Near Tong'an
Fujian Province
People's Republic of China
1709 hours

"Listen, sir!" RM2 Knowles said. "Gunfire!"

Morton heard it, a far-off chatter of automatic weapons fire. A lot of it.

Among SEALs and other Special Forces operators, it was an axiom that, for most missions, if you had to open fire, the mission was already a failure.

At a guess, Tse and his parafrogs had just put their collective webbed feet deep in the middle of it.

Morton crawled out of the communications hide and made his way across the forested slope to another roofed-over trench, where his 2IC was waiting. "Hey, Jammer."

"Yessir. I hear it."

"We can't stay here. Chinese helos have been circling around all day. I don't want to wait for the word from SOCOM."

"Roger that, Skipper. What about Tse's men, though?"

He nodded. That was the problem. Technically and officially, the Taiwanese parafrogs were on their own, especially after they'd strayed from the operations plan.

But the SEALs and the commandos had worked and trained together, shared the mission this far together, sweated out the wait together. It would be just plain wrong to light off for the sea, abandoning Tse and his men to their fate.

"Jammer, we're going back to help Tse."

"Aye aye, Skipper. I don't like it, but aye aye."

"Good man."

"Are you going to tell headquarters?"

Morton grinned in the darkness of the hide. "Why? It would just confuse them some more." He was still angry at the confusion, and the fact that the SEAL Team appeared to have been left dangling in the breeze.

"When do you want to move out?"

Morton listened for a moment to the crackle of gunfire. If anything, it was increasing in intensity. "Immediately," he decided. "Tse's men don't have the expendables for a sustained battle, and we can't afford to wait. Tell your people to saddle up. We're moving out now."

"Roger that, Skipper."

Another helicopter flew overhead from the east, banking north, toward the sound of the gunfire.

Morton wondered if the SEALs were going to be in time.

USS *Seawolf*
Victoria Harbor, Hong Kong
1712 hours

A mournful whistle sounded to starboard. Garrett and Lawless both turned, raising their binoculars. The Russian GKS vessel was still moored in the harbor; through the binoculars, Garrett could see several officers on the ship's weather bridge staring back at them through binoculars of their own. One of the Russians raised his cap in salute.

Lawless replied with the same gesture. "Seems kind of strange being buddies with those guys, doesn't it?" he said.

"Times change, Captain. And we're still facing their technology, if not their animosity."

"You got that right. Uh-oh, they're flashing us. How's your Morse?"

"Rusty, sir, but passable." He trained his binoculars on the flickering pulse of the Russian vessel's semaphore lamp. "Looks like . . . 'you . . . have . . . tail.' "

"What the hell?" Lawless said, lowering the binoculars.

"A Chinese sub, Skipper. Has to be. Following in our baffles. We can't hear her, but that GKS over there has some pretty sensitive listening gear. They may have a sonar track on our shadow."

"Figures they would have a sub waiting to follow us out."

"This could be a problem, sir."

"Not so long as we're still at peace, Mr. Garrett. And please God we stay at peace until we're clear of this damned harbor. . . ."

Garrett turned in the cockpit, raising his binoculars and scanning the waters aft of the *Seawolf*. He couldn't see anything. And yet . . . "Do you think a submarine could follow us through this channel *submerged*, sir?"

"Queensly asked me that. I wouldn't care to try it myself. But it's possible."

"Let's see. The main channel's marked at twenty to twenty-five meters' depth. *Seawolf* carries an eleven-meter draft, and our sail adds ten meters or so on top of that. It would be damned tight for us."

"What about an Akula?" Lawless said.

"About the same. Ten meters' draft. The Akula's sail is pretty squat, though. Maybe five, six meters? They'd have a bit more room to play in."

"Not much. Especially with harbor traffic this heavy, I wouldn't want to try it."

"No, sir. But I'll tell you what does worry me . . ."

"What's that?"

"A Kilo, sir. Six and a half meters' draft. Five meters or so on the sail. And only seventy-three meters long."

"Hmm."

"If I was skipper of a Kilo, and my orders were to keep tabs on the Yankee-dog *Seawolf* submarine in my harbor, I might gamble that by following in his baffles, submerged, I could trust *him* to clear the surface traffic out of the way."

"He'd have to tuck in real close."

"Yes, sir, he would."

Both men trained their binoculars aft again, searching for a periscope, a swelling on the surface of the harbor, anything that might hint at an unseen companion astern.

"Lookouts! Keep a close watch astern. We may have a tail."

"Aye aye, sir!"

"I'll tell the sonar crew," Lawless said, picking up the handset.

"Even knowing," Garrett said, "I don't know what we can *do* about it."

"Try prayer," Lawless replied.

It sounded reasonable. There wasn't a whole lot else available to them right now.

Tuesday, 20 May 2003

Guangdong Administrative District Fleet Naval Headquarters
Guangzhou, People's Republic of China
1726 hours

The war began in earnest at approximately 1730 hours, Tuesday, May 20, and it began in the office of Li Guofeng.

Admiral Li was a survivor, one of the old guard of the PLA who'd somehow retained position and rank through the swirl of purges, reorganizations, and administrative house cleanings that had been the norm for any long-term military career within the People's Republic. He still favored plain olive-drab working uniforms without the gold braid and finery of rank, a holdover from the days of Mao when rank, theoretically, at least, was considered counterrevolutionary and bourgeois.

The man who'd just entered his office held similar taste and similar tenure. General Zhang Yun Hai was the commander of the Fujian District ground forces and, as such, was one of the most powerful men in the PLA. Since Fujian was opposite the Strait of Formosa from the old enemy, Taiwan, the local militias and PLA forces received the best of men, equipment, and military appropriations, second only to the Beijing District itself. It had long been established that the final reunification of China would begin from Fujian, with local forces invading Taiwan. Too, if the rebels in Taipei were ever foolish enough to attempt an invasion of the mainland itself, the blow would surely fall there.

Technically, the two men were at the same level of rank, but Zhang was nominally Li's superior by virtue of a year's seniority. Li was in overall command of PLA fleet assets in Fujian and here in Guangdong and was charged with the defense of the PRC coast from Hainan to Fuzhou. They shared command with a third man, General Lung Ziyi, who was in charge of the Fujian District's PLA air units, but Lung was in Beijing now, and Zhang was in control of the local air force. Neither of them trusted Lung, a newcomer and a decided sycophant with the political cadres in the capital.

They sat in Li's office, drinking green tea and studying the map spread out on the desk between them. Several aides were with them, marking the locations of enemy and neutral vessels and aircraft in the area.

"But can we get the Americans to break off the negotiations?" Li was saying. "World opinion will stand against us if we attack while in the midst of negotiations."

"Beijing should not have allowed the negotiations in the first place," Zhang said. "It is diverting us from our true will, our true course of action."

"They vacillate, unsure which way the winds are blowing. We need to help things along."

"Agreed. But—"

He was interrupted by a knock on the door. "Come!" Li said.

An orderly on the admiral's staff stepped inside and saluted. "Comrade General! Colonel Wong to see you, sir. He says it is most urgent."

Li exchanged glances with Zhang. "Send him in."

Colonel Wong Hui Ling was on the HQ staff for the Fujian Military District and as such reported directly to General Zhang. However, during Zhang's visit to Guangzhou, he'd stationed himself in the Fleet Communications Center, where he was monitoring the situation along the coast. A small, thin, acid-faced man, he was known to be extremely ambitious . . . and therefore dangerous politically. The trick was to keep him so busy with important and heavily detailed work that he didn't have time to play politics.

"Comrade Admiral," Wong said, saluting. "Comrade General, an important radio message just came in. It's from Tong'an."

"Ah!" Zhang said. "They have taken the bait?"

"So it would seem, sir. Elements of the Xiamen Guard and local militia have engaged a strong force in the hills above Tong'an. We believe them to be Taiwanese commandos."

"The reinforcements have been moved into place?"

"Yes, sir. As ordered. We have them trapped."

"It would seem, Comrade General," Li said slowly, "that this gives us the opportunity we have been looking for."

"Indeed. With enemy commandos on our shore, at the same time as we are engaged in peace negotiations with the West, it will be *us* with whom world opinion stands."

Li swept his hand across the chart on the desk. "We have a number of possible naval targets here. The American carrier elements are still too far at sea for an effective strike, but some of their frigates are already within the strait."

"Is it wise to attack the Americans as well as the Taipei rebels?" Zhang wondered. "If we restrict our strikes to Taiwanese forces, we can more effectively maintain our contention that this is strictly an effort to reunify China."

"We have discussed this, General," Li said, "many times. The Americans came to Taiwan's defense when we began lobbing missiles at Taipei. They deployed a number of fleet elements, including their new Seawolf-class submarine to the strait. We need to demonstrate, without equivocation, that *we* control the Strait of Formosa. Not Taipei. And not the Americans." Reaching out again, he pointed at a blue symbol drawn on the map, seventy kilometers off the coast near Xiamen— and the rebel stronghold on Kinmen Island. "This ship. What is it?"

"Sir," an aide said, leaning forward to study the symbol, then checking the notebook in his hand. "That is an American vessel . . . a Perry-class frigate, the *Jarrett*. FFG 33. We believe she is performing an antisubmarine sweep ahead of the arrival of the American carriers."

"That ship might also be operating in support of the commando forces ashore," Zhang added. "Providing technical or communications support."

"That, at least, would be a viable claim," Li said. "Comrade General? I suggest that this is your next target."

Zhang considered for a moment, then nodded. "I agree." His eyes strayed south along the coast, to Hong Kong, where another blue symbol had been drawn. "And what of the American submarine *Seawolf*?"

"*Changcheng* is already tracking her, in concert with one of our diesel boats. I dispatched her down the Pearl River this afternoon, and she should be in the Hong Kong operations area by now. Her orders are to keep the *Seawolf* under observation, to follow her if she leaves port . . . and to be ready to sink her at our command."

Zhang nodded. "Good. This entire operation depends on your submarines, Admiral. The *Changcheng*, especially . . . but the diesel boats as well, operating in support. We will need to free the *Changcheng* from her escort duties in order to use her against the American Seventh Fleet."

"I agree."

"But the American should be sunk in international waters. Not in Victoria Harbor."

"Yes. As of our latest reports, the *Seawolf* is still at Hong Kong. We expect her to leave momentarily, however. There was an . . . incident in Kowloon last night, with some of the *Seawolf*'s crew. The American sailors were under arrest. MMI hoped to interrogate them. Unfortunately, the local authorities freed them before MMI personnel could get there. We expect, however, that this will goad the Americans into putting to sea once more. They will not wish to be trapped inside that harbor or its approaches."

"Hmm. Which would be better, then? To sink her at the dock, and screw *gwailo* opinion? Or retain the semblance of legality, and sink her in international waters?"

"Best, General, would be in the harbor approaches.

The water is shallow, the channel too narrow to allow for maneuvering. She would be an easy target."

"But that would still make us look bad in the world's eyes, Comrade Admiral."

Li shrugged. "General, if war has already broken out—and the sinking of the USS *Jarrett* will be nothing less than a final and complete declaration of war—what matters it where we sink the *Seawolf*. If anything, sinking her in one of the Hong Kong approach channels makes recovery work simpler. Imagine what technological and military secrets must be stored aboard her!"

Zhang nodded, thinking about this for another moment. "Very well. Timing is critical, and I do not want to attack the *Seawolf* while she is tied to the dock. Perhaps we could intern her instead?"

"If they are still at the pier, of course." That would be infinitely preferable. The secrets to be won . . .

"If not—"

Another knock sounded.

"Come!" Li said impatiently.

"Comrade Admiral!" the orderly said, handing Li a message flimsy. "This radio traffic just came in from Hong Kong."

Li read the paper, then smiled. "Our decision has been made, General. The *Seawolf* left her pier a few minutes ago."

"So, she is still in Chinese waters?"

"Yes. Moving into the east approaches to Hong Kong."

"Then I suggest we commence the next phase of the operation at once." He looked at Wong. "Colonel. You will give the order to our detachment at Tong'an. Target the American frigate."

"Yes, sir!"

"If I may suggest, as well, General," Li said, "one of the new diesel boats is positioned here, not far from Kinmen. It could serve as backup in the attack."

"An overwhelming attack, from sky and sea." Zhang clasped his hands behind his back, staring down at arcane symbols scrawled on the map. "And so it begins."

"And so it continues, Comrade General. We merely complete what was begun when we swept Chiang from the mainland, fifty-four years ago."

"Patience is an extremely rewarding virtue, Admiral," Zhang said, "if a difficult one to observe. Fifty-four years . . ."

"The Middle Kingdom has traditionally followed the long, sure path, Comrade General, even if the journey takes a century."

"I wonder where it will lead us?" Zhang asked. "I wonder. . . ."

Near Tong'an
Fujian Province, People's Republic of China
1740 hours

"Skipper! Look!"

Morton raised the binoculars to his eyes, looking down into the clearing. The SEALs had made a quick passage across the hills above Tong'an, closing on the sporadic sound of gunfire up ahead. They'd reached a spot overlooking a crossroads in a woods-shrouded meadow and had gone to ground when they saw several PLA troops moving along one of the dusty roads.

With a rumble of heavy engines, two massive vehicles lumbered out from beneath heavy canopies of camouflage netting and woven tree branches. They appeared to be Chinese variants of old Soviet Zil-135 eight-wheeled trucks, carrying forty-foot, two-stage rockets on their beds. Troops were bustling around them, obviously getting them ready to fire. An armored personnel carrier squatted at the edge of the forest, standing guard.

Morton glanced at his watch. It still wasn't time to hear back from SOCOM, even if they still had the satcom antenna set up. Sixteen SEALs armed with assault rifles—they wouldn't have a chance against those troops down there. They had no antiarmor weapons save for plastic explosives and their laser designator, but you had to get right up to the target to use the plastique, and the laser required someone on hand to deliver the guided force package, an aircraft or a ship capable of firing Copperhead rounds.

Besides, SEALs weren't intended to take part in heavy, stand-up slugfests with an alert and well-armed enemy. It would be suicide to try.

The SEALs could do nothing but watch, helpless, as the PLA soldiers suddenly scattered into the surrounding woods, the missiles elevated slightly, and then with a shrill whoosh one of the weapons hissed off its launch rail on a contrail that filled the meadow with a billowing white fog.

Seconds later the second missile fired, following the first on streaking contrails low across the hills and forest toward the southwest.

Were they opening fire again on Taiwan? Or was this something different?

Morton knew he had to get some answers from HQ,

and fast, because until he did, he was fighting blindfold and with hands tied. *And* he had to find Tse and his commandos.

If he had just been dropped into the middle of World War III, he wanted the hell to know about it.

Strait of Formosa
Off the Fujian Coast
1805 hours

The wind was picking up, with the promise of a rain squall sweeping in from the northeast. The USS *Jarrett* plowed ahead through increasingly heavy swells, heading south just outside the twenty-mile international boundary.

The first warning of any threat came from her radar watch as one blip, then a second, appeared on her screens, angling in from the northwest. There was a critical moment's delay as the radar operator attempted to verify the sighting. No one wanted a repeat of the deadly accident that had taken place in the Persian Gulf, when a frigate much like the *Jarrett* had accidentally downed a civilian airliner, thinking it an oncoming missile.

There could be little doubt, however, once hard course plots were made. The incoming objects were skimming the waves, streaking directly toward the *Jarrett* on intercept courses at just under the speed of sound. Targeting profiles matched entries in the ship's target library: an improved Hai Ying land-launched solid-fuel-booster surface-to-surface missile, mounting a five hundred kilogram warhead, a range in excess of a hundred kilometers, and a speed of Mach 0.9, known in the NATO code lexicon as "Silkworm."

Operating this close to a potentially hostile shore, the *Jarrett* was already at full alert. General Quarters was sounded nonetheless, as Captain Bennings ordered the helm hard over. By presenting his stern to the oncoming missiles, he narrowed *Jarrett*'s target area sharply and also gave a clear field of fire to the Mark 15 CIWS mount above the *Jarrett*'s fantail helicopter deck.

The Close-In Weapons System, CIWS, known affectionately throughout the service as "C-whiz," was a Vulcan/Phalanx point-defense gun designed to destroy antiship missiles. The multibarrel M61A1 gun cycled at an incredible rate—hurling fifty 20mm depleted uranium rounds per second; the gun was served by two radars—one tracked the target and a second tracked the outgoing rounds. A computer compared radar data and constantly adjusted train and elevation automatically, to bring the two radar pictures together and deluge the target with a literal hail of destruction.

The maximum horizontal range was only about fourteen hundred meters—less than a mile; there was no second chance if the technology failed.

And the technology did not fail. The first silkworm missile was brought under direct fire at maximum rage. The CIWS above *Jarrett*'s helipad swiveled, elevated, then sounded with its characteristic shrill, high-pitched whine, sending a stream of depleted uranium across the ocean swell astern. It fired . . . corrected . . . fired . . . corrected again, then loosed a final three-second burst dead on target. A dazzling flash half a mile astern marked the missile's death as the warhead detonated. Three seconds later the boom of the explosion reached the *Jarrett* across the open water.

Immediately, the CIWS barrel pivoted slightly and began firing again, using short bursts to walk the rounds into the second target. There was no explosion this time; the Silkworm broke apart under the barrage, chunks and pieces tumbling in smoke-trailing arcs into the water.

On board the *Jarrett*, cheers broke out, first in the combat center, then spreading throughout the ship. Captain Bennings barked an order over the ship's loudspeaker system, demanding quiet. The ship had just been fired upon, and they had to assume that they were now at war. More missiles might be fired at any moment.

Jarrett's sonar watch picked up the faint hum of the next attack minutes later . . . a spread of three torpedoes coming in from port. Bennings barked new orders, swinging *Jarrett*'s knife-edged prow hard to port in an effort to turn into the torpedoes, to minimize the ship's target silhouette and perhaps to get inside the torpedoes' arming radius.

But it was already too late. Three wire-guided homing torpedoes fired from the PLA Navy submarine *Hutiao*, the "Leaping Tiger," went active, their onboard sonars pinging shrilly off the *Jarrett*'s hull. Once active, their wires were cut, allowing them to swim free as they acquired their own solid tracking locks on the American frigate.

There was, unfortunately, no undersea equivalent of the CIWS. Moments later the first torpedo struck the *Jarrett* on her port bow, detonating with a savage explosion that ripped a fifteen-foot hole through her thin hull. The second torpedo missed or failed to detonate . . . but the third, running deep, passed directly under the stricken frigate's keel and exploded, nearly lifting the 2,700-ton vessel clear of the water and snapping her spine.

The *Jarrett* sank swiftly, most of her crew still at their battle stations as the frigate broke in half and the sea came crashing in. A pall of oily black smoke towered above the Strait of Formosa.

Weather Bridge
USS *Seawolf*
Eastern Approaches to Hong Kong
1807 hours

"You know," Garrett said thoughtfully, raising his binoculars to his eyes again, "I'm getting a really uneasy feeling about this. I think that destroyer to port is moving to cut us off."

Seawolf had made the turn around Hong Kong Island and was moving south now, picking up speed as she neared open water. There was less traffic in the water about them, and the shorelines to east and west were receding at last. For the past ten minutes, however, a Luda-class destroyer had been coming up on them fast from astern, passing them to port a good thousand yards off.

Now, though, the Luda's sharp prow had swung over and the lean, gray vessel was slicing through the water at twenty-eight knots, reaching past the *Seawolf* on a course that would put her squarely across the American sub's bow in another few minutes.

The Luda was a deadly looking craft, similar in design to one of the old Soviet Kotlins. Over 130 meters long, displacing 3,250 tons, she was long and sleek of hull, with a bridge house that appeared too large for her low hull, twin stacks widely separated by surface-to-surface missile tubes, and with armament of every description bristling on her deck from the twin 130mm turret mount on her bow to the conventional depth charge racks on her long, flat fantail. Her weaponry included 37mm and 25mm antiaircraft guns, ASW rocket tubes, depth-charge mortars . . . an arsenal geared to hunt down and kill submarines.

"I think you're right," Lawless said. Picking up the phone handset, he said, "Weps. This is the captain."

"Ward here, sir" crackled over the sail speaker.

"Give me the update on our loaded warshots."

"All tubes loaded, per your orders, Captain. Tubes One and Three are flooded. Outer hatches closed."

"Give me a track on target Romeo One-one-niner, and update."

"Aye aye, sir. Romeo One-one-niner now at relative bearing three-three-four, range nine-nine-oh, speed two-seven knots. We have solid tracking data on radar and sonar."

"Target Romeo One-one-niner, Tube One."

"Target Romeo One-one-niner, Tube One, aye, sir."

"Only one?" Garrett asked. The usual practice was to assign two fish to a target.

"I'm still worried about our shadow. I don't want to—" Lawless stopped, his gaze locked on the Chinese destroyer. "Uh-oh. This may be it."

A semaphore light winked from the Luda's starboard bridge wing. Garrett raised his binoculars to his eyes and spelled out the words as each Morse letter flickered across the open water. "Heave . . . to . . . or . . . I . . . fire . . ."

One of her bow guns flashed, as if to punctuate the order. The bang followed a couple of seconds later, as the shell keened across the Seawolf's bow and struck the sea, raising a thundering geyser of water ahead and to starboard.

"Lookouts below!" Lawless shouted. The sail lookouts promptly dropped through their hatches. "You, too, Number One."

"Captain—"

"I'm right behind you, damn it. Clear the bridge!" He already had the phone handset to his head. "Conn! This is the captain! Take us down!"

Garrett dropped through the open hatch in the weather bridge deck, catching the ladder halfway down and sliding the rest of the way to the first level on the rails. He hit the deck and looked up, waiting for Lawless to follow.

A thunderous cacophony filled the sail, like jackhammers pounding on sheet metal. Garrett shouted with stunned pain, hands to his ears. The Luda had seen the lookouts leaving their posts, perhaps noticed *Seawolf* beginning to settle into the water at the skipper's command, and opened fire . . . probably with light antiaircraft guns.

Garrett grabbed the ladder railing and scrambled back up, poking his head up through the round and open hatch. Another fusillade of enemy fire swept the *Seawolf*'s superstructure, rounds slamming into her sail.

Captain Lawless was slumped against the cockpit's starboard side, huddled down, as if cold. "Skipper!" Garrett grabbed his arm and pulled; Lawless's head lolled around, left eye staring, revealing the gaping horror where the right side of his skull had been. Blood and brain tissue and chips of bone were splashed across the deck and bulwark in scarlet surprise. The left side of Lawless's binoculars were still gripped in his left hand; his right arm ended at the wrist.

There was no time to retrieve the captain's body, no time to think. Reacting by trained instinct alone, the conscious part of his mind numb, Garrett dropped back through the hatch, slamming it shut above him and dogging it tight.

More rounds slammed into the sail, one punching through with a violent bang. Garrett kept dropping through the sail levels, sealing the last hatch above him as he dropped through into the control room.

Lieutenant Tollini and the COB met him, staring. Everyone on the bridge was staring, and it took Garrett a second to realize that his uniform was covered with blood. "Mr. Garrett . . ." Dougherty said.

"The skipper's dead," Garrett said sharply. "Dive the boat!"

"We're going down to periscope depth, Captain," Tollini said. "That's about as deep as we can go without bottoming out."

It took Garrett another moment to play back in his mind what Tollini had just said. The diving officer had called him "Captain."

"Are you okay, sir?" Dougherty asked.

He nodded. "Ask me again when we're clear of this, COB."

This wasn't the way he'd wanted to return to command . . . but as the second man in the rank hierarchy, he was captain after the captain's death. Men failed. Men died. The crew and the boat kept going.

"Maneuvering!" he called. "I am taking command. Bring the helm left, forty degrees. Make revolutions for fifteen knots."

"Coming left to four-oh degrees, aye. Make revs for fifteen knots, aye."

He hit the intercom button by the periscope station. "Sonar! Conn!"

"Conn, Sonar, aye!" Toynbee replied.

"We're coming left forty degrees. See if you can pick

up our shadow back there when we drop him out of our baffles."

"Roger that, sir."

"Weps. I want you to *swim* the warshot out of Tube One. Wire-guide it around to port for a baffles shot."

Ward looked startled. "Aye aye, sir. Swim the fish."

This was a relatively new tactical capability for American submarines. Though they generally still launched torpedoes the traditional way, it was possible to drive a torpedo out the tube without the usual burst—and noise—of compressed air.

This allowed for relatively silent launches and more flexibility in targeting. Wire-guided Mk 48 ADCAP torpedoes were steered by a crewman on the submarine, using a computer-joystick arrangement that sent electrical signals down the slender wire tying the torpedo to the boat. Gone were the days when steam-driven torpedoes were fired more or less straight at a target using a periscope fix and plotting data off of a mechanical angle-on-the-bow computer. Most modern submarines didn't even have stern torpedo tubes; *Seawolf* mounted four forward tubes slanted outward through her hull from the torpedo room. Once a fish was clear of the sub, it could be steered in any direction.

A loud ping sounded through the control room.

"Conn, Sonar," Toynbee reported. "Active sonar from the destroyer. He's pinging us."

Not that he needs to, Garrett thought. He knows exactly where we are. But the turning maneuver might possibly muddy their sonar picture for a critical few moments.

"Conn, Sonar! I have our shadow, designated Sierra One-five-four. Got him on the scatter off that active ping."

"Tell me."

"Two hundred twenty meters astern, bearing three-four-seven. I've got faint screw noise now, too, same heading. We're tentatively IDing him as a Kilo."

Which made the most sense. A diesel boat could follow *Seawolf* soundlessly, tracelessly . . . and was small enough to be handier in these tight and shallow quarters.

Another ping echoed through the hull.

"COB? What's the draft on a Luda-class destroyer?"

"Four meters, Captain. Uh . . . five and a bit, if you add the sonar dome under the bow."

"Damn," he said. "This is going to be tight."

And then all eyes went toward *Seawolf*'s overhead and forward, where they could hear the deep-throated *chug-chug-chug* of the destroyer's twin screws, steadily approaching. . . .

Tuesday, 20 May 2003

Control Room
USS *Seawolf*
Eastern Approaches to Hong Kong
1814 hours

"Conn, Sonar! Destroyer changing aspect. He's turning into us!"

"Helm! Come hard right!" Garrett ordered. "Make revs for twenty knots!"

It was, he thought, a little wildly, an uncanny dance . . . but one ad-libbed rather than choreographed. *Seawolf* had turned left toward the destroyer; the destroyer had turned right toward *Seawolf*. Now *Seawolf* was veering off to the right, hoping to catch the destroyer off his guard.

And all the while, *Seawolf*'s lone torpedo, still connected by an unraveling strand of slender wire, was circling far around to the left, coming up now on a moving point two hundred yards astern of the twisting submarine.

"Captain!" Ward announced from the weapons control board, just behind the helm station. "That last maneuver put our fish astern . . . two hundred yards."

"Hold it a moment more," Garrett said. He closed his eyes, picturing the positions of the dancers in this ballet in three dimensions . . . the Luda-class destroyer, the *Seawolf*, the torpedo, the Kilo. . . .

Ping!

"Sonar, Conn! Do you still have our tail?"

"Negative, Skipper. Too much back-scatter off the seabed."

But he was still back there, somewhere . . . and almost certainly readying a torpedo or two of his own.

Wait . . . wait . . . The Kilo skipper would be copying *Seawolf*'s maneuvers, but each imitation would be delayed by a number of seconds, the time it took for his own sonar crew to pick up the change in *Seawolf*'s sonar aspect, evaluate it, and repeat it.

"Sonar crew. Pull your ears! All hands. Brace for collision!" *Now!* "Weapons officer! Detonate the torpedo!"

Ward already had his thumb poised above a large, red button. When he pressed it, 650 pounds of PBXN 103 high explosives detonated with a thunderous crash two football fields astern of the *Seawolf*'s screw.

The shock wave was enough to send a shudder along the length of *Seawolf*'s hull, rocking her hard. Seconds later they could hear, they could feel, the looming mass of the Luda directly overhead, as *Seawolf* twisted hard to starboard beneath the destroyer's keel. The shock-wave caught the *Seawolf* and gently nudged her forward . . . and also up, just a little. A shattering, tearing

crunch sounded from above the control room, and the
deck tilted to the right.

Then *Seawolf* righted herself. Garrett clutched the
periscope railing hard, willing the sub to keep moving.
If her upper works were fouled with the destroyer, if
the damage was too severe . . .

"Jesus!" Tollini said, looking back at Garrett from
his station at the dive board. "I think we just scraped
off the bastard's sonar dome!"

"Helm. Come to heading one-five-zero. Slow to
eight knots. Maintain silence throughout the boat."

Minutes dragged past, as *Seawolf* slowly and quietly
crawled away from the clash, her sonar ears again
probing the water astern, trying to piece together a co-
herent picture of what was happening. The destroyer
appeared to have heaved to, and there were some unpleasant fluttering noises that might have been hull
damage of some sort. Toynbee also reported that they
could hear the Kilo, blowing her tanks and surfacing.

That was good news, at least, nearly the best they
could expect. Garrett had not targeted the Kilo directly
because she was so hard to pick up on passive sonar. In
any case, what he'd wanted most to do was brush the
Kilo off and wreck her sonar picture of the *Seawolf*.

The detonation of a Mk 48 ADCAP torpedo between the Kilo's blunt prow and *Seawolf*'s screw had
undoubtedly done just that . . . and quite possibly had
been close enough to the unseen Kilo to cause substan-
tial damage as well, to her sonar suite if nothing else.

The explosion had also deafened the destroyer, and,
if *Seawolf*'s accidental brush with its keel had done
what Garrett thought, the destroyer might have been
permanently deafened when the bulbous dome containing its Jug Pair sonar was carried away.

The control room was enveloped in complete silence as minute followed minute and *Seawolf* continued moving southeast at a slow and steady pace. Twice Garrett ordered changes in course and speed to help throw off enemy tracking attempts, but she continued her overall run—if her ultrasilent creep along the sea floor could be called a "run"—toward the southeast and the safety of deep, open water.

Near Tong'an
Fujian Province, People's Republic of China
1818 hours

"Yellow Dragon, this is Blue Dragon. Yellow Dragon, Blue. Do you copy?" Patiently, Morton repeated the call. The sounds of steady gunfire from up ahead had ceased for a time, but now there were continued brief, sharp flurries of automatic fire, punctuated once by the crump of an exploding hand grenade. A gentle rain had begun falling, somewhat muffling the gunfire.

The SEALs had crept as close to the battle as they could without being discovered. Now they needed to make contact with Tse.

"Blue Dragon! Blue Dragon! This is Yellow!" The voice was Tse's, sounding tired and haggard. "What the hell are *you* doing here?"

"Pulling your tail out of hot water. What's your tactical situation?"

"It was a trap," Tse replied, his voice carrying a taste of bitterness. "The Silkworm launchers were there to draw us in. We're on a hilltop about twelve kilometers from our original OP, map coordinates . . ." He began rattling off a string of alphanumerics. Morton already had his plastic AO map out and swiftly localized Tse's position. As he'd suspected, they were on the hill just ahead.

"I would estimate a full PLA brigade in our immediate area," Tse went on. "I have two dead, four wounded, and we're low on ammo. Situation is desperate."

A sudden sharp sound over the tactical radio channel corresponded with a loud *whump* from the hill ahead. "They're starting to bring in artillery. We're not going to hold for very much longer."

"You can hold for fifteen more minutes," Morton told him. "Stay low, get ready, and stand by for a fast E and E on a bearing of . . . one-seven-four. Do you copy that?"

"I copy, Blue Dragon. And . . . whatever happens . . . thanks."

"You can thank me when we get to the sea, Yellow Dragon. Stand by."

TM1 Jorghenson crawled over to Morton's position. "We've got visual with the bad guys, Skipper," he said. "Light MGs, assault rifles. They're not dug in and they're not watching their backs."

"Okay, Swede. Let's see what we've got."

They moved forward through the steady drizzle, until Jorghenson tapped his shoulder twice and pointed. From a concealed position behind a fallen log and within a clump of bushes at the edge of a clearing, Morton could see three Chinese soldiers crouched behind boulders at the side of a dirt road twenty yards ahead, their backs to him, their attention focused on something farther up the slope. Pointing again, Jorghenson indicated that more PLA fire teams were located there . . . there . . . and over there.

Two more came running up the road, puffing with exertion. One carried a Type 56 machine gun—a close copy of the old Soviet RPD—the other a couple of boxes of linked ammo. An officer stepped out of the trees ahead and waved them on.

The SEALs faded back into the woods. Silently, using hand signals, Morton spelled out what he wanted. *First squad . . . with me. Second squad . . . set claymores . . . along that road.*

As the word was spread, SEALs began materializing out of the forest, black-faced, nearly invisible against the underbrush. They used sign language and touch, for the most part, but whispered instructions over the tactical channel where necessary. First Squad began spreading out along the clearing, moving around its fringes, closing on the unsuspecting PLA troops who were busily focused on their own prey.

The PLA officer vanished into the shrubs at his back as a black-clad arm swept around his mouth and a SEAL Mk 1 diving knife sliced through jugular, carotid, and windpipe. Another Chinese soldier grunted, then collapsed, the thump of his falling louder than the double-tapped 9mm Hush Puppy rounds that silenced him. Sound-suppressed H&K fire cut down the two men with the machine gun in mid-stride; a nearby PLA soldier saw them fall and shouted. An instant later a 40mm grenade detonated between him and another soldier, flinging them apart like torn rag dolls.

The SEAL squad surged forward then, a general advance that caught the PLA soldiers from behind and completely unprepared. While SEALs were not intended for heavy combat, their tactics and weaponry allowed them to survive short contacts through a sheer, overwhelming viciousness of superior firepower. They stuck with suppressed weapons—H&Ks and Smith & Wesson

Hush Puppies—for as long as possible, but once things went rock-and-roll, Whiteman began cutting loose with his M-60, and the men with M203 grenade launchers, Douglass and Knowles, began popping 40mm rounds at every likely concentration of enemy force.

In moments the Chinese troops along the southeastern side of the hilltop were dead, wounded, or fleeing in utter confusion. Morton gave the call over the tactical channel for Tse and his men to come on down.

Minutes later the Taiwanese commandos were jogging down the slope, carrying their dead and wounded with them. Tse met Morton at the edge of the clearing and shook the American's hand. "Thank you, Commander. I . . . don't quite know what to say."

" 'Thanks' will do fine for now. Let's get the hell out of here."

"Affirmative to that!"

Bullets snipped among the leaves overhead. The PLA forces were reorganizing. The Taiwanese and their American escort began moving south along the dirt road, the last men in the column walking backwards laying down heavy bursts of rearguard fire.

Five minutes later the first Chinese troops came down the road, a couple of platoons on foot, and more piled into the backs of four trucks. The SEALs of Second Squad, well-hidden in the forest, waited until the lead elements were already past before triggering the first pair of claymore mines . . . then the second . . . then the third. . . .

The claymores, each with its distinctive, convex-curved "This side toward enemy" face, had been mounted on their tripods in a staggered array that blanketed the road from both sides. Packed with seven hundred ball bearings apiece and a kilo and a half of shaped high explosives, claymores acted like titanic shotguns when triggered, slicing through vegetation, flesh, and even light armor in broad, expanding swathes of bloody destruction. With the kill-zones of the mines overlapping, the Chinese troops on the road were shredded by blast upon blast upon devastating blast.

PLA troops outside the kill zones immediately plunged into the woods beside the road, seeking to avoid further emplaced mines; thirty yards into the forest, they ran headlong into another line of claymores, set by the retreating SEALs to further discourage close pursuit.

The survivors were not eager to follow closely. The SEALs began leapfrogging backward, one line of men crouching in the brush, covering the rest as they fell back, then falling back in turn while the other SEALs covered them. Before long, contact with the enemy was broken, and there were no further sounds of pursuit.

The rain fell harder, as thunder—natural thunder as opposed to the manmade variety that had echoed off the hills earlier—boomed. The SEALs and their Taiwanese allies continued moving south, then east, back toward their insertion point.

Control Room
USS *Seawolf*
Eastern Approaches to Hong Kong
2040 hours

Gradually, as the fast-paced minutes of the skirmish lengthened into hours, Garrett ordered *Seawolf*'s speed increased, putting more and more distance between the submarine and any possible search and pursuit.

From the sounds dwindling astern, the PLA Navy had lost the *Seawolf* completely in the explosion and in the next few moments of chaos. A dozen other naval vessels, from patrol boats to a second Luda, were converging on the area, and Toynbee was even able to report the presence of helicopters passing overhead, so sensitive were *Seawolf*'s underwater ears.

An initial survey of the damage to the boat was completed. The sail was partly flooded. It was sealed off from the rest of the boat by watertight doors, but the periscopes and electronic masts still worked. Handling was a bit sluggish; with water in the sail, *Seawolf* was top heavy and clumsy but still answered well to the helm.

And there'd been only one casualty—Lawless.

The crew was silent, at first.

"Skipper?" Lieutenant Ward said after a long time.

"Yes?"

"Didn't you run into a Chinese ship with your *last* command?"

Ward's tone had a sparkle to it. He was attempting an uneasy joke, hoping, perhaps, to lighten the atmosphere inside the control room.

Good man, Garrett thought. Thanks for the straight line.

"Actually, what I hit last time was a Chinese Kilo-class submarine," he said. "Not, properly speaking, a *ship*. This time, though, I thought I'd try to ram the destroyer instead. At command school they call this 'innovative tactics.' What do you think?"

Gentle laughter and nervous chuckles fluttered through the control room.

"I'd say, sir," Ward replied, "that any tactics that let

you walk out of an enemy harbor full of ASW assets is a good one."

"Thank you, Weps. And good work on swimming that fish. *That's* what helped us break contact." He waited a beat, then added, "You know, people, I'm going to have to think about this. Hitting the enemy target with a *torpedo* instead of with my submarine. That's such a wild idea, it just might work!"

It was a weak joke, he thought, but this time the laughter was louder and harder, without the nervousness. While a skipper was expected to show no weakness, he thought he could afford a bit of self-deprecation. The crew would need a strong bond to get them past a double assault on their emotions . . . the abrupt transition from peace to war, and the death of Captain Lawless.

"Sonar, Conn. What do you have nearby?"

"Nothing close, Captain," came the reply. "We're in the clear."

"Up periscope."

The Mark 18 scope slid smoothly up through the overhead, and Garrett took his place at the eyepiece. In the fast-dwindling light he could just make out the humps of mountains to the northwest. Walking the scope through a full 360, he saw no surface vessels on the horizon at all.

"Radio Shack. What do we have up there?"

"Lots of traffic, Skipper. We're recording."

At Garrett's command, *Seawolf* released a souvenir of her visit—a radio transmission buoy keyed to send an account of the action just past after an hour's elapsed time. It informed those higher up the chain of command that the *Seawolf* had been slightly damaged and that Garrett had taken command after Lawless's death. If enemy listeners homed on the brief, burst transmission, they would find only empty ocean.

"Down scope," he said at last. He grinned at Tollini. "You know, that's a hell of a note, when the only defensive maneuver we can make is 'down periscope.'"

"We used to say that on board the *Miami* when we pulled duty inside the Persian Gulf," Dougherty put in. "The water's so shallow there you feel like a bug on a plate."

"Should get better from here on out, Skipper," the diving officer said. "Bottom is dropping fast . . . we're passing the hundred-foot mark now."

"Good. Mr. Simms . . . plot us a course north toward the strait, best possible speed. We'll need to surface after it's dark to make repairs to the sail. And we'll need to see what COMSUBPAC has in mind for us. Until they tell us otherwise, though, I'm assuming we're go for our original mission—to listen for Chinese subs in the Strait of Formosa."

"Those orders'll likely read 'listen for, find, and *sink*' now," Dougherty said.

"Agreed. It would be nice to get in a few licks of our own."

A radioman entered the control room, a message flimsy in hand. "Captain? Flash-priority urgent. From COMSUBPAC."

"Well, they're on the ball!" COB said.

"They don't have our update yet," Garrett said. He scanned the decrypted message.

TO: CO USS SEAWOLF, SSN21
FROM: CINC COMSUBPAC
DATE: 20 MAY 01

USS JARRETT, FFG33, SUNK BY ENEMY ACTION FORMOSA STRAITS 1815 HRS 20 MAY. A STATE OF WAR IS

CONSIDERED TO EXIST AT THIS TIME BETWEEN THE US AND THE PRC. YOU ARE DIRECTED TO TAKE SEAWOLF INTO THE STRAIT OF FORMOSA AND COMMENCE OPERATIONS ALONG MAINLAND CHINESE COAST, ENGAGING ALL ENEMY TARGETS WITH SPECIAL EMPHASIS ON PRC SUBMARINE ASSETS.

There was more to the message—signal codes and communications protocols, for the most part, and a purely gratuitous warning not to allow *Seawolf* to be trapped in Hong Kong, but the body of the message was brutally to the point.

America was at war, and *Seawolf* was on point.

Near Xiamen
Fujian Province, People's Republic of China
2340 hours

Rain hissed down through the forest canopy, soaking already swampy ground. Morton and three of his SEALs, plus Commander Tse, huddled beneath the partial cover of a south-facing rock shelter, an overhang that deflected the worst of the downpour. Knowles and Haggarty had set up the LST-5 with the dish antenna trained on the southern sky, relaying their transmission through the comsat to Coronado.

"You were dead right," Commander Randall's voice said, through crackles of static and the watery roar of the storm. "It *is* a cluster fuck, and some heads are going to roll all the way from Taipei to Washington."

"Copy that, sir," Morton said. "But it's not helping us here and now."

"I know. But I want you boys to know we have *not*

forgotten about you. We're putting together a recovery effort now. And Navy Intelligence has a man going out to one of the carrier battle groups to coordinate things."

"That's good to know. What do we do now?"

"Continue your E and E to the coast. Check in at your scheduled times for updates. And for God's sake steer clear of the PLA."

"What about the Silkworm launch vehicles, Commander? We're still in a position to call in air strikes. As long as we're here, it would be a shame to waste an in-country asset."

"It would be a shame to lose that asset in a gunfight with regular army troops," Randall replied. "This thing is a lot bigger than one SEAL platoon, Commander, and way over our heads. Your orders are to get your people out of there."

"Aye aye, sir."

"Talk to you at your next check-in, Jack. Randall out."

They began packing up the satcom radio. "So?" Tse asked him. "What's the story?"

Morton sighed. "It sounds like one of those cases where the right hand didn't know what the left hand was doing. Some of your people decided it would be a good thing to involve SEALs in a ground op on the mainland. Some of my people, with business interests in Taiwan, decided that that would be a wonderful idea and approved it, but apparently the approval didn't go as high as J-SOCOM. The op was what they call 'compartmentalized,' with only need-to-know personnel in the loop.

"The only trouble with that was, they weren't expecting that last minute peace overture from the President. The State Department negotiators were off to Beijing, and nobody at that level knew we were on the ground here." He chuckled. "New Orleans all over again."

Tse frowned in the rainswept darkness. "Please?"

"Sorry. One of the great mistakes of military history. The Battle of New Orleans—one of the great military victories for the United States—was fought in 1815, something like six weeks *after* the Treaty of Ghent ended the war we were fighting against England at the time. Back in those days, news traveled by horseback or by ship, and battles could be fought between forces that technically were at peace but who hadn't gotten the word yet. You don't expect that to happen with satellites, computers, and high-speed data connections, but things have gotten so top-heavy lately, with departments and directorates and a hundred different headquarters, control hierarchies, and command structures . . . most of them not talking to one another." He sighed. "Commander, did you know that in 1983 the American invasion of the little island of Grenada nearly *failed* in complete confusion . . . because different branches of the U.S. Armed Forces were using different time tables? No one had bothered to check to see whether the orders were being issued for the Grenada time zone or for Eastern Standard time, an hour earlier. Units in different services couldn't talk to one another because they hadn't agreed on common communications frequencies. Some Navy SEALs died because they were dropped in the wrong place at the wrong time, in heavy seas, too far from land. We can fight any enemy in the world, but we can't master our own cumbersome chain of command."

"Perhaps," Tse said, "we need an electronic form of bureaucracy. To do for bureaucracy what electronics did for communication."

"Hmm. A way to do much more, even more slowly?"

"Or to do it more quickly, but with even more confusion."

"Sometimes I think the only thing that is standing between civilization and absolute disaster is the fact that bureaucracy gets in its own way. It's so damned clumsy it's not a serious threat to anyone."

Morton stared off into the rainswept darkness. "Let's saddle up, people. We can make good time in this storm."

"The PLA will not be anxious to track us in this," Tse agreed. He looked at Morton. "Commander Morton. Some of us will still be remaining behind."

"I figured as much. You have your own war . . . and your own orders."

"We appreciate your help back there. More than we can say. And we will ask you to escort some of us back to Taiwan, with our dead and wounded. But the rest of us . . ."

"Understood. But your men are low on munitions."

"If we could have some extra 5.56 and 7.62, that would help a lot. Until we can arrange for a resupply air mission."

"Damned if I want to lug that shit all the way back to Taiwan." Reaching down, Morton thoughtfully tapped a metal case resting beside the wall of the overhang. "You know, I haven't seen our laser target designator. We must have dropped it up the trail a ways. If you happen to see it, make sure it doesn't fall into PLA hands, okay? I mean, it has directions on how to use it, frequencies for calling air strikes, all kinds of sensitive information I wouldn't want the enemy to have."

Tse grinned. "We'll see what we can do."

Morton put out his hand. "You take care of yourself, Tse."

"And you, Commander. It has been good serving with you. *Very* good."

The two parties separated at that point, Morton and his SEALs, along with ten of the Taiwanese commandos, moving on toward the coast, while Tse and his men faded back into the storm.

Morton wondered if he would ever hear of those men again.

COD Aircraft Sierra-Alfa Five
Over the Western Pacific
2355 hours

Captain Frank Gordon was miserable. The COD aircraft—the acronym stood for Carrier On-board Delivery—was a C-2A Greyhound, literally a bus for hauling personnel, supplies, and mail back and forth among far-flung naval air stations and bases and the U.S. carrier battle groups at sea. With two turboprop engines and a ferry range of almost 1,500 nautical miles at 260 knots, it was ideal for the job it was designed for . . . but not exactly the latest thing in comfort.

Especially while bouncing around the western Pacific in the middle of a class-two storm.

He was strapped into a passenger seat just abaft the cockpit. A Greyhound could carry thirty-two passengers in addition to its three-man crew, but this flight was empty except for Gordon, a distinction of sorts, he supposed. He wouldn't have been quite so worried if he wasn't seated directly behind the pilot, who was clutching the steering yoke and peering ahead past the steady *thwick-thwick-thwick* of the windshield wiper, as though trying to penetrate the murk by sheer force of will . . . and muttering obscenities under his breath.

This, he decided, was fitting punishment for any sin he'd ever committed in the line of duty. As the Greyhound bucked and side-slipped in the turbulent air, he was repeatedly glad he'd had little for dinner . . . and miserably sorry that he'd had anything at all.

"Okay, Captain Gordon!" The copilot had to shout to make himself heard above the roar of the engines and the howl of the storm. "Just got word from the *Stennis*! They'll have a Hawkeye ready to go airborne the minute we bite steel!"

Gordon could only nod understanding. The E-2C Hawkeye was essentially identical to the C-2, a twin-turboprop design with folding wings for carrier stowage, but with most of its interior space taken up by electronics. The naval equivalent of the big Air Force E-3 Sentry AWACS aircraft, Hawkeyes mounted a powerful APS-125 radar inside a rotating radome above the fuselage and served both as radar pickets and to coordinate combat communications among ships and aircraft.

"Don't worry, Captain! We'll have you down in one piece and airborne again in a jiff!"

He nodded again and wished the copilot would leave him alone. He was trying so hard not to be sick.

The string of muttered obscenities from the pilot grew fiercer. "*Where* the fuck is that damned postage stamp?" he heard the man say aloud, and decided he must mean the aircraft carrier they were hunting for. It was tough enough to spot something as tiny as a carrier in the middle of all this ocean. Add midnight darkness and a howling storm . . .

"Okay! Okay! Got 'em!" the copilot said. "Call the ball."

"I'll give them a fucking ball. Okay. On track. Easy . . ."

Gordon tried to peer past the pilot's shoulder but could see absolutely nothing except blackness. What the hell were they looking at? The Greyhound slewed sharply sideways and the swearing upped a notch, the pilot battling the wind through his yoke and rudder control pedals.

Suddenly, it felt as though the seat dropped away beneath Gordon, then slammed up hard to meet him coming down. There was a shriek of tires on steel, a surge of acceleration as the pilot threw the throttles full-forward just in case they missed their catch . . . and a final, violent yank as the Greyhound's tailhook snagged a taut arrestor cable on the deck.

The pilot cut back the throttles and began taxiing the aircraft through the storm. They were down, and Gordon still couldn't see much outside but blackness. No . . . wait. There were some lights, high up and to the right . . . probably the pri-fly bridge overlooking the flight deck.

"Told you we'd get ya down in one piece, sir!"

"Just fucking wonderful" was all Gordon could say.

Because now that he was down, he had to change aircraft and go up into that mess again.

Some days it didn't pay to get out of bed . . . particularly those days when you never got to go to bed in the first place.

Wednesday, 21 May 2003

Control Room
USS *Seawolf*
Southwest of the Penghu Islands
0830 hours

At forty knots, *Seawolf* cruised east across the stretch of shallow ocean between Hong Kong and Taiwan in less than eight hours. The Penghu Islands—until recently known by their Portuguese name of the Pescadores, or Fishermen's Islands—were a scattering of low, flat islands and atolls stretched across the Formosa Strait about halfway between the mainland and the southern tip of Taiwan. They were of little importance to anyone save the local tourism industry and as a median strip in the strait, dividing it into the broader west channel along the mainland coast and the narrower but deeper east channel next to Taiwan.

Garrett had been seeking the deeper water of the

eastern passage. The average depth offshore from
Hong Kong was fifty meters or less; west of the Penghu
Islands, the bottom averaged twenty meters and
shoaled to as little as ten meters—far too shallow for
the *Seawolf* to remain submerged.

Which meant those waters were too shallow for Chinese subs as well, and they would be looking for the
same, deep waters. The undersea valley between the
Penghu Islands and Taiwan would be prime hunting
grounds for PLA Navy Kilos.

The sun was high when *Seawolf* came to periscope
depth. Garrett walked the scope, confirming that the
horizon was empty. A recent line of storms had passed
through on their way into Asia, and the broken clouds
caught the golden morning colors and scattered them
across the sky.

The sky was filled with radio waves as well as color.
As soon as *Seawolf*'s radio mast broke the surface, the
radio shack began recording multiple repeated calls.
Most urgent was a series of coded messages giving *Sea-
wolf* a forward controller contact, code named Crystal
Ball. When contact was established via UHF, Crystal
Ball turned out to be a Navy E-2C Hawkeye off the
Stennis, serving as a forward battle controller and as
coordinator for the *Stennis*'s far-flung air squadrons.

Garrett was not surprised when he heard the voice at
the other end of the line as he pressed a radio handset
to his ear. "Commander Gordon! What the hell are you
doing out here?"

"Trying to get what is laughingly called 'the big picture' by the Beltway insiders," Gordon replied. His
voice sounded worn and very tired, and Garrett
guessed the Naval Intelligence officer had been awake
for a long, long time.

Well, Gordon had been a submariner once, and he knew what port-and-starboard watches were like.

"And what does the big picture look like so far?"

"Like shit. The PLA is out to prove that they rule the Strait of Formosa, and is threatening everyone else with death and destruction if they try venturing through. Four hours ago they closed the strait to *all* shipping, military and civilian, and set out to prove it by sinking a Filipino freighter and a Japanese oil tanker."

"Missile attacks?"

"Negative. Submarines. We think the Kilos have just started earning their keep. Which is what you're going to do. Confirmation just came down the line. You have temporary command of *Seawolf*."

The words scarcely sounded real. Even a temporary command was more than he'd been expecting. There were, he imagined, plenty of people back in the World who'd have preferred to see another skipper flown out to the *Seawolf*, but this was war, and every moment counted.

"Thank you, Commander. So . . . it sounds like the *Seawolf* is going to go sub hunting."

"Affirmative . . . but you have another mission first."

"That being?"

"A platoon of U.S. Navy SEALs—sixteen men—plus ten Taiwanese commandos are stranded on the mainland near Xiamen. J SOCOM is organizing an extraction with Mark-5s, but we want *Seawolf* to move in and offer support. The Mark-5s may not be able to penetrate the coastal defenses."

"That is damned shallow water in there," Garrett said. "*Seawolf* may have to walk in."

"You can fly in if you have to, but get those people out of there."

"What's the rush? I thought you'd want SEAL teams on the ground right now."

"These boys went in just ahead of the current unpleasantness and were basically overlooked when State began playing kissy-face with Beijing. Their Taiwanese opposite numbers walked into a firefight, our boys bailed them out . . . and they're coming out now with wounded and low ammo."

"We'll get them, Commander."

"Good. I know you will. Retrieving those SEALs is your primary mission. Your secondary mission—which you will pursue so long as it does not interfere with your primary mission—is to find every goddamn Kilo you can run to ground and blow it out of the water. We suspect at least one Kilo is in the AO near Kinmen. She took part in the sinking of the *Jarrett* last night and is believed to be positioning herself to interdict traffic in the Xiamen area. We want that bastard sunk."

"Aye aye, sir. Any other good news?"

"Only this: You have two carrier battle groups coming into the theater within the next twenty-four hours—the *Stennis* and the *Kitty Hawk*. *Kitty Hawk* will be taking up station off the northern tip of Taiwan. *Stennis* will be stationed off the south tip. Neither carrier can be allowed to enter the battle zone until we are certain the submarine threat has been eliminated or greatly reduced. The CBGs have their own ASW assets, of course, but they will not be able to cope with ten Kilos. We want you to cause some attrition on the enemy forces before the big boys arrive on the scene."

"Roger that." Hell. Every Chinese submarine along the coast would be eager to score an American carrier. Once they knew those CBGs were on the scene, the underwater stretches of the Formosa Strait were going to look like rush hour.

"You'll have some help from other U.S. submarine forces in the area. The *Jefferson City* and the *Salt Lake City* will be arriving ahead of the *Stennis* CBG. They should be in your AO within the next eight hours. The *Cheyenne* is en route from the Indian Ocean and should be in your area late tomorrow. Ah . . . and your old friend, the *Pittsburgh*, will be attached to the *Kitty Hawk* group. Try not to run into her with the *Seawolf*."

"Fuck you, sir," he replied in a deadpan voice. "Fuck you very much." He saw the radioman, who was jacked into the conversation, struggling to control his expression and wondered how long it would take for the story to spread throughout the boat.

"This is where we find out if all the money we spent on the *Seawolf* was worth it," Gordon said. "Good luck, Tom."

"Thank you, sir. We'll do our best."

"I know you will, Tom. Congratulations on your confirmation."

"Thank you." He didn't let himself think about the possibility of temporary becoming permanent. There were too many variables, too much in the way of politics involved. They wouldn't let him keep the *Seawolf* once this fracas was over, but another command, perhaps? Another L.A. boat?

This was at least a golden opportunity to get his career back on track. The promotion boards might select him for O-5 yet.

That was a worry for the future, though. Right now, it sounded like *Seawolf* was the only submarine asset in the Strait of Formosa, and that was damned thin odds. Ten to one? Worse, when you counted the Chinese Akula loose out there, the former *Nevolin,* and infinitely worse when you remembered that even before their recent Russian shopping spree, the PLA Navy had boasted a submarine fleet of ninety-one old Romeo-class diesel boats, fifteen even more ancient Whiskeys, plus eight or ten of their more modern Han- and Ming-class nukes. Whiskey and Romeo attack boats might be antiques by today's standards, but in a defensive role, dashing out from coastal hides to strike at shipping or passing American naval forces or lying in silent ambush among the tangled labyrinths of coastal islands from Hainan to Luda, they were still deadly. The People's Republic was not yet able to project her submarine force across oceans as easily as the United States, but her submarine forces made her a dangerous regional player and the obvious mistress of her corner of the world ocean should the United States decide to pull back from the western Pacific.

Not an option. Quite aside from any vital interests the United States possessed in the region, Garrett had strong personal reasons not to want to see the Chinese dragon swallow this quarter of the planet.

Kazuko would be back in Tokyo by now. He was glad she was out of the fire zone.

"Mr. Simms," he said as he left the radio shack and reentered the control room. "Plot us a new course."

"Aye aye, sir," the navigator said, looking up from his chart table. "Where to?"

"Into harm's way, Mr. Simms. Into harm's way. . . ."

**Control Room, PLA Submarine *Changcheng*
South China Sea, south of Taiwan
1005 hours**

They called him Sinbad.

Hai-tziun shan-tzo Hsing Ling Ma—the rank was

the equivalent of a Russian *kapitan pervogo ranga* or an American naval captain—was something of a celebrity within the ranks of the PLA Navy. He was an ethnic Hui, for one thing, a Chinese Muslim of Eurasian descent, from the province of Yunnan, near China's border with Burma, Laos, and Vietnam. Such high rank rarely came to non-Mandarin officers, and only exceptional performance through the course of an exceptional career could have brought him to the post he now held—commander of the Akula-class nuclear attack submarine *Changcheng,* the *Great Wall.*

His nickname actually was the Chinese equivalent of Sinbad—Ma Sanbao, a figure unknown to the West but something of a historical icon to people in southern China, Burma, and other parts of southeast Asia. The original Ma Sanbao had been born in 1371 and, like Hsing, was also a Hui from Yunnan. "Ma" was the Chinese equivalent of "Mohammad," and Sanbao's original name had been Ma Ho.

As a child Ho had been castrated by Chinese troops chasing Mongols out of the southern provinces—a curious custom they'd evolved to pacify the male locals, whether Mongol or not—and made an orderly in the Chinese army. Perhaps because of the hormone imbalance, he had grown to great height—probably not the eight feet legend attributed to him, but a giant, certainly, among his own people. By the time he was twenty-five, he'd won influence as chief of all of the emperor's thousands of eunuchs, made powerful friends within the imperial court, and been given the name "Cheng."

In 1405, three years after the ascent of a new emperor to the nascent Ming throne, he was made an admiral. Eighty-some years later, an obscure Genoese navigator in the service of Spain was given the grandiose title "Admiral of the Ocean Sea," but that admiral had only three ships in his command; Cheng Ho's fleet numbered 317 vessels, many of them far larger and more seaworthy than Colombo's caravels.

The Ming Empire was undeniably *the* world naval power of its day. They possessed enormous fleets, with magnificent ships far larger and more modern than anything yet developed in the primitive backwaters of Europe, vessels with three decks and towering masts capable of ocean voyages of thousands of miles. Between 1405 and 1433, Admiral Cheng Ho set forth on seven separate voyages—the original "Seven Voyages of Sinbad"—which took him to Ceylon and the Persian Gulf, to Arabia, to Egypt, and perhaps as far as the southern tip of Africa.

There were even rumors that the Ming fleets discovered new lands far to the east as well; certainly, they reached the southern shores of Africa from the east fifty years before Vasco da Gama did the same from the west and were within a historical footnote of discovering Europe. Had they done so, world history undeniably would have been vastly different, and the whole long, sad, and bloody chronicle of European colonization of Asia, of opium wars and puppet governments, of western hegemony, the Boxer Rebellion, and centuries of shame and national loss of face would never have happened.

For one brief, gleaming moment of history China had unknowingly held within her grasp the key to world domination. The ascent of a new emperor to the Ming throne in 1433, however, ended all possibility of that. Turning inward, suspicious of foreigners and foreign-barbarian ideas, the Ming Dynasty had ceased its explorations, disbanded its fleets, and even passed laws against building ships of more than one deck. The magnificent fleet that might have circumnavigated a world rotted on the beach, and Cheng Ho vanished, his name erased from the records by jealous, vengeful, or fearful enemies.

China *could* have discovered the West rather than the other way around, and how might that have changed the course of world history? Hsing Ma had used that argument frequently while campaigning for a stronger, deep-water navy for the PRC and especially for a stronger submarine force, one that could project Chinese power as far afield as Europe or the American West Coast. That, undoubtedly, at least as much as his religion and ethnic heritage, was why he'd received the nickname of Ma Sanbao.

Perhaps as a reward for his diligence in promoting the PLA Navy—or perhaps simply because he was a strong political supporter of Admiral Li Guofeng— Hsing had received the coveted command of the *Changcheng* and orders to take her into action against the Americans. The U.S. Seventh Fleet had intervened in Chinese affairs in the Strait of Formosa more than once since 1949. This time, it was vowed, the balance of naval power would be in the hands of the Middle Kingdom. Key to winning that power, however, was the destruction of the new American submarine *Seawolf*. Then other American submarines would have to move into the strait . . . and movement meant noise, and an advantage in any undersea game of *xiang qi*.

Seawolf, unfortunately, had eluded the *Tai Feng* at Hong Kong, where trapping and capturing her would have been easy, and recovery efforts simpler if the attempt had ended with the American's destruction. Now the enemy vessel was loose in the *Taiwan Haixia*—the Formosa Strait—and trapping her would be difficult. Fortunately, Hsing thought, he held several key advantages.

First of all, until the American carrier fleets arrived, the *Seawolf* would be largely alone, save for ASW assets flying off of Taiwan. With the *Changcheng* as the flagship of a wolfpack of Chinese submarines, supported by PLA ASW aircraft and vessels operating off the mainland, it should be fairly simple to cast a net that would snag the American vessel. Too, the operational area between Taiwan and the mainland was excruciatingly shallow—a disadvantage for Hsing's submarines, but a greater disadvantage for the American. There would be no thermal convection layers beneath which a submarine could hide from sonar, no deep trenches in which to lose pursuers.

And best of all, the American submarine's movements could be anticipated, even predicted with some precision. The *Seawolf* would almost certainly be hunting for the *Hutiao*, the Kilo-class diesel boat that had torpedoed the USS *Jarrett* yesterday. With the *Tiger Leaping* as bait, hard up against the Fujian coast, the *Seawolf* would be as vulnerable as a tortoise on its back.

Hsing planned his campaign like a carefully plotted game of *xiang qi*, the ancient Chinese version of chess that, like its western counterpart, used lesser pieces— pawns, guns, carts, horses, ministers, and officers—to trap and pin the opponent's leader, the red *suai* or the black *jiang*, a situation called *jiang shi*. He had already signaled three other Kilo-class subs to join his pack . . . and sent orders to the captain of the *Tiger Leaping* to remain in the vicinity of Kinmen.

And now, with almost leisurely deliberation, Hsing began to draw tight the net. . . .

Near Xiamen
Fujian Province, People's Republic of China
1323 hours

They'd reached their insertion point that morning, taking the risk of traveling by day in order to put yet more distance between themselves and any pursuit. The storm had moved on, but the ground was soaking wet, slowing travel to a slippery, uncertain-footed scramble through mud and dripping vegetation. All of them, SEALs and commandos both, were chilled and miserable despite the wet suits beneath their camouflage. The cold and the damp reminded Morton forcibly of the less pleasant aspects of Basic Underwater Demolition/SEAL training—BUD/S—and of Hell Week in particular, when SEAL recruits were kept soaking wet and running on the thin edge of exhaustion, lucky to pull down forty hours of sleep total in an entire week.

The training was that grueling so that the SEALs knew they could survive such conditions, knew they would survive and continue to hurt the enemy. Knowing he would survive, however, was not the same as enjoying that survival. *Just a little farther*, he told himself. *Just another few kilometers . . .*

Morton crouched in the underbrush at the edge of the forest, studying the narrow channel between the mainland and Kinmen through his binoculars. They would not be going back that way. Half a dozen PLA patrol boats were crisscrossing the narrow channel, and it looked like heavier craft were bombarding the Kinmen defenses. The invasion of Taiwan had begun, apparently, and it had begun, as had long been expected, with landings on tiny, isolated Kinmen or at least with a heavy naval bombardment. Morton could see what looked like a Luda-class destroyer out there, plus several smaller vessels, probably Jianghu missile frigates. A pall of black smoke hung above Kinmen, and he could hear the thump and rumble of big guns across the water.

Their Draeger rebreathers and swim gear were where they'd left them, buried and hidden at the edge of the woods above the beach. They would not be able to make the crossing by daylight, however, not with those patrols out there. And the four wounded Taiwanese wouldn't be able to swim underwater in any case. They would need to wait for darkness . . . once more.

Morton accepted six volunteers for the perimeter watch and told the rest of the men to get some sleep. Shivering, he decided he would not sleep himself just yet. Instead, he worked with Knowles to set up the LST-5, pointing the antenna at the southern sky.

They were going to need help on this one, and lots of it.

Sonar Room
USS *Seawolf*
South of Kinmen Island
1520 hours

The captain, Queensly decided, was being cautious. He liked that.

They'd crossed the Strait of Formosa at midday, but they'd taken their time, running at twenty knots and taking the 150-mile journey in seven hours. They could easily have halved the length of time necessary for the crossing, but the skipper had a paranoid streak about him, and he took it slow so the sonar team could actually have a chance to hear something.

At the end of the run, Garrett cut the speed even more, idling along the coast at five knots, trailing the TB-23 towed array astern and giving the boys in the sonar shack a really good listen. At speeds over twelve to fifteen knots, the efficiency of the boat's passive sonar arrays was reduced considerably. At speeds of over twenty knots, it was almost impossible to hear anything at all, because of the rush of water over the acoustical pickups.

In any case, even *Seawolf* made noise when she cruised along at better than twenty knots, and the skipper was being careful about any noise at all. The crew was padding around barefoot or in their socks, and the word had quietly been passed: Silent routine means *silent,* or the skipper'll see you walk home, see?

Queensly wasn't concerned with noise on the boat . . . not with the whispered conversations or the mounting tension. He was doing what he liked to say the Navy paid him to do, which was to see with his ears.

Everyone has their own modality, the means by which they best pull in information from the world around them. For most, that modality was sight, with hearing second and kinesthesia—the sensing of body position and movement—a distant third. Ken Queensly, however, had been born with a defect in both eyes that left him nearly blind, able to make out shapes and shadows. So far as the state of Ohio was concerned, he'd been legally blind. He'd gone to special schools, gone through special training, and for a time had even had a seeing-eye dog. Simply living in a world of gray and formless shapes had given him an almost magical way with hearing. It wasn't that his ears were that much sharper than those of sighted people; he'd simply been able to draw a lot more information from the sounds he heard than could most.

When he was fourteen a new laser surgery technique had given him sight. It wasn't perfect—he would always wear glasses—but the shapes now had solidity and meaning. He could *see*.

And yet Queensly's primary modality remained his hearing, perhaps because his brain had simply been rewired that way. When he joined the Navy at eighteen, a standard test of his hearing had shown he could recognize faint mechanical noises behind a susurration of natural noise, could pick up on acoustical patterns others missed, could distinguish easily between sounds that seemed identical to others. In short, he was a born sonar technician, and in due time, after attending C-school at New London, that was what he'd become.

Perhaps the strangest part of the story of which Queensly was aware was that there were plenty of sonar techs in the Navy who were as good or even better than he was, yet had never been blind. Some people, it seemed, had simply been born with supernatural hearing, and the Navy recruit testing was designed to identify those people so that they could be properly trained.

Queensly was using every bit of his expertise now, both natural and trained, as he sat in his chair at the sonar console, head encased in earphones, eyes closed, reaching out with his mind . . . out . . . out . . . *listening*.

He could hear the whisper of *Seawolf* moving through the water and easily discounted that. He could hear a forest of clicks and snaps in the distance . . . shrimp, or other biologicals. He could sense the bottom, a kind of dead feeling, flat and muddy and very shallow beneath the *Seawolf*'s keel. Far off, there was a rumble of sound, many vessels, he thought, and the pounding of what might have been gunfire transmitted through the water.

And closer . . . just a few miles off . . . a steady beat of sound, a kind of chugging noise . . .

He opened his eyes and studied the waterfall on the console screen in front of him, reaching out after a moment to flick selector switches that narrowed in on the low frequency end of the signal. There . . . a faint, faint straight line against the background hash. But he'd *heard* it first.

"Chief? New contact. I've got a diesel boat snorkeling."

Each of the four sonar stations was manned. Queensly was listening to broadband signals from the towed array, while Rog Grossman handled the broadband input from *Seawolf*'s spherical bow array, Tommy Juarez watched the high-frequency input from the port and starboard hull sensors, and Chief Toynbee ran the spectrum analyzer and served as watch supervisor. The sonar officer, Lieutenant j.g. Neimeyer, stood in the doorway, apparently doing his best to stay out of the way.

Toynbee called up the signal on his screen. "Got it. Conn, Sonar," he added, speaking softly over the intercom circuit.

"Go ahead, Sonar."

"Designating new target, Sierra One-eight-three, Skipper. Bearing two-nine-five."

"Do you have a range yet?"

Queenie looked at Toynbee, who nodded. He touched the intercom button on his console. "Sir? Range uncertain, but I think he's close in to shore. I'm getting a bit of back-echo that's kind of . . . muffled."

He couldn't explain what he heard or how he knew what he knew, but in his mind's eye he could sense that diesel engine chugging along with the muffling presence of the shore just beyond.

"Got it, Queenie. Thanks." There was a pause. "Outstanding job."

"Thank you, sir."

He felt a small warm thrill at that. Queensly was in danger of falling in love with the captain. At least, that's what Toynbee and the others laughingly said. It didn't make sense that a submarine skipper should be able to walk on water, but Garrett inspired that kind of loyalty. Jesus! The man had come down to that filthy, stinking jail himself and charmed them right out from under the noses of those Hong Kong cops. . . .

Right now, he would follow Captain Garrett anywhere, and he would certainly give the skipper his very best. He continued trying to pierce the dark waters about the *Seawolf*. There was something . . . something. . . .

Seawolf possessed the most advanced, most sensitive underwater listening equipment in the world, gear so sensitive the sonar crew liked to joke about what they heard on surface ships or other submarines—snatches of conversation, scenes of passionate sex aboard a cruise ship . . . or the fall of thirty-seven cents—three dimes, a nickel, and two pennies—on the deck of the ship's store aboard a Los Angeles-class sub passing miles away. Toynbee swore he'd once been able to tell the chief snipe on board the DDG *Arleigh Burke* exactly what was wrong with a pressure coupler on his number three LM-2500-30 gas turbine simply by the sound it transmitted through the water as the *Burke* passed the *Seawolf* off the California coast.

Seawolf's sonar suite was the brand new BSY-2(V), affectionately known as "Busy-Two." Computer enhancements and electronic filters allowed the sonar techs to strain each individual thread of sound from the background, clean it up, strengthen it, stretch it for

analysis. Nicks, dents, and out-of-balance shafts gave
each turning screw a slightly different quality of sound
that could be used to identify one ship from another, as
individual as fingerprints even on sister vessels. A library of recorded sounds let *Seawolf*'s sonar crew
match up the sound prints of thousands of ships from
countries around the world.

And yet, despite all of the technical gimmicks, all of
the bells and whistles, *the* most delicate, sensitive, and
vital listening device on board any American submarine was the Mark I Mod 0 ears of the sonar tech, and
the brain between them. Electronics were wonderful . . . but the human brain was capable of feats that
seemed nothing short of sheerest magic.

What Queensly was picking up now, pulling it away
from the background hash and the slow chug of the
diesel engine snorkeling up ahead, was less a distinct
sound than a *feel*, almost an absence of sound, a dead
zone in the water. Sonar techs sometimes joked among
themselves about hearing holes in the water, but there
was, sometimes, something about the quality of background noise that seemed to change in a particular direction, suggesting that there was something there in a
manner that felt more like extrasensory perception
than mere hearing.

Seawolf's TB-23 towed passive array was particularly sensitive to sounds to either side of the boat,
though Queensly could hear that snorkeling submarine
which was just a little off the port bow now.

"Chief?"

"Yeah?"

"I think I have something to port. Off the port
beam." He looked up at his screen, adjusted the frequency input. Nothing there that he could identify by
eye. And yet . . .

"I don't see a thing, Queenie."

"It's there, Chief." He was certain of it. "It's big, and it's moving. And . . . it's *quiet*."

"You sure?"

"Absolutely."

"Sonar, Conn."

"Go ahead, Sonar."

"Uh, sir . . . Queenie has a possible new sierra . . . bearing . . . Queenie?"

"Bearing one-nine-zero. Extreme range."

"Bearing one-nine-zero, extreme range. Designate Sierra One-eight-four."

"You got a make on it yet?"

"Negative, sir. It's real stealthy, whatever it is."

"Okay, Chief. Stay on it."

"Will do, sir."

"Tell Queenie he's got a free shore leave if he can hear them talking over there and tell me what they're saying."

Toynbee chuckled and tossed Queensly a wink. "You got it, Captain."

The warm feeling grew stronger.

And as the minutes passed, so too did the nonsounds of the hole in the water to port. Something, Queensly thought, was stalking them.

The hunter was on the point of becoming the hunted.

Wednesday, 21 May 2003

Control Room
USS *Seawolf*
South of Kinmen Island
1536 hours

"Conn, Sonar," Toynbee's voice said over the intercom. "Updating Sierra One-eight-three. Redesignating contact Master Four-one." When sonar contacts, designated "sierra," were identified through more than one signal or set of sensor data, they were given "master" numbers.

"Definitely a Kilo-class diesel boat running submerged on snorkels," Toynbee continued. "Range now estimated at thirty thousand yards. Target heading two-six-niner."

"Very well." Garrett keyed the sound-activated ship's intercom. "Now battle stations torpedo, battle stations torpedo. All hands, man battle stations torpedo. Torpedo Room, Fire Control. Make Tubes One

and Three ready in all respects, including opening
outer tube doors."

"Make Tubes One and Three ready in all respects,
open outer doors, aye," the weapons officer replied
from the fire control console.

"Conn, Torpedo Room, loading Tubes One and
Three, aye aye."

In fact, six of *Seawolf*'s eight torpedo tubes had been
warshot-loaded since Hong Kong—one through four
with Mk 48 ADCAP torpedoes, and Tubes Five and Six
with Tomahawk cruise missiles, in case they were
called on to strike at a land target. It would take only a
few moments to flood one and three and open the outer
doors preparatory for firing.

But Garrett wanted to get closer, and he also had
some tactical planning to do. He walked over to the
starboard chart table, joining Lieutenant Simms and
Master Chief Dougherty.

"How accurate are these charts, Lieutenant?" he
asked.

Simms frowned. "Not as accurate as we'd like,
though the Taiwanese have been pretty good about
helping us update old charts. The bottom here's at
about thirty meters."

"*About* isn't good enough. Not if we have to run.
Where's Master Four-one?"

"Right here, sir." Simms pointed to a red grease pencil track, updated with new sonar reports every few
minutes. The target was running almost due west several miles south of Kinmen Island.

"Kinmen," Garrett said, thoughtful. "That's Quemoy, isn't it? Nationalist Chinese?"

"Well, the Nationalists are out of power, sir,"
Dougherty said. "But it's Republic of China and not
People's Republic."

"That's what I meant. The good guys." On his chart Kinmen was an inch-wide blob. "You have something that shows Kinmen up close?"

Simms pulled out a finer-scale map, showing a bow-tie-shaped island—Kinmen—with a smaller island—Liehyu—two kilometers to the west.

"Looks like it gets real shoal here," he said, pointing to the bite on the south side of the big island. Soundings there, in meters and in feet, showed water only a few meters deep in places.

"Yessir," Simms said. "That's Liaolo Bay, and we'll want to avoid it."

Garrett pointed to the strait between Kinmen and Liehyu. "This channel looks passable."

"Barely, sir. It's deep enough for the local shipping. Eighteen meters. We'd be broaching on the way through."

"But it gets deeper north of the island."

"Yessir. Twenty-five meters. And even deeper to the west, off Xiamen."

"Okay. Thank you."

"Yes, sir."

Garrett caught the glance Simms exchanged with the COB, a look that might have been translated as *What the hell does he have in mind?* And COB gave a slight shrug, as if to say, *Beats the hell out of me.* In fact, Garrett wasn't entirely sure himself what he planned to do, but he wanted to keep his options open.

His major decision at the moment was a tactical one: whether to spend one torpedo on Master Four-one, or two. The usual practice was two, just in case the guiding wire broke on one, and just in case the targeting and range data weren't as accurate as hoped. A careful skipper would slightly lead the target with one shot and slightly trail it with the other, to guarantee a good lock once the fish acquired the target.

But there was also the ghost contact off to port, Sierra One-eight-four. If that was a Chinese sub—and Garrett was willing to bet money that if it wasn't a Kilo, it was the Akula-class *Nevolin*—then things were going to get damned interesting as soon as he took his first shot. It might be wise to save a couple of fish for a snapshot reply. The worst aspect of the unfolding combat situation was the feeling that *Seawolf* was in a pocket. The target was now almost due north, just this side of Kinmen Island. West was the ghost contact. Garrett had already decided that if he were skipper of a Chinese boat out there, he would be working together with at least two other submarines to trap *Seawolf* against a hostile coast.

Yeah, if he was coordinating this hunt, he'd have one boat about where that ghost contact was . . . and another *here*, to the south, and another *here* to the east, neatly boxing the *Seawolf* against shore and shoal water.

And Garrett never assumed that his opposite number on an enemy sub was any poorer at tactics than he was. That kind of half-assed thinking could get you and your whole command dead, fast.

Returning to his station by the periscope stage, he hit the intercom switch again. "Sonar, Conn. Estimated range to Master Four-one."

"Conn, Sonar. Estimate Master Four-one now at twenty-eight thousand yards."

"Very well. Alert me when we're at twenty thousand yards."

He wanted to be at knife-fighting range for what he now had in mind.

Sonar Room
USS *Seawolf*
South of Kinmen Island
1542 hours

"Twenty thousand yards?" Neimeyer said, eyebrows raised.

"I think the skipper wants to put our fish right down the guy's throat," Toynbee replied, not taking his eyes off his console screen. "Sir."

Craig Neimeyer swallowed. He was a thin, gangly kid from Kansas City, Missouri—"Misery," as he'd always called it, until he'd finally left home for good and joined the Navy. *Seawolf* was his first sea duty, and he was still in the process of finding his legs.

He knew that, and he knew he would have a year or so of paying his dues before he could wear the coveted submariner's dolphin on his uniform above his ribbon rack—before he was accepted as a real submariner. And he knew it would take that long to learn all of the boat's systems. At twenty-seven, he was quite a bit younger than many of the experienced hands, like Toynbee and Grossman, and only a handful of years older than the youngest newbies, like Queensly.

In fact, not counting his four years of Annapolis, Neimeyer had about the same level of experience as Queensly did. In other words, he was a raw kid, wet-behind-the-ears newbie, still fair game for orders to requisition a skyhook, a left-handed wrench, or a bucket of camouflage paint, or the old nuke-sub-mariner hazing gag of Nair in the shampoo bottle.

The hell of it was, while he'd trained in sonar and associated electronics systems at New London after his graduation from Annapolis, he still wasn't entirely sure what he was supposed to be hearing when he actually stood a sonar watch. People with as much experience as Toynbee left him feeling completely inadequate, and a talent like Queensly's left him in awe. He knew how to swap out the circuit boards of a BSY-2(V), but sorting anything useful out of that colored-light cascade on the screen or, worse, from the hiss and gurgle and whoosh he heard over a set of sonar headphones, felt forever beyond him.

The best he could hope for was to stay out of the way and try to be useful.

He watched Queensly, who was sitting at his console, eyes closed, an almost beatific expression on his features as he reached out with his mind, with his very soul, into the surrounding darkness. His life, Neimeyer realized, depended on the keenness of Queensly's hearing at least as much as it did on the ability of the skipper to make good tactical decisions . . . perhaps more so at this point.

"Conn, Sonar," Toynbee said after a long pause. "Estimated range to Master Four-one, now twenty thousand yards."

"Sonar, Conn, stand by . . ."

Neimeyer closed his eyes, his knuckles whitening against the edge of the spectrum analysis console.

All his life, he had been very much in control—of his emotions, of his life, of his decisions.

Not being in control was a decidedly uncomfortable proposition.

Control Room
USS *Seawolf*
South of Kinmen Island
1604 hours

"Firing point procedures," Garrett said at last. "Master Four-one." The whole boat was silently waiting on him, on his orders, and it felt now as though a vast weight had been lifted.

"TMA complete," Ward said sharply, referring to the target-motion analysis conducted by the BSY-2 operators and the fire-control coordinator. It sounded like he'd been counting the seconds until he could say his piece. "Target now bearing three-five-five, range twenty thousand. Target course two-seven-one, speed ten knots."

"Very well," Garrett said. He drew a deep breath. *This is it.* "Match sonar bearings and shoot, Tube One."

"Match sonar bearings and shoot, Tube One."

There was a silent pause. In the old days, aboard diesel fleet boats, they would have heard the hiss of the torpedo exiting the tube in a burst of compressed air, have felt the bow-upward lurch as the submarine lost the torpedo's weight. *Seawolf* was big enough, was massive enough, that there was no sensation of having fired at all.

"Tube One fired electrically," Ward announced, reading the arcane shift of lighted panels on his combat systems board.

"Conn, Sonar. Torpedo running hot, straight, and normal."

"Sonar, Conn, aye. Fire Control. Set unit one off-course twenty degrees to the right."

"Set unit one off-course twenty degrees to the right, aye, sir," one of the ratings at Ward's combat systems panel said. He was a young third class, steering the ADCAP torpedo at the end of its unspooling wire through a joystick on his console. He looked for all the world like a teenage kid playing a video game.

And in a sense, that was exactly what he was. Most of the men on board the *Seawolf* were kids; the average age was twenty-one.

"Running time to target," he said.

"Running time to target, nine minutes, thirty seconds," Ward replied.

And this was the toughest time in an attack run. Up until the point where the torpedoes were actually fired, the captain of a submarine was insanely busy, coordinating data coming in from the TMA board, the sonar shack, and the torpedo room. Now, though, there was nothing to do but wait for an agony of unholy minutes . . . wait, knowing that at any moment the enemy might hear the approaching torpedo and realize they were under attack, knowing that the ghost out there— or other, unheard enemy submarines—might have heard the launch and be closing now to firing positions . . . knowing that he could not turn or maneuver the *Seawolf* at all, or even close the outer doors and reload the torpedo tubes, because doing so would cut the slender wire that was fire control's link to the speeding fish. Break that electrical link, and the torpedo would be lost, too distant, as yet, from the target to find it on its own.

And Garrett was mindful that his primary mission at the moment was not the sinking of that Kilo out there, but the rescue of a team of SEALs on the Chinese beach somewhere ahead beyond Kinmen Island.

But the Kilo was standing squarely in *Seawolf*'s path, and that, Garrett thought, was the Kilo's very bad luck.

Nothing was going to block *Seawolf* from her rendezvous.

Near Xiamen
Fujian Province, People's Republic of China
1605 hours

Jack Morton was tired of waiting. One of the Chinese commandos was in a bad way, his belly torn open by a finger-sized scrap of shrapnel, and Doc McCluskey didn't think he would last out here another twelve hours.

More than that, however, the PRC attack on Kinmen had thoroughly screwed things for the SEALs. Even without wounded men in tow, swimming back to Kinmen beneath the keels of enemy frigates, amphibious ships, and patrol boats was not exactly his idea of a good time.

"We've been trying to dispatch a Mark V package to your area," Captain Randall had told him over the satellite link. "But the fighting off Kinmen makes deployment a problem. You're going to need to get offshore a ways."

"Copy that," Morton had replied. "We have a couple of options there. Then what?"

"A submarine is operating in your area. They have orders to pick you up, *if* you can get far enough offshore to make contact."

"And how far is far enough?"

"The bottom's pretty shallow between Kinmen and the mainland," Randall had replied. "But if you can make it into the Xiamen shipping channel . . ."

Morton had led First Platoon down a wooded, brush-covered slope to see about doing just that. He'd left them at a temporary camp, well hidden from the air and the water, and with Sergeant Zhu Fengbao, the senior Taiwanese commando remaining with the SEALs after Tse's departure, worked his way down the slope to a vantage point overlooking the shore.

West of Kinmen, and within sight of that island, was another island, almost perfectly round and connected to the mainland in the north by a causeway bearing a road and a railway line. Once called Amoy, Xiamen Island had been designated a special economic zone, and in the past few years it had gone through something of a building boom. The Beijing government had been trying to lure foreign investment there, especially from the "rebel province" of Taiwan. The hope had been to attract overseas Chinese to live out their retirement on the island; in fact, wealthy Chinese investors had been buying up property at a rate guaranteed to send housing prices soaring.

From the spur of mainland northeast of Xiamen and within sight of the causeway, Morton and Zhu had a clear view across several kilometers of water of the low, gray sprawl of Xiamen Island, dotted with new high rises and construction. A steady stream of military vehicles was moving across the causeway bridge from the north, and Morton could see several large artillery pieces being set up in a clearing on the island.

The city of Xiamen itself was invisible on the far side of the island, on the west coast, and the shipping channel ran south to the open sea, its location clearly marked at the moment by a pair of freighters and a PLA frigate.

This side of the strait was thickly forested, with channels and inlets beneath the heavily drooping branches of mangrove and thick stands of bamboo. The water was shallow and muddy, more like a tropical river in appearance than a seacoast, with steep banks and very little surf. An armed trawler idled in the channel, perhaps thirty yards offshore.

From the cover of the heavy foliage above the shore, Morton studied the craft through his binoculars. It was typical of the trawlers used along the mainland coast by militia, police, and customs agents, with a six-meter hull, a displacement of perhaps two hundred tons, and mounting two 12.7mm machine guns, one forward of the squared-off, midships superstructure, one aft. He counted about ten men on board, then passed the binoculars to the man beside him, who studied the crew's uniforms for a moment.

"I think they militia," Zhu said. "Only pieces of uniforms. No police. No immigration. More like fishermen."

"They're not real squared away in the discipline department," Morton said, taking the binoculars back. "Looks like they're having a party over there."

Zhu shrugged. "There nothing they can do while battle is fought," he said. "They wait for outcome."

"Are those *women* they have on board?" Morton asked. Several people were gathered on the forward deck, and three of them wore brightly colored garments that looked anything but military.

"Local girls, maybe," Zhu said. He grinned. "They think, 'Might as well have fun while we wait.' "

"And we might be able to use that to our advantage," Morton said. "Come on, Sergeant. Let's get back to the others."

Quietly, they slipped away through the underbrush and back up the hill.

The gods of war had just handed the SEALs a golden opportunity, and Morton was determined to take advantage of it.

Control Room
USS *Seawolf*
South of Kinmen Island
1612 hours

"Captain!" Ward announced. "Unit one has acquired the target."

"Outstanding," Garrett said. That meant the torpedo was now picking up the target's acoustical signature with its own on-board sonar homing system. "Bring the unit left to bearing on-target."

"Bringing torpedo left seven-nine degrees, to bearing on-target, aye." The third class at the weapons console brought his joystick hard over to the left. After firing, Garrett had ordered the course of the torpedo offset behind the Kilo-class submarine up ahead, with the result that the torp was now passing astern of the target. Turning now, the torpedo was bearing once again directly on the target, but coming in from astern.

"Unit one now bearing on target," Ward announced. "Unit one has acquired target."

"Range to target."

"Range to target estimated at twelve hundred yards."

About thirty seconds to target.

"Torpedo Room, Conn! Cut the wire! Close outer door on Tube One. Reload Tube One with Mark 48 ADCAP."

"Conn, Torpedo Room. Cut the wire. Close outer

door on Tube One. Reload Tube One with Mark 48 ADCAP, aye aye."

"Conn, Sonar! Master Four-one has just fired a torpedo! Correction, two torpedoes now in the water!" There was a pause. "Torpedoes are changing aspect. Looks like a snapshot astern."

Garrett grinned. Ward looked at him from the weapons console and tossed a jaunty thumbs-up. The Kilo had heard *Seawolf*'s torpedo coming in from a stern quarter and just loosed two fish of its own—the technical term for an unaimed shot was "snapshot"—back along the course taken by the incoming torp.

"Conn, Sonar. Master Four-one is now making revolutions for twenty knots. Snorkeling has been secured. He may be trying to descend."

"Good luck to him in thirty meters of water," Garrett said. The enemy skipper had a shockingly limited number of tactical options open to him right now. He could try to outrun *Seawolf*'s incoming torpedo, though the Mk 48 had three times the Kilo's speed. He could try turning into the torpedo, hoping it hadn't yet armed. He could pop noisemakers to decoy the torpedo. He could hope that his snapshot would frighten the firing submarine into changing course, thereby cutting the wire early . . . not realizing that the wire was already cut and the torpedo was on its own.

"Conn, Sonar. Target has released countermeasures. Our unit has just gone active."

Which had just convinced the Kilo's skipper that his only hope now was to outrun the torpedo, unless he could decoy its sonar with a noisemaker. Seconds dragged past. . . .

"Conn! Sonar! Unit one has detonated. Sir . . ." There was a hesitation.

"Go on, Sonar. Don't keep us in suspense."

"Sir, we're getting breakup noises. We got him!"

Several of the men in the control room grinned, and two mimed a high-five. Their training and discipline kept them from giving a cheer, though, and Garrett was proud of them.

"Sonar, Conn. Reel in the towed array." They were about to be pulling some high-speed maneuvers, and they would lose the towed array if they tried it with the cable dragging astern.

"Conn, Sonar. Retrieving towed array, aye aye."

"Helm, steer directly for Master Four-one."

"Steering course three-five-five, directly for Master Four-one, aye, sir."

"Conn, Sonar," he heard at last. "Towed array is retrieved and stowed."

"Very well. Maneuvering, make revolutions for thirty knots."

"Make revolutions for thirty knots, aye aye."

He saw Tollini's left eyebrow creep higher on his forehead and the glances exchanged by other officers and men in the control room. Thirty knots was damned fast for water this shallow. It also all but guaranteed that the enemy would hear them in these confined waters, while at the same time making it impossible for them to hear the enemy.

"Conn, Sonar!"

"Sonar, Conn. Go ahead."

"Sonar contact, designated Sierra One-eight-five, bearing two-six-four, range approximately forty thousand yards. Possible Kilo, moving at two-zero knots." A hesitation. "Sir, we're losing him in our wash."

The ghost to the west had just come out to play.

Near Xiamen
Fujian Province, People's Republic of China
1625 hours

Morton slipped quietly into the water beneath a big mangrove tree overhanging the edge of the bank. He'd donned his Draeger rebreather, mask, and fins, and was carrying his H&K. The water was almost opaque, but he'd taken a compass bearing on the target from the shore and swam now in the indicated direction with a slow, steady beat of his fins, guided by his wrist compass.

Unseen around him in the murky water were the seven SEALs of First Squad, along with two Taiwanese commandos, Sergeant Zhu, and a corporal named Chen Huiexin. Moments after beginning the swim, he sensed the looming shadow of the PLA militia patrol boat ahead and above; putting out his hand, he touched the rough, barnacle-encrusted steel hull.

He waited, checking his dive watch, counting down the seconds, sensing his comrades gathering about him and around the hull. At the agreed-upon moment, he moved to a point just left of the patrol boat's single screw and lifted his head above the water.

He found himself looking up into the surprised face of a Chinese sailor, who was standing on the patrol boat's fantail, leaning against the aft railing. Morton brought his H&K up out of the water, but before he could trigger it, the sailor's expression of surprise turned to one of pain as he twisted back from the railing, his throat and upper chest opening like the bloom of scarlet flowers.

Morton hauled himself up over the fantail one-handed. Other SEALs were clambering onto the deck as well; MN1 Curt Hauser had cut down the militia sailor with a silent, three-round burst from his H&K and now was sweeping the patrol craft's after deck with deadly suppressing fire.

Morton swung over the railing and dropped to the deck beside Hauser, where they were joined a moment later by Knowles, Bohanski, and Zhu. A Chinese crewman lunged for the aft 12.7mm mount and was shot down. Another man emerged from the pilot house with an AK but didn't make it all the way up the ladder and onto the deck before a sound-suppressed burst punched him back through the deckhouse door.

Other SEALs were swarming over both sides of the anchored boat—hulking, black-clad figures in masks and rebreather gear that gave them a terrifyingly anonymous deadliness. A Chinese sailor on top of the deckhouse pitched over the side and plunged into the sea. Another threw up his hands, begging in a high-pitched singsong before Chen slammed him down with the butt of his M-16 carbine.

Screams and shrieks erupted from forward and from inside the deckhouse. A naked woman emerged from the doorway and raced on bare feet for the aft railing. Morton reached out, grabbed her wrist, and took her feet out from under her with a sweep of his left foot, knocking her facedown to the deck. A naked man emerged from the deckhouse with an automatic pistol and was killed.

Morton signaled, and two SEALs plunged through the deckhouse door, heading for the engineering spaces below. Chen and two more SEALs from forward took the bridge.

In seconds the patrol craft was secure. Of twelve Chinese militiamen on board, nine were dead and three were prisoners, along with four terrified civilian women. No SEALs or Taiwanese commandos had been hurt.

"Yar, my captain!" Knowles said with a grin, brandishing his H&K. "We be pirates . . . and the ship be ours!"

"Let's get her under way, then," Morton replied. "Meadows! Valienti!"

The two SEAL snipes, both enginemen first class, stepped forward. "Sir!"

"Fire her up. Hauser, you and Jorghenson raise the anchor."

"Aye aye, Skipper!"

"Knowles, with me. The rest of you, secure the prisoners." He looked across the water toward Xiamen Island, then east, toward the low, shadowy shoreline on the horizon that was Kinmen, now darkened by a rising pall of smoke. "We have to find an American submarine out there, somewhere," he said, "and it would be nice to find her and get the hell out of here before the bad guys do."

Wednesday, 21 May 2003

Control Room
USS *Seawolf*
South of Kinmen-Liehyu Channel
1638 hours

"Conn, Sonar! We're passing Master Four-one to star-board."

"Thank you, Sonar. Stand by."

That the sonar shack had been able to pick up any-thing as *Seawolf* sped through the water at thirty knots was little short of astonishing . . . that, or the Chinese Kilo was very close aboard indeed and making a lot of noise where it rested on the shallow bottom.

The tension in the control room now was slowly ris-ing to an unbearable pitch. At this speed *Seawolf* could easily ground in the rapidly shoaling water, broach to on the surface, or even slam headlong into the twisted wreckage of the sunken Kilo.

"Maneuvering!" Garrett called. "Slow revolutions! Do not, repeat, do *not* cavitate, but bring us down to steerage way."

"Slowing to steerage way, aye aye, sir."

"We're slowing, Skipper," Tollini announced after a moment, as the massive bulk of *Seawolf* dragged more and more slowly through the water. "Fifteen knots . . . twelve . . ."

"All hands, this is the captain. The bad guys just saw us sprint for the wreckage of that Kilo we plugged. Beyond that is the channel between Kinmen and Liehyu Islands. With a bit of luck, they'll think we're going through that channel. Let's not do anything to disabuse them of the idea. Maintain silence throughout the boat."

Steerage way was slow—a knot or two, just enough to maintain steering control of the *Seawolf* as she crept along the bottom. This was the moment when her silence truly was golden, rendering her acoustically as a hole in the otherwise noisy water.

"Helm, come left ninety degrees."

"Helm coming left nine-zero degrees to new heading, two-seven-eight degrees, aye, sir."

"You have the conn, Mr. Ward," Garrett said. "I'll be in the sonar shack."

"I have the conn, aye, sir."

Walking aft and port to the sonar room door, Garrett looked in. The tension there was, if anything, greater than on the control deck. The three sonar techs and Chief Toynbee were hunched over their glowing console screens, heads encased in earphones. The sonar officer, Neimeyer, stood by the sound spectrum analyzer, his eyes wide, sweat beading his face.

"Mr. Neimeyer," Garrett said quietly. "Have your people keep their ears sharp. You are our eyes now."

"S-Sir?" Neimeyer looked as though he hadn't understood. Garrett frowned. The young j.g. did not look good.

"Are you all right, son?"

"They're . . . they're *out* there, Captain, moving into attack position!"

The quaver in Neimeyer's voice told Garrett what he needed to know. The sonar officer was at the breaking point.

"Mr. Neimeyer, you're relieved. Chief Toynbee, take over as acting sonar officer."

Toynbee met Garrett's eyes. He looked both relieved and scared. "Aye aye, sir."

"What do you have?"

"Sierra One-eight-five is closing, sir. Redesignating now as Master Four-two. He's a diesel boat, making revolutions for eighteen knots, on a heading of zero-four-zero. Straight for us, Skipper."

"Keep on him, Chief."

"Captain?" Queensly said, touching his headset, eyes still closed.

"What is it, Queenie?" He'd heard the others calling the young ST "Queenie" and used the nickname now to help reduce the tension.

"I have a second contact, sir. Designate Sierra One-eight-six, bearing one-seven-eight, range twenty-seven thousand. And . . ."

"What is it?"

"I can't be sure, sir, but I think there's another contact behind the first. Very, very quiet, but I thought I was picking up some low-frequency tonals for a second there."

"Tonals from Sierra One-eight-six, maybe? Or a bottom echo?"

"No, sir. A second contact, farther away than the first." He shook his head. "It's gone now. But it *might* have been a third boat cavitating as he picked up speed."

Garrett frowned, picturing the tactical situation. One boat coming at them from the southwest, another from almost due south. He'd been expecting a third boat boxing them in to the east, but this new ghost contact was to the south, behind Sierra One-eight-six. Was it a third boat caught out of position, on its way to the east? Or might it be the hunter himself, the mastermind behind the Chinese attack boat deployment, following behind his hounds?

Neimeyer turned on Garrett, grasping his shirtfront with surprising strength. "They're closing on us!"

Garrett broke Neimeyer's grip with a twist and a straight-armed block. "Get hold of yourself, son!"

"Don't you understand?" His eyes were wild now. *"Don't you understand . . . ?"*

Garrett took a step back, cocking his fist for a blow to Neimeyer's jaw. Before he could swing, though, Chief Toynbee had dropped his headset, risen from his chair, and grabbed Neimeyer from behind. The young officer twisted, then screamed. Toynbee felled him with a single, brutally hard elbow smash at the base of the man's skull.

"COB!" Garrett snapped as Neimeyer slumped in Toynbee's arms.

"Yessir."

"Get this man out of here. Get him to sickbay."

"Aye aye, sir." Dougherty took Neimeyer's limp form from Toynbee. "Upsy-daisy, sir. Here we go. Eisler! Snap to! Give me a hand!"

"Have the doc take a look at him."

"We'll take care of him, sir."

Garrett stepped aside as they dragged Neimeyer out of the sonar shack, then locked eyes with Toynbee. "Striking an officer, Chief?"

"It goes harder on officers who hit their men. Sir."

"I see." He grinned. "Well, it's a good thing no one hit anyone."

Toynbee nodded. "Yes, sir, it sure is! Thank you, sir."

"For what? Listen . . . we're going to be creeping along this new course very slowly for some time. We can't trail the towed array, but it should give you a chance to listen hard to port. Keep me updated."

"Aye aye, sir. That we will do!"

"Captain?"

"Yes, Queenie?" The young ST seemed oblivious to the small and violent drama that had just been played out a few feet away from him.

"We're getting . . . transient noises, sir. Kind of like a rumble, far off. It sounds kind of . . ."

"Yes?"

"Sir, it sounds like gunfire. *Heavy* gunfire, like artillery or something. I think someone is shooting at someone else."

Which made sense. If the PRC had declared war on Taiwan, one of their first targets would most likely be the ROC garrison on tiny Kinmen.

"Thank you, Queenie."

"I'm also getting what might be a number of surface contacts. Too confused yet to make out anything certain. There are a lot of bottom echoes, sir."

"Great work, son. Stay on it. If you hear them goddamn sneeze, tell me."

"Aye aye, sir."

Garrett returned to the control room, where several sets of eyes followed his movements. He couldn't tell whether those looks expressed fear, respect, or hostility after they'd seen Neimeyer dragged from the sonar shack. At this point it scarcely mattered. It was vital that Neimeyer not make any noises loud enough or persistent enough to carry past *Seawolf*'s hull and into the surrounding ocean, and vital, too, that he not panic and possibly hurt someone, or accidentally engage some piece of machinery that would tip off the enemy.

Walking over to the chart tables, he joined Lieutenant Simms, studying the high-resolution map of Kinmen and Liehyu. *Seawolf* was now passing the gap between the two islands, traveling slowly west. The fact that Queensly had picked up the sounds of surface vessels and gunfire here suggested that the sounds were being funneled through the narrow strait from the north, from the far side of Kinmen.

An invasion of Kinmen by the PRC? Or simply a close-in shore bombardment?

COB joined them a few moments later.

"How is he, COB?"

"He's doin' okay, sir. The doc is giving him something to sedate him."

"Thanks, COB. Have Ritthouser keep me informed."

"Already told him that, sir."

"Outstanding."

He was sorry about Neimeyer, but there'd been no alternative. The safety of the boat and of the entire crew had to take precedence over any one man.

He thought about Captain Lawless, alone on the weather bridge.

In silence, then, *Seawolf* drifted slowly west.

Now, again, came the waiting. Some wit with undeniable military experience had once remarked that life in the wartime military was ninety-nine percent boredom, one percent stark terror. On board a submarine that was even truer, with hours spent stalking the enemy, or listening for him, or hiding. Once the order was given to fire, there were a few minutes of high-riding excitement, as torpedoes flashed through the water . . . but then the noise and excitement were gone, replaced once more by tedious waiting, by listening, by slow, gentle, and above all *quiet* maneuverings. Somewhere out there at least three more submarine skippers were ordering their sonar crews to comb the ocean for *Seawolf*, to pick out any scrap of noise she might make, to close on her for the kill.

Toynbee appeared at his side. "Skipper?" the sonar chief whispered. "Master Four-two and Sierra One-eight-six pulled a sprint and came up close to the wreck of Master Four-one. They're passing astern of us now."

"And the ghost?"

"If he's there, he's still out there to the south."

Garrett nodded. Not much longer before this was settled, one way or another.

Near Xiamen
Fujian Province, People's Republic of China
1651 hours

Jorghensen suggested calling the patrol boat the "Runcible Spoon," and somehow the name stuck. Morton wondered, though, who was the owl and who the pussycat.

With the engines fired up and Chief Bohanski at the wheel, they'd maneuvered the little craft in close to the shore. The Second Squad SEALs and the rest of the Chinese commandos had waded out to meet her, bringing along the wounded and the two bodies of the comman-

dos killed at Tong'an. In minutes they were motoring
away from the shore, steering for the middle of the strait.

The seven prisoners, all of them fully clothed now,
had been secured hand and foot with plastic ties the
SEALs carried with them for prisoner handling. Zhu
had argued that the captives should be killed—a necessary combat expedient in a desperate situation, but
Morton wasn't ready to go that route yet.

"Damn it, Zhu," he'd said, furious. "There are alter-
natives to murder."

At his orders, the prisoners were hauled below deck
to the boat's tiny mess area and lounge, where they
now took up all of the furniture and most of the available deck space. Under other circumstances he might
have killed the combatants—American Special Forces
operatives were prepared to kill civilians when it was
absolutely necessary to preserve a mission—but things
hadn't reached that point yet. The desperate, terrified
expressions in the eyes of the prisoners, military and
civilian, had been enough to convince him they
wouldn't have much trouble from the captives . . . not
for the moment, anyway.

Her diesel engine chugging fitfully and belching
smoke from the water exhaust aft, the *Runcible Spoon*
steered for the center of the channel, then turned east.
Dead ahead, smoke rose in black pillars from the fires
burning on the island of Kinmen.

Artillery rumbled and boomed from Xiamen.

"They do it again," Zhu explained, pointing to the
island. "When Mao try to take Kinmen before, he put
big guns on Xiamen . . . called Amoy by West. Fire
half-million shells at Kinmen."

"A hell of a bombardment. It's amazing that little island is still above water."

"Yes. Just so. Someone calculate all those shells

something like ten percent of *all* artillery shells in PRC inventory then. But Kinmen hold."

"Do you think it will hold this time?" Morton asked.

"It will. It must." There was a moment's hesitation, a darkness behind the eyes, a hint of deep pain. "I from Kinmen. I have wife and three children there. Also mother, father, sister, other relatives."

He'd been angry with Zhu for suggesting that the prisoners be summarily killed, even though he understood the hard, cold, rationale behind it. Zhu's expression, though, reminded him that the most bitter of wars were *civil* wars . . . and that over five decades of hatred between Taiwan and the mainland had left some very deep scars indeed.

What must it be like for Zhu to be here, he wondered, relatively safe aboard the captured patrol boat, while his family tried to survive that holocaust of fire and steel on the eastern horizon? He understood now why Zhu had elected to return instead of staying with Tse. He wondered if the other Taiwanese aboard had similar motives.

How long could the PLA be held at bay?

Control Room
USS *Seawolf*
South of Liehyu Island
1659 hours

"We're updating Sierra One-eight-six to Master Four-three," Toynbee said softly. He pointed at the chart between them. "And we're calling a new sonar contact Sierra One-eight-seven, due south, range forty thousand. About here."

"The second ghost?"

"Yes, sir. He sprinted for just a few minutes, long enough for us to nail him by his tonals. Then he went quiet again. Vanished."

"What about Masters Four-two and Four-three?"

Toynbee grinned, a crooked showing of teeth. "*That's* the good news, sir. They kept going right on past us. We lost 'em in our baffles, but a few minutes later Queenie picked 'em both up on the starboard array. It looks like they're moving into the channel between these two islands." He looked up at Garrett, respect softening his weathered features. "*Damn* it all, Skipper! You planned it that way! You suckered 'em!"

"We just encouraged them to think the obvious, Chief."

But he was pleased by Toynbee's praise. *Seawolf* had made a mad and noisy dash at thirty knots straight toward the noisy wreckage of the first Kilo—and toward the channel between Kinmen and Liehyu just beyond.

The enemy might expect to lose the '*Wolf* momentarily in the noise from Master Four-one. They would look at their charts and see the channel just beyond, an apparent escape route for the trapped American sub. At least two of the hunters were moving into the channel, trying to track the fleeing *Seawolf*, unaware that the American had gone death-silent and changed course, creeping off to the east.

Too bad all of the Chinese boats hadn't come to the same conclusion, he thought. The ghost, Sierra One-eight-seven, was still hanging back, a good twenty miles to the south. He might be waiting to see if the American had really gone through the strait. He might be hanging back to keep an overview of the whole situation.

Or he could have continued creeping forward at

dead slow, maintaining silence just as *Seawolf* was, in order to close the range.

That thought deflated Garrett's pleasure a bit. He felt the tension building again, like a cold, clammy giant's grip on throat and heart and gut. His head throbbed beneath the bandages he wore. The stress of the moment was gnawing at him, and he could feel the fluttering beginnings of an anxiety attack. Shit, he was no better than poor Neimeyer, scared half to death, broken by stress, by battle tension, by the sheer responsibility of his command.

These men were looking to him to get them out of this mess. And here he was, playing it by ear and relying on sheer, cussed luck.

Fuck that! He didn't have time right now, didn't have the luxury of being human.

He walked over to the helm station, where Dougherty stood just behind and between the two enlisted ratings manning helm and planes. The planesman had precious little to do in such shallow water, but he sat bolt upright, hands gripping the control yoke, eyes riveted to the plane angle indicators. The helmsman sat to his right, gripping the steering yoke, his eyes on the heading indicator.

"Steady as we go," Garrett said, and hoped the order was enough. For all of them.

Near Xiamen
Fujian Province, People's Republic of China
1742 hours

"What the hell is going on over there?" Morton asked aloud. He was on the *Runcible*'s bridge, a pair of binoculars raised to his eyes as he studied the islands and surface ships across perhaps eight miles of sea.

Zhu stood at his side, also watching through binoculars. "Helicopters," he said. "ASW warfare, yes?"

"That's what I'm thinking."

The *Runcible* was cruising slowly south, rounding the gently curving coastline of Xiamen Island and passing between that island and the twin ROC islands of Kinmen and Liehyu to the east. The shipping lanes south from the port of Xiamen lay somewhere a few miles ahead and farther around the island itself, to the west.

Sounds like express trains warbled overhead—artillery shells on the way from Xiamen to Kinmen. *Nothing,* Morton thought, *like an afternoon cruise through no-man's land.*

From here, the northern end of the strait between the two ROC islands was just visible. There were several surface ships in the area, including a big Luda-class destroyer and several patrol boats of various sizes and descriptions. Two helicopters—from here they looked like American Kaman SH-2Fs but with PRC markings—circled above the strait between Kinmen and Liehyu like hungry buzzards.

A thuttering roar sounded from astern. The two men peered up through the bridge windshield, watching as a large Zhi 8—a licensed copy of the French Frélon heavy helicopter—rotored low overhead. Very low. The pilot, evidently, was trying to keep below the arc of artillery shells passing overhead on their way to Kinmen.

"The American submarine," Zhu said. "Perhaps enemy find."

Morton didn't reply. If the American sub that was supposed to pick them up was over there . . .

As he watched, something dropped from the belly of one of the Kamans, and Morton recognized the sawed-off cylindrical shape of an ASW torpedo. They *were* hunting a submarine over there. Morton felt a hard, cold lump growing in his throat.

Their chances out here alone were not good. For the moment, no one was paying any attention to them, a solitary patrol boat cruising off the coast of Xiamen Island. If they approached the ROC islands, though, they were sure to be given a thorough look-over by the Chinese forces of both sides of the battle. Hell, it wasn't like they could just cruise into the port of Kinmen and tie up at the dock, even if they could make radio contact with the defenders on the island and make themselves believed.

For a long moment he watched the smoke crawling up against the sky. A geysering fountain of water erupted from the sea. A hit!

If the American sub was sunk, the only alternative Morton could think of was to round Liehyu and make for Taiwan, a hundred-and-something miles across the Strait of Formosa.

Waters no doubt patrolled by trigger-happy PRC warships that would be suspicious of a lone coastal patrol craft . . . as well as by ROC and American forces that would be just as suspicious and just as eager at the trigger.

His pirate ruse was beginning to look like a singularly bad idea.

Control Room
USS *Seawolf*
West of Liehyu Island
1750 hours

"We're here, Captain," Simms said, pointing at the red wax marker line drawn on the chart. "Three miles southwest of Liehyu Island. Xiamen Island is here, about eight miles northwest. The shipping channel is here . . . ten more miles." He shook his head. "We don't know the SEALs could have made it out there, though."

"I intend to find out, Mr. Simms. We're not leaving our people behind."

"No, sir. But how the hell are we supposed to find them?"

"Captain?" Toynbee stood at his elbow.

"Whatcha got, Chief?"

"We're not sure, sir. *Something* is going on over in the channel between the two ROC islands. We've picked up pulses from dipping sonar . . . and an underwater explosion."

"An explosion! A mine?"

Toynbee shook his head. "Queenie thinks it was a small torpedo, sir. Probably a 400mm ASW fish dropped from a helo."

"The devil you say!"

"Confusion to the enemy," Toynbee said, grinning his crooked grin.

The old naval toast was appropriate here. Unless Garrett was mistaken, the Chinese surface vessels near Kinmen had picked up one of those Kilos moving north through the channel and attacked it.

"That gives us a chance, gentlemen," he said.

Near Xiamen
Fujian Province, People's Republic of China
1750 hours

"My God, that gives us a chance," Morton said, watching the spectacle unfold through his binoculars.

Several long minutes had passed since the explosion of a helo-dropped ASW torpedo on an underwater target. Morton had been about to give up the vigil when he'd seen a long, low, dark gray rectangle breach the surface. From here he could make out the periscope mast. Several surface ships were moving in close alongside now.

One submarine conning tower looked frustratingly like another, especially when there wasn't anything else visible to allow a guess at length and height. But that conning tower looked odd . . . and hauntingly familiar, considerably longer than it was high.

He studied the scene a moment longer, warm hope growing. "Yes!" he announced. "The sons of bitches scored an own goal!"

"Sir," Logan said. The 2IC didn't have binoculars and could only see a confusion of smoke and tiny, distance-blurred shapes on the horizon.

"That's a goddamn *Kilo* that just surfaced! One of theirs! I think they just put a torpedo into one of their own submarines!"

There was no mistaking that squat silhouette now, not when he'd stared down at an identical sub's conning tower in the North Pacific just a few years before.

"Then that means . . ." Zhu said.

"It means our sub is still out there and probably raising a hell of a row. Break out the signal gear, boys. Go!"

They might just be able to get out of this. . . .

Control Room
USS *Seawolf*
West of Liehyu Island
1754 hours

"Captain!" Toynbee was breathless with excitement, leaning out of the sonar shack to pass the word. "We have Blue Dragon!"

"Jesus!" Garrett hurried to the sonar shack. "Where? How far?"

Juarez was standing over the WLR-9 Acoustic Intercept Receiver, a console at the far end of the sonar shack behind the BSY-2 consoles that picked up incoming sonar signals from other ships or enemy weapons, warning *Seawolf* when she was under active sonar observation. "Approximately five miles, sir," Juarez told him. "Bearing two-nine-five. They're using a hand-held transponder and Morse."

"What message?"

"Just their call sign, Blue Dragon, and a coded request for extraction, with wounded. They appear to be at sea in a small boat, approximately two hundred tons. We're tracking it now with the Busy-Two. Designated Sierra One-eight-eight."

"Shit." Wounded personnel meant that they wouldn't be able to swim down to the *Seawolf* while she remained safely submerged. And if the *'Wolf* dared to surface, she'd be picked up by every shipping and coastal radar on this part of the China coast.

And there was worse. It was at least another two hours and more until sunset, and every Chinese ship in the region, including those stalking submarines, were going to pick up that Morse sonar transmission and home in on the source at flank speed. It was going to be extremely crowded around those SEALs very soon.

"Maneuvering!" he called. "Come to new heading, bearing on sonar contact with Sierra One-eight-eight. Make revolutions for forty-two knots."

They were abandoning all pretense of stealth now. *Seawolf* was now in a deadly, flat-out race, with the SEALs at the finish line . . .

. . . and with survival as the prize.

Wednesday, 21 May 2003

Armed Trawler *Runcible Spoon*
Near Xiamen
Fujian Province, People's Republic of China
1833 hours

"We still don't know that one of our subs is out there," Knowles said. "And this damned thing could alert every PLA destroyer and submarine within ten miles that we're here."

He was referring to the banger, the small sonar transponder that dangled now over the side of the patrol boat on the end of a twelve-foot cable. For the past ten minutes Knowles had been crouched next to the case that held the battery and the signaling key, dutifully tapping out the coded contact message in Morse. The pulses of sound bearing that message were spreading throughout the surrounding waters. If an American sub were in the neighborhood, she would hear it.

373

But so, too, would those ASW ships on the horizon, just eight or ten miles away.

Morton stood next to him, watching the ships on the horizon through his binoculars. "We'll give it another five minutes," he decided. "Then we'll wait an hour and try again." He looked at the sky. The sun was just setting behind the mountains to the west, and twilight was shadowing the ocean. There was still plenty of light, however. "We may have to wait for full darkness before the sub drivers'll come in close enough for a pickup."

"*If* they come in. *If* they're willing to surface to take on our wounded."

"Yeah, Wheel," Chief Bohanski said from the railing nearby, using the SEALs' slang term for the skipper of a platoon. "Suppose they decide not to come? I mean, figure the economics . . . a half-billion-dollar submarine, or sixteen SEALs and some Taiwan commandos? Kind of a no-brainer, ain't it?"

"It's the *Seawolf* operating in this area, isn't it?" Jammer Logan said with a grin. "That's *three* billion dollars or so."

"I thought she was in Hong Kong."

"I imagine she put to sea," Bohanski said, "when the current unpleasantness began."

"Let's hope so," Morton said. "Because if someone doesn't come get us—and I don't care if it's *Seawolf* or a garbage scow—it's a long hike back to Taiwan."

Morton continued to study the entrance to the narrows between Liehyu and Kinmen. The PRC ships there appeared to be in complete confusion. He couldn't be sure, but he thought that several surface vessels were taking the crew off the Kilo-class sub that had just surfaced.

"Man, that has to hurt," Logan said, using his own

binoculars at Morton's side. "Shooting yourself in the foot that way."

"The PLA doesn't have the experience we do of surface ASW forces working close together with submarine assets. And there's nothing like a little invasion to make things real confused."

"It looks like goddamn goat-fuck over there. That's a technical term, you know."

"Roger that."

"Hey, Skipper?"

"Hmm."

"The chief has a good point. Why would they risk an asset like a nuclear sub in a place like this? They ought to send in a couple of Mark Vs, or some SDVs."

"Mark Vs, or just about any other surface special warfare asset we have, are going to be vulnerable to PLA surface ships . . . or aircraft, for that matter. And SDVs have a limited range, and they still couldn't get the wounded out." He lowered the binoculars and shook his head. "No, a sub is our best hope. It can pop up, take us all on board in a few minutes, and be underwater again before the Chinese know we're here."

But he wondered. It would still be best to wait for nightfall, of course, but he was just now considering the possibility that there were Chinese submarines out there as well as American. If that Kilo boat was the only one in the area, great. *She* wasn't going anywhere, except possibly to the bottom. But one Kilo suggested the possibility that there were other Kilos as well, or some of the older Chinese boats, Romeos and Whiskeys. And any of them could be creeping up close at this very moment, homing on the sonar pulses Knowles was tapping into the sea.

Chances were, though, that the Chinese subs were scattered far afield, setting up a blockade of the Strait of Formosa or positioning themselves to intercept the U.S. Seventh Fleet when it arrived. He was more concerned about that destroyer off to the east than he was about more Chinese subs.

Even so . . .

He'd read an account of an operation during the closing years of the Vietnam War, in 1972. An American Air Force officer had been shot down several miles behind enemy lines, at the beginning of a major North Vietnamese invasion, the "Easter Offensive," as it was called.

As it happened, that officer, a lieutenant colonel named Hambleton, had possessed highly classified information pertaining to U.S. ballistic missile strategy. It was imperative to get him out, because if the NVA got him, they would be sure to turn him over to Soviet advisers, and the secret data he possessed would be compromised.

Repeated efforts to reach Hambleton had failed, however. Helicopters had been shot down, and the crew of an OV-10 Bronco spotter plane was forced to eject behind enemy lines as well. In all, something like nine men had died trying to rescue one, and the command authority in charge of the rescue operation had all but written the officer off. After almost two weeks on the ground without food or fresh water, Hambleton was all but dead anyway.

One man, though, a Navy SEAL serving as an adviser to a team of South Vietnamese naval commandos, had refused to give up. He'd led a South Vietnamese team in and rescued one of the Bronco fliers. Then he and one South Vietnamese sergeant disguised themselves as Vietnamese and traveled upriver in a sampan, eventually reaching Hambleton and bringing him back. The odds were impossibly long, but the SEAL had done it, winning, in the process, the second of three Medals of Honor awarded to Navy SEALs in Vietnam.

The story—made into a movie starring Gene Hackman years later—was one of those touchstones of SEAL history, a story every SEAL knew and remembered . . . even if Hollywood's version of things had rewritten the plot to eliminate the SEALs' part.

But the story also cast an interesting light on Jammer's question. How valuable was one man? Or sixteen? Or twenty-six?

How willingly should a submarine with 120 men on board risk itself for a handful of commandos?

There was no easy answer to that one. In wartime, sacrifices were made. In wartime, men were risked, and men were lost. But SEALs, ever since their inception at the beginning of the Vietnam era, and going back to the Navy Underwater Demolition Teams from which the SEALs had been formed, always operated under one rule of honor: They *never* left behind one of their own.

Navy submariners, Morton knew, operated under a similar philosophy. They took care of their own and would do anything possible to rescue stranded American military personnel.

"Better cease transmission, Knowles," he said. There was still no sign that the distant Chinese warships had noticed them, but he was growing increasingly nervous about the possibility of enemy subs in the area.

An American submarine might be willing to come here to pick them up, but he was damned if he was going to serve as bait for Chinese sub-hunters.

Control Room
USS *Seawolf*
Xiamen Channel
1833 hours

Twice in the past ten minutes *Seawolf* had slowed to less than twelve knots, giving the sonar shack a chance to listen for the acoustical homing signal from Blue Dragon, then accelerated once again in a short, sharp burst of speed. They ought to be very close now.

"Maneuvering, slow to five knots."

"Maneuvering, slow to five knots, aye, sir."

Garrett hit the speak button on the sound-powered phone. "Sonar, Conn. Get your ears on. What do you hear?"

"Conn, Sonar." There was a long pause. "Sir, we've lost the signal."

Damn! "Sonar, Conn, aye. Last bearing and range on Master Four-four?"

"Bearing two-nine-zero, range . . . close. About two miles, sir."

"Mr. Simms? What time is local sunset?"

"About eighteen-thirty hours at this latitude, sir." He glanced at the big clock on the control room bulkhead. "A few minutes ago, in fact. It'll be light for another forty minutes, though."

"Very well." He stepped up to the Mark 18 scope. "Up periscope."

He rode the scope as it slid up from its well, walking it about for a full 360 before bringing it to a halt on the indicated bearing.

The light was fading fast on the surface, which was one bit of good luck for the *Seawolf,* and there were no surface vessels close by. No . . . there *was* something. It looked like an armed trawler, a coastal patrol boat of perhaps two hundred tons, riding the swell perhaps a mile away.

"Radio Room, Conn."

"Radio Room, aye."

"See if you can raise Blue Dragon on their tactical frequency."

"Radio Room, aye aye, sir."

He watched the target a moment more. It appeared to be wallowing slowly in the swell, moving west toward the Xiamen shipping channel.

"Conn, Radio Room."

"Go ahead, Radio Room."

"Sir, we have Blue Dragon. They report they're in an armed trawler at—"

"We have them targeted. Tell them to prepare to transfer to the *Seawolf*. Tell them to move smart. We won't have much time."

"Aye aye, sir."

"You're surfacing, sir?" Ward asked.

"No choice," Garrett replied. "They have wounded."

"It's a pretty big risk."

Garrett was thinking of the last time he surfaced under the eyes of a hostile vessel. He'd come *that* close to court-martial that time. "Maybe. But our people up there are running out of options, and time."

"Conn, Radio Room. Message transmitted and acknowledged."

"Down scope!" As the periscope slid back into its well, Garrett looked at Ward and added, "I'm gambling that one submarine looks pretty much like another, at least to a casual observer. Chief of the Boat!"

"Yessir!" COB replied.

"Who on board has the most experience with Stingers?"

"That would be me, sir. And possibly the MAA."

"Okay. I want you and Yolander on the deck detail, with Stingers."

"Aye aye, Captain!"

"And tell off a deck detail. We need to hustle those people off their boat and get them belowdecks on the double. I don't want to be on the surface for more than fifteen minutes. Got that?"

"Got it, sir."

"Maneuvering. Come to course two-nine-zero, bearing on Master Four-four. Make revolutions for ten knots."

"Coming to course two-nine-zero, bearing on Master Four-four, aye. Make revolutions for ten knots, aye."

"All hands, this is the captain. Make preparations to surface."

Seawolf turned slightly, moving northwest through the murky water. Garrett kept his eyes on the bridge clock. At ten knots she would cross a mile in about six minutes. Coming up close alongside the SEAL boat, however, would still require more art than science. *Seawolf* could precisely target the patrol boat with a pulse from her active sonar, but if the SEAL transmission hadn't attracted enemy notice, a pulse from *Seawolf*'s powerful bow sonar was certain to do so.

He waited out the minutes.

Another worry played at the edge of his thoughts. He remembered the discussion in the mess hall about the Japanese ship *Ehime Maru*, the *Greeneville*, and Commander Waddle. If *Seawolf* surfaced at just exactly the wrong spot, she could send the SEAL boat to the bottom.

"Maneuvering. Slow to steerage way. Up periscope!"

He rode the scope to the surface and walked it around. *There! Less than two hundred yards ahead!*

"Maneuvering, come to one-nine-two. Ahead slow . . . make revolutions for five knots."

"New course one-nine-zero, aye. Make revolutions for five knots, aye."

He stepped back from the scope. "Bring us up."

"Now surface, surface!"

The deck tilted beneath his feet.

Armed Trawler *Runcible Spoon*
Xiamen Channel
Fujian Province, People's Republic of China
1840 hours

"Sir!" Bohanski shouted, pointing north. "Submarine periscope off the starboard quarter!"

Morton swung around, raising his binoculars. Yes! A periscope was dragging a thin, white wake through the water a hundred yards away, getting closer. But was it *Seawolf*? Or a Chinese sub? The radio call over their tactical channel minutes ago had sounded like a voice from heaven, but there was no reason to begin singing hallelujahs just yet.

The top of the submarine's conning tower appeared above the waves, slowly growing taller . . . and taller . . . and taller. Definitely an American submarine, with a conning tower as high as it was long. And at the base of the sail forward, against the deck, there was the sloping, streamlining foot that marked her as a Seawolf-class submarine.

"There's our ride home, Chief," he said.

"She looks mighty damned good from here, sir."

"She'll look better when we're on board. Is everybody topside?"

"They're bringing up the wounded guys now."

"Very well." He turned his binoculars toward the

Kinmen-Liehyu channel, peering through the gathering twilight. No sign yet that the surfacing *Seawolf* had been noticed.

But it wouldn't be long now.

Sail
USS *Seawolf*
Xiamen Channel
1842 hours

"Crack the hatch!"

Garrett stood back as an enlisted rating named Caswell turned the wheel and pushed the hatch up and back. Water sprayed down from the opening overhead, but both men scrambled up the ladder and onto the weather bridge.

Damage control parties had repaired the sail, plugging the cannon-shell holes and draining the flooded portions. The ocean, Garrett saw with a small tug of relief, had cleansed away all traces of Captain Lawless's bloody death.

Seawolf had come about and was moving south now, beneath a flame-red sky. The Chinese armed trawler was seventy yards ahead, just off the starboard bow. Through his binoculars Garrett could see a number of men clustered on the boat's deck, black-clad, black-faced.

And some of them were waving.

He picked up the intercom handset. "Maneuvering, Bridge!"

"Bridge, Maneuvering, aye!"

"Come right three degrees. Slow to two knots."

"Come right three degrees. Slow to two knots, aye, sir!"

"Bridge, this is Radar Watch. We're being painted. Search radar, at various frequencies. No weapon locks yet."

"Radar, Bridge. I copy that."

He heard a clatter from astern and turned in the cockpit. Sailors in bright orange life jackets were spilling out of the forward stores hatch and onto the deck just abaft of the sail. Ritthouser was supervising the extraction of four Stokes stretchers—coffinlike affairs that looked like they were made of chicken wire, used to transfer wounded personnel from ship to ship.

Two men, Dougherty and Yolander, carried bulky-looking pipes over their shoulders—Stinger antiair weapons. They took up positions well apart on the after deck, scanning the sky.

Seawolf faced three threats now: enemy submarines, surface vessels, and antisubmarine warfare aircraft. The closest known enemy sub was still ten miles away, as were the nearest surface ships. No aircraft had been reported on radar.

But aircraft could reach the *Seawolf* from over the horizon and from any quarter in a scant minute or two.

And they *would* be coming. And soon.

Seawolf gentled toward the Chinese trawler, closing the gap between them. Someone in the trawler's pilot house was doing his bit as well, edging the clumsy looking craft closer to *Seawolf*. Soon the trawler was off the starboard beam and ten yards off. Someone on the forward deck hurled a monkey fist. Someone on *Seawolf*'s aft deck grabbed the line and began pulling it in, hauling in the heavier piece of line to which it was tied. In moments a line-handling party on *Seawolf* had the line secure to a deck cleat and was dragging the trawler in close alongside.

"Conn! This is Radar Watch."

"Go ahead."

"Sir, I have a target, designated Romeo One-five, bearing one-zero-eight, range five miles. Speed one-five-zero, on an intercept course."

Garrett turned his binoculars in the indicated direction, toward Kinmen. There it was . . . a Kaman SH-F2. Someone had picked *Seawolf* up on their surface radar and was coming to investigate.

"I've got Romeo One-five on visual. It's an ASW helo." He turned, leaning over the lip of the cockpit. "Deck there! Hostile aircraft approaching from the southeast!"

He saw Dougherty wave acknowledgment as both Stinger men repositioned themselves, facing port. Several SEALs had already leaped across from the trawler's forward deck and were helping to pass the Stokes stretchers back to the Chinese boat. Sailors from the *Seawolf* were helping other men across.

Garrett watched the incoming helicopter. The ASW torpedoes it carried had a much longer range than the Stinger antiair missiles. The one thing the Seawolves had going for them now was the fact that the Chinese were going to be damn careful this time. They'd just scored an own goal and nailed one of their own subs. They wouldn't be eager to do that a second time and would come in first for a close look.

The Stingers might be a surprise, too. Kilo-class boats were reported to have antiair missiles stowed in a launcher on the aft portion of the conning tower, behind the periscopes, but of all the submarines in the world, they were the only boats to have antiair capability. The Chinese helo crew wouldn't be expecting shoulder-fired AA missiles on an American sub.

He hoped.

The helo dropped lower, skimming the waves a thousand yards off, turning slightly to reveal the PRC markings on its tail boom.

"I've got tone!" Dougherty yelled from the deck. That meant the heat-seeking head of the Stinger missile inside his launcher had picked up the helicopter's engine exhaust and now had locked on target.

"Take him down, COB!"

"Clear behind me!" Dougherty yelled. The Stinger launcher had a nasty back-blast, which would burn anyone standing behind the COB and likely send him tumbling into the sea as well.

A sharp hiss split the air, and the missile streaked out from *Seawolf*'s aft deck, riding a white plume of smoke. The contrail reached toward the helicopter, swinging sharply as the target abruptly jinked to the left and popped a flare. For a stomach-twisting moment it looked like the missile was going to miss, decoyed by the hot-glowing flare.

But it was already too late, the missile too close. The contrail connected with the Kaman's tail boom and exploded with a white flash.

The helicopter staggered, then slewed into a hard spin as the tail rotor broke away in a cloud of debris. Tilting wildly, trailing smoke and burning fragments, the helo slammed into the water half a mile off the port beam.

The deck crew and SEALs cheered. They were swaying the first of the casualties across to *Seawolf*'s deck now.

There was no time for celebrations, however.

"Conn! Sonar!"

"Sonar, Conn. Go ahead."

"We have company, Captain. Sierra One-eight-seven is making revolutions now for forty knots, bearing one-five-five and on an intercept course. Sounds like he's in a hell of a hurry." A beat. "Captain, we're redesignating Sierra One-eight-seven as Master Four-five."

"Sonar, Conn. That's *four*-zero knots?"

"Four-zero knots, aye, sir."

Which meant that Sierra One-eight-seven—no, Master Four-five now—was not a diesel-powered Kilo. Its combination of stealthy characteristics and high speed could only mean one thing.

The Chinese Akula was out there, closing now, and fast.

The question was how long it would take the Akula to get a firing solution. *Seawolf* had minutes now, no more, before she could expect a torpedo salvo from the enemy.

"Deck there! Hurry it along, on the double! It's time to get the hell out of Dodge!"

They were bringing the second wounded man across now.

Armed Trawler *Runcible Spoon*
Xiamen Channel
Fujian Province, People's Republic of China
1845 hours

"Get the rest of them across, Jammer," Morton said. "Sergeant Zhu? With me."

He led Zhu below decks to the mess deck, where the prisoners remained trussed up hand and foot. He drew his SEAL knife and jammed it, point down, into the wood of the mess table.

Seven pairs of eyes stared at him, with expressions ranging from fury to terror.

"Tell them we're leaving them now, Sergeant. I'll leave this knife so they can free themselves."

The plastic binders on their wrists could not be broken or untied. They had to be cut. It would take one of the prisoners a few minutes, at least, to free himself and the others.

And by then the SEALs and their allies would be gone.

Control Room, PLA Submarine *Changcheng*
South of Liehyu
1845 hours

Shangxiao Hsing Ling Ma had been hovering over the sonar officers for some minutes now, as if to wring every scrap of information out of them by the sheer emotional force of his presence. They'd easily picked up the sounds of the enemy submarine minutes ago, as it sprinted at forty knots, stopped, sprinted again, stopped . . . as though searching for something.

Headquarters had reported the presence of enemy commandos ashore in Fujian Province. Hsing assumed the American submarine *Seawolf* must be attempting to pick them up.

The American captain was clever. He'd torpedoed the hapless *Tiger Leaping*, then raced for the sound of her broken hull. *Red Star* and *Monsoon* had followed . . . apparently assuming that the American had continued north through the Xiamen-Liehyu passage.

With a radio mast above water, he'd picked up the news minutes later. A helicopter at the north end of the channel had spotted *Jijie Feng*—the Kilo-class *Monsoon*—close by the fleet bombarding Kinmen. Someone had panicked—heads *would* roll for that!—and loosed an ASW torpedo. The *Monsoon* had been hit and badly damaged. She'd surfaced at once, and the crew was being taken off save for the damage control parties on board, but she was out of the hunt for now.

The American sub had surfaced, apparently to make its rendezvous.

The range was extreme—over twenty-five kilometers—but it was worth a shot.

"Fire number one!" he ordered. "Fire number two!"

It would at least frighten the Americans, and they might even get lucky.

Sail
USS *Seawolf*
Xiamen Channel
1847 hours

"Bridge! Sonar! Torpedoes in the water, Set-53! I have two, repeat two contacts, bearing one-five-five, originating Master Four-five, range thirty-two thousand yards, speed forty-five knots."

Set-53 was a standard 650mm torpedo, with a range of fifty-four nautical miles at a speed of thirty knots, or twenty-two miles at forty-five knots. Thirty-two thousand yards was a hair under sixteen nautical miles.

At that range and forty-five knots, it would take over twenty minutes for the torpedoes to arrive. *Seawolf* had time.

But not much.

"Bridge, Radar!"

"Go ahead, Radar."

"One of the surface ships is getting under way, sir. Designate Romeo One-six. Bearing zero-nine-four, range thirty-seven thousand. Intercept course at twenty-five knots."

"Bridge, Sonar. We confirm that. Redesignate Romeo One-six as Master Four-six."

The Luda-class destroyer; a hulking, sharp-edged brute. He could see the mustache of her bow wake in the gathering gloom.

She had spotted the *Seawolf* and was thundering on, an all-out charge.

Correction. *Seawolf* didn't have much time at all. . . .

Wednesday, 21 May 2003

USS *Seawolf*
Xiamen Channel
1848 hours

"Bridge, Sonar."

"Sonar, Bridge." What *other* good news was there? Garrett wondered. "Go ahead."

"Two more torpedoes in the water. Set-53. Bearing zero-five-zero, range ten thousand! Intercept course at forty-five knots!"

"Acknowledged."

"It's Master Four-two, sir! Looks like he made it through the channel and is swinging around from the northeast!"

Two enemy subs and two sets of torpedoes, inbound toward the *Seawolf*. And a destroyer halfway between the two, inbound and loaded for bear.

It was *really* time to go. "Deck there! How much longer?"

"Another couple of minutes! We're bringing the last casualty across now!"

They'd rigged lines between the two vessels and were swaying a Stokes across the gap between them. Several SEALs and Chinese commandos were dragging two still shapes in dark green body bags across the trawler's aft deck as well.

"We don't *have* two minutes, COB! Speed it up! Clear the deck!"

"Aye aye, sir!"

Garrett turned to Caswell, the young rating who'd accompanied him to the bridge as lookout.

"Clear the bridge, son. Get below."

"Aye aye, sir!"

"Bridge, Radar!"

"Go ahead."

"Master four-six has increased to thirty knots. And . . . we have multiple air targets, now. Bearing two-zero-zero, incoming at three hundred knots."

Those last might be fast ASW helos or slow-moving jets—fighter bombers. This was getting damned bad, damned fast.

"Conn, Bridge! This is the captain."

"Bridge, Conn, aye." It was Tollini's voice.

"Stand by to pull the plug. When I give the word, go deep enough to polish her belly. Flank speed, dead ahead."

"Aye aye, sir!"

"Weapons Systems!"

"Weapons Systems, aye," Ward replied.

"Match radar bearings and shoot, Tube Six, Master Four-six."

Tube Six's warshot was a harpoon missile, Garrett's best option right now for a surface target. It was a lot faster than a torpedo, which would give the oncoming Luda less time to try to evade it or shoot it down.

"Match radar bearings and shoot, Tube Six, Master Four-six, aye aye, sir." There was a pause. "Tube Six fired electrically, sir."

"Very well. Match sonar bearings and shoot, Tube Three, snapshot on Master Four-two!" The Kilo was much closer than the Akula, only five nautical miles off; the torpedoes she'd just loosed had a running time of just over six minutes.

That was a bit too close for comfort.

"Match sonar bearings and shoot, Tube Three, snapshot on Master Four-two, aye aye. Tube Three fired electrically. Sonar reports torpedo running straight, hot, and normal, sir."

Well off *Seawolf*'s port bow, the water foamed and boiled suddenly. The harpoon canister, floating to the surface at a forty-five-degree angle, carried the missile out of the water, then jettisoned its nose cap and aft section. The harpoon's booster engine ignited, and the missile streaked from the water, angling toward the east.

Flight time to the destroyer was only two minutes. Following its track as it skimmed low across the waves, Garrett watched it near its target, watched fountains of water kicked high all around it as the destroyer opened up with every 25- and 57mm AA weapon that could bear.

Apparently, though, the Luda had nothing like the American CIWS, and the missile kept going. At the last moment it angled up, rising sharply, a pop-up maneuver to bring it down on the target's lightly armored upper deck from above.

The quarter-ton high explosive warhead detonated with a towering pillar of white smoke, stopping the Luda dead in her wake. Seconds later another explosion went off . . . and then a third.

"Bridge, Sonar! Explosion and secondaries, Master Four-six! We're getting breakup noises. Master Four-six is a dead-un, Skipper!"

"Got it, Sonar." Garrett could see the destroyer beginning to develop a heavy list and going down by the bow. Fires raged on the deck around the ship's forward twin 130mm gun mount and just below the bridge.

Things were happening rapidly now. One of the air contacts resolved itself into a Jian 7, the Chinese naval version of the venerable MiG 21, thundering in low from the northwest. Yolander triggered his Stinger, sending a missile streaking up toward the interceptor, which banked sharply, scattering flares.

This time the decoy worked and the Stinger missed, but the MiG circled well clear toward the north, cautious now.

More minutes passed, as the last of the wounded commandos, strapped tightly into his Stokes, was lowered feet first through the narrow aft hatch. The last couple of SEALs leaped the gap between the trawler and the *Seawolf*, landing on the broad, sloping deck and scrambling up with the help of outstretched hands from the waiting *Seawolf* sailors.

"Cast off the line!" COB shouted. "Cast off! Clear away!"

The *Seawolf*'s end of the line was tossed overboard; there was no time to secure it. Dougherty and Yolander tossed their empty Stinger launchers over the side rather than try to manhandle them down the narrow hatch. Dougherty waved the last of the SEALs and the deck party below. "Come *on*!" he shouted. "Come *on*! What do you guys want, a guided tour of Beijing? *Move it!*"

The last of the sailors vanished down the hatch. Dougherty waved at Garrett. "Deck clear, deck party secured and below!"

"Maneuvering, Bridge. Flank speed, full ahead!"

"Bridge, Maneuvering. Flank ahead, aye!"

"Dive! Dive! Take us down!"

Garrett was already dropping down into the conning tower hatch and slamming the hatch tight above him. Dogging the hatch, he hurried down the rest of the ladder, dropping into the control room.

He checked the clock. "Sonar! Range to nearest torpedoes."

"Two torpedoes closing from zero-five-zero, range two thousand. They have acquired. The Kilo cut them loose a moment ago."

He'd cut it a bit closer than he'd hoped.

"Conn, Sonar. Unit Three, our snapshot, has acquired the target."

"Captain," Ward said. "The snapshot might have scared them off, made them change course."

"Maybe," he said, nodding. It didn't matter now. *Seawolf* had her own problems. "Helm, come left forty degrees."

"Come left, forty degrees, aye, sir."

That would put the incoming torpedoes squarely astern. *Seawolf* had a top speed nearly equal to that of the Set-53 torpedoes. If she could stay ahead of them for thirty miles or so, they would run out of fuel before they could close the gap.

But *Seawolf* had to reach her top speed first, and you didn't accelerate a ten-thousand-ton submarine from zero to forty-five in less than several minutes.

"Helm. What's our speed?"

"Passing ten knots, sir."

"Sonar! Range to nearest torpedoes?"

"Range fourteen hundred and closing."

"Sonar. Give me a count on the range."

"Aye aye, sir. Torpedoes now at twelve hundred yards, closing. Eleven hundred yards . . . one thousand yards . . ."

"Speed twenty knots, Captain."

"Very well."

"Range to torpedoes nine hundred yards. Eight hundred . . ." There was a much longer pause. "Seven hundred." Then, "Six hundred fifty."

"Speed thirty knots."

Seawolf was moving faster now, racing through the ocean depths, open sea ahead.

"Conn, Sonar! I have an explosion on a bearing matching Master Four-two! We hit him, sir!"

This time there was a cheer from the men in the control room.

"As you were, people." It wasn't time for celebrations yet.

"I'm getting breakup noises from Master Four-two. He's on the bottom. Master Four-six is sinking as well."

"Range to nearest torpedoes."

"Five hundred fifty yards."

"What about Master Four-five?"

"The Akula is still closing at forty knots, sir. Range twenty-five thousand yards. His fish are at fifteen thousand yards, closing slowly."

A pair of black-clad, dripping forms entered the control room from the aft doorway. "Permission to come aboard, Captain."

Garrett looked at the SEAL with surprise. His face was black with grease paint, but he recognized the voice. "You! Commander . . . Morton, isn't it?"

"Son of a bitch! Captain Garrett!" He looked at his companion. "Jammer, that's the *second* time this guy has pulled me out of the drink!"

"Permission to come aboard granted." Garrett grinned. "But let's not make a habit of this, okay?"

"I'd rather not, Captain, if it's all the same to you."

"Range to nearest torpedoes."

"Conn, Sonar. Range now four hundred yards."

"Helm? Speed?"

"Speed now forty knots."

The torpedoes were closing now at a rate of five knots. They would close the gap in another three minutes.

He kept watching the clock. The two SEAL officers stood death-silent, aware now of the danger stalking them all, yard by yard, from astern.

"Two hundred yards."

And then, "One hundred yards."

"Weapons systems! Release countermeasures!"

"Countermeasures away!"

"Helm, come right one hundred degrees!"

"Helm right one hundred degrees, aye!"

At this speed, the deck tilted sharply as the *Seawolf* leaned into the turn. At forty knots, they were effectively dogfighting with those torps.

"Torpedoes bearing straight!" Toynbee's voice called. "We suckered 'em!"

"They still might reacquire." The torpedoes had picked up the sound makers released by the *Seawolf* and failed to match her hard-right turn. Once they'd punched past the decoys, however, they would begin circling, following an automatic program to search for another target.

And *Seawolf* was the only target within range.

More minutes dragged past, as *Seawolf* raced toward the northwest. After putting a fair distance between her screw and the torpedoes she changed course again, heading south once more.

Sonar reported that both torpedoes were pinging, searching with their active sonar, but the signals were weak, too weak, perhaps, to pick up the *Seawolf*. After five minutes one torpedo reacquired the American submarine, but by then the *Seawolf* had opened up the range again, and the torpedo fell far astern.

The warshots from the Akula had long since been lost.

And the *Seawolf* reached the open sea.

Control Room, PLA Submarine *Changcheng*
South of Liehyu
1915 hours

"Captain! An urgent message, in from Fleet Headquarters."

Shangxiao Hsing accepted the message flimsy and read it, scowling. He was being ordered to break off the attack. There was a more important target approaching.

Perhaps it was just as well. The American *Seawolf* had eluded his carefully prepared box trap and managed to sink two Kilos and a destroyer directly, as well as being responsible for severe damage to a third Kilo. He had one Kilo left in his small wolf pack, the *Heilong*— the *Black Dragon*. With the American out of the box, the odds were not as good as Sinbad would have liked.

And the battle elsewhere was not going well. Minutes ago an American Los Angeles-class submarine had sunk the Kilo-class *Nan Yu* north of Taiwan. Two more, the Kilo-class *Jade Dragon*—the *Yulong*—and a PLA Romeo submarine, had been spotted by Taiwanese antisubmarine forces west of Taiwan and sunk from the air. And one, the *Tai Feng,* had been damaged in her encounter with the *Seawolf* in Hong Kong harbor and returned to port at Guangzhou.

Of the original ten Kilos purchased from the Russians, only three were left, and they all were scattered to the south. Four attack submarines—even if one was a nuclear-powered Akula—would not be sufficient to close the Strait of Formosa.

And yet, the day might yet be won, despite the black defeat of China's new submarine arm.

An American carrier! The message reported that an American carrier battle group, built around the supercarrier *Stennis*, was now approaching the southern tip of Taiwan. Hsing knew if he moved quickly, he could be in position to hit the carrier from ambush.

And there would be another encounter with the *Seawolf*. He was certain of that.

"Raise the captain of the *Heilong* on the radio," he said. "We have new orders."

Control Room
USS *Seawolf*
Southwest of the Pescadores Islands
2230 hours

"So, Skipper . . . why are we back here?" Ward asked.

"I think he just likes the deep water," Dougherty suggested.

Garrett smiled as he took a sip of coffee from his mug . . . the big, white one with the word CAPTAIN above the name USS SEAWOLF across one side. "It is kind of nicer to have some water beneath our keel," he admitted. "But we're hunting for that Akula."

"The Akula?" Simms said, puzzled. "What makes you think he's on this side of the strait?"

"Because the *Stennis* battle group is coming through here pretty quick now. If you were skipper of an Akula, and you had a choice between an American sub and an aircraft carrier, which would you take?"

"Tough to say, really," Dougherty replied. "I mean, both a *Seawolf* and a supercarrier are pretty high-value targets."

"True. But the Akula skipper was running a wolf pack of at least four Kilos. He lost all four going after us. He might decide that a carrier is an easier target. And . . . it's a target with a much higher profile. Beijing is bound to figure that a CBG can do them more damage than one submarine, and pictures of the *Stennis* burning on CNN would be such a powerful moral boost to them, and such a blow to U.S. prestige. I know which one I'd choose."

"Conn, Sonar! Multiple targets, bearing one-zero-zero. I've got them in a convection zone . . . range about fifty miles."

"That, gentlemen, is our cue. If we can hear the *Stennis*, so can the enemy. Battle stations torpedo."

Control Room, PLA Submarine *Changcheng*
Southwest of the Pescadores Islands
2245 hours

"Multiple targets, Captain," the chief sonar officer reported. "We have identified two frigates . . . an oiler . . . and . . ."

"Yes?"

"An aircraft carrier, sir! We have them!"

Hsing nodded. "There will be at least one, perhaps two Los Angeles-class submarines in advance of the squadron. We will let them pass, then move in concealed by their wakes. Our target is the carrier."

"A missile attack?" the weapons officer wanted to know.

"No. The American carrier possesses high-speed cannon as a defense against sea-skimming missiles. We will take her with torpedoes."

"Yes, sir."

"Do you wish to pass orders to the *Heilong*, Captain?"

He considered this. "No. We will do nothing to give away our presence. The *Heilong* will choose her own attack plan. Executive officer! You may sound battle stations."

Silently, the *Great Wall* crept into position.

Control Room
USS *Seawolf*
Southwest of the Pescadores Islands
2320 hours

"Conn, Sonar. I have an explosion, bearing two-seven-three, extreme range. Sounds like a torpedo detonation, sir."

"The carrier?"

"Negative, sir., I have the *Stennis* at twenty thousand yards, dead ahead. This is out in front of the CBG someplace."

Garrett nodded. "The battle group's sub escort," he said. "They've run into something."

"Maybe we won't get to play, you think, Skipper?" Dougherty said.

"Somehow, I don't think that Akula skipper is the type to charge a CBG head-on. My guess is that he's lying back in deep water, just like us, hoping to sneak in on the carrier's wake. If we——"

"Conn! Sonar!"

"Talk to me."

"I have torpedo tube doors opening, sir! Bearing two-five-nine. Range uncertain, but he's damned close!"

"Weapons! Give me a TMA on that target!"

"I need time for the TMA, sir. We don't have the range yet. . . ."

"This is no time to polish the cannonball, dammit!" The expression was an old submariner's term, meaning to so work and rework a Time Motion Analysis that the shot was ruined. "Sonar! Go active! Nail that bastard!"

It was more important now that *Seawolf* know exactly where her adversary was than that she stay invisible. *Seawolf*'s bow sonar, the most powerful in the world, sent out a high-pitched, ringing ping.

"Conn, Sonar! Range to Master Four-five is twenty-three hundred yards! Sir! He's fired! One torpedo in the water!"

"Weapons Systems! Match sonar bearings and shoot, Tubes One and Two, Master Four-five!"

"Firing Tubes One and Two," Ward said calmly. "Match sonar bearings and shoot, target Master Four-five, aye aye."

"A second torpedo in the water! Make that three . . . four . . ."

"Tubes One and Two fired electrically," Ward announced.

"What is the enemy's range to the *Stennis*?"

"Thirty thousand yards, sir. Running time eighteen minutes."

"Okay. We have time. Weapons, match sonar bearings and shoot, Tubes Three and Four, Master Four-five."

"Match sonar bearings and shoot, Tubes Three and Four, Master Four-five, aye. Tubes Three and Four fired electrically."

"Offset unit three thirty degrees left. Offset unit four thirty degrees right." He wanted a spread that would come down on the enemy boat like a charging stampede.

"Units one and two have acquired the target, Captain," Sonar reported. "Units three and four have acquired."

"Cut the wires and close the outer doors. Reload Tubes One, Two, Three, and Four. Helm! Come left ninety degrees. Maneuvering, make turns for forty knots!"

For a long thirty seconds nothing happened. Running time from *Seawolf* to the Akula was a minute and a half. It would be close. . . .

Control Room, PLA Submarine *Changcheng*
Southwest of the Pescadores Islands
2321 hours

The sound of the enemy's active sonar pulse had rung through the *Great Wall*'s hull like the clanging of a gong. "Enemy submarine!" the sonar officer cried. "Close to starboard! Range twenty-two hundred meters!"

Hsing Ma caught his lower lip between his teeth, his fast-dwindling store of options an agony of failing hope. He had four torpedoes running, targeting the American carrier, but it would be long minutes yet before they could acquire the target for themselves. If he changed course to avoid or attack the American, he would break the wires directing them.

"Four enemy torpedoes in the water to starboard!" the sonar officer called. "They are going active. They have a target lock . . . on us!"

There was no way around it. If the *Great Wall* was to have even the faintest hope of surviving this, Hsing had to jettison his own torpedoes.

"Cut the wires on all torpedoes!" he snapped. "Helm, come hard right, ninety degrees! Torpedo Room! Close outer doors on One through Four. Open outer doors on Tubes Five and Six and make ready to fire!"

Seconds counted now. If he could turn into the enemy's oncoming spread of torpedoes, perhaps he could get inside their arming radius . . . or sucker them with decoys. Perhaps . . . perhaps . . . perhaps . . .

The deck tilted sharply, and Hsing grabbed hold of the railing encircling the periscope station to remain upright. "Enemy torpedoes . . . range four hundred and closing!"

"Release countermeasures!"

"Countermeasures released."

"Enemy torpedoes closing, range six hundred . . . five hundred . . ."

Hsing thought of Ma Sanbao, the original Sinbad the Sailor. What had ever happened to him? The dynastic histories had no record of him after 1433 and the sudden, inward turning of the Ming Empire. Presumably he'd died or been murdered by his enemies, and yet there were persistent, half-mythical rumors that he'd made an eighth voyage, a voyage toward the east and the rising sun, to unknown lands beyond the Great Sea.

The destiny of nations, of whole peoples and civilizations, turned at times on such tiny details. The ancient Sanbao had come so close to reversing the tides of history; the China of the Mings might have discovered Europe and constructed a bridge to a future where the Middle Kingdom dominated its enemies and ruled in peace and harmony.

And the fortunes of the People's Republic might well ride upon the fate of a single submarine and the skill of her captain.

"Range two hundred . . . one hundred . . ."

And her captain's luck. Hsing Ma closed his eyes and prayed. . . .

Control Room
USS *Seawolf*
Southwest of the Pescadores Islands
2322 hours

"Master Four-five has cut his wires!" Toynbee yelled. "His torpedoes are running free!"

Garrett closed his eyes. He was not a particularly religious man, and he doubted that God chose favorites in the squabbles among the tribes of humankind, but sometimes things came down to the point where prayer was the only available option. By forcing the enemy to cut his torpedo wires, *Seawolf* had just saved the *Stennis*, at least for the moment. If the Akula could avoid *Seawolf*'s attack, however, the outcome of the ensuing, deadly duel would be anyone's guess. *Seawolf* had been created to counter Akula and her kind and had the tactical advantage, but the two were the most silent, most deadly hunter-killers of the world ocean. The ultrasilent Akula, the so-called Walker-class boat, could so easily vanish into silence and in her turn close on *Seawolf* for a final kill.

"Conn! Sonar! Change in target aspect! He's turning . . . releasing countermeasures. . . ."

Garrett nodded. The enemy skipper was doing what he would have done . . . dogfighting his boat, trying to outmaneuver the torpedoes. He might be turning away, hoping to mask his retreat behind his decoy array . . . or he might be turning toward *Seawolf*'s torpedoes in an attempt to get inside their arming range.

By offsetting the attack angles on two of his fish, Garrett had countered both possible maneuvers as best as he could, giving them the optimum chance of acquiring their target, no matter which way it turned.

A dull rumble sounded through the *Seawolf*.

"Conn! Sonar! We have an underwater explosion! Unit one hit Master Four-five!"

A second later another explosion sounded, followed moments later by a third.

Even without the help of sonar, the rumbling detonations were clearly audible in the control room. Moments later they could hear a deep, groaning, creaking noise . . . the mournful cry of a vessel's spine snapping, the death song of the other boat.

"Conn, Sonar! We got him!"

"What about his torpedoes?"

"None have acquired their target, sir. They're starting to circle."

But *Seawolf* was already sprinting away, moving at twenty knots . . . at thirty . . . at forty . . . and the fast-moving enemy torpedoes would have to circle far around before they had a chance of acquiring the American submarine.

Ahead, the *Stennis* battle group sailed on into the night, most of the six thousand men and women aboard her completely unaware of the drama that had unfolded astern.

And in *Seawolf*'s control room, Commander Tom Garrett joined his crew in a wild and lusty cheer.

Inwardly, though, the sudden release of the building stress had left him feeling weak . . . almost depressed. He wondered about the enemy submarine's commander, about who he was, about what he'd been thinking. He'd come so close to scoring a kill on the *Stennis*. But for *Seawolf*'s intervention . . .

Still, for all the complex technology of modern weapons, weapons platforms, sensors, and computers, combat was yet decided by luck and by the people who manned them. Battles—and the subsequent fates of nations and rival peoples—were not determined by robots. Not yet.

Garrett was fiercely proud of the Seawolves, the men under his command.

EPILOGUE

Tuesday, 17 June 2003

Headquarters Building
SUBRON 11
San Diego, California
1512 hours

"You can't keep the *Seawolf,* of course," Rear Admiral Bainbridge told him gruffly. "You know that, don't you?"

"Yes, sir. I do."

He stood at attention in front of the admiral's desk, immaculate in his dress whites. Somewhere outside, in the San Diego Navy Yard, *Seawolf* was tied to a pier, as dock workers began replacing her temporary repairs with something more permanent.

Of course he couldn't keep her. Others were in line for that command . . . and more than likely, the affair of the *Pittsburgh* and the Chinese Kilo was still too well remembered at SUBRON 11.

"If it's any consolation to you, you've been put in for

407

the Navy Cross. What you did out there was nothing short of spectacular."

"Thank you, sir. But my crew deserves most of the credit."

There was little else he could say. Besides, he wanted this agony over with, damn it. Kazuko had flown to Hawaii two days ago and was waiting to meet him at her hotel in Honolulu. All he needed to do now was complete his official mission debriefing with Bainbridge, and he would be free for five glorious days in a bit of well-deserved leave.

Hopefully, the hotel amenities would be a bit more pleasant than those in Hong Kong.

"So noted, Commander. So noted. You'll be pleased to know, by the way, that your efforts in the Strait of Formosa may have paid off in bigger ways than any of us imagined. Thanks to your dogfighting out there, the PLA lost all but three of her best attack boats. Their invasion fleet pulled back from Kinmen. The PLA troops that had already hit the beach there were killed or captured within hours. You might also be interested to know that the Taiwanese commando group left on the mainland tracked down those vehicle-mounted Silkworms and laser-targeted them for F/A-18 Hornets flying off the *Stennis*. Taiwan is now secure, and there are indications that Beijing is going to fold. You and *Seawolf* may just be responsible for winning the war."

"That is good news, sir."

"Hm. It gets better, son. We can't give you the *Seawolf*, but we have picked out a new assignment for you. *If* you want it."

"Thank you, sir." He closed his eyes. Was it going to be Adak after all? Or a desk job back in Washington or here at San Diego?

"I don't know what the hell someone was thinking,"

Bainbridge went on. "With your record . . . running into other submarines *and* destroyers, surfacing in hostile waters, I'd think the powers that be would be a bit leery of giving you a new command."

"A . . . new command? Sir?"

"How would you like to command the *Virginia*?"

The *Virginia*! First of a brand new class of attack submarines! She was smaller than *Seawolf* and had only half the weapons. But she was brand, spanking new, with fully computerized controls and all of the incredible stealth characteristics of the *Seawolf*, and more. She was the lead boat of a whole new generation of submarines, a weapons platform designed to operate in utter stealth and invisibility, close in to enemy shores. She would be an invaluable addition to America's arsenal in the War on Terrorism . . . and against any other enemies who sought to challenge America at sea.

"I . . . I . . . don't know what to say!"

"Try 'thank you.' Actually, I think *Seawolf* is too much the Golden Fish to entrust to sub drivers like *you*."

Garrett was able to chuckle at the gentle dig. "Golden Fish" was the nickname the Russians had hung on their Alfa-class attack subs. Faster than anything else in the ocean, and deeper-diving, the Alfas had also been incredibly expensive. Like *Seawolf*. The *Virginia* and her sister boats were each a fraction of the cost of a *Seawolf*.

It wouldn't make them expendable by any means. But in modern war, Navy vessels were expected to go into harm's way. Less expensive meant more flexibility in their deployment. More daring. More resourcefulness. A wider range of mission options.

And greater responsibilities for their skippers and crews.

"Thank you, sir!"

"No, Commander. Thank *you*. And well done." He extended a hand. "Congratulations. Just don't run into anything else, okay?"

"I think, sir, that my driving is a *lot* better now."

And Garrett shook the admiral's hand.